Rebecca Thornton is an alumna of the Faber Academy Writing A Novel course, where she was tutored by Tim Lott and Esther Freud. She lives in West London with her husband and two sons.

Read what bloggers are already saying about

THE
EXCLUSIVES

"*Prep* meets *The Secret History* meets *Mean Girls* – **a stunning debut novel.**"

Esther Walker

"**A compelling, dark and well-written coming-of-age story** with a well built-up plot, a great setting, and an intriguing cast of characters; a read I really enjoyed!"

A Spoonful of Happy Endings

"I loved this . . . An impressive debut for sure . . . **This one will stay with you.**"

Liz Loves Books

"Freya and Josephine are inspired characters and the denouement is simply electric. **An utterly brilliant read!**"

Booksmonthly.co.uk

"**An absorbing debut from Rebecca Thornton** with a slowly unfolding mystery that will keep you guessing throughout . . . it may just be the book you've been waiting for."

Daisy Chain Book Reviews

"**I haven't read a book quite like this one** . . . I could only wonder what the result would be when the whole thing went up – I was't dis . . . . .oves Books

THE
EXCLUSIVES
Rebecca Thornton

twenty7

First published in Great Britain in 2015 by Twenty7 Books

This paperback edition published in 2016 by

Twenty7 Books
80-81 Wimpole St, London W1G 9RE
www.twenty7books.co.uk

A CIP catalogue record for this book is
available from the British Library.

Paperback ISBN: 978-1-78577-012-8
Ebook ISBN: 978-178577-007-4

1 3 5 7 9 10 8 6 4 2

Typeset by IDSUK (Data Connection) Ltd
Printed and bound by Clays Ltd, St Ives Plc

Twenty7 Books is an imprint of Bonnier Publishing Fiction,
a Bonnier Publishing company
www.bonnierpublishingfiction.co.uk
www.bonnierpublishing.co.uk

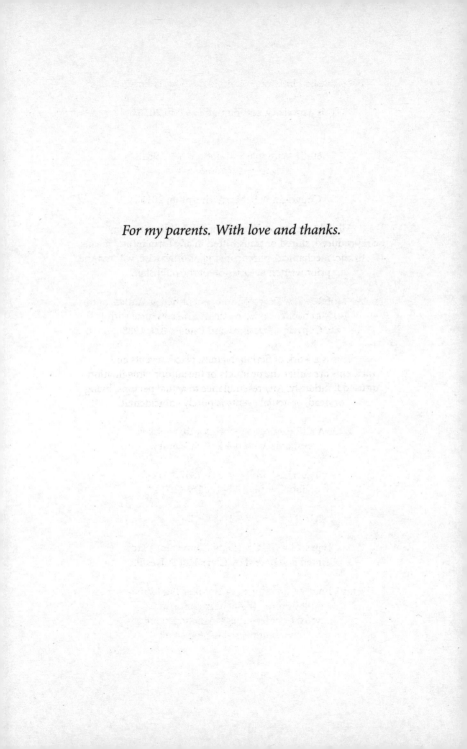

For my parents. With love and thanks.

JORDAN, 2014

Everything changed when I was given the badge. I only had it for four months, but I wore it that whole time, just above my left breast. Blood red, with gold lettering: *Head Girl.*

Four months was all it took. Four months with that stupid badge. And, now, all these years later, I imagine telling my colleagues what happened with Freya, over flasks of coffee, the dirt of an archaeological dig tickling our lungs.

You were just young, they might say, laughing. *Young, naive and stupid.*

Young, yes. Stupid, no.

But I would laugh with them and say, *Yes, yes, I was.* As if the words could salve the ache that flowers across my chest. I couldn't tell them though. Of course I couldn't.

And then last night, for the first time in eighteen years, Freya got in touch.

She is coming here to Amman. 'On business', so she says. The email arrived just before I had climbed into bed, worn and heavy with exhaustion from the day's digging. My computer had pinged an alert and there it was, in cold, black type: **Freya Rogers**. I had wanted to delete it straightaway but my hands had cemented themselves flat to my chest. *What does she want?* My mobile had

1

rung two minutes later, a green glow on my bed. *My God. That's her, too,* I had thought. It wasn't, of course. Barely anyone has my number but, by then, she was everywhere. In the yellow walls, the distressed wood-framed mirror, even the catch of laughter from downstairs. I had gone to the bathroom before opening the email, looked at my reflection, close up, but all I could see was Freya. The beauty of her. *'I'm coming back for you,'* she had said once. 'No,' I had replied to the mirror. 'No, you aren't.'

Back in my room, I had worked up the courage to read what she had written. The email had looked odd. I was used to seeing her small, clumsy handwriting, sloping as it reached the edge of the page. She was Freya Seymour before, and I think of what else she used to be: freckly, blonde, with legs and hair that tangled all over the place and a smile that made your heart spin. I had to read the email five or six times and even then I could hardly make sense of it. I was still unable to breathe, the base of my skull thick with fear.

Josephine,

I do hope you are well. I'm not sure if you still have this email address. I heard from Verity that you are currently based in Amman. She read your name in The Times *and I'm there, doing some pro bono business training in a couple of months. So long has passed and I hope you might like to meet. I know it's out of the blue but, even after everything that happened, I hope you say yes. I really must see you. I know your dig is going on for a year, so let me know if you'll be around in September.*

Freya Rogers, née Seymour.

Freya *must* see me? And had felt it necessary to sign off with her married name? She probably wants to show me she's moved on, that she's no longer the girl from the past.

And even now, a day later, as the sun's rays tighten my skin, my colleagues digging around me, I continue to re-play the words in my head: Verity. Verity Greenslade: former Deputy Head Girl. I still like to think everything was her fault, but of course it wasn't. And then I realise they are still friends, and the sun hazes and I need to lie down. I screw up a dusty tunic behind my head and lie on a chunk of rock. *Freya – what would I say to you? And what do you want from me?* I smooth down my overalls and take off my gloves, setting them next to me. My hands have gone cold and dry and my insides feel like they are rotting. The shadow of a colleague bears over me.

'Are you OK?'

I squint up. It's Jeremy, our intern. 'Of course,' I reply. 'I'm great. Just trying to cool down for a minute.' Willing him to go away, I shut my eyes and he walks off. Beneath the sunlight, a perfect vision forms. I can see Greenwood Hall down to the last, dark brick. I can see that disgusting, open-mouthed gargoyle, perched on the side of the school chapel, that Freya and I used to pretend to kiss and the missing piece of stone where we used to leave each other coded notes. *4 4 A 3 FIRE.* I recall our messages that would lead one of us to a secret part of the woods where the other would be waiting, cigarette in hand.

I inhale, relieved. The memories are not always like that. They surface, on the whole, when I least expect them, freewheeling out from my subconscious. Peeling an orange for breakfast and Freya's face forms. 'Here,' she is saying, dressed in her school sports kit. 'Last orange segment. Quick. I saved it for you.' And sometimes it's just a sense of her: a low-level disquiet. There's one in particular, though, that I've come to expect. Rely on, almost. The glint of a coin. That little Spanish peso she used to thread through the shoelace of her boots. 'This is my lucky charm,' she would say. 'This and you.' The vision of her army boots is a sharp one too. She wore them all the time when we went clubbing. The scuffed toe, the little fluorescent beads; her calves lost in the top of them. And then, without warning, the image will shift. I see her in perfect detail, twisted mouth, red eyes. Coming at me. I don't ... can't ... think of everything that happened. Just the bit where Freya found out what I'd done. Her face. My God.

I get up, unable to lie for much longer – I need to move with my thoughts. How *dare* she? All this time later, when I'm half-way across the world. I pick up my spade, squeezing the handle until my fingers are numb. I drop it and, instead, pick up a rock lodged between two big stones. I squeeze that. I don't feel anything but, when I look up, Jeremy is in front of me again, looking at the dry sand. Three drops of blood soak into the ground.

'Josephine?'

'What? What do you want?' I snap.

He steps back. I must look as if I'm about to hurl the rock at him. I laugh, a mean laugh, but Jeremy doesn't say anything, just walks to the medical kit, which is lying on the sand next to a big white van, left there after an earlier incident with a tin opener.

'Here, let me sort that out for you.'

Without the will to resist, I let him tend to my hand.

'It's small but quite deep. What did you do?' he asks.

'Nothing. It's nothing.'

Nothing. Is it? And as the sharp, pleasant sting of antiseptic infuses itself into my cut, I wonder what Freya would make of me now – what she remembers of me then. Does she think of the weekends spent at her house, the chocolate fug of our midnight feasts in the den? Or the holiday in Cornwall, where she helped me wrench out my first tooth with a red thread torn from her favourite knitted jumper? Or does she just remember the bits at the end? The bits that are full of shattered hope and betrayal and...

The sun, it's so hot, but I start to shiver. I tell the team I'm leaving early. They all look worried. 'I'm fine,' I say, tapping my watch. 'I've got to finish that paperwork, remember?' No one says anything.

'Get back to work.' Jeremy motions for everyone to start digging.

'See you later,' I say. 'We can all have a drink together.'

Mia, the team assistant, is now squinting at me, her hand like a baseball cap over her eyes. I quickly pick up my faded pink cloth bag, stuff in the leftovers from my lunch – a half-eaten piece of Arabic bread and a sweaty slice of cheese – and disappear.

I make my way through the dust, back to the main road. It's a half an hour walk and I'm barely able to hold myself up but, somehow, I manage to get there, whilst mentally composing variations of emails back to Freya. *Hi Freya, that's fine. Would be great to see you ...*' No, that could never happen ... *'Freya, I'm sorry, I'm very busy and can't manage to get any time off at the moment ...*' That's more like it, that's what she would be expecting me to write. So maybe, just maybe, I should surprise us both.

I wonder what I might say if I saw her, how things would change if she came back into my life. If, together, we would be able to make sense of everything: the shards of memory, the cloaked edges of my mind. Or if seeing her would destroy everything I've worked towards. Everything I've made my life into without her, spent years creating and shaping. Maybe we would be able to reach penance? Forgiveness? I don't know. And when I'm thinking about forgiveness, I know I can't ignore her and I know what I have to say.

I start running, and hail a taxi back to my hotel room. 'Duwar Al Khamis. Fifth circle,' I say, throwing two notes at the expressionless driver. I need to get to my computer and tell her what's going to happen. To stop the vision of her face flashing its way through my mind. And so, hair scraped back from the burning sweat, with the low echoes of a *muezzin* from outside, and a cooling Turkish coffee for company, I begin my reply.

1996

It's the start of the Upper Sixth, autumn term. There's a group of us outside, waiting to be called into Announcements. The Gothic building is set against a grey sky and there's the heaviness of expected rain. I am pleased about the lack of surrounding colour, as though nothing is expected of me. But, of course, it is. I stand apart from the other girls, who are all plumped with the possibilities of the new term ahead. The huge, shiny black iron gates stand opposite me. People often hoot when they drive down from the town past the school, gearing up towards the motorway. 'Posh girls,' they shout, making rude gestures. As we wait, a boy in a passing car winds down the window, wiggling his tongue through V-shaped fingers. I wave wildly in return. The boy looks frightened and the car swallows him back down. A light tap on my shoulder makes me turn around. It's her, of course.

'Hi, Freya. OK?' I say.

'*I'm* OK, but how are you? Nervous?'

'Hmmm. No, not at all. I'm alright,' I say.

'Good. I'm glad. As long as Verity doesn't ... you know.'

'I know,' I reply. 'I couldn't take it.'

'Me too. Don't worry. It's not going to happen. And even if it does ...' says Freya. *If it does.* I think of my mother: the sweep of hair, all puffed up at the front so she looks an inch or so taller than her five foot six frame. The upwards thrust of her chin when she thinks she's been wronged and the tired drop of her eyelids. And the rest of it. *Do not let your mind go there,* I think. *It will not happen. It will not.*

Freya points out a bead of sweat on my forehead. 'I know it's going to be OK,' she says. A bell rings, the sun comes out and we both go inside. The question of where to sit during School Announcements has been bugging me for a week. Main School is huge. It easily fits the six hundred students: rows of blue-backed plastic chairs, surrounded by glossy, light wooden benches. If I'm too near the main stage, where the teachers congregate, I'll look expectant, eager. Too far and I run the risk of tripping over a wayward foot. Freya solves my problem, as is so often the case. Grabbing my arm, she pushes me into the third row from the front, near the end of the aisle.

'Here.' She hands me a faded green hymn book.

'Thank you.' I flick to page thirty-seven. The piano music begins, with Mr Tredegar playing. 'All things bright and beautiful,' we sing. As the last note is delivered with a flourish, the headmistress, Mrs Allen, stands.

'Girls, good afternoon. Please sit.' She claps her hands tight and the sound echoes around the room, stilling everyone into silence. 'Since there is no chapel today, let us say the Lord's Prayer.' We lower our heads and I can hear Verity nearby, loud and brusque, like she's telling someone off.

'...For thine is the kingdom, the power and the glory, for ever and ever. Amen.'

'Amen,' we all repeat. I tap my forehead, breastbone, left shoulder, right shoulder; a ritual of habit, more than a sign of belief.

'Welcome back, everybody. I hope you all had wonderful summers. Right. I'd like you to give a warm welcome to the new girls who've arrived at the school, from both the UK and abroad.' There's bored clapping; even the teachers can't feign enthusiasm.

'Thank you everyone. There's a new girls' tea later next week. Your Housemistresses will give you details. And now ... for the school notices. First, I would like to extend thanks on behalf of the entire school to the ten retiring Prefects and to the Head and Deputy Head, for their incredible hard work throughout the past year. They've worked tirelessly to keep the school together, and I'd like you to give them all a round of applause.' We all clap dutifully but everyone wants Mrs Allen to hurry up and announce the new Prefects and Head and Deputy Head Girl positions. 'I'll read out the Prefects in a few minutes. Before that, I've just got a few things to say.'

The usual school notices are read out. How much we've all raised for charity (*Yes!* I've won, with my general knowledge quiz raising one thousand and forty-three pounds), updates on dances with boys' schools, and Sarah Maynard for School Games Captain, surprise surprise. Freya and I giggle as Sarah walks to the stage, head bowed. 'She's so annoying,' Freya says, clapping extra hard to cover the bite.

'Lastly, girls, before the big Announcements, I've got some other news. It's about the Anne Dunne Scholarship this year. As I'm sure you all know, Anne Dunne was the founder of the school. She set up the scholarship as a way of bringing out the best in our girls. There's no financial reward, however the chosen person will gain automatic entry into Miss Dunne's former college, Somerville, at Oxford University. As long as she gets a minimum of three A levels, of course. As you know, Miss Dunne was a huge champion of women going into further education and Oxford are delighted to be involved.'

I don't need to look around to sense that people are staring at me, as though my winning is a given. Sally Aylsford has turned around, giving me a weird, encouraging nod. I can even feel Freya looking at me out the corner of her eyes.

'And some more news about the Anne Dunne this year. We've decided to open up the scholarship to our sister schools – St Catherine's, St Margaret's and Lady Goring's. Each school will put forward three of their top girls and they will go and have an interview and sit one or two general knowledge exams.'

Opening it to other schools? Why? I think. Sally is still staring and I force myself not to make eye contact. I do a quick mental calculation of how this might lower my chances of winning. And then consider the fact I might not be put forward at all. The thought translates into a smile and Sally sits bolt upright, smiling back at me and revelling in misjudged complicity.

'So, we'll make final announcements about who we will be putting forward for the scholarship in a few weeks. No decisions have been made as yet, so please work hard until then. And ... now the moment you've all been waiting for.' Mrs Allen clears her throat. 'I'm going to read out this year's Prefects. Please make your way to the front of the stage and Mrs Bevell will present you with a badge and certificate.' Freya looks at me. 'From

Clifford House, your Prefect is … Mrs Bevell, please could you pass me the list?' Mrs Bevell draws her hands to her face. 'Gosh, sorry. Here we go.'

'From Clifford House, we have Emma Jameson.' The school goes wild as Emma gets to her feet and goes onto the stage. Emma is one of the popular ones. The list continues and I get to my feet, along with pretty much the rest of the school, after Freya's name is called. 'I told you,' I mouth at her. She clasps her hands together and grins.

'And Josephine Grey, who has been made Prefect on account of her all-round achievements.' Mrs Allen beckons me up. 'Come and join the others.' I walk, head very still. The school is clapping and my feet feel light.

'Thank you,' I say. Mrs Allen's hand squeezes mine. The other Prefects pat my back and I can see Verity looking at me, mouth pressed white.

'Well done, well done,' they say.

Freya smiles, rides up on the balls of her feet. 'Think we can go for a fag after this?' she whispers. I widen my eyes in warning, and ignore her.

'And now we have our Deputy and Head Girl announcement to make,' Mrs Allen says. The air around me grows thick and, again, I feel all eyes on me. Chin up, I pull my back straight. I stare at a tiny point in the ceiling above Mrs Allen's head.

'We've come to a final decision, girls. It was no easy task, believe me. Our decision is based on academic achievement, integrity, a responsible nature –' Mrs Allen looks around the room and takes off her glasses '– and, above all, the ability to lead. Five hundred and eighty-two of you here at Greenwood, with over fifty staff, and the girls we've chosen as both Head and Deputy Head, will be expected to be moral and academic guides to each and every one of you.' Freya shuffles next to me. 'And so our Deputy Head this year ...' She pauses. 'Is...'

The entire school looks from me to Verity. Mrs Allen is busy getting the badge ready. 'Sorry, girls. The Deputy Head this year is ... a great leader who has shown a fantastic attitude both in her personal and school life. She'll be a strong role model ...' It suddenly crosses my mind that she might be talking about me – she hasn't mentioned sports, which is Verity's big triumph. I wipe my hands on my skirt and force a smile. 'If you'd like to come up and get your badge, and everyone please give a cheer to ... Greenwood's new Deputy Head, Verity Greenslade.' My insides swell with relief and I exhale, very slowly. I remain outwardly calm, clapping softly. Verity strides up to shake Mrs Allen's hand. She turns to face the school and places a squeezed fist in the air. She's still looking at me, though, eyeballs set with fury.

'Thank you, Verity. I'm sure you'll do a fantastic job.' Mrs Allen takes an envelope from Mrs Newcross and flicks it open. The badge.

'Right. On to the big announcement. Head Girl. I know you've all been waiting for this for a long time.' The room stills and Freya nudges me, giving me a thumbs-up by her skirt. 'Verity's never going to forgive you,' she whispers. It's true. If I'm made Head Girl, she probably won't. Ever since Dominique, Verity's older sister, was made Head Girl of Greenwood Hall and went to Oxford three years ago, Verity's been absolutely hell-bent on following her lead.

'And now for our new Head, who was a unanimous choice by the whole staff. She's been one of the school's most successful students since I've been here, if not *the* most successful. We are truly proud of her. She's been a real asset to the Greenwood Hall name and I'm delighted and honoured to announce her as your new Head Girl. If you'd all like to give a huge round of applause to –' Mrs Allen gives a half-smile '– the wonderful … Josephine Grey.'

Five steps forward. Mrs Allen pins the badge to my school jumper, mouth pressed in concentration. I hear the roar behind me as I stand on the stage. The catcalls make my blood fizz and Mrs Allen pats me on the shoulder. 'Well done. I knew you could do it,' she whispers. The other teachers are all on their feet.

'Thank you, Mrs Allen. Thank you very much.'

It's OK, I think. I feel like collapsing with relief. *I'm Head Girl. I'm OK.* I'd already been Head Girl once before. Head of Mayfield, the small primary school at the end of our road. My mother had been there when my name had been called at Sports Day. All the other mothers had been dressed impeccably and she, in her holey tights, smelling of ammonia and God knows what else, had caused everyone to move away from us. She with her slow, weary voice, who hadn't congratulated me. Just stared, until my father had led her away and told me to go back to school and that he would collect me later.

'Head Girl – well done. Keep it up. You keep it up,' he had whispered. And I had. Even throughout the troubled years, I had kept it up. I had to. And now, for the Anne Dunne. The Anne Dunne, Oxford and then everything will be perfect.

Mrs Allen is squeezing my shoulder. 'Josephine? You are very welcome. We are really honoured to have you as our Head. I know you won't let me down. One of the best students we've ever seen here. Very, very well done again.' I close my eyes briefly then take my place next to her, with Verity on my other side. Verity sidles up to me and whispers, 'Well done you, Josephine. Reckon we'll both be put up for the scholarship as well? Fight for Head Girl now a fight for the Anne Dunne?' She rubs her hands together and puffs at the air, as though she's about to start running a race. I ignore her.

Mrs Allen winds up the school notices and thanks all the girls and staff for attending. Time to tell my parents. My father works for the Prime Minister, his right-hand man, and it's not often I can get hold of him. I use the payphone in the main school and leave a message with Sally, his secretary. She mutters a quick 'Well done' and hangs up. Ma is distracted. 'Good, good.' She's breathing heavily, as though she's run to the phone. I know she won't have been more than ten footsteps away. She hangs up as I'm recounting the moment my name was called. There's a small tapping noise on the other end of the receiver. Three or four in a row and then there's silence. I don't really know what I expected but I still feel like I've been punched in the throat. I put down the phone and Freya appears. 'You OK?' she says.

'Fine. Just phoned my mother.'

'Oh,' she says. 'Are you … I mean, was it…?'

'I'm fine. Yes. It was fine,' I reply. Freya's chewing on her bottom lip and I don't have the energy to expand on the subject matter, or to reassure her that I'll be alright.

'Well, just because I'm the only one around here that knows,' she says, 'it doesn't mean that you'll ever be a burden. You can talk to me whenever. OK?'

Again, she's said just the right thing. I let her pull me along and we decide to go straight into town. She's going to smoke and I'll keep her company. We sign out of the school in the Records Book: '4.30 p.m., 7th September, 1996, Head Girl celebration, Café Doombar. Out for one hour, Freya Seymour and Josephine Grey (Head Girl! Woohoo!),' Freya writes. 'No one ever checks this damn thing anyway,' she says.

'Better be on the safe side,' I reply, although my new Head Girl badge is already making me feel invincible. We slide through the school gates, the metal heavy against our bodies. We head down through the concrete subway tunnels, the opposite way from town, and find a car park away from the school. It's old and stinks of piss. We crouch next to an emergency exit.

'Hey, Frey, I can't smoke at school anymore. You know that, don't you?'

'I know,' she replies. 'I shouldn't either, but I guess I don't have as much to lose.'

'Hmmm,' I say, thinking of Oxford.

'Oh, what about the scholarship too? Are you excited?' asks Freya.

'Why would I be excited?' I reply.

Freya takes a step back and frowns. 'Well, you know, 'cos, you'll probably get it, that's why. And then you won't even need to bother trying for Oxford.'

I feel my bones jarring. 'Do you reckon?' I say, in what I think is a casual tone.

'Well, don't you?' Freya laughs. I don't reply and she exhales a heavy stream of smoke into the air. She hands me her lit cigarette. I don't take it.

'For God's sake. Hold it for one minute. Just need to tie my shoelace.' As she bends down, I take a drag and Freya looks pleased above her shoe. 'Upper Sixth special exeat in three days. Shall we go out on Saturday night, then?' she suggests. 'To celebrate? It'll be our last real chance, I guess? Before we have to really start working and stuff.'

'Yeah. OK, then. We can celebrate. Or commiserate over the fact we won't have any more time off until the end of term. Where?'

'How about that club? You know the one we went to last time?'

'The Fridge?'

'Yeah. That one. There?'

'OK, great. Just us, like usual? Will be nice to spend time with you before we never see the light of day again.'

''K. Sounds lovely. Just us, of course.' Freya offers me some more of her cigarette.

'No. Come on, let's go.' I start moving. We walk back to the school, taking the long route through the lacrosse fields and the back of the woods. We have taken off our school jumpers so no one can smell smoke on us and we arrive back at our boarding house cold and damp. We go to my dormitory where we change out of our uniforms and into after-tea mufti – Freya borrows some of my clothes and both of us end up wearing long skirts, Doc Martens and white T-shirts. We can't talk freely. There's a girl, probably a Junior, crying on the bed next to mine. Her trunk is still full of clothes, although her personal pinboard is covered in photographs of her family and posters of men with long hair and guitars.

'Alright?' Freya calls to her.

'Fine. Just ... just my parents have just left,' she says.

'Ah,' says Freya, 'it gets better, don't worry. I promise. Look at us, we're still here.' She laughs, not unkindly, and opens the top drawer of my bedside table. She pulls out my Acqua Di Gio and sprays us both. 'Just so you smell nice.' She glances around the room. Two more squirts and she's satisfied. 'There. That'll do.'

Mrs Kitts our housemistress knocks on my door and comes in without waiting for a response. I shove both mine and Freya's school jumpers under one of the beds and open the window.

'Phew. Hot,' Freya says, giggling. *Shut up, Freya,* I think.

'Yes. It's quite stuffy, isn't it? Ah, Josephine. The new Head,' she says, clasping her hands in prayer. 'And our wonderful Prefect too. Both Fallow girls, eh? So proud to be your housemistress.' She looks at Freya, eyes shining. I'm always surprised by how much thinner Mrs Kitts is up close. I can see her collarbone jutting out of her cream silk blouse.

'Girls, it's House Meeting soon. Special one for you two. Congratulations,' she says, nodding at me. 'And Eleanor? If you need to talk to me, or you are upset, come and find me or one of the girls. Have you been designated your House Shadow yet?'

Eleanor blows her nose. 'Yes. I'm meeting her later so she can show me round.'

'Great,' says Mrs Kitts.

'OK. Shall I ring the gong in about half an hour?' I check my watch.

'That will be perfect. Freya, if you could come with me to go through your UCAS form.' Mrs Kitts holds out a hand and then pulls it back. Freya looks at me and I nod for her to go. I don't say anything else as they both walk out of the room. I sit and absorb the past few hours and relive that moment when Mrs Allen reads out my name. *Josephine Grey. Head Girl. Josephine Grey.* The words loop in my brain.

After House Meeting, Mrs Kitts calls me over to tell me that Mrs Allen wants to see me straight after tea. 'Just for a quick congratulations handshake and agenda meeting,' she says. 'Only you and Verity.'

I run to the shower, scrubbing away any possible remnants of smoke and change my clothes yet again. It takes ten minutes to get to Mrs Allen's study from Fallow boarding house and I walk as fast as I can, through the dew-soaked grass and across the chapel courtyard. Verity is already waiting outside Mrs Allen's study, looking calm. She doesn't even bother looking at me when I sit myself down on the wooden bench next to the grandfather clock. Mrs Allen opens her door a few minutes later and ushers us both in.

'Josephine, where would you like to sit?' says Verity. She almost curtsies as she smiles at Mrs Allen.

'I'll sit here,' I say, folding myself into a large, cushioned pink velvet chair. She pulls up a wooden chair next to me.

'Girls, well done. Really well done, both of you. How are you feeling?'

'I'm feeling great. Thank you, Mrs Allen. And, Josephine, well done again, you look like you feel great too!' Verity leans over and rubs my arm.

'I'm good. Thank you. Thank you for putting your trust in us,' I say.

'Well, you both deserved it. Right. Just a few things before choir. The school newspaper this year. Josephine. So, as per tradition, you'll be doing the edit. Verity, you too?'

Verity nods and makes a big show of pulling out a notebook, scribbling down the words: '*The Lens*', in a jaunty scrawl.

'Budget is a bit higher this year,' says Mrs Allen. 'I'll go through the costs with you, Josephine, in the next couple of days. We'll be publishing in time for the Christmas holidays, as usual, and, as you know, this term is always busy so it would be good if you got things moving before you get swept up with other stuff. Is that all in order?'

'Yes. Thank you,' I say.

'And I need some co-ordination help with the Anne Dunne scholarship.' Verity stops writing and looks up. 'Nothing big … but we need to sort out logistics with the other schools. Again I'll be going through that with you soon.'

'Do we know who is being put up for the scholarship yet?' Verity asks. *Me,* I think.

'No,' says Mrs Allen firmly.

'Right. Sorry, sorry. Just wondering,' Verity puts her head down into the pages again.

'OK, so, girls, I think that's it, other than to again say a huge well done. Upper Sixth privilege in a few days, with your extra exeat. I suggest you take a much deserved break before you come back and it all gets going.'

'Thank you, Mrs Allen,' says Verity. 'Right. It's six o'clock. Jo, bit early but shall we go and get supper together?' Verity extends an arm for me to take.

'Thank you, Mrs Allen,' I say. 'That's lovely, Verity.'

Mrs Allen opens the huge oak door and we both leave, walking down the empty corridor in total silence, stopping only to look at Main Notice Board. There's nothing new tacked up, other than rows of photographs of the new girls, eyes bright with hope.

And then, as we finally get to the dining hall, Verity and I go our separate ways without giving each other so much as a second glance.

By the time exeat comes around, I'm exhausted. Right before home-time, I find myself sleeping on the floor next to my desk, curled up around piles of textbooks, marked with hundreds of Post-its, like sprouting yellow teeth. And then it hits me again. I'm Head Girl! And as I keep looking down at the badge, glinting in the light with all its promise, I think about how Freya and I will celebrate. Just us two. Our last unburdened night out. It's got to be wild. It is, after all, our last night of freedom before my future begins.

2014

It's been nine days since I replied to Freya. I spent the next two days alone, barely able to speak to anyone, thankful that it was the weekend. The others were off, sunbathing on the roof terrace of one of the five-star hotels, while I was left alone in the shimmering heat. I continued to work, stopping only to douse myself in warm bottled water and to eat handfuls of peanuts that had served as my only food intake since Freya's email.

I had only managed to send the email after spending hours hunched up on the bed, writing and rewriting replies. A swell of memories had filled my head as I typed: Mrs Allen's glasses, perched on the shelf of her bosom as she read out School Announcements, and how I felt when I found out I was Head Girl; the surge of power that that little red badge gave me. It made my spine stretch high, towards the cream-coloured ceiling of Main School. Smaller details popped up, unbidden – the skirt Freya wore that fateful night, denim with little skulls and crossbones lined across the waistband, the result of hours decorating with a penknife and some glue. I found it the day after, scrumpled up in the bin. I took it home and kept it. Never admitted that to another living soul.

Dear Freya, I had written ('Freya' had sounded too passive aggressive, 'Hi Freya', too fake.) *I hope you are well. Time has gone past quickly. Thank you for your email. I'm sorry, I can't see you. Things are extremely busy at work at the moment and I'm probably going to be off again soon, so not sure where my next post will be. I wish you luck with everything.*

I had deliberated on how to sign off for a good three hours until my head felt like someone had kicked it.

All best wishes
    J.

Send. Done.

And since then, nothing. I've managed to keep myself from constantly clicking the refresh button on my emails, wondering if she's playing some sort of game. *Bitch,* I think, then curse myself for getting caught up in it all. *You wanted this,* I tell myself. During work days, I have to keep putting down my tools to check my phone. Refresh my emails. Everyone's noticed and I hear Mia asking Jeremy if everything's OK with me. 'I'm fine,' I interrupt.

Nine days and I haven't left my room other than to work and to make two quick trips to the supermarket, stockpiling my fridge with food for packed lunches. On the tenth night, my colleagues come and knock on my door.

'Join us for a drink?' they ask, blinking nervously.

'No. I'm OK. Thanks, though.'

'Sure?'

I nod and since last night no one has bothered coming. Against my best intentions, I check my email. There's one from

Toby announcing that he's coming to see me on his way back from Iraq.

> *Josephine, Josephine. I'll be swinging by Amman, mainly to see you but also for a story on the Syrian refugees. Dine with me? I've got some interesting stories for you. Other things afoot too, so will be good to talk. Arrive day after tomorrow. With you at seven, earliest. Fondest, T.*

Toby always has interesting stories. I'm a keen recipient of his time in war zones; blood, guts, guns, he's had it all and for some reason, he keeps coming back to boring old me, who's had a pair of hands in dust and mud for the past ten years. I wonder if he'll take my mind off things as he normally does and I'm interested to know what other things he's got to talk to me about – Toby's always one for surprises. I reply.

> *T, I would love that. I'll have a whisky and soda waiting for you in the bar of Hotel Mamounia, for when you arrive. No flak jackets allowed. J.*

Send.

Refresh.

Nothing from Freya. Stop checking, I tell myself. And then I wonder again if this is all a stupid little game. If she's doing this to torment me.

I pour a drink, a ginger beer from the minibar fridge. Then I choose vodka, from the little bottles lined up in front of me. I splash one into the plastic cup and, before I know it, it's gone.

Filled with bravado, I have another one. A glass of cold white wine follows and I sit, staring at my computer. I didn't want to see her. But why hasn't she written back? I should be pleased. But she can't have given up that easily, can she? Before I know it, my fingers are flying across the keyboard in a mixture of panic and defiance.

Freya, I hope my email got through to you. Connection is tricky here sometimes, especially when I'm out and about on a dig. I hope you understand that we can't see each other. I do hope you are well. Josephine.

Send. Frantically click the back button. Too late. It's gone. I feel a sense of relief that I'm the one that's ceded the power. Not to have it in my hands anymore feels good. But then the panic really sets in and I start trembling. *Fuck,* I think. *What have I done?* I feel like I did with Toby the first night I met him, greedily scouring his mind and then scribbling my London phone number on the back of his hand in the sticky-floored bar. 'It's OK to feel vulnerable,' I mutter. *No,* I think. *I've been there, done that and it's not.*

I hear a knock and it's Jeremy. He's twenty, fresh from university and doesn't ever appear to give much thought to his classical good looks.

'Just checking you're OK. No one's heard from you in yonks.' He smiles.

'I'm great.'

'Good. What are you doing?' He walks into the room and I shut my computer.

'Nothing, just catching up on things.' I'm desperately trying to forget the email I've just sent.

'Come on, let's go down and get some drinks.' I start to shake my head but Jeremy holds up his hands. 'No buts. We've all decided. You've been on your own up here long enough.'

My shoulders sag in defeat. 'OK,' I say and, before I can think much further, I grab my torn, leather wallet and old silk shawl that I bought from a market in town, and we leave the room. There's no phone signal downstairs in the bar and three times during the night I go back to the room to check my email. Nothing. Jeremy buys me shot after shot of tequila and I end up necking them all. My colleagues have never seen me take so much as a sip of wine and are all cheering me on. Jeremy spends the first half of the night laughing then looks worried. 'Josephine,' he says. 'I think we'd better get you to bed.'

'At least someone cares,' I shout. Jeremy hauls me up to my room and I can hear Mia wolf-whistling.

I turn to her. 'Is this what you do to everyone when they first come out for drinks?' I ask.

'No. I think people were just surprised to see you out and wanted to...'

I grab on to the dark wooden table. Mia puts her hand near my arm.

'Wanted to what?' Even through my drunken haze, I can hear my voice, sharp at the edges.

'Nothing, nothing. We just wanted to have a good night out, that's all.' She takes a step back.

'Come on,' says Jeremy. He looks over at Mia. 'You get back soon too, OK?'

*   *   *

It's five in the morning when I wake up needing to be sick. I slide my palm across the other side of the bed. Empty. *Thank God,* I think. Toby and I have no set rules but the intern who is fifteen years my junior might have him riled. Other than that, I don't remember much of the night beyond the look on Mia's face when she saw Jeremy taking me upstairs. A few other flashes here and there – Mia and Jack dancing on the terrace and me smoking apple-flavoured shisha and drinking red. Red? After white and tequila? *Why?* I think, getting up to be sick. The only benefit is that I'm too ill to think about Freya for a whole day. I have a general sense of unease but it's almost comforting. An antidote to the clear lines of her face that have come to taunt me almost every minute since her email arrived.

'Fun last night.' Mia winks at me when she turns up late to work. I've made sure I arrive before anyone else this morning. I don't reply. Just carry on working. Sweating and working.

My hangover is still with me the day Toby is due. I thank the sun for lifting the colour in my cheeks and, of course, duty-free mascara. I dab some three-year-old concealer under my eyes, pressing down the dusty lumps into my skin. It makes me look haggard so I rub it off with a piece of tissue. Freya still hasn't replied. I will enjoy tonight with Toby, I think. I leave my mobile in the bedroom and hope that Toby will remember where I've told him to meet me. I slink down the stairs, feeling a strange combination of freshness and fatigue. I'm wearing his favourite outfit of mine: my pale-blue jeans, flip-flops and a plain white fitted T-shirt.

'I love you in that,' he had said the last time we met. 'Plain. Shows off your beauty.'

I had snorted when he told me that. It's the only time I've ever heard him use the 'L' word. I'm wearing a tiny squirt of jasmine scent, and my hair is tied back. I cut a fringe a few months ago and the remnants of it still hang in my eyes. I sit and order two whiskies, one double for him and one single for me. I don't know why – I hate whisky. I take a small sip. It's seven forty-five before I begin to wonder if I should call in at the front desk and see if his plane was on time. I'll give it another fifteen minutes. It's now eight o'clock and I signal for the waiter, to come and bring me some more peanuts. He gives a little bow as I point to the china bowl. Jeremy, Jack and Mia are all on the other side of the bar, drinking what look like Margaritas. Jeremy keeps glancing over and I pretend to be watching the couple on the next table. Eight thirty. Eventually Jeremy walks over and asks if I'm alright.

'I know you're waiting for someone but wouldn't you like to come and join us?' His thumbs rest on the top of his jeans. 'Come on?'

I smile but it comes out as a wince. 'Thanks so much. I'll stay here. I'm enjoying the cool air. Thanks, though. We might come and see you later. Whenever he gets here.' There, that's subtly told him. He raises an eyebrow.

'OK then. Well we're just over here if you want us.' He leaves.

To hell with it. I order another whisky. I ask the waiter to take away Toby's drink. I'm only halfway through my glass when I see him. He's wearing thick, black, mud-covered boots. His jeans are all ruched up at the top where he's pulled his belt tight and his black T-shirt is tucked in. His press pass is still around his neck, a plastic-encased picture, straight-faced and brown hair all dishevelled and he's carrying the black holdall which I know will have the same few things inside: a notebook, a couple of pairs of boxer shorts, the same style of plain green toothbrush he always has, a copy of *The Great Gatsby* and his good luck charm – a small teddy bear given to him by an Iraqi orphan.

'How typical,' I always laugh when I pluck it out, although I am looking forward to its familiarity. And I'm about to tell him this despite him being so late, but, when he sits down, he looks worried. His unshaven look has pushed the boundaries of contrived reporter and grey flecks have started to appear. 'Whisky.' He points to my glass and mouths 'another' to the waiter, who scuttles off behind the bar.

'J, I'm so sorry.'

'It's OK. I don't mind at all. I knew you were coming.' I cover my nerves with a false laugh.

'No. Really. I'm sorry.' He has his chin in his hands and he's rubbing at an invisible speck on his left cheek.

My stomach feels like it's filling with helium. 'What's happened?'

'I'm in trouble.'

'In trouble? What do you mean?' Images of Kalashnikovs, bombs, beheadings, threats flit through my brain. My muscles tighten. The fear defaults my mind to an image of Freya's face.

'I'm having a baby.'

Absurdly, my first thought is to jump up and congratulate him.

'A baby?' I repeat.

'Yes. I'm sorry, J … I'm really sorry. She's called Anna. I met her in Syria last year. We took the assignment in Iraq together. She's a photographer.'

I snort, despite myself.

'I know, I know. Original.' He slugs back his whisky and puts a hand over mine.

'Don't patronise me, you fucker,' I say, but lightly. I can hear punctuated silences on Mia and Jeremy's table as they flick interested glances over the rims of their drinks.

'No. I'm sorry. I really am. I know you and I … it's a strange relationship…'

'Yes, yes I know. We aren't *together* together.'

'I know but that doesn't make it acceptable. I should have told you. You deserve better than me.'

How is this happening straight after Freya got in touch? Has she set off some weird chain of events? Don't be ridiculous, I tell myself. She doesn't have that power over me. *Oh but she does.* Or rather, the memory of her does. And then I think of my mother, the flick of her cigarette lighter, the looseness of her stare.

'What, you should have told me that you were shagging someone else? No need, darling.' I try to keep the malice out of my voice. I want to throw my drink at him and scratch his eyes out. I start to feel choked.

Toby draws himself closer to me, inspecting my face, my eyes, as if he's really seeing me for the first time. 'Josephine? Josephine? Are you OK? You're shaking.' He's leaning towards me now, taking my hands. He flicks at the plaster on my palm. 'What happened here?'

'I'm cold. And nothing. Just a cut. Don't try and distract me,' I warn him.

'Sorry.'

'How old?'

'Twenty-five.'

I think of her, all young, smooth and tanned. She's probably model height, with no need to wear make-up, or wrinkle-reducing moisturiser. I think of how much time I've spent in the sun recently. And then suddenly, out of nowhere, I feel desperate to talk to Freya. *She would have known what to do,* I think. *Pull it together, Josephine. Pull it together. You're in danger of* . . .

'So how else was your time? Anything else interesting to tell me?' I say.

'J . . . Are you OK? You seem . . . You look thin as well. Really thin. Is there something else going on?'

'Me? Yes of course I am. I mean, of course I'm alright. Why wouldn't I be?' I take his hand, imagine stabbing it with the little cocktail umbrella. 'Don't worry at all. We never promised we'd be faithful. We never even put a label on us. So of course it's fine.'

'OK.' I take pleasure from the fact he looks hurt.

'So go on then . . . Tell me more about your time away.'

'Well . . . If you're sure?'

'I'm sure.'

And for the next three hours he talks until the midnight breeze picks up and I'm rubbing down the hairs on my arms. I want to ask about the baby. I want to ask if he's going to be in its life. I want to ask if he's going to hold the little creature in his arms and give him or her his finger to suck on, if he's going to change its nappies and love it and look at its little chest, billowing up and down. But I don't. Instead I ask him about Kalashnikovs and bombs and beheadings and threats, and, all the while, I'm thinking about Freya and wishing I could confide in Toby about what has happened, ask him what I should do. That he could help me. But instead I know that when we go to bed that night we'll talk about what we normally talk about: nothing. Undress, wash our faces, brush our teeth. He'll comment on my T-shirt nightie and I'll smile and he'll run his hands up and down my body and give me that knowing gaze which makes me feel reassured but a bit queasy and I'll let him turn me over and he'll go for a good five minutes and I'll make a few moans and groans and it'll be just the same as it always is, except this time the emptiness will feel even more endless. Almost exquisitely so.

1996

'Upper Sixth Fallow girls, you're all here, I think? Have a good exeat,' Mrs Kitts says. We're all lined up, shaking her hand before we go home for the weekend.

'Thank you,' I reply. 'I'll try and get some rest.'

Mrs Kitts winks. 'Make the most of Upper Sixth privileges. Are you getting the train?' she says.

'No, I'm going to Freya's tonight for dinner, her dad's coming to pick us up.' Freya waits next to me, weekend bag in hand. We watch as parents come and pick up eager offspring. Kate Green's mother wafts in all glamorous, greeting her daughter as though they've been parted for a decade. Freya looks worried, desperate to spare my feelings. 'Ridiculous. So over the top,' she says, squeezing my hand. I laugh, but can't think how to respond.

Rollo arrives two hours later, when all the other sixth-formers have left. He blames work but I've never known him – or Freya, for that matter – to be on time. When we finally get to London, after an hour-long drive, it's already time to eat.

'I'm making you a celebration dinner,' he says. 'Both of you. Head Girl and Prefect. Leon? Anything you have to celebrate with us?'

'No, Dad.' Leon, Freya's brother, is sitting on the sofa, reading a magazine with a bikini-clad girl on the cover.

'Any other news, girls?' Rollo asks.

'Josephine's going to be a scholar soon too, aren't you, J?' Freya says.

'Really, Josephine?' says Rollo. 'You didn't tell us about this?'

I glare at her. She knows how I hate talking about this sort of thing – as if there isn't enough pressure. 'There's nothing to tell. Just that there's the Anne Dunne Scholarship up for grabs soon. What about you, Freya? Wouldn't you like to try for it?'

There's a warning tone to my voice that I try to dampen. It doesn't work and Rollo looks up, frowning.

'Yes, darling, what about you? Why hasn't Mrs Allen put you up for it? What have you done wrong? That woman, always overlooking you. Do you want me to ring up the school?'

'Well … nothing … I just … the names haven't been announced yet.' Freya looks at me confused, wanting help. I don't give it to her, in the hope she'll shut up about the damn scholarship.

'Dinner time,' says Rollo, and we all take our seats at the table.

'Want some bread?' Leon asks me.

'Thanks.' I take two slices and pass the basket to Rollo, who waves my hand away.

'Trying to lose weight,' he says, pulling back the red liquid from his wine glass. 'So, Head Girl, eh? Have you told your father? And your mother? She gets out soon, doesn't she?' Rollo asks. The table goes silent and I don't know how to respond.

'I've told him. He seemed pleased. As for Mother … she's fine. She's coming home soon? How do you know? Did *he* tell you?' I catch Rollo looking at Freya and she shrugs.

'Your father –'

'Because he didn't tell me,' I say.

'Dad, pass the bread over,' Freya says breaking the silence.

'There's none left. Sorry. Speaking of the devil, how is your father?' he goes on.

'*Dad*,' warns Freya.

'Sorry. Aren't I allowed to enquire after my oldest friend? We keep missing each other.'

'Yes, yes, of course,' I say. 'He's on good form. He's been work-ing hard. He flew off to South Africa last night.' Rollo looks as though he wants to say something but doesn't, just pushes a handful of crisps into the side of his mouth.

'Want us to go and check on your mother?' he says, when he's finished eating. 'Leon, you'll be here, won't you? I'm away for the Paris News Conference.'

Freya's brother pushes his hair back and nods his head. 'Of course. Whatever you need me to do. She's still … she's still at …?'

'No,' I say, louder than intended. 'No … I mean … yes she's still there and no, please don't go and see her. She'll be fine.' Rollo leans over, takes his napkin out of his collar and squeezes my shoulder. I want to throw his hand off.

'Well, we're going out tomorrow, Dad.' Freya's giving me that look – the one that says, it's OK, I've got your back and I give her a small smile. 'Just me and Josephine. Isn't that right, J? It's a celebration night out for us both. Oh yeah, and we're staying at Josephine's tomorrow by the way.'

Rollo looks up from his soup.

'Amy's there, don't worry,' I say, referring to our long-standing housekeeper, who has taken to spending about ninety per cent of her time out of the house.

'And where are you two going?' Rollo says, staring at me.

'We're going to the cinema, followed by a ... pub?' I look at Freya. She's widening her eyes, which I take as her signal that I'm saying the right things.

'Yes, Dad,' she says. 'We're just going to the pub. You can't stop us. We're legally allowed. At least, nearly.' Freya smirks at me. The bait's worked.

'You can go to the pub. I don't mind. Just don't...'

'Yes, Dad, we know,' replies Freya, tying her hair with a bobbled blue hair elastic into a knot on the top of her head. 'Can I borrow some money please?'

'Sure. How much do you need? Enough for a taxi back to J's. J, do you need money too? Has your father left you any?'

'I've got some, thanks. He left me extra, since he's away this weekend. Hey, want to join us tomorrow night?' I ask Leon, who is threading his fingers through his hair. I feel bad for asking – it's meant to be just me and Freya and I'm already thinking of my line of defence for later, but I look over and she's smiling.

'Thanks, but actually I'm going to a footy game in Manchester tomorrow. Would've done, though.'

I feel hollowed out by this, so I smile as quickly as possible. 'Great, who are you playing?'

'Some douchebag team. West Ham.'

'Oh right.'

'Right. Ice cream anyone?' Rollo leans back in his chair and opens the freezer behind him.

'Dad. Tomato soup and ice cream? I thought we were going to have a special exeat supper,' says Freya.

'Well, you have another exeat this term. Oh and half-term as well, so I've got another two chances at pulling one out of the bag, haven't I?' The table goes silent. 'Sorry, folks. Can't quite seem to do it like your mother.' And I see Rollo's Adam's apple retreating into his throat. 'So, ice cream?'

'Please,' I say, skidding my bowl over to him. We never have such a thing as ice cream in our house – Father only instructs Amy to buy the basics – so I leap on it gratefully.

'Right. Film, guys?' Rollo rubs his hand together and picks up the ice cream.

'*Dad.*' Freya throws her hands up in the air. 'No more. Come on. Look,' she says, pointing at his stomach. 'I mean what would Mum say?'

'She would have laughed. Laughed at how you can't even cook a meal without her,' I say, looking at Freya. For one minute I think I've said the wrong thing. And after a few seconds Rollo shouts: 'She would have found it hilarious. I mean look at me!' Rollo grabs his stomach. Freya laughs and so does Leon.

'Thanks, J,' Rollo says. 'Always make us feel better. I do know. That you know what it's like, I mean.'

'Not exactly,' I say, 'but sort of.'

Freya grabs my hand. We all troop into the den and Freya pulls out the beanbag that Molly their Labrador used to lie in before she died. It's still covered in her hairs, which always make me sneeze.

'J?' She points to it.

'No,' I reply, pointing back at my nose.

'Ah yes. Doh.' She flattens herself on it and Rollo, Leon and I sit on the cream sofa. Rollo is resting his feet on the beanbag and Leon and I are squashed up on one half, my elbows squeezing into my ribcage for fear of getting too close. *Leon.* He's never resented my presence in their house. Never asked why I'm there. Accepted me all those years ago, when things really started going so wrong with Mother. I find myself desperate to snuggle into him, unsure if this is because I love him, or because he represents everything in Freya's family that I don't have in mine. I had wanted a brother, so badly it had hurt. Father had sat me down by the big fireplace in the drawing room when I was six, my hot palm in his. 'Darling, you know ... your mother,' he had said. 'The timings ... They are not quite right. She's going away. I'm sorry.'

'Warm enough?' asks Rollo. I nod. It's never cold here. Everything always feels warm; the white fluffy sofas, the light cream carpet, the ornately carved Indian tables, even the marble kitchen surface, which gets more and more cluttered every time I visit. There are still the framed collages, lining the walls: pictures of when Freya and I had first met, up until we were about fourteen and Freya's mother had died. There's the photo I love: the one that was taken the day Freya and I first laid eyes on each other. We had been four and hated each other at first sight. I had threatened to cut off her pigtails, secretly pulling at my own short hair, willing it to grow. 'It's no good,' I had heard my father say to Rollo one lunch. 'You can't force them to get on.' And then when things started to unravel with both of our mothers, things changed, our friendship sealed overnight. And then Leon. I can feel him next to me, as Indiana Jones plays in the background. The intake of each breath, the warmth of his arm next to mine. I can't concentrate on the film. I'm counting the breaths next to me and thinking of the scholarship and our celebratory big night out tomorrow and what I'm going to wear and if we should leave early to avoid the nightclub queue and if I can get my prep done on the train back to school.

'OK, bedtime.' The film ends, and Rollo heaves up off the sofa and doesn't look back.

'Night,' we all shout in unison.

'Me too,' Freya says and rolls off the beanbag. Leon and I are left to flick through random TV channels. There's *The Word*, showing an uncircumcised versus a circumcised penis and it's too awkward to move and I begin to feel light-headed.

'Right, bed for me,' Leon says. He musses my hair in an annoying, overly fraternal way and leaves me to curl up on the sofa.

I watch the news and then a video until three in the morning, until my thoughts settle into sleep. Five hours later, I wake up to a loud cough in my ear.

'Didn't make it to your room last night?' Rollo sits on my feet. I want to yelp but manage to hold back.

'No, sorry.'

With my parents away so often, I have my own room at Freya's house. It used to be her mother's dressing room and it's large and bright and yellow. I love it. It's full of my books and Freya's old clothes, boxes of her mother's jewellery which they couldn't bear to get rid of: thin gold necklaces, chunky coloured bracelets and feathered earrings, hanging off a large white dressing table mirror. It still smells of old perfume and there's dust in the corner but it's mine. It's about four times smaller than my own bedroom but it makes me feel safe. It makes me not want to go back to the coldness of my own house.

'Pancakes?' He pats my knee and I smile. 'Girl after my own heart,' he laughs.

However, when Rollo brings me my breakfast, I find the nerves and excitement of the night ahead are all too much, and I am completely unable to eat.

2014

The dig is going as planned. If we are on target, we'll get more private funding, so I'm working the team extra hard. We rise at dawn, when it's grey and chilly, and work away as the flamingo-pink sun orbs its way over our heads and sinks back into the valley below.

We take sandwiches with us, wrapped in wax paper and soggy with the heat. I still haven't eaten much since Toby left. He had stayed two nights until he returned to London.

'Got to file my story,' he said just before he left, patting his breast pocket where his Dictaphone normally sits.

'Internet?' I asked.

He had said nothing about the baby and we had carried on talking as usual, but I could feel his guilt. It was in every attentive movement: the pulling out of chairs, opening doors and noticing when my glass had been empty. And there was the 'hovering hand', constantly, near my back. A guilty hand that could never quite bring itself to touch me.

When I took him to the airport, he had patted my head like a faithful pet.

'Speak soon?' I said. I had wanted to say a hundred other things but, instead, I had a grin so fixed that it hurt the backs of my eyes.

'Sure,' he replied. And now, as I chewed at the foamy bread and ham that I brought for my lunch, I still didn't know whether he had meant it.

'You look tired,' Jeremy observes as I scrunch up the rest of my wrapping.

'I'm OK,' I say, shielding my eyes.

'You sure? You look thinner, too. How about a drink tonight? I promise we don't have to go mad like last time,' he says.

'I've got some work to do. But thanks.'

'I'm not going to stop asking you, you know.' I think of Toby.

'Well. OK, look let me get some stuff done and I'll see how I feel.'

'Good.'

'Back to work.' I hand him a spade. We work hard and, by the end of the day, I'm gasping for a shower. I am sodden with sweat. I clamp down my armpits so Jeremy can't see the seeping patches under my arms. I wonder why I care. Despite my earlier protestations, we end up in the hotel bar once again, scoffing salted peanuts and drinking ice-cold beers in frosted glasses. It's just us two and I've washed and put on make-up – Mia commented on my face when I passed her in the lobby. I felt self-conscious and wiped my cheeks.

'No, no, you look really nice,' she said. 'Just that we don't dress up much here.' I feel bad I didn't ask her to join us.

Jeremy and I talk until midnight. He laughs and rolls a cigarette and I'm suddenly, painfully, reminded of Leon expertly rolling tobacco, crumbling smooth Moroccan hash into a Rizla, smoothing it down with his butternut-coloured fingers. Leon, who still talked to me, even when things had got to breaking point with Freya, and told me not to worry and that of course it seemed desperate, hopeless – but that it would be OK. And as Jeremy is flicking the flint of his silver lighter, I feel as though I'm about to cry.

'You look sad,' Jeremy says.

'I'm OK. I'm just … thinking about things.' I turn my head, hoping he'll shut up.

'What's the matter?' He reaches over, cups my chin and I feel so angry with him, so intruded upon, that I find myself pushing his hand onto the table.

'Whoa,' he says, and I feel even angrier. I want to tell him to stop being so fucking nice and to grow a backbone and just … for God's sake.

'I'm so sorry,' I say. 'Just having a tricky time at the moment. Toby.'

'Toby?' He raises his sandy-coloured eyebrows and again, I feel inexplicably annoyed.

'Toby. He's got someone pregnant.'

He puckers his mouth into an 'O' shape and I nod. His mouth stays in the same position and, although I haven't smoked since school really, I hold out my hand for his cigarette.

'He's quite pitiful really. Would never commit. Poor girl who he's got pregnant won't know what's hit her,' and, as I say the words, I know how horribly untrue they are but I carry on. 'He's so emotionally defunct. He'll probably scar that poor baby for good. And let's hope it doesn't inherit his temper. Or his nose.'

'I thought he was very good-looking.' Jeremy stubs out his cigarette and starts rolling another. I screw up my face.

'You look seriously ugly like that,' he laughs. I am so relieved and grateful he hasn't said something sweet and kind that I punch his arm and laugh. In fact, it's made me feel so much better that I contemplate kissing him. Later on, though, he doesn't try. I make a clumsy movement towards his face but he hugs me and goes to his room.

'Bastard,' I say out loud but at least this time I'm smiling.

The next day Jeremy comes to see me again with a large pizza box. 'Here,' he says. 'You don't have to eat with me or anything. But you look like you're fading away.' Normally I would be pleased with a comment like this but I've begun to worry about how little I have been able to eat since that first email. Every mouthful makes me feel sick. Chewing is too much effort and every time I swallow the food sticks in my chest. 'Thanks,' I tell Jeremy, pulling the box from him. He steps back, releasing his hands in surrender. 'Alright, alright, I get it. You're either hungry, or you don't want to talk,' he laughs. I shut the door in his face and go back to my computer, and still after fifteen days I'm waiting for Freya's reply.

1996

It's three hours before our celebratory night out. I haven't eaten lunch and I can just about fit into the black skirt I bought last month. *Yes yes yes.* We left Rollo after Freya had eaten her pancakes and got the bus all the way to my house. There's a huge display of lilies on the mantelpiece in the corridor; Amy's trying to make the house look nice. Then I see she's left a short note under the big, glass vase: *My mother's sick – had to go see her. Fresh flowers and beds made. A*

'Freya, looks like we're alone tonight. Hooray. Amy's buggered off. We've got the house to ourselves.'

Amy has been with us for eleven years and now feels at ease to do what she wants. My father wouldn't notice if she was there or not, as long as his bed is made in the morning. Freya does a little bottom wiggle and I follow suit, feeling immediately foolish. 'You dick,' she laughs.

'Deep Forest or Massive Attack?' she asks.

'Hmmm. Massive Attack.'

Freya fiddles with the large hi-fi system next to the hall and comes back in.

'How do I look by the way?' she asks, presenting herself in her short denim skirt. She's wearing big army boots artfully left undone, fluorescent beads threaded through the laces, and a green fur-hooded parka jacket.

'You look amazing, as always.'

She grins at me.

'You too, your legs look long in that skirt.' She slicks on some pink lipgloss and hands it to me. I shake my head and point to a nude colour that I'm holding.

'What about my make-up?' I prompt. I want her to say I look pretty.

'Fine.' She curls her lashes and pouts. 'Here, put some more mascara on.' She hands me a black tube. 'Gotta make the most of your eyes. People would kill for that green. And your hair too. It's too flat. Hang on.' She works her fingers through my scalp. 'There. That's better.' She steps back and nods. 'Lovely.'

'Do you think Fred and Guy will be there again?' I ask.

'Hmmm. Not sure. But I know that hot guy you fancied last time said he was coming this weekend.' Freya puckers up her lips and runs her hands down her body.

'Shut up,' I laugh.

'I'm sure he liked you back. He asked where you were when you went to get drinks. And, well, of course he would fancy you. Obviously.'

I want to ask her why but stop myself, convinced I won't be able to live up to her answer. 'What about you?' I redirect. 'What if Guy is there. Think you'll ...?'

'Me and Guy? Nah. Too immature.'

'Immature? Freya, he's twenty! And you seemed pretty into him last time.'

'I know. It's just that ... Don't. I feel bad about that. Anyway, I've gone off them. Him, I mean.' Freya shuts her eyes and smiles, hugging herself as though she's lost herself in a dream of someone else.

'Wanna eat?' she asks suddenly.

'Nah. I can never eat before we go out, you know that.'

'Fag?'

'Yummy, that'll do.' We both spark up, and Freya rolls a joint too.

'Want some?' she asks. 'It's nice. I got it from that guy at the Serpent's Summer Rave. Remember? Mr Rainbow ... the guy with the orange trousers.'

'Hmmm. Vaguely. I'm alright, thanks.'

'Come on J. It's a spliff, it's not going to kill you. They aren't drugs-testing, you know.'

'I know. It's just. You know...'

'Head Girl?' Freya exhales and puffs out little rings of smoke. They float out of her mouth like little polo mints.

'Well. Yes. You know. If I have some now, I'll want other stuff later on. I've just got to keep my head clear. I might smoke some of that in a bit –' I point to Freya's hand '– and, anyway, I'm just ... my mother ... you know.'

'Oh.' Freya stops for a second, afraid she's upset me. 'What about her? She won't find out, you dummy.'

'No, no it's not that. It's ... it's just that I've heard it can ... I just read something in the paper last Sunday, that's all.'

'It can what? What did you read? What are you on about?'

'Nothing,' I finish lamely.

'OK, well, it's ... they're fine. I mean, it's good. Like, if you want some, you'll be fine. Anyway, will you look after me then? I think this is really good stuff.' Freya giggles and pats her bra.

'Yes. I'll look after you. I'll have a few drinks later. And a few smokes. Nothing much else.' I feel guilty, pretending I'm only staying sober to look after her, but I can see no other way out. I can no longer risk it.

An hour later and both of us are starfished on the deliciously cool marble-floored entrance of my family home, waiting for our taxi. I'm still smoking cigarettes. Freya's eating crisps and rolling up another joint.

'I can't move,' she giggles and slides her legs and arms up and down. The doorbell rings and I look at Freya.

'Please?'

'Sod you.' She hauls herself up. 'You lazy toad. You wouldn't make anyone else do that apart from me.' She looks in the hall mirror, bares her beautifully white teeth, looks from side to side and then opens the door.

'Taxi?' says a thin, hooked-nose man clutching his car keys. We both laugh for no particular reason.

'We'll be there in a sec,' I say. 'Quick, Freya, hurry up, stop looking in the mirror.'

The taxi flies through puddles, the raindrops on the window blurring the lights and the people and the shop windows.

'Oh shit. Have you got your ID?' I suddenly ask, rifling furiously through my bag.

'Yup.'

'Thank God,' I say, and apply another layer of nude lipstick. 'We can't queue and then not even get in – do you remember that time with those French guys? When you couldn't even speak.'

Freya laughs. 'We were only a year off for God's sake. OK quick, let's practise. You were born in nineteen seventy-nine and your birthday is the twentieth of August.'

'No, you dimwit,' I flick her head. 'That's my real birthday.'

'Oh, crap. Yes. OK, so hang on, you were born in nineteen seventy-eight and your birthday is January eleventh. Right?'

'Yeah. That's right. Now you go.' The taxi driver is looking in his rear-view mirror at Freya.

'Shhh,' she says to me, giggling and darting her eyes towards the front seat. 'He's going to dob us in to the club bouncers and tell them we're underage. Then they might phone our parents.'

'Don't be absurd,' I say. 'He's looking up your skirt.' She bends double, pulling it down.

'Come on, pull yourself together, quick,' I say. 'We're nearly there.'

'OK. Hang on ... when was I born?'

'Freya, come on! You can't screw this up – it's our last one remember? I'm not spending it wandering the streets looking for somewhere else to go because we can't get in. OK?'

'Don't worry,' she says, linking my arm and squeezing it softly. 'It's going to be amazing. Don't stress. This night ...' She opens the taxi window and shouts at the top of her voice, 'This night, Josephine and Freya, best friends, best night ... this night is going to be one that we never, ever, *ever* forget.' She turns and looks at me. '*Capisce?*' she says.

'*Capisce*,' I reply.

2014

I've taken three days off to go to the Dead Sea with Jeremy and Mia. The last time I took a break from work was when I went to France for my great-aunt's funeral, two years ago. I had thought about asking Toby, then decided it would have been too full-on, even though by that point, we had been seeing each other on and off for over a year. I had returned to work more unrested and alone than ever. All those sunny days, full of false hope, had highlighted to me that, since Freya, there was no one I wanted to spend prolonged time with. And nor, perhaps, them with me.

But when Jeremy asked me if I wanted to join them, I surprised myself in not hesitating to say yes. When I had agreed, I had almost jumped with shock: the sheer relief of not being in Amman, where Freya thinks I am. Although she said in her last email she wasn't due for another few weeks, ever since she hasn't replied I've been quietly terrified she would turn up unannounced. Jeremy hadn't flinched when I agreed, smiled and told me he would hire a car and could I please leave my bags by my door so he could carry them downstairs.

We leave on Thursday evening, the start of the Jordanian weekend, driving down the dusty pink roads towards the Dead

Sea. I'm in the front, next to Jeremy. Mia is curled up in the back, asking us to help her compose texts to her ex.

'What a complete twat,' she says, punching the keypad of her phone. 'Listen to this ...' she says, and reads us another of his messages. I pull out my phone.

'Bet I can beat you,' I laugh and read out one of Toby's latest.

'*All good here. About to go to the wilds of Afghanistan to hunt some stories. Will keep you posted. Fondest, T.* I mean what's that all about? He thinks he's so war chic.' I snort. Mia laughs and Jeremy lights up a cigarette. I think I've said just enough about Toby so that it looks like I don't care but when Mia's still laughing and sarcastically calling him war chic a few minutes later, I wonder if they know what I'm thinking. I laugh too, but the idea that Toby, the only person I've allowed into my life since Freya, has cut me out so easily, strangles me without warning. Was that how Freya felt too?

'Mia, can I have a cigarette, please?' I ask. She hands me the packet and a green lighter without looking up. I take one out and light it, sucking the smoke and the hurt right back into my lungs.

We stop and get some beers for the evening, along with some *za'atar* bread and cheese to grill. We are staying in a small flat, lent to us by one of the private investors funding our dig. It's right on the sea, near the Mövenpick Hotel. It's quiet and clean and we sit outside, sniffing the salty sea, intermittent gusts of drainage blowing in our direction.

I light a cigarette. My third one since Jeremy first handed me his roll-up the other day. I feel young, smoking, even though I'm aware every drag is deepening the lines on my face. We talk, all three of us, until three o'clock that morning. Mia has forgotten about her ex and me about Toby. They both ask me about my life, my school days. 'You're such a closed book,' Mia laughs, loud with drink. 'Come on, give us some stuff about yourself.' I'm sure they're asking so they can report back to the rest of the team, who have always been trying to glean information about me. No one can seem to accept I want to keep myself to myself. With good reason, perhaps. But then I look at them, waiting for me to talk and they both look so ... so open, so eager, so kind, that I unwrap my arms from around my stomach, and resolve to relax.

I mentioned Freya to them briefly, once before, never in detail. I try her name out again on them, see how it sounds, how it rests in my throat.

'There's not much to tell, really,' I say. 'I went to a strict boarding school. We weren't given any freedom and I had a best friend, Freya. We were ... our families knew each other and I used to stay with them a lot as my father was often busy at work.' I stop to look at them, see if I've given anything away but neither of them move. 'Go on,' says Mia. 'And well, not much else really.' I shrug. 'Then I got a degree and you pretty much know the rest. Very boring. And now I'm here, with you guys.'

'Well, you must have something else. You've told us bits about Toby ... what about your family? Parents? Siblings? What did your father do?' Mia swigs some more beer, throwing a glowing cigarette butt across the garden.

'You'd better go and stub that out,' and then, aware I sound bossy, 'I'm terrified of fire.' Mia gets up, carries on talking with her back towards us.

'Are they still alive? Do you get on?' Jeremy is leaning forward with his elbows on his knees.

'No siblings. My father still works. He's at Number Ten. He's very much alive. My mother, she's … she's. Yes, she's also alive …' No one has ever asked me about my family, not since school. I haven't let any conversation get that personal and, if it has, I've managed to steer it back to safer ground. 'Why are you so interested?' I give a shrill little laugh.

'Well, we do work together,' says Jeremy. 'Practically lived together for the last seven months. Everyone knows everything about each other on a dig, except you. Mysterious.'

Is that what I am? 'So,' he continues unabated and my heart sinks. 'What does your father do at Number Ten? And how did he meet your mum? He must have some amazing stories.' Mia walks back to us, cupping her cigarette butt. She puts it on the table and lights another. 'Here,' she says, throwing me one. She catches me looking at the cigarette butt. 'Don't worry, it's out,' she says. I don't answer her. Instead, I light my cigarette and think of Mother, how elegant I thought she was when I was young, with her black cigarette holder, cherry-red nails. And then, later on, the piles of half-empty fag packets that overflowed from her old Hermès bag; the one she always wore around her shoulder, covering her like a protective talisman. She would only ever have one or two puffs before she would extinguish the cigarette with a weak grind of her foot.

'My father,' I say, eventually, 'yes … he's pretty interesting. He's now the Permanent Secretary.' If either Jeremy or Mia is impressed, they don't show it, so I carry on. 'My mother, nothing much about her, I'm afraid. She and my father met at a party when she was about eighteen. She came from a real aristo family, so obviously my father thought he would marry well. She was beautiful and accompanied him to all his smart dinners as he worked. She tried different things – setting up different businesses but nothing really worked, and then I was born and she ended up staying home a lot more ...' *just not with me,* I wanted to add.

'Ah,' says Mia, as if this explains everything. Despite the relief of silence, I feel a prickle of irritation. I slump back, unwilling to talk much longer and reluctantly they finally get the message in my strained shoulders and accept that I'm done. Mia senses the awkwardness and starts changing the topic, telling us that she also went to a really strict school.

'It was exhausting,' she laughs. 'Always having to be top dog. I'm pretty sure it's going to an all-girls school, don't you think? Jeremy? You were OK, you went mixed, didn't you?' Jeremy nods and both look to me.

'My school,' I say, 'yes, it was very, very strict. Did you board, Mia?' I'm starting to feel uncomfortable talking about my school days and hope that Mia will take up the conversation.

'No. I was desperate to, but hearing you now makes me glad I didn't. I had a very Enid Blyton impression of boarding,' she says. I tell her it would have been nice if it had been really like that.

'We did have that thing of competing all the time though,' she says. 'Undercurrents of it everywhere. Whether it was boys, weight, academia. And if we failed? God forbid if we failed at anything. I was lucky, I could go home and hide in my bedroom. I suppose you could never do that being a boarder, could you?

It must have been like living in a constant spotlight.' Mia's on a roll now and totally animated in her stream of consciousness, speaking faster and faster. 'Like, shoot me now if you screwed up an exam or did anything wrong? I mean – what happened if you had an argument with someone and wanted time out?' I want her to stop right now, because I don't know how to answer this one and I think of those big iron gates at the front of the school – the way they were a protection from my home life, but at the same time hemming us all in. I go quiet, thinking of what Mia has just said, and about my own failures with Freya. Mia, too, is absorbed in her own thoughts and the conversation winds down. Jeremy suggests we play charades; a game I normally hate but it's distracting them from talking to me so I try to get into it. We pull off bits of bread, drinking beer after beer, occasionally leaning over to clink the necks of our bottles and I realise I've had something close to fun. We go to bed and Jeremy has already put my and Mia's suitcases on the single beds in our shared room. He will sleep on the pull-out sofa bed in the front room. 'So I can chase off burglars,' he laughs as he comes to our room to say goodnight.

'Oh no, don't freak me out.' Mia slugs back another beer and unfolds her long legs off the chair. 'I'm off to bed now.' She's bra-less; shaking out her curly, auburn hair. I glance over at Jeremy, who, to my relief, is not looking.

'Me too,' I say and Jeremy looks up.

'Need anything?'

'I'm OK. Thanks so much.'

I haven't shared a room with anyone, other than lovers, since school. Mia snorts and shuffles in her sleep and I find it oddly comforting. I can hear Jeremy clicking away on his mobile phone and I wonder who he is texting. We wake up the next morning and walk to the Dead Sea, where we have Turkish coffee and spend hours and hours floating in the dense water.

The rest of the holiday goes by quietly and by the end of it I realise that since that first night I have only thought about Freya fleetingly. Even the darkness of the bedroom hasn't jolted me into conjuring up her face. Her hair. I feel an emptiness when the time comes for us to go back to the city. Jeremy hoists our luggage into the car and we drive back in silence, through the desert and small villages, lit only by moon-struck houses along the road. We arrive back at the hotel and stand in the reception. Work-mode descends upon us, shoulders stooping with the effort of it all.

'See you tomorrow?' Jeremy looks at me.

'Sure.'

'What time?'

I realise I'm still his boss, yet I don't know if he's joking with me.

'Your normal time,' I say, realising this sounds like a dig at the fact he is always twenty minutes after everyone else. 'I mean. Just normal time,' I add, awkward in my attempt to be kind. Jeremy smiles and punches me on the shoulder and again, realising I'm his boss, steps back apologetically. Everything is out of sync. I know I'm not good at making these situations better so I wave goodbye to Mia, who is smirking.

'See you tomorrow then.' I turn and fish for my keys. I switch off the air conditioning in my room, which is rattling above my head, and even though I know I shouldn't, even though I try convincing myself to just leave it alone, I can't resist one look, preparing myself for the usual spam, the insignificant names. I coach myself into not expecting anything as my emails take ages to load, the timer dominating the screen, but finally they do, and with a sickening jolt there it is. All this time I have been longing for Freya's reply, but now it's here, I'm too fearful to look. My heart is twitching in my chest and my throat runs dry. *But this is what you wanted*, I tell myself.

> *Josephine. I did get your email. I'm sorry you don't want to meet but I think it is really important that I see you. I am willing to come to wherever you are … I am keeping up to date with the dig and hope it's all going as planned. As I said, I'm on business but I can take time off and we can discuss things properly.*

That was it. At first, I am disappointed. Firstly at the brevity of her message – she hasn't signed off and secondly because she's called me Josephine, rather than J. When the disappointment subsides, I feel a total lack of control. Yes – I had been expecting her to reply – a friendly note, perhaps, saying she understood and that she hoped I was well. Instead, this? The Freya I knew never used to be so assertive, so bossy and, because I'm not going to see her, I'm powerless to come back at her. Her tone has only made me resolve what I had decided earlier, though. That I will never, ever, do what she wants.

And she's keeping up to date with the dig. *How?* I think. I quickly Google myself to see what's been written and I find three new articles – two in *The Times* and one in the *Telegraph*. Then I start looking deeper.

I Google Freya every so often and have never been able to find anything on her, no matter how hard I've looked. For years I would do it every day, though, recently, less. And since she's emailed me I've been too overwhelmed to do an internet search for her, in case, somehow, she finds out. Rationally, I know the thought is ridiculous. But that's what she's done to me. I think of my mother, all huddled up and shaking whenever anyone came near her. In an effort to distract myself, I type Freya's name into the search bar, tapping the keys really hard.

I still can't find anything on her, with her married or maiden name. Nothing. How can she leave so little trace? I look on Facebook, logging in with Toby's password, and she is not there either. Nor Twitter, nor LinkedIn. I start looking up other names from the past and there's Sally Aylsford, on Facebook, with a bottle of beer in one hand, diamond ring glinting in front of her face. '*He finally asked!*' says the caption. I scroll down her friends' network for any hint of Freya, any pictures or tagged posts, but she's still not there. Verity – are you there at all? I type in her name in Sally's network and nothing comes up either. Paranoia sets in and I wonder why they are both so inaccessible. *Are you hiding from me?* Even in my head I sound utterly mad and I realise it's time, once and for all, to stop all this. I'm still overcome with fury that even now Freya thinks she has enough power over me she can tell me what to do. Is she trying to show me she's changed? That the dynamics of our friendship no longer exist? She used to tell me she wished she was like me, not caring so much what other people thought.

And now, it seems she's trying to prove her point in her ridiculous little email. As if we are still how we were at Greenwood Hall and everything in between is just an awful dream. I set an auto-responder on my email account: *This address no longer exists.* I feel a mix of nostalgia and relief – Freya and I set up that email together as part of an IT project, when the internet first reached Greenwood. That part of my life, finished. Closed.

Next I create a new email address: Earthseaproject@google-mail.com – a reference to my favourite book trilogy. I store a few of my most important contacts there – my father, his secretary, Amy, Toby and one or two of my old friends from previous digs, who might come in handy. I wonder who else I would have had on my list ten years ago. Not many more, that's for sure.

Dear All, I type, blind copying everyone into the email.

My old email is no longer in use. Please contact me here. I would be incredibly grateful if you didn't pass this email on to anyone that may ask for it.

I stop typing here and wonder if I am sounding crazy then realise I don't care – the thought of Freya finding out where I am is worse.

I then write to all my colleagues from my work email address and tell them that it is no longer in use either, and that I'd be emailing a new work contact out later that week. Next, I email Amy and ask her to start the ball rolling to get my English mobile number changed. *You know all my details,* I write. *Please go as far as you can and if you need me to finish or sign anything, just email me or ring me on my Jordanian number. Thanks Amy, J.*

I feel much, much better and I start to shut my computer when I hear another email pinging into my inbox. It's from Anne, my mother's carer. It reads:

Hello my dear Josephine,

I've been trying to get hold of you on your mobile for a few days. Please could you ring me, your mother is very sick. I'm so sorry. I know you don't like being disturbed when you are away but I've spoken to the doctors who all agree that you need to come back. To say goodbye. I'm so, so sorry to write this on the computer. No voicemail on your telephone. She finally got her own way, she was desperate to go this time. Once again, I'm so sorry for the shock.

God bless.

Anne xxx

I'm waiting to be flooded with grief, or something, but nothing happens. All I get is my mother's voice telling me she wants to cut my hair. The most random of things, and I can't work it out. The voice repeats itself over and over – when I was little, about six or so, she would snake her cold, white hands around the back of my neck, whilst holding a pair of blunt scissors. As I'm trying to rationalise and process my thoughts, I'm struck by a series of insignificant details. How noisy the air conditioning is in my room. How the brown curtains have a weird stain on them just to the left of the wall. How the light fitting in the ceiling is slightly off-centre. Odd. And then I start to shiver. I try to switch on my phone but the battery is dead. Jeremy, I think. His room is on the other side of the hotel, so I run to reception and ask them to ring up.

'You alright?' He appears three minutes later, in nothing but a towel and flip-flops.

'I...'

'You what?' He looks amused, then worried.

'It's my mother.'

'Your mother?' He frowns.

'She's very ill. Not sure what's wrong.' There's a silence. I'm sure he's wondering why I've called him and I barely know myself and I find that all the efficiency has gone and shock has set in and I am talking very, very fast and I need a drink of water.

'Sorry, I ... I just ... I didn't know what else to do. I don't suppose you have any water to hand, do you?'

'No. No need for sorry. Give me the company credit card, or tell me where it is. I'm going to book you a flight today – back to London, is it?'

I nod. 'That would be great. Thanks so much, Jeremy. I normally do this kind of thing myself, it's just my phone ...' I hold out my old mobile to show him the blank screen.

'Don't be silly, you don't need to explain. Come here.' He takes me by the arm and orders me a hot chocolate at the hotel bar. 'Stay there,' he says, squeezing my shoulder. I sit down and wonder if my mother is aware of what is happening. If Father is with her. If she's scared. She never seemed scared, all that time, even when she first went away. Just looked back at us, hissing and spitting at Father and calling him the devil and pointing at the sky, jabbing at the clouds with her fingers, seeing shapes within them that I couldn't possibly imagine. And then Father's voice comes to me – 'You look just like her' – and my mouth goes dry again. I've managed to keep myself sane all these years. During school, after school. Busy, successful and sane, and I wonder if this is it … that when Mother dies, whether it will be my turn. And then the fear really kicks in.

Jeremy's back in half an hour, with a printout, a wallet and my passport, which is kept in the safety deposit box.

'Josephine? Are you OK? You look dreadful. I mean, I guess that's no surprise given what you've just heard but…'

I gesture at the passport. 'Thank you.'

'No worries.' He still looks concerned. 'Your flight leaves in five hours. Sorry, I couldn't get one earlier. Here, your passport and there's two hundred dinars in there too.' He hands me the wallet.

'Thank you again.' I wish I could start crying like a normal person but, instead, I feel totally disconnected. All I can think about is whether the plane will be cold and if I should change into my trainers. And then I realise, if I'm going back to London, I might very well bump into Freya. The thought brings me back into myself. Terrifies me. I clamp my mouth shut to try to stop the shivering. And then I wonder what kind of person I am to be thinking about Freya at a time like this.

'Right,' I say, forcing myself to speak. 'I'll email you when I'm in London. Could you let me know how the next few days go? And you and Mia can be in charge of things. I'll tell the big bosses. Mark's kind, he'll be fine with it, as long as he knows you guys are on it. If you just give me a brief rundown of what's gone on during the day, I'll write back with instructions.'

'Listen, don't worry. We've already done the timetable rota for the next three weeks at our last meeting so we're all up to speed. Just go, have a quick shower and I'll meet you in fifteen minutes outside your room and we'll get a cab.'

'We?'

'Yes. I'm coming with you to the airport.' I'm both annoyed that he thinks I'm incapable of getting there myself and secretly pleased he's making an effort.

'Thank you,' I say softly, 'I appreciate it.'

1996. THE MORNING AFTER...

I haven't slept properly. Floated in and out of dreams, flashes of the club. Despite my vows to stay off them, the drugs are still in effect – I didn't take much so I could stay in control, but they must have been strong, or maybe I was a lot drunker than I thought. I can feel my heartbeat somewhere near the base of my throat, echoing up to my brain.

When I open my eyes, something doesn't feel quite right, even though Freya seems to be sleeping soundly on the bed. It's not just the comedown. It's a feeling of dread and change. I'm untethered, my spirit floating aimlessly somewhere in the universe with my twitching, restless body left behind. I remember snatches of what was only a few hours ago, and I start to shiver. Normality, I think. That's what I need, so I go to the kitchen and pull on my school jumper, which is hanging up next to my coat in the hall. My Head Girl badge catches in my ponytail and my hair elastic snaps undone. I curse and then I feel the huge lump on the back of my head. It stings and, as I gingerly touch it, I can feel crusted blood. Where did that come from? I touch it some more and, when I pull away my fingers, they are warm and red. I feel the rest of my head and then look down my arms, legs and feet. My breath keeps catching but an inner voice tells me to pull myself together. *What is a Head Girl meant to do in this situation?* I ask myself. *I am Head Girl and so I've got to take control.*

I set about cleaning every single surface I can find: the insides of cupboards, the fridge, the oven, shelves. The kitchen is already clean – Amy keeps a tight ship – but there is something gratifying about the mechanical nature of my movements. Whenever I stop, I get weird little lights creeping into my mind. Are they real? I try to bat them out of the way but it doesn't work. I clean some more and as I buff the surfaces over and over, urging my mind into repression, I begin to think of Freya: Freya who is always so open, who always says what she thinks, an open book in every way, unable to conceal her feelings. My mind tries to draw back to the memories of the previous night but nothing specific surfaces. Just a lurch in my stomach and an impending fear that something awful has happened. If Freya remembers, though, *she will tell,* I think. *Freya will tell.* The drugs, the booze. She will let it all out.

At first, it's a thought that doesn't gather weight but then I think about the school finding out. And Father, Mother, Rollo, Leon. My mind leads on to the consequences of this happening. We would no doubt be expelled. No Head Girl badge, no university, no future, no nothing. And even worse, if all of that happens, if I lose the perfect facade I've created, then I'll have lost everything and I have an image of me, years down the line, just like Mother – she had been the perfect wife before it all fell apart; the look of absolute terror at the things she's seen, heard, the cocktail of medicines and then the slump of her eyes as the drugs blend with her soul – and I know now that my mission, my overriding mission, on top of school, on top of the scholarship, on top of everything else, is to get Freya to keep her mouth shut, so that everything can be as it was: she a Prefect and me on track to get to Oxford.

The kitchen looks perfect now. I go over the surfaces once more with a new, yellow dishcloth I find under the sink. If everything is perfect, glistening, clean, nothing else can go wrong. This is the true face of the world.

But it's another hour before Freya comes down. Hair brushed, she's wearing one of Mother's grey cardigans, which stops just above her knees. It's covered in burrs and, more strangely, what looks like white party popper string. She's put on mascara, concealer and blusher although it's not enough to hide the light grazes that scatter her cheek and chin. Her nose is rimmed with a bloody crust. Her legs are shaking and she's hunched over. She looks so frail. Her neck is still filthy, streaked black all over. She sees me looking and opens her arms, waiting for her to take me into them.

'You look nice. I'm cooking breakfast for us, though technically it's not exactly morning but still a first meal is a first meal,' I say, not moving from the hobs. I am serene; even when bacon fat spits on my cheek.

'J?' she says uncertainly. Her eyes are tearing up.

'OK so let's eat. How many eggs?' I cook and serve without waiting for a response. The white gelatinous wobble on my plate is making me feel a bit sick but I force it down anyway, in great lumps. Freya is still standing in the same position, watching me eat.

'Last night,' I say as the silence hangs thick between us. 'What happened at the club ... Just try and forget about it, OK?'

I'm shaking the ketchup bottle and nothing's coming out. I feel like smashing it on the floor, lying on the broken glass. Instead, I calmly poke my knife down the bottle-neck. The sauce trickles out, along with a drop of blood that slides its way down from my neck to my arm. I catch Freya watching and quickly wipe it away.

'Josephine.' She's talking but her teeth are chattering and I can't make out what she's saying. The dirt on her neck makes her look like a tramp and her hair needs a wash.

'No buts … Just try and forget about it.' The sauce relents, splurging all over my plate. 'Remember, I'm Head Girl, you are a Prefect. We are both taking our Oxbridge entries soon and we've got to get on with things.' I'm sure this will work. I know how important Oxford is to Freya. It's an obsession of hers – in living memory of her mother, who also went there. But then she sinks onto her knees, holding her hands up in what looks like prayer. 'Please,' she says. 'Please.' She curls herself up on the floor so I can't see her face and lies there whilst I calmly eat my food. *At least Amy and Father are not due to return soon,* I think.

'Like Mrs Allen always says –' I watch her, trying to work out if she's even breathing '– I know it might be tricky but just, "onwards and upwards". So carry on as if nothing happened, alright? If they find out what we were up to, what we were doing, it'll be an instant expulsion. I don't know about you but … I only did half a pill. And what the fuck was in it anyway?' For a moment I feel my composure slipping. *Rein it back, Josephine, keep it together.* I take a breath and continue, 'It's not worth the mess we'd get into.'

'But it wasn't ...' She lifts her head, then goes silent, gazing off into a distance far beyond the walls of my kitchen.

'Stop thinking about it,' I order.

'But ... J, I've got to tell you...'

'Just don't ... I don't want to hear another word. Do you hear me?'

She rests her head back down and neither of us speak. The 'mornings-after-the-night-before' are usually spent dissecting every detail of our night out. Flirtations (who had the hottest guy after them), the music (was it too heavy?), the people (did we bump into the usual crew?). They're normally washed down with Diet Coke and laughter but this time we are quiet, absorbed in the excruciating treadmill of our own thoughts.

'But ...' Freya turns her head up and looks at me, desperate, and her legs are making little jerky movements, although the rest of her is still. I tell myself it's the after-effects of all the drinking and the pills, nothing else.

'No buts. Are you seriously telling me you want to destroy all of our successes so far? Everything that we've worked for? We can't let it all go down the drain. For what? For one night? *One night,* Freya? Years of hard work? And you were the one that pushed me into it. Remember? I said I wasn't going to take anything. And if anyone finds out about the pills ... So, please, just stop bloody thinking about it.' I'm talking, yet barely aware of what I'm saying. My mind keeps pulling back to the glare of those eyes.

'Think of our school motto. Remember? *Per Asperrimus ad Parnassum.*' I realise I sound like Verity but it's too late. Freya sobs and tears spill out of her eyes at the same time and her legs start stiffening and jerking again and she's crying. I slowly close and reopen my eyes as if she's a difficult toddler throwing a fit in a supermarket aisle. 'Come on,' I say.

Per Asperrimus ad Parnassum. Through great difficulties to the heights of success. Head Girl. I'm Head Girl now and I have a responsibility to lead and guide. Make things right. Head Girl. My duty to show courage and be of great, great success.

Boom. Doof. Boom. Doof.

I push the noise of the club out of my head, but it comes back again, louder and more insistent. I let it stay there for a bit and then pick up our plates and take them to the bin. My head feels like it's being smashed from one wall to another. Drink. The half a pill. And then I remember the lump on my head. I try to change tack. I put the plates and cutlery in the huge silver dishwasher, and walk over to where she's lying. 'It's OK.' I lie down beside her and smooth her hair. It feels stiff and then I see bits of dirt and other things nestling between the strands. 'It's OK. Look, don't worry. It's OK.' Freya looks up at me, hand resting on her stomach. She's stopped crying.

'Really? Do you really think so? I mean ...' Freya's eyes search mine but I can't tell if she's engaging with me.

'Yes of course, of course.' I don't know how I'm managing to sound so calm, when my head is feeling the way it is. 'It's all going to be OK,' I say.

She gets up. 'So that means we can tell someone? I don't think I can go on if we don't. I can't. I just can't.'

I bite down on the inside of my cheek to stop myself screaming at her. I'm finding it difficult to keep my patience.

'No, no, Frey. We can't tell anyone. Just trust me on this one. We can't. We'd probably be sent to rehab of some kind.'

Her eyes finally focus, and she looks like she's listening. 'Really?' she says, disbelieving.

'Yes. Really. So remember. Nothing.'

She is silent, thoughtful and I think finally this is starting to sink in. I feel a bubble of relief.

'OK,' she says. *Come on, Freya. Stick with me on this one.* But she starts up again. 'What about … I mean … what if? Last night? Surely we need to …' She's digging around in one of the kitchen drawers, where we keep all of our phone books. She throws a Yellow Pages onto the counter and starts flicking through it. 'Here,' she says. Her finger can't meet the page but I'm looking at her, willing her to stop.

'It's fine.' I grab the book and put it back in the drawer. 'I don't know what you are thinking. But it's fine. Honestly. Alright?'

'But … I need your help. Will you? I mean … practical things too.' I have no idea what she's talking about and then she's pointing to something in her pocket and I can't see exactly what it is but I think I know what she's getting at, and I wonder how I could be so stupid as not to have thought about that myself. And so I tell her to stay where she is. I go upstairs, remembering something I saw in Amy's room and I explain how it's going to work and Freya says are you sure that's the right thing to do and I say yes of course and she says thank you. She seems to accept what I've said and, when I think she's finally pulling it together, her face crumples and she starts to plead with me again if we can talk to someone, even tell her father. 'Anyone, just anyone,' she is saying, her voice desperate and I want to slap her because she's talking absolute gibberish now and I can't really make anything out so I stand up and clap my hands instead of stinging them on her tear-stained cheek.

'Right,' I say brightly, 'I know what will make us feel better. Shall we watch *The Sound of Music*?' It's one of our favourite morning-after films. We always end up singing and talking about Nazi rule, then singing again. Freya dresses up sometimes, white handkerchief pulled tight around her head like a bonnet.

'Adieu, adieu to ye and ye and ye,' she usually sings. This time, however, we both sit in front of the whirring video, too tired to blink. Freya's pulling a thread from Mother's jumper, winding it through her fingers.

'So what do you think about the scholarship?' Freya asks, as Julie Andrews is breaking out into another song. She sounds nearly normal, if a little flat, and for the first time I am relieved she is bringing up something ordinary, even if the notion of conversation right now is excruciating.

'What about it?'

'Who else do you think they're going to put forward?'

'Dunno.'

'Melody Swaffham? What if you don't get put forward?' I laugh but my stomach's niggling. It's nothing too obvious, like someone is gently flicking it from the inside, just the after-effect of the drugs, I suppose. And then, thoughts start ricocheting around my head, pinballing their way through the flailing network of post-night-out brain cells. No scholarship, no automatic entry to Oxford. What if I don't get the scholarship and then don't get into Oxford either? The flicking starts pulsating, growing, until it feels like someone is grabbing my insides and shifting them around. Mother's face keeps appearing. Snarly and misshapen.

'What about you?' I force myself to say.

'What about me?' And then she loses it. The tears. She's shaking so violently I think she's fitting.

'Come on, Freya. For goodness sake! Seriously. It's OK.' I don't know, though, if it is, and I catch myself wondering if it might have been better if, last night, both of us had died. But we didn't. And so … 'It's your fault, you got all those pills in. Who would believe us anyway?' I say, hoping this will pull her together and shut her up once and for all. She leaves the sofa and I make a half-attempt at shouting after her. Five minutes later she comes back with a coat she's borrowed from my room.

'May I?' She starts to put it on. It's an old grey duffel that Father bought me from Switzerland. She keeps getting her arm stuck in the wrong sleeve. Over and over. I grab it from her and drape it around her shoulders.

'Here. Let me do it.' She's putting on a pair of her old Converse trainers that she left at my house the last time we went out. She leaves the laces undone, stuffing them under the tongue.

'I don't want to wear those boots,' she says. 'The ones I was wearing last night. I'm taking them. I'll shove them in a skip somewhere. And the skirt. I've thrown it away.'

The thought of her staying is too suffocating, I'd like nothing better than to just be on my own but the pragmatist in me is terrified that if she leaves in this state, she'll go and tell Rollo. So I use my last card.

'Freya, listen, don't go quite yet.' She turns her head, going to the gilt-edged mirror on the other side of the room. She's looking at her neck.

'Look at me.' She turns and stares. Blank eyes.

'Your mother. You have to stay silent for your mother. Alright? She's looking out for you, wherever she is.' Her eyes start flickering. Burning right through me and, for a minute, I wonder if she's going to hit me.

'Freya, your mother loved you so much. She'll make sure you can deal with this, wherever she is now. But if you tell anyone, if you tell a soul, seriously – one soul – then you won't get into Oxford. Do you get that? You won't be able to make her proud. You won't be able to make your dad proud. He needs this, Freya. He needs this just as much as you do. He needs to be able to tell himself he did a good job on you and Leon, without her being there. He loves you so much too, Freya. He loves you. Don't let him down. Don't let your mother down. So do you promise? You promise not to say anything?'

She regards me carefully for a moment, through narrowed eyes, and I realise I am holding my breath.

'My mother. You're right.'

I breathe out and she's looking skywards now. 'Mother. I've got to make her proud, don't I? Get into Oxford. That's what she would have wanted for me. More than absolutely anything in the entire world.' She bends down as though she's trying to catch her breath, and comes up again.

'Yes. More than anything in the world,' I echo. 'She wanted you to follow in her footsteps. Be brave like her. She would want to look at you now and say you have had the best opportunity you could have had. Lived the best life you could. Make her proud.'

The window's open and a breeze brings in a sweet smell of flowers. Freya seems to take this as a sign. Robotically she says, 'I've got to make her proud. Of course. No, I won't say anything. I promise you. But you'll help me get through this, though, won't you? We'll help each other?' I give her a small nod and a smile and I'm hoping to God she can't see through me but it's too late. She takes a step backwards and the trust evaporates.

'Bye then,' I say lightly, 'see you at school tomorrow.' The space between us unfurls as she waits for me to break the silence. I don't. I want to leave it on a striking note, so that she thinks about her mother and what it would mean if she told anyone. She moves her hand, slowly, from the doorknob and turns towards the stairs. A moment later I can still hear her feet, whispering on the carpet. I go back into the room and turn up the volume on the television.

That night, I go to the kitchen to make some tea. When I dump the tea bag into the bin, I see the jewelled glint of the denim skirt that Freya had been wearing. The band of skulls and crossbones that we had spent hours gluing on together. I pick it out, shaking off bits of eggshell and bacon fat and toast crumbs. I smell it. Smoke, CK One and something else: a slightly soury, metallic smell with damp undertones that hits the back of my throat and makes me panic. I take the skirt, stuff it under my bed. I then pack my bags and leave, scribbling Father a note.

Couldn't wait for you, I write. *Had to go back in time for choir practice.* Love J? Or Josephine. In the end I go for just J and place an Eiffel Tower paperweight over the thick, cream paper. I order a taxi on Father's work account. I intend to get the train but, since it's only half an hour away and knowing Father won't object to the cost, I end up asking the taxi driver to take me all the way back to school.

'Put it on your account?' he asks, stilling the fir tree that dangles from his rear-view mirror.

'Please,' I say, hunting for a tip. I give him five pounds and spend ages counting out the change. The iron gates loom over me like vultures and for a moment I can't bring myself to go in.

The girls seem settled into old routines when I get back. That first afternoon, I hear of three arguments in our year, so-and-so told so-and-so that so-and-so slept with so-and-so. Kitty Archwright has accused Flora Jones-Bardam of sabotaging her friendship with Olivia Buckingham and so on and so on.

Whispers fill the school. The younger girls press themselves against the corridor walls as the older girls swish past. Teachers already look tired and the new girls are brazen with having passed initiation in the form of midnight dares (run down the front stairs in just your bra and knickers, ring the gong in the middle of the night, that kind of thing). Eleanor from my dorm has long forgotten her homesickness and is all jokes and shrieking and I have to tell her twice to be quiet after bedtime. I go to bed with the rest of the girls, even though lights out for non-sixth-formers is at ten o'clock. I wonder if Freya came back on the seven o'clock evening train like she normally does, or whether she decided to come back before class tomorrow morning. When I think of her, I'm all prepped not to be able to sleep, terrified that after last night I'll scream out, but my brain and body are totally numb. I can't feel a thing. As soon as I shut my eyes, I'm gone.

2014

The ride to the airport is mercifully quick. Neither of us speaks. Jeremy tries to hug me as I am about to walk through the departure gates but I hold myself rigid against his touch. He lets his arms fall to his sides. 'I've got everything,' he says. 'I promise. Don't think about work.' I nod and turn away.

I've always loved plane rides. I even look forward to the compartmentalised food plates, where everything is neatly packaged and set in front of me. I love the swooping feeling of the plane taking off, even the turbulence. It is the only time these days I will watch a film. Today's offering is some romcom that I've never heard of but which requires little concentration. I feel guilty every time I sit back and relax. I should be thinking of Mother. The green cashmere cardigan she always wears, her nails yellowing from all the smoking. I've only seen her three or four times in the past two years and on each occasion she was more and more hunched and silent, the drugs taking hold of her shrivelling body. The air stewardess comes round with a clinking tray of glasses.

'Wine?'

I take one, reclining my seat and then the name drops into my brain like a boulder.

Freya.

It's OK, I tell myself. I will never see her again and she will never know of the volcanic swirl that has been erupting in my stomach since I read her email. I imagine what would happen if we met again and it goes something like this:

'*Freya!*'

She would look at me, giving me the swift up and down she always does when first meeting someone, and then flick her ponytail onto her left shoulder and twirl the end through her fingers.

'*J!*' No, I shake my head remembering the formal tone of address in her last email. '*Josephine.*'

'*How are you?*' I would stand a few steps away from her for fear she might try to touch me, and she'll understand, always able to read my cues like no other. And then I fear she will start talking about it, about school, and that night and the horrors that follow. What would I do then?

'*You could have helped me,*' she would say.

I could have helped you, I would think.

I try to shift myself out of my reverie but the dialogue continues to whirr: *I could have helped myself. But that's OK, Freya, because you have no bearing on who I am now. The memories – they have no power over me. None.* I will stay in London only as long as necessary and then I'll leave, back to Jordan. *But her email was so persistent.* The plane starts to judder and the vibration of the captain's voice through the loud speaker tickles my ears, warning of turbulence. The voice is jarring and, as I think of bumping into Freya in London, I start to panic. The narrowness of the plane seems to be too small and constricting for the noise in my head.

My lungs shrivel and I cannot breathe. It is that night all over again, the music pounding in my ears. *Doof. Boom. Doof. Boom. Make it stop*, I think, and the plane flails, wings rattling.

Flashes flit through my brain, things I have not thought of since they happened: the sweet smell of the smoke machine mixed with sweat, strobe lights, the whoosh of chemicals taking hold of my body, the eyes of the dragon tattoo staring at me, daring me on to do what, I never knew, and then again, Freya's eyes. They are with me right now: it is like someone is wringing all the fear from her and it has risen up into her face trying to burst its way out. Her eyes are huge, shimmering with terror at what is happening.

My thoughts start skidding, piling up into one big mountain of entangled horrors. The whirrings slow down, replaced by echoes of memory from what followed that night: my behaviour when we got back to school and how Freya reacted. An image of Rollo forms and he is smiling, squeezing me tight in the soft pit of his arm. He is telling me that no matter how bad it gets with my mother, he'll be there to pick up the pieces.

'I promise you, I promise you,' he is saying and I start to cry.

I drop my head between my knees and I feel a light hand on my shoulder. I am too weak to throw it off.

'Excuse me? Miss? Excuse me? Would you like something? Water?' The immaculate, russet-haired air stewardess smells of violets and face powder.

'Vodka,' I murmur. I can hear the liquid being poured and the ice being chucked in and I drink it gratefully. The huddled mass of thoughts disperses and subsides.

'You look better now, sweetie. Do you want some food?'

'No thanks.' *Do not call me 'sweetie' again,* I think. The next two hours speed up with the help of a few more vodkas and by the time I go through arrivals and bag retrieval, the episode on the plane feels like a dream I had pretending to be someone else. London sinks back into my psyche as though I had never left. The thick, sweet smell of Amman replaced with warm gusts of hamburger odours wafting out of restaurant extractor fans; the bright lights of the baggage reclaims and the people, marching about their way with much more intent than the cigarette-clouded languor of those in Jordan.

When I arrive at my parents' house, I find Father is out. All the furniture and ornaments remain in the same place as that fateful night with Freya. I had emailed Father from the airport with my flight details, so he knew I was returning. The initial hollowness that he hasn't stayed in to be with me is quickly replaced by relief that I can postpone any discussions about Mother. I can unpack, relax. Try to find some warmth and cosiness in the draughty rooms and corridors of home. I find a note on the kitchen table, underneath an empty glass vase.

Josephine, Welcome back. Got dinner with the PM – couldn't reschedule. Only round the corner. Will be back afterwards and hope for a catch up drink with my favourite daughter. Your mother is steadier today. We'll get Max to drive us to see her tomorrow. X

There's also a letter from Amy, with a new mobile and phone number. I spend time copying over my contacts wondering how many of them I'll ever use. I climb the stairs to the top of the house. After the dust and sand-covered floor in my room in Jordan, the thick, white carpet feels luxurious under my toes. My old bedroom takes up the entire top floor, with a large en-suite bathroom attached. The same wartime prints are still hanging on the walls from when I was about six. Freya would always tack pictures around my room, of men from bands I had never really heard of. 'Eddie Vedder,' she would say. 'He's *so* hot!' After she left I would always take them down.

I sit down on the huge white bed, fresh and plump, and from underneath it pull out a wooden box full of letters and old keepsakes that I haven't looked at for years. Not since I left Greenwood. Everything is kept in plastic sleeves, filed in order of year. I take out a green one that's splitting at the seams. There are postcards, birthday cards, letters, flyers and little notes in there. I tip them all out on the bed, then lay them out in date order.

Freya used to write to me often. I would always find little notes and cards under my pillow at school, wishing me luck for an exam or for no reason at all. '*Josephine,*' she's written on one card. '*Happy Birthday to my oldest and bestest. Giving this to you a few months early because I've got us tickets for the Serpent's Summer Rave next week. Love, F XXX*'.

And another: '*J, Good luck for your exams. Not that you'll need it, obviously! Number one student ... One day maybe I'll catch up with you. Love, F xxx*'.

And then I find it – a small, crumpled flyer, a muddy footprint shading the black and white outline of a dancing figure. It's the flyer from that night. '*THE FRIDGE, THE ANNUAL RETURN TO PEACE PARTY, 9 p.m. to 6 a.m. AFTERPARTY AT BANANA MOON.*'

I sit and look at the familiar shadings, the Buddhist symbols curling their way around the page. *Freya*, I think. *What happened to you?* And then I wonder if it really was that night that ruined everything, or whether something else was at play – whether our friendship might always have been doomed.

I find an old diary, corresponding to that time. In it are daily entries about work, the teachers, Freya of course, boys. Until after that night. Then it goes blank, other than a few scribbles about my Head Girl jobs and what Mrs Allen needs doing. I throw the whole lot back into the box and push it right under my bed, then remove it and take it outside and put it in a cupboard which has all my old school folders in it dating right back from when I was four years old. I flick through a few; my writing was so neat, so old-fashioned, even then. I close the cupboard door quietly, placing my head against the mahogany. I push a large chest of drawers against the cupboard, to shut away the contents and keep them further away from me. Afterwards, I feel like the breath is being squeezed out of me, like an old, wheezing accordion, so I go downstairs, slug back my sixth vodka of the day and go to bed, restless but somehow exhausted.

He doesn't look up when I come into the kitchen. Flicks the pages of his newspaper whilst writing notes on a small yellow pad next to his empty bowl. 'Hello,' I say, my voice small. He's still in his dressing gown. Patterned blue, perfectly pressed and turned up at the sleeves.

'Josephine, coffee?' He finally moves his eyes away from the news and stares just to the left of me, as though he's embarrassed at being in his nightwear. 'Nice to see you. Sorry about last night. Are you alright? Had a good flight?' He doesn't wait for me to answer, so I know these questions are merely perfunctory. 'Your mother's comfortable. She's …' His eyes take on an unfocused look. I nod, letting him off the hook. 'Here,' he says, 'drink this.' He takes a blue mug from the shelf and pours it full.

'Thanks.' I sit and read the newspaper over his shoulder until we get to the Sports section.

'Right. Best get ready. We'll get a car to see your mother? Will you come?'

'Of course.' I give a sarcastic laugh. 'I didn't come all this way to see you.' Father looks down, swills his empty cup around and wipes his mouth with the back of his hand. He looks as though he's about to say something. Shuts it again and clears his throat. 'I mean … I was joking,' I say, surprised at his reaction.

'I'll get dressed,' he says. 'Meet me back down here in fifteen.' He sounds sharp, professional. I want to tell him again that I was joking but something stops me. The fear that I'll sound insincere; that it'll make it worse.

I'm ready in ten minutes. I'm wearing the brightest coloured clothes I can find: a light-blue jumper and a brown scarf, which don't go but the oddness of the colours takes my mind off things. Father comes down three minutes later, in a smart suit.

Max, Father's driver, arrives to take us to the hospital. He swings round to the Wentworth-Miller patient wing. I stride into the hospital quickly before I become fearful.

'Room three hundred and two,' says the receptionist, as she recognises Father, who is coming up behind me. We go down to her room, past gilt-framed pictures of roses; red, yellow, orange and pink. Nothing but roses. I start to feel weird, looking at them all. They're so beautiful. So perfect.

Neither of us bothers knocking at her door. When we enter, she looks like she's staring outside the dark-glassed window but, when I get closer, I see her eyes are shut. She's thin and smells of sick. Her skin is yellow and her arms are puckered with tape holding down tubes that are sticky with blood.

'Hello,' I say. I look over to Father, who is gripping the end of her bed. Neither of us says anything more. She's not with us, mentally, at least. I don't know whether she's sleeping, or just heavy with drugs. I notice her breasts drooping down each side of her ribcage. Those same breasts that used to cushion large diamond-egg necklaces, sapphires, or the flat gold lizard she used to wear, with the ruby eyes. I walk over and take her hand and motion to Father to do the same thing. A young-looking doctor, hair knotted up in one of those tortoiseshell crocodile clips that always remind me of Freya, knocks on the door.

'Can I come in?'

'Please.' Father pulls up a chair for her but she waves it away.

'Thanks so much. Better not sit down or I'll never get up again. Right. You are her husband and daughter, is that correct? I'm your Consultant. Miss Mainwaring.' We both nod. She clicks her biro and makes a few notes on her clipboard.

'Mr Grey, how are you doing? If you would both step outside for a moment, I'd be grateful.'

'Yes, yes of course.' Father adopts the tone of an eager school-boy and we follow her back through the door.

'Right. Well, as you know, Mrs Grey's very heavily sedated at the moment. She ... well, we think she hasn't got long. I'm so sorry. I don't know how much you know, Josephine, but she overdosed, aspirating on some of her vomit. She now has pneumonia.'

'How long?' I ask, before Father has to.

'One, maybe two days.'

'How?' Father sags against the wall. I don't know if it's from relief, or pain.

But I don't want to hear any more. I go back into her room, leaving him with Miss Mainwaring. There's something unnatural about the way she's sleeping, which might be the medication. The corners of her mouth are twitching and there's a knot of hair curled up by her right temple. Her ear lobes are free from the pearls she always used to wear, which sit on the side of the bed. I pick them up, hold them against my lobes. I had never wanted to have my ears pierced, not since Mother had told me that if I did, she would buy me the same pearls so that we could be like twins.

And then I hear a movement. I think it's her. I'm too afraid to turn around, so I put the earrings back and stand, frozen. Her eyes are shut but I start to remember the last time I saw her and I can almost hear her voice. The whisper: 'You, Josephine. You and me. We're the same. You will always be my daughter.' I stay turned away for a while and when I do turn, she looks dead. I walk over and lift her eyelids. I look through the hollows of her eyes, the black pupils. 'I hope you are comfortable,' I say, taking her hand. I'm shaking and can't pick it up properly. I lean over and kiss her, something I don't ever remember doing. She's still breathing. The trace of veins on her eyelids looks like she's smudged purple eye-shadow on her sockets.

Eventually, in some sort of unspoken tag team, I go and sit outside whilst Father is with her, for at least an hour. I focus on a small crack in the ceiling and I remember staring at that little point above Mrs Allen's head, when she had announced Head Girl. How I had wished for Mother to react to my news in the right way. How I longed for her to tell me she loved me and that she was proud. And how I hungered for that badge. Wished on it so hard I thought I might burst. That badge was the symbol of the perfect trajectory to success – Oxford, a first-rate career that would, of course, mean I would never, ever end up like her.

Max is waiting for us outside the hospital. My senses sharpen, I feel as though I'm faced with an onslaught of one hundred hurtling juggernauts and have to work out which way to leap. The suggestion of death inhabits everything I look at. The broken branches of trees, the old lady across the road stooping to pick up her plaid purse, flower petals drooping, despite the sun. Father is wearing an odd, shiny smile, lips pulled right back to the top of his gums. He's acting like he's just closed the business deal of the century. His eyes are glowing, darting from one point to another. It crosses my mind he's tried to anchor himself with some sort of pills, but then I see his teeth sinking into his bottom lip. Something he does when he's nervous, and I realise it's a massive dose of adrenaline, careering through his body. He can barely keep himself still. Finally, he gets into the car and Max asks us where we are going and he doesn't reply. Just looks at me, totally dazed.

'Any restaurant nearby, Max,' I say, speaking for us both. 'That would be great. Thank you.'

We find a small, empty Italian cafe. When I get out of the car, the sun hurts my eyes, my legs tickling with weakness. My neck is heavy; iron clad. Seemingly unaware we've stopped and parked, Father sits, waiting for someone to do something. I open his door. He frowns. 'We're here,' I say. 'At a restaurant.' He gets out, holding onto the door frame and still wearing that weird smile, fiddling with a red handkerchief from his pocket.

'Here. Come on,' I say. He takes my arm and leans into me. I bolt myself upright to stop myself from falling.

We sit down in the restaurant in total silence. I take charge, asking the small, buck-toothed waitress for the menus. She nods, licking her two front teeth. 'Can we also have a bottle of wine, please?'

I sit up straight and place the menu in front of him. He doesn't open it so when the waitress comes back and pops the cork, I order for him. 'Two margheritas too.' I have no idea whether he even likes pizza but the action makes me feel strong. Like I've got everything under control.

'She's comfortable,' I say, bolstered by my apparent emotional strength and Father's lack thereof. 'That's all that matters. OK? She's going to be comfortable.'

Our wine sits, untouched. The pizza finally arrives. That too sits congealing on the brown-speckled plates. Father picks up and sets down his glass, without drinking anything.

'She looks like a...'

He doesn't finish and I don't try to fill the void of his lapsed sentence. I take a large sip of my own wine.

'Everything OK?' The waitress leans over me to put down the salt and pepper, her necklace dangling in my face.

'Fine,' I reply.

'So funny, isn't it?' he says suddenly.

'What?'

'Just ... She won out in the end, didn't she? I didn't even see it coming. She seemed peaceful the other times. Today ... she didn't. Why is it so cold in here?'

'It's not,' I say, passing him the brown Indian print scarf I'm wearing. 'Have this.'

He folds it over his legs like a napkin.

Unexpectedly I ask him the question that has always haunted me. 'Why did you marry her?' The question comes as a surprise to both of us.

He takes a moment to consider this. 'Because she was such a mysterious beauty before. God that makes me sound awful, doesn't it.' He rubs his face, skewing his dark eyebrows. It makes him look comical; at odds with the painstakingly put-together front he normally displays.

'Before what?'

'Before things really went wrong. Before the pregnancy.' Abruptly he stops talking. In a physical attempt to displace his own thoughts, he wraps my scarf around his waist like a cummerbund, squeezing the ends together and tying small knots into the black fringing.

I swallow hard. 'Before the ...?'

'Pregnancy. You, I mean. She was OK before that. Looking back on it there were signs, of course. They only started getting worse later on, though. When she stopped her medication. And then it just ... it totally spiralled. And none of us could get a check on it.'

Pregnancy. It was my fault. The perfect circularity of this both comforts and scares me and then I wonder: if my birth triggered her illness does that mean her death will trigger something in me? The thought is irrational, I know. But it gathers pace, creeping and crawling under my skin. Father's now smiling, as though he's telling me a story of long lost beauty and love.

'And then of course,' he goes on, sliding his finger around the rim of his wine glass, 'and then it got worse and worse of course. The hoarding in case of war. Her "devil voice". And then, the bathroom incident. After that it was just a nightmare. Terrifying.' There's nothing in his face to give away that he actually thought any of it was terrifying. As though he's telling me it's a very nice day and that he's off to work soon. The absence of any obvious emotion makes me think that it was, indeed, too terrifying to deal with at all.

'What bathroom incident?'

'Just … just the beginning of the worse parts. You'll probably remember it all very differently.'

My mind wanders back. I think of her when I was young. My first memory; not really a memory: an imprint. The wholeness of her, even though she never quite seemed complete. The heavy smell of talcum powder and cigarettes, the impossibly high heels. Her slender calves and the awkwardness of her touch. Hugs with me would make her leap backwards, as though she had been slapped. And then the imprint becomes clearer as the years pass, forming into cogent outlines. The precision of her walk, which later on became a shuffle. And then the gross protrusion of her belly as her back became more and more hunched. The thinness of her legs and arms. The stare. Those eyes, always looking for something. Never finding. Those tight scars, laddering right up her arms. The way I felt when she came near me: like a skinned rabbit, ready to be gutted. And now, her organs shutting down, purple eyelids. Blanched skin. I take a bite of pizza but the dough starts to swell in my throat.

I point to the bottle-green water carafe, which is near my father. He doesn't notice and the waitress is forced to intervene, whacking my back until my heart feels like it might pop out of my blue T-shirt. I think back to what my mother said to me. That she and I are the same. My brain feels like it's melting and Father's face starts drooping. Jowly and wax-like. Like the faces of that night with Freya. And then I freak out and I wonder if I'm freaking out because of the association, or whether the hallucinations have started, just like they did for Mother and I try and slow down my thoughts but ... but ...

'Umm, actually ...' I begin to say.

'Yes?' He looks up. *It's OK*, I think. *I don't sound mad.*

'Nothing. Nothing. Just wanted to ...' *Yes*, I'm thinking. I can still talk. Still make conversation. Still be normal. There are no hallucinations. No voices. And then it hits me again. A hint of something. It feels like my thoughts have swerved off course. Like the centre of each one is being sucked into some weird vortex. Shit. I'm beginning to unravel, so I tell my father I'm going to the bathroom and I run the tap and take great gulps of water because, of course, if I can still open my mouth, drink, swallow, repeat then I'm still functioning and I'm still OK and I'm still not like her. I sit on the loo sweating, tearing bits of loo roll off and then I start needing to pee but I find I can't.

When I make it back to the table, Father has finished my wine too. I signal to the waitress to bring me some more and I down it. 'You too?' I say to him, pointing to my glass. He nods. After three more and a vodka and orange, my thoughts unclench and the fruity liquid steamrolls calm through my blood. I slump back into my chair and eat the cold pizza.

When we get back home, we say a quick goodnight. I lie awake in my room, sluggish from drink. My mind has settled. I'm too scared to move in case the panic sets in again, so I forgo my desperate need for water, instead counting the headlamps from passing cars. Mother's probably dead now. I wonder if I'll be able to sense it when she goes. The thought brings a lift of freedom, then guilt.

Two hours later I can still hear Father rustling papers in his study. The tone of light outside my bedroom window starts to shift; the blackness gearing up towards a blueish-violet. The static in my brain peaks and drops, until it eventually flatlines. And dreaming of Freya and Mother morphing together, haloed in beautiful golden hair, I fall asleep.

1996

The next morning I wake up at six thirty and get dressed, my back turned to the rest of the sleeping dormitory. I pull on my blue woollen school cape that I wear on special occasions. I'm giving my first speech as Head Girl during morning chapel. I haven't had any time to prepare – although I had thought, or rather fantasised, about it for the entire year before I was appointed. I'm going to talk about personal strength and that's OK because, after the weekend, I feel strong. Or rather, I am not feeling much, which seems to me a very good thing indeed. Gives me space to concentrate on Freya, Oxford, the scholarship and *The Lens*.

I sit on the staff table at breakfast (which no one thinks odd – they've probably assumed it's a new school policy) to escape the chance of anyone talking to me. After I've eaten a piece of toast, I walk up to chapel and stand at the old wooden lectern. The girls and teachers file in. Everyone is facing me, sitting upright and eager to hear what I have to say. Shafts of sunlight from the stained glass windows throw themselves onto the stone aisle, brightening up the dark wood pews. The choir balcony balustrade that lines the chapel walls is overhung with attentive heads and the teachers at the back are all standing up to hear what I have to say.

'Be of good courage,' I say as I lean forward into the pulpit. My voice echoes pleasantly around the brick walls. Everything I say seems directed at Freya and what happened over the weekend. At first I can't see her in the congregation but then finally I spot her, and what is she doing but laughing, with none other than Verity Greenslade. I stop. Firstly, as Deputy Head Girl, Verity is not meant to be talking during chapel and secondly, Freya hates her for trying to compete with me so much over everything. I've never really had that much of a problem with Verity but I know that, on plenty of occasions, Freya's wanted to do more than pull at those bouncing, brown curls of hers.

'She's always looking down at me from that snubby little nose of hers,' Freya complained. 'And the way she's obsessed with beating you at everything. Don't you get sick of it? I mean it must be exhausting for her.' I've always compared Verity to an enthusiastic games teacher's assistant. Harmless but too perky for my liking. *What could they be laughing at?* Freya looks up and catches my eye. She looks ashamed but they don't stop talking. I glare at Verity and make a subtle nod towards Mrs Allen, who half stands and shushes them both. Freya looks cross and, instead of being pleased, I feel worried. I have to be careful with Freya right now.

'And now for our hymn.' I lift my chin. ' "Holy, Holy Holy!", number sixty-seven.' The organ starts and I sit down. I can see Verity and Freya – shoulders shaking, hands clamped over their mouths. Verity would never normally behave like this, especially now she's in a position of power. Verity's now looking straight at me, one eyebrow raised. *What is going on?* I think.

After chapel, I wait by the entrance of Main School, purely out of habit. I'm still thinking about Verity, but Freya and I normally meet every morning to walk to class. She's not there when I turn up. When I start to leave, though, I can see her looking at me from the end of the corridor. She's washed her hair, at least. She's doing this weird thing with her hands, wiping them on her jumper over and over. A bell rings and a crowd of girls rush through the space between us. She flattens herself against the wall and raises her arm in front of her face, like a shield.

I run over and drag her into an old sports changing room which is being renovated into sixth-form study space.

'You alright?' I ask as she slides down the wall onto the floor.

'Fine,' she replies. Her voice sounds deeper than usual.

'You looked … you looked like you were going to faint out there.'

'People. All those people,' she replies and I can hear her tongue working at the back of her throat, trying to swallow.

'Yes,' I reply, unsure of what to say next.

'Listen. What happened with Verity just then in chapel … I'm just feeling …' For a moment, the old, kind Freya is back. I speak quickly, to try to let her know that I don't mind. That it doesn't matter. That we should just get back to normal.

'Forget it. It's nothing. Well, best get to class then,' I say. 'Bell rang and they'll wonder where we are. Head Girl can't be late.' I laugh to show I'm joking but I can feel that instead of smoothing things over, it's coming across all wrong.

'Wait! Wait, please. I need to speak to you. I need help with this,' Freya says, pulling my hand back down. Her wrist is so thin and it makes me think of my mother's limbs; the sharpness of her elbows and wrists and the memory of her triggers a physical sensation – like someone's pressing into my chest. I realise that if Freya can make me feel like this now, things would only get a lot worse if any of this got out. She smiles shakily and I want to reach down and hug her but stop myself just in time to think about how the course of things would change if I did.

'With what?' I say. I follow Freya's eyeline around the room thinking she's clocked someone, but I look around and it's just us. She's squeezing her finger and then I see she's wearing her mother's old silver ring, despite jewellery being banned during school hours.

'What do you mean, *with what*? With what happened. I need your help. If we aren't going to say anything, the least I need to be able to do is talk about it. With you, I mean. I need to know what to do. You've always been there for me, J – we've always been there for each other … Please don't let's stop now.'

'I … I thought we'd agreed. I thought we agreed not to discuss anything,' I reply. 'That it was over. That we had to concentrate on our lives.'

'*You* agreed. But not me. Can we meet after school today? Go for a coffee or something? Just please … just to talk it through?' I think she's about to cry but she squeezes the ring again and shuts her eyes. 'So?' she says, turning to face me.

'Freya. I … if we talk about this once, it'll just drag it out. We've got to just focus. Come on. It's class. I need to …'

'You're saying no? Is that it? That you won't talk to me about it?'

'There's really nothing to talk about. I don't know what you want to rake over? I told you –' I sound all shrill and Freya looks at me, frowning '– I don't want to end up in some rehab place. Do you? That's what'll happen.'

'But what about the rest of it, J.' Freya sounds calm. 'We can't just let it go.'

'The rest of it? The booze and stuff? Under-age clubbing? We can and we will.'

'The rest of it,' Freya repeats. She's now kneeling looking down at me. 'You know what I'm talking about, don't you, Josephine?'

'I'm not getting expelled for some stupid half a pill,' I hiss.

Freya looks shocked, confused – and then seems to give up on the conversation. She shrugs. 'I don't know if you are deliberately ignoring this or not.' Her words ignite a blast of emotion and a jolt of memory from the club night. Blood and sweat. Its unwelcome appearance forces me to push it away, deep into my subconscious.

I don't reply and we sit in what I think is quite a companionable silence. I think she's understood that I'm not going to talk. And then, she leans over and pinches me, hard, on the leg. I'm so shocked, I laugh.

'Just checking you are alive,' she says, and then she pinches me again, this time digging one of her nails deep into the skin of my thigh. 'Are you? Are you alive?' She's still got her nail in my leg, twisting it round like a screw.

'Look. Come on, Freya. Enough of this.' The pain makes my ears ring and my voice won't submit to what I want it to do and I'm beginning to shout.

'OK. If that's what you want,' she replies. 'But just so you know, I will never, ever –' she's standing up now, her legs kicking out like a show pony '– forgive you for this. Do you hear?'

I'm still reeling from the sting of her nail and the fact she's physically tried to hurt me – Freya shouted at me the last time I stood on a spider. But the implication that she'll keep silent is a relief somehow. I reassure myself that she's just saying things now she doesn't mean and I know Freya. I know that she'll soften in time. That she'll realise in the end, that I'm right.

'I have to go, OK. We'll catch up later,' I say, my voice comforting, I think, but she's looking at me with an expression I don't recognise, and which makes me catch my breath. Later in class and then dinner and finally in bed while I try to find sleep which does not come, I am still trying to figure it out, running through various epithets in my mind in a long and varied list searching for its meaning, but ultimately without success.

Freya and I don't see each other for a few days, which I am secretly relieved by. We both need a bit of space, I reason, and I put it down to the fact of both of us being very busy; there's the scholarship announcement looming and my UCAS application and essay for Oxford due in. I've got two free sessions today, which I'll use to study. I make my way to the Mann Library to read the newspaper. All the tables are full, so I walk to the end of the room, trying to find somewhere to sit. Thankfully, no one looks up from their books; I feel like being anonymous today. I'm trying to be quiet, but the floor is stone, and I can hear my footsteps clacking around the room. I find a free space near the big, latticed windows overlooking the tennis courts. The thwack of the ball is going to irritate me, I'm certain. Bracing myself for annoyance, I realise that Verity is sitting on the next table. She's reading *The Times*. I've already got a copy of the *Independent* and I can see that she's only on the second page.

'Verity,' I say. 'Can we swap when you've done?' I flag up the *Independent*, for her to see.

'Sure,' she says. 'I'm going soon anyway, to help Freya get organised for the thing tonight.' I can see her eyes narrowing, trying to detect whether I'm going to Freya's 'thing'. I have no idea what Verity is talking about and then I remember that Freya had organised a small party in the house kitchen. Once a month, we are each allowed a couple of glasses of wine, given to us by our housemistress. Freya hosts a gathering with a few select guests to celebrate this honour. She'd been discussing it last week. Working out who to invite, whether to smuggle in some vodka. I wonder what it means that it's still going ahead and whether I should turn up and try to get things back to normal.

'Ah, yes, of course,' I say. 'Freya's been talking about that for absolutely ages. Sent out the invites about a month ago.' I smile, knowing Verity was of course, not on the original invite list. 'I think I might even have lost mine.'

'Oh,' Verity falters and looks at her watch.

I smile and look up at the stone-arched ceiling. 'Well, anyway,' I say, 'I can't make this one. I'm studying.' A look of bovine confusion crosses Verity's face. 'Have a really lovely time, though.'

Verity starts to leave then turns back round. 'You're talking about Freya's monthly gathering? It's not that. It's something different. That was last night. It was great. No, no, tonight's another thing altogether. I'm thinking of starting up a new society and I've asked Freya to help. To get some people together.' Verity's lip is twitching and I'm at a loss for words. Her mouth puckers up to one side and she flicks her curls over one shoulder.

'Ah. Well good luck with that. God, I can't even find time to go to the bathroom at the moment,' I say, keeping tight control of my voice. 'So, if you're going soon, may I?' I begin to take *The Times* and she's caught between wanting to keep it for herself to annoy me and making another big show of going to see Freya. She hands me the paper.

'OK then. Perhaps we'll catch you later.' The emphasis on the 'we' stings me as it's meant to and I sit down, opening the paper, unable to concentrate. Ten minutes later and I still haven't managed to absorb anything. That Verity has the power to do this to me is making me furious, and I begin to get a headache. I go and lie down, and wonder if I'm still tired from what happened. And then I wonder if Freya is feeling tired too. Clearly not if she's so busy partying and chummying up to Verity. But perhaps this is a good thing? I mean, if she's doing that maybe she's moving past it. Maybe this is her way of forgetting too.

However, by a few days later when I'm due to go through my final UCAS application with Mrs Kitts, Freya and I are still avoiding each other. Or rather, Freya is avoiding me. It's been a week and I'm so busy that I shouldn't have time to think about the distance between us, although, of course, it creeps into my mind every so often. I've tried to find her a few times but the last time I saw her, walking across the lacrosse pitch, she had turned in the other direction. I thought at first she hadn't seen me but then she had kept turning her head to check I wasn't following her. Looking back now perhaps I should have run after her, pleaded with her to talk to me. I need to keep her onside, after all. Instead, I had been so shocked, so angry, that I had thrown my lacrosse stick on the ground. 'Jesus, be careful, that caught my foot,' Lindsay Pardell had said. And then realising it was me said, 'Josephine, sorry, sorry. Just that hit me pretty hard.' I feel constantly on edge – every time I'm called to a meeting, I think that Freya's opened her mouth.

'Josephine?' Mrs Kitts is saying. 'Put whatever's troubling you away. Josephine, stop losing concentration, it's not like you.' She crosses her legs and her black skirt rides up her thighs. She sees me looking and she pulls it back down.

'So, if you get an interview, they're probably going to want to know how much you know about Eisenhower. I hear History's getting more and more popular so we've got to cover all bases.' I'm praying, given Father's lifelong inculcation into me that History is so all-important, that I will have all bases covered. 'Yes,' I reply. 'That's fine.' I look at Mrs Kitts and carry on talking. 'Will they ask about my personal hobbies, do you think? I've written about them on my application.' She's handing me a notebook full of reading matter. Our fingers touch and I pull my hand away.

'They'll want to know you are well rounded, yes.'

'I hope I'm not,' I say, blowing up my cheeks. Mrs Kitts looks surprised I've attempted a joke and forces a brittle laugh.

'Sorry. Lame,' I say. 'So I can tell them about the societies I run? And of course I'll have the editorship of *The Lens*, so that'll be great.'

'Oh, yes of course. I forgot Head Girl edits the paper.' Mrs Kitts is leaning forward and the insides of her nostrils glow pink in the light. 'That's excellent, they'll like that very much.' We run through some more History discussion and, when we finish, she clears her throat and looks at me shrewdly.

'How do you think Freya is, by the way?' she asks.

'She seems OK.' I pause and she doesn't fill the silence. She waits for me to say more and I want to know why she's asking, if she knows anything, but I'm fuming and upset at the mention of her name, so I collect my things and disappear. It's only when I leave that I realise my anger towards her has replaced any feelings from that night. The numbness has started to dissipate and all my emotion, energy, seems to be targeted at Freya ignoring me and working out how I'll stop her from telling anyone.

I go to the School Hall, where I've called a meeting for *The Lens*. The school newspaper has been running for nearly one hundred years now and I'm honoured, as Head Girl, to edit this year's edition. I'm determined to make it the most spectacular publication yet. I've asked Father to get an interview with the PM. He's agreed, of course; he's desperate for me to make this year's paper the best as well.

'Show Rollo a thing or two,' he laughed when I last spoke to him. Rollo is Editor of the *Sunday Herald* and will also be thrilled if I produce a good paper. The meeting is at four o'clock. Normally Freya and I meet at the school gates at three thirty, just before tea. I know Freya won't be there, but I take the route past the gates, just in case she is waiting. She isn't. Disappointed, I walk into the Big Hall and there are already about forty girls in the room. I remember Freya has promised me she'll help but, again, she doesn't show up. Verity, who is meant to be helping me edit, is not there either.

'Girls,' I call. My voice comes out higher than normal. 'You can all sit down,' I say, adopting Mrs Allen's brusqueness. 'Right. So you're all here because you've expressed an interest in helping out with *The Lens*. As you know the school newspaper is read avidly, and not just in these four walls.' I stop and guide my hand around the room. 'This year's paper simply has to be the best. It's our one-hundredth edition and so we want to be part of something that's going to make us proud. I want each and every one of you to write, edit and get the greatest quotes you can. Remember, make everything entertaining, readable, sharp. Yes, Annie?' I look down towards Annie Rogers, who is grinning at me like a friendly elf.

'How do we know what we're all writing?' she asks.

'Well, Annie.' I've ended up sounding patronising. 'Well,' I start again, 'when you initially all signed up to help, I listed your names and subjects on the Main Board outside here.' She nods. 'Now, each category has four people attached to it. I want all of you to hand something in and I'll be choosing the best ones to publish.'

'When do you want the pieces in?' Mary-Louise asks from the corner of the room.

'Erm, end of next month latest, please. I've left editorial instruction on the Main Notice Board, so you can have a look there for word count and tone.' The room is quiet.

'Oh and we also need anonymous titbits for the "Guess Who?" section. Obviously that's the fun bit every year and so we need to make it good. Please post in my pigeonhole and spread the word.'

'What kind of gossip?' Mary-Louise puts up her hand again. 'And where's Freya? She said she would work on a piece with me.'

'Freya's been called to a meeting.' I force a smile. 'And, as for gossip, absolutely anything at all. Have a rifle through the old editions of the paper and you'll see the kind of thing, but this year it has to be explosive. I want lots of people talking about it.' The girls nod and I signal for them to disappear. A dismissive wave of the hand which makes me feel at first powerful and, soon after, foolish.

'Thanks very much,' I call, as an afterthought.

The next few days are spent with Freya still avoiding me. I see her a few times but every time she clocks me, she whips her head in the opposite direction so I can't even see her face. All of this is distracting me from my work, making me hot with fury. In the boarding house, she works hard at ignoring me. There are two entrances to the house, one for the Juniors at the back, and the big yellow door at the front is for the older years. Every time I see Freya, though, she's making her way round to the back gate. In the Dining Hall, she turns up late, scouting around for me and purposefully walking to the other side of the room. Freya and I usually take our places in the back left-hand corner but when I decide to brave it one night and sit there, I find Verity in my place, who gives me a half-wave, before her lips disappear into an undisguised smile. Freya looks straight down, just carries on pushing the food around her plate. *Fuck you, Verity,* I think. I will not turn back now, but all the other spaces on the table are taken. I put down my plate on the corner, next to Gracie Lovell, before going to get a chair from another table.

None of the other girls at the table speak. They are all busy looking at me or Freya, pulling their mouths into sympathetic shapes. I haven't told anyone that Freya and I aren't talking, so either it's totally obvious to the entire school, or Verity's been shooting her mouth off.

Finally, Gracie asks for the salt. Freya doesn't make any eye contact with me at all. I notice rough patches of skin, just below her elbows and around her neck, where it's all pink and a weird greenish-blue colour and she's tried to cover it up with foundation, normally banned on the school premises. It's probably killing her – I've never, until now, seen Freya's skin look anything less than perfect. I don't taste any of the chicken on my plate, just cut, chew, cut, chew.

Gracie turns to Freya and says in a loud, self-satisfied voice, as though she's brave enough to be doing everyone a favour, 'You guys have to make up, you know.' She throws me a look. And tilts her head back and laughs. 'It's weird you not talking. Makes things awkward for everyone. What are you arguing about any-way?' There's a bit of food stuck in the crossover of her two front teeth. Everyone looks down in a hurry, so no one has to tell her. Gracie arrived late to the school and has been trying to make everyone's business her own for the past few years. Freya had always told me she was well meaning, until we discovered she had been pitting Freya against me in an effort to become closer friends with us both.

'Doesn't she realise we tell each other everything?' Freya had said. 'Stupid girl.'

I'm reminded of this as Gracie gives us both a falsely sym-pathetic look. Verity half stands up and leans over to Freya, puts her arm round her shoulders, darting poison at me with her eyes. 'Freya's fine. Aren't you? I'm looking after her.' Freya doesn't say anything, just wipes her nose.

'We can't really tell you what's been going on,' Verity is saying. 'It's something between Freya and Josephine.'

What do you know? I think and shoot a furious look at Freya, who is still staring at her plate. I force myself to breathe. Freya isn't that stupid, I reason. She's just toying with me, trying to get a rise.

'Girls, that's enough. Surely you all have plenty to be getting on with besides idle speculation,' I say. I'm aware I sound like a total idiot, but there's nothing else I can do. Everyone falls silent and Freya tries to put her fork down but it drops onto the floor. But later when Mrs Kitts calls me into her study after supper, my heart palpitates with fear that Freya has said something.

'Are you alright?' she asks. Her cat, Twiggy, leaps onto my knee.

'Yes, I'm fine,' I say. 'Why?' Twiggy is rubbing her nose against the pad of my thumb and I stroke her black fur.

'You seem … I don't know. Tired. Not on it. Are you feeling alright? Is this all too much?'

She doesn't know. My heartbeat starts to stabilise.

'Is what too much?'

Twiggy purrs.

'Everything. Head Girl, A-level mocks, *The Lens*, just … everything.'

'No.' I lean in to Twiggy's stomach and breathe in her animal scent.

'Good. I just thought…'

'No, I'm fine. Really.'

'Really?'

'Yes. I'll let you know if there's a problem.'

'Good. Because we're always here to help. Whatever you need. You've handed in your essays to Oxford now, so that should be a big weight off your shoulders.'

I want to ask about Freya but I don't trust my voice not to tremble, so I nod my head and, when I walk out, Freya is standing there, outside Mrs Kitts's study, waiting to come in. She doesn't look at me. I make a very slight movement, as though I'm about to stop her. Not quite enough that she could be entirely sure I'm doing so, but just to give her an opportunity to respond. She doesn't. Just marches right on into Mrs Kitts's flat and I see her combing her hair with her left hand as she knocks on the door. But this time I am not going to let her just ignore me. I need to know what she is playing at. So I wait for her to finish, sitting outside Mrs Kitts's flat for a full hour before she comes out. But before I get a chance to say anything I see a smug look on her face, as though she's privy to some highly sensitive information. She raises an eyebrow and smooths down her hair. My blood races, at what they might have discussed. 'Freya.' I jump up. My voice is shaking. 'Freya!'

She turns to face me and the dry patch of skin flares red. 'What do you want?'

'I just ... I wanted to talk to you.'

'Why? What's there to talk about? You don't seem to want to talk about anything at all, do you? Just had to make sure I was quiet. Didn't care about me.' She's now snarling like an angry cat. I walk towards her.

'Go away,' she's shouting. 'Get the fuck away from me. Don't touch me. Don't come near me, you fucking bitch!'

I can hear girls outside and I want to tell her to shut up but I daren't. I've never seen her like this.

'You don't even care now, do you? Just worried someone will hear you.' Freya opens the door, swinging it back so it slams against the wooden chest that holds our house trophies. They rattle and, for one minute, I think they're all about to fall to the floor. 'Here, everyone can fucking hear now!'

'Please, please Freya, please be quiet. I just wanted to chat, alright? I can explain…'

'Explain? Explain what? You wanted me to be vulnerable so I wouldn't tell anyone, didn't you? Well, let me tell you something. I've told people. Don't worry, I've made sure they won't say anything. But you'd better watch your back.'

'Who? Who, Freya?' And I grab her shoulders to shake the answer out of her but she rears back and knocks my fingers away with a savage blow, hissing at me. I wipe away flecks of saliva from my face. In all the time I've known Freya, I've never, ever seen her so much as raise her voice. Before these past weeks, the angriest she'd been with me was when I kissed a boy she liked three years ago. She didn't speak to me for half an hour, before she had reached over and taken my hand. 'Stupid boys anyway,' she had said. And now, she's here, eyes being pulled back into the top of her skull, lips white then red. Her hair is still immaculate and, out of nowhere, she sits down, winded.

'No one. Just screwing with you. I probably won't say anything, but I can't be sure.' She's smirking. Looking at my reaction, waiting for me to beg. I want to, but I can't seem to speak.

'OK,' I finally whisper. The threat in her words ... she's never played games with me like this. She looks taken aback that I haven't pleaded, then tired and her limbs soften in their stance.

'Just go,' she whispers. Mrs Kitts opens the door and points to the phone receiver. 'Girls, be quiet,' she's mouthing. She looks at Freya, who then looks at me with her lips all pursed and I finally leave. I decide to go to the library for some solace. As I leave, I see Verity outside the front door.

'Josephine,' she says, curls bouncing. 'We've got our weekly meeting with Mrs Allen today, don't forget,' she says.

'Oh, is that why you're up here?' I had forgotten. I can't believe I had forgotten. All this Freya stuff is knocking me off my game. That has to change.

'Oh, no it's not now. Freya and I, we arranged to meet ...' She looks towards the woods, where we normally smoke together. 'I won't ... I mean ... I'm not. I'm just keeping Freya company whilst she ... in fact, I'm just walking her to the edge of the woods and she'll go on from there.'

I walk off but she follows me, threading her arm through mine. I can't very well push her away so instead I drop my arm and, in the end, she is forced to remove hers.

'We're just hanging out,' she says, defensively. 'But we can hang out too.' Her eyebrows shoot up towards her low hairline and she does a little jig. 'Mrs Allen said we had to work together, remember?'

I narrow my eyes. I can sense Verity wants something from me.

'No, seriously. I mean, just 'cos you and Freya are ...'

'Are what?'

'Well, you know…'

'No, I don't.' I will not give her the satisfaction. She does that stupid jig again and pretends to swipe an imaginary tennis racket in the air.

'Oh, well anyway. We've got to work together as a team now. So let's try and not make things awkward, eh?' How dare she try to push this on to me.

'Yes of course,' I reply, before realising that, where Freya's concerned, getting close to Verity might not be such a bad thing. 'Want to come for tea? I was going to the library but…'

'Well …' She looks back up towards the house and I know she's waiting for Freya to come back down and my heart begins to beat out a curious rhythm.

'OK, no worries. I'll make my own way down.' I find myself doing an odd little skip, to show her I don't care but I trip and my ankle folds in on itself. It doesn't hurt very much but I feel myself about to burst into tears. *You stupid fool.* I smile again and walk off. I feel like every part of me is being dragged to the floor by some invisible, iron weight and my heart spikes with the pain. Could Freya have really told someone and if so who? And how can I shut her up?

2014

The next morning, the hospital rings. It's me who picks up the phone. I'm calm. The interruption from the dark, snaking corridors of sleep is a welcome relief.

'It's Doris. From the hospital. It's about your mother.' I get ready to say I'm sorry. That we'll come and sign the death certificate if needs be. I open my mouth, eager to sound pulled together. 'She's fine. Rallying. It's just a courtesy call really.' I hang up, thinking of her heart and the strength with which it's beating. Whether it's getting fainter and fainter, or whether the thrum of it jolts the flow of blood back around her body. I go and tell Father. He's on his way out and, when I give him the update, he snatches a big, black umbrella off the wooden pegs by the door in an act of what I can only describe as impatience. For a few seconds, I'm shocked, then realise that I feel the same way. I want to get back to Jordan. I want to leave the claustrophobia of this half-death, half-life limbo.

Five days later and she is still going. I've vowed to get up to speed with paperwork and research and my days are spent in the British Library and the evenings with Father, in The Ivy. Petrified I'm going to bump into someone I know and have to face the usual barrage of questions, I ask Father to book the tables at the back of the restaurant, in a quiet corner. He looks worried by this. 'Why?' he keeps asking, and then I realise he has had to deal with these forms of paranoia before and I reassure him. 'Just feeling tired. Don't want to have to deal with everyone.'

Most of all, though, I'm scared I'll bump into Freya without warning. Caught off guard when I'm at my most vulnerable and I won't have rehearsed what to say. I sneak around the streets of London, swerving around every single person with blonde hair, regardless of how tall, how short. I wonder if she is still even blonde. I'm sure I would sense her, though. The serenity of her, amongst the thrum of strangers. My internal radar is on overdrive, trying to pick up cues and movements of what I once knew to be Freya. It's exhausting and I wonder if it's a form of latent grief, this paranoia, or whether it's just the start of things to come.

The only person I can tolerate right now would be Toby. I text him to say I'm in London. '*Great news, me too,*' comes his prompt reply. '*Frontline Club, tonight. I'm giving a talk on Afghanistan. I'll leave you a ticket at the front desk.*'

I text back quickly, annoyed at his presumptuousness and annoyed I'll end up going, despite the risks involved. The talk is insanely boring. Not least because I have heard these stories a million times before. I scan the room and wonder if the mother of his child-to-be is there. The talk winds up and Toby gives me a smile from the stage. 'Any questions?' asks the person leading the discussion. I raise my hand and ask about withdrawal of troops from Iraq. Toby looks stumped. I have no idea why

I've asked it. We've been over this topic of discussion so many times. It's one of those heated, passionate subjects that we have differing opinions on that are always, always followed by him leading me to bed. It is a joke between us, if one of us mentions Iraq, we know it is a coded plea for sex. He reddens and so do I but I carry on staring.

'Well?' I say.

Toby stutters and gives a half-laugh. 'Right. Anyway, so … I …' But by then I am not listening to his answer because I've forgotten to switch my phone on to silent and I look down and it's Father, who has texted to tell me I am to ring home straightaway.

'She was comfortable when she died,' say the nurses at the hospital. There was a small mention in *The Times* of Mother's death, only in relation to my father's work, and now it is up to me and Father to plan the funeral. I have never done anything like this before. I get to work in a matter-of-fact way, alone. It's helping, me hiding behind my computer. I haven't seen anyone since I found out. Toby had taken me home after his talk and made me whisky and hot water. Bloody whisky. He had not said anything about my behaviour, instead, asking if I wanted to stay the night.

'What about your girlfriend?' I had said, shivering. 'What's her name again?'

'She's not my girlfriend. She's the mother of my child.'

'Well, maybe you *should* make her your girlfriend.'

I had wanted to take that back but I was too tired. Too exhausted after realising again and again that Mother was finally dead, waiting for her spirit to dovetail mine. I hadn't stayed. Father had texted, asking me to go home and, for once, I had done the right thing. Two days later, I still couldn't really get my head around the fact that she had gone, or make sense of what she had been like when she was alive. I still haven't cried. My skin has gone dry, though, and I keep rubbing moisturiser over my body, with little effect. I feel oddly alive and awake but I figure it's the shock.

And then that night, like a monster creeping up from beneath the bed where I am already shivering and scared, I receive an email from Freya.

Josephine, I'm so sorry to learn of Alice's death. I remember her as a good woman, when she wasn't ill, and I am send-ing my condolences to both you and your father. I know you don't want to see me, but I am afraid I just can't accept that. There are things we need to talk about. I would also like to say sorry about your loss in person, so how about we meet in London before you go back to Jordan? I could come and visit you at your home, or wherever you are now? If not, I'll still look you up in Jordan. As I said I really need to talk to you. If you could send me your postal address, I'd be grateful. Freya.

She's written to my new email address. I quickly Google florists, to distract myself from trying to work out if she's following me. But she's inside my head. *How the hell has she managed to get my contact details?* I check my new phone. Nothing. Then I get back to my computer again. Whilst I'm typing, a peculiar sensa-tion overcomes me, as though the room is tilting and takes on a strange phosphorescent glow. Then my head begins to throb and Father knocks on the door.

'Here,' he says, putting a cup of tea next to my computer.

'Thank you.'

'You alright? How are you feeling? It's all a bit strange, isn't it?'

'I'm doing fine. Thanks.'

'Well, if you ever need to talk. Your mother, she…'

'She what?'

'She … she … I don't know. I just feel like we never really spoke about things.'

He rubs his knee. I laugh. That has to be the understatement of the century. He goes on.

'We had to hide it from you. I did, rather. Me and Amy. We couldn't tell you what it was really like. The episodes. The voices. The self-harming. You were too young and when you got older it just seemed wrong, but I thought you always must have known.'

'I'd better get back to the florists,' I say, sounding curter than I mean to. I know how difficult it must have been for him.

'J…'

'Yes? I'm fine, seriously.'

'OK.' He gets up to leave and I point at my screen.

'I got an email from Freya. Did you give her my email address? Or give it to Rollo?'

I try to flatten out her name but I can feel my voice wavering. Father sits back down and rests his right elbow on my desk, smoothing away a tea stain with his left hand.

'Of course I didn't. No. Freya? As in … Freya?'

'Yes. As in … yes. Her.'

He whitens. 'What did she say?'

'Just how sorry she was about Mother.'

He gets up to leave the room again. I know he blames me for destroying his relationship with Rollo. I want to tell him I miss Rollo too, but instead I flip down my computer screen and lie on the bed. Three hours later and the thoughts are still hurtling through my brain. They consist of the following:

1) My mother being burnt into ashes (because whichever way I look at it, that's about the sum of it). What then? *What then?*

2) Who we will invite to the funeral and who will turn up. *Where is Mother now?*

3) The email from Freya. Her tone of voice. Telling me what to do.

4) The picture of the flyer from that night. The outline keeps appearing, at first, just the outline. Then, slowly, the image shifts, becoming more and more menacing. The man on the flyer has started to take on a devilish form.

Interspersed with all these disconnected thoughts are flashes of green light and Freya's eyes and odd snatches of the smell of sweet cigarettes in the club. There goes the thump of the music and, although I try to revisit that night, I can't get beyond the strobes and the dance floor that jumps up and down with our feet. Has Freya forgotten too? Is that why she wants to see me?

Please, I think. *Just remember.* But the only things that stick out are run-of-the-mill events: music, dancing, hands in the air and, for us at the time, drugs. And then it hits me:

that smell. That grotesque smell of musty sweat and sharp deodorant, the flash of brown hair, the pupils ferociously juddering around the room, the glint of crystal stones on Freya's denim waistband, the sensation of pleasure mixed with a deep, deep, empty and inwardly rolling pain and then I turn over onto one side, throw up in the bin next to me and pass out.

I'm wearing a fitted black suit, a tucked-in white shirt and pointed flat pumps. I look like I should be conducting a business meeting but it feels appropriate to the occasion. I wear my hair in a ponytail, with more make-up than usual. Father and I have sent out fifty invitations to the funeral and for a tea afterwards, in the Church Hall. We've had everyone respond; impersonal letters, since most of them didn't know her.

Walking up to the church, I see a few MPs with their spouses. There are Mother's two nurses from the hospital and the doctor she's had for years. Amy is waiting for me by the side of the church. She hugs me and tells me she's always there for me, no matter what. The day is cold and blue and the cherry blossom trees are throwing pink petals in our hair.

'Hello,' goes the form. We shake hands. … 'We're so sorry about your mother,' they say. No one says anything else. No one asks how I am. Which is a relief, really.

'Thank you,' I reply, gesturing for the guests to walk inside the church and take a seat. The priest appears and says how sorry he is in a low, sombre voice and I feel like laughing. In fact, I almost snort and Father glances at me concerned; perhaps he thinks I'm crying. I pretend to wipe my nose.

The service is quick. The priest asks us all to sing, sit, pray, ask God to look after the deceased, pray, sit, stand. He's conducting the small congregation like he's commanding a fully staged opera. Father gets up to read. He's using his work voice, all composed and serious. Halfway through, he stops, rearranges his tie and clears his throat. 'And let us also please remember Gordon and Kitty, my wife's late parents.' Everyone bows their heads, like we used to during school chapel. There's a lady with blonde hair, curled up into a chignon. She's wearing a pink fascinator and for a moment I think it's Freya. She keeps looking at me, but there's no upward turn to her lip, no emerald sparkle to her eyes. She's assessing my grief. I make a self-conscious attempt at wiping my eyes. Then it's one of Mother's friends reading. A school friend who went quiet when we asked her to say a few words. In the end she had agreed, as long as we paid her train fare from Berkshire. She reads a twee, generic little poem about love and the stars. And then it's me. I walk up to the lectern and clear my throat. *You are in charge of a team of people, get it together,* I think. It works and I find myself totally disconnected from the wide-eyed people and the wooden box in front of me.

Halfway through it hits me, as my gaze falls on the coffin, that there is a dead body and it is my mother's, little less than two metres away from me, and I stumble on my words. And, out of nowhere, I remember a faint touch on my hand, a little rubbing motion. I don't know if I am remembering or hallucinating.

'This hand comes from me,' she is saying. 'Your daddy and I made this hand, and isn't it beautiful?'

I look down at my hands now, holding the reading, and they are rough, builder's hands. The nails are chipped and smudged, where I've tried to varnish them with grey polish. Would Mother still think I've got beautiful hands now? Would she see through the hard physical labour that I've put them through for the past ten years, to the things I've tried to rub out? The service comes to an end, with the coffin rattling into the roaring fire behind.

We congregate in the hall and I feel a nothingness I know will only be filled by food and wine. There are steaming pork buns, mini steak and kidney pies, fish and chips in paper packets, mozzarella and sundried tomato skewers and sweet-chilli prawns. I take a few pork buns and help myself to the largest glass of white wine on the table.

'Well done. We got through it.' It's Father and he's clutching a half-finished cigar.

'We did. Yes. Not a bad turnout?' We look around the room. People milling around acting like it's a networking opportunity. I can't bring myself to talk to any of them. My mouth doesn't seem to work properly and I'm very light-headed.

'Want a cigar? Outside?'

'I'd rather have a cigarette,' I say brightly, pretending to be normal in the hope that it'll make me feel better.

'Cigarette? Since when did you take up smoking again?'

'Ha. Just need a distraction.' I force a little laugh.

'Come on then. I've got some Camel Lights. Remember you used to steal them to take back to school with you?' We walk outside, pushing past a group of Father's colleagues, who are between huge mouthfuls of pork bun and champagne.

'Why did you bring that up, me taking the fags? Harbouring it for all these years?'

Father takes a step back. 'Sorry, I didn't mean anything … Mother and I … that was one of the laughs we used to have, about you nicking cigarettes.'

'Oh. I didn't mean to snap,' I reply, contrite.

'It's OK. You look pale. Have you eaten?' he asks.

'I'm fine.' *Why does everyone keep asking me that?* I watch the people walk past the church, voyeurs, looking at our faces. Interested in what grief looks like on these two people smoking outside the church hall. They all seem so distant, these strangers, like I'm looking at them from underwater.

I take a cigarette and lean into the flame. I feel awkward smoking in front of a parent and inhale extra loudly to prove to him I'm doing it right. *Pathetic,* I think. And he offers me another when I've extinguished the last and, even though my head is fuzzy and I feel like I'm about to faint, I take it. My third inhale and I feel someone tap me on the shoulder. *Please not now,* I think. If I turn around too quickly, I might be sick. I turn to Father, who is looking past me and smiling, arms outstretched.

It's Rollo.

Despite the years, I am pleasantly surprised beneath the initial shock to discover he hasn't really changed. The skin around his neck is a little looser but I still recognise that yellow tie, the one with the small blue Scottie dogs embroidered onto it. His glasses are a little more modern. He's got thick, black-rimmed frames that magnify his eyes into watery pools and he's wearing a tight-fitting navy suit. 'Josephine.' I can hear him but I'm too busy looking behind his shoulder, heart skittering across my chest, to see if Freya's with him. Of course there was a possibility she would turn up. Why didn't I think of it?

'Josephine?' Father shakes my shoulder and motions with the flat of his palm towards Rollo. 'Are you alright?'

I think I'm about to have a heart attack so, without saying a word, I walk towards Mother's doctor and stand there, looking at him, waiting for him to say that I am to go to the hospital immediately. My eyes feel dry and exposed. He doesn't stop his conversation, so I carry on standing where I am relieved he doesn't think I'm about to die.

From the corner of my eye I can see Father and Rollo, talking. Father's looking over at me, palms skywards and giving me a questioning, sympathetic look. I can make out him mouthing the words 'upset' and 'sorry'. I mentally kick myself for not even thinking that Rollo would turn up, after all these years. Has Freya told him she's tried to get in touch with me? How much does he know? Suddenly, I'm so overwhelmingly terrified she's going to appear that I put down my glass and walk out.

I walk around the streets of London, up Sloane Street and on to Knightsbridge, all the way through Green Park and Piccadilly. I stop a few times to have a drink in some of the places in the back streets, standing silently at bar after bar, and I only realise the time when I walk into a pub with a green sign and gold writing on it, and they are calling last orders. I down a shot of tequila and order a double vodka and a thick-lipped man – he looks like he works in the City – comes up and puts his arm around me. For some inexplicable reason, I pull up my chin and stick out my chest, twirling my hair. 'Why are you crying?' he asks, thumbing at my face. He stinks of booze and aftershave. 'I'm not,' I reply.

'You are. You are. Your collar is soaked. Got a boyfriend?' he says.

I don't reply, just pull him by the elbow and take him to a bar down the road that I know will be open for at least another three hours.

1996

Freya and I have not spoken since the incident outside Mrs Kitts's office. Thoughts of her gather speed in my head at many intervals during the day, mostly when I'm silent and alone. I haven't really seen her either; once or twice in class where she now sits right at the back and in chapel, as a Prefect, where she's stationed at various points shushing the younger girls. I am relieved when anything happens to distract me from her. And then finally I get the biggest distraction of all: it's the day of the Anne Dunne Scholarship announcement, where we will find out who the teachers have put forward. Mrs Kitts had told us at House Meeting the day before. 'Girls, you'll find out about who has been put forward tomorrow. The list will be posted on the chapel doors, ready for the service in the morning,' she had said.

At breakfast, it's all I hear about: in the queues, at the table, when we take our trays to the kitchen. Chapel is supposed to be at eight thirty every morning but it's been put forward to eight twenty, because of the announcement.

I think about lagging back but decide to face things head-on. There's a scrum to the chapel doors, the noise peaking then falling silent as a large group of girls from the year below rush to the yellow paper, pinned to the cork board. There's a few gasps and the crowd turns around, hunting for someone. Gracie sees me and my stomach swoops expectantly, but she doesn't react. Then I see Freya coming down the hill and someone shouts to her.

'Freya! Quick, quick! The Anne Dunne, you've been nominated!'

Freya breaks out into a sharp walk and a massive cheer erupts. *Freya?* I think. *Freya?!* She's undoing her hair from the messy bun on her head and she's now running. Opening out her arms like she's scored the lacrosse goal of the century and she's the old Freya again. Luminous, hair flying, smiling. She's all over the grounds, swooping and whooping and, out of nowhere, Verity appears, and takes her hands and they dance around like two wood nymphs, screaming and shrieking.

Verity can afford to be excited that the other nominee is Freya; after all, she is really no competition whatsoever, and then I slow down and realise that Freya being nominated is the best thing that possibly could have happened. For me, at any rate. She will be so distracted, so busy studying, she'll totally forget about telling anyone what happened. *Bring it on,* I think. It's almost worth taking myself out of the game so she has more of a chance. Let her and Verity fight it out, but then I remember why I am doing this in the first place. Why this is so important. And she's there, in my head, arms all skinny and cut and that smell of almonds and the devil that chases her. Then it comes to me that no one has congratulated me. Surely I've been nominated? But girls are flying past me and no one has said a word. *How could this happen? How?!* I ball my hands into fists by my side and bite the inside of my cheek, releasing iron and warmth into my mouth.

The girls next to me are swept away with Freya's pleasure and everyone is still cheering as she makes her way down to chapel. I look round to see if anyone else thinks her nomination is strange but no one is with me – everyone seems genuinely pleased and, although I'd always been quite happy with only Freya in my life, this gives me a sensation of loneliness. That no one, not even my own mother, would ever find my achievements this exciting.

I'm meant to be leading prayers today but I can't face it. Everything starts blurring. I have not been nominated. *You will cope,* I think. How? *Get a hold of yourself!* Then someone walks past me and claps me on the back. 'Well done,' they say. I smile. It's a third-former, whose name escapes me but I recognise her from choir.

'Well done?' I reply.

'Yes. Well done!' She points to the chapel door and I realise that, of course, I have been nominated and that for all the other girls, it was totally expected and that is why no one has bothered to congratulate me. I walk through the chapel doors, sliding my vision towards the paper. There it is:

NOMINEES FOR THE ANNE DUNNE SCHOLARSHIP

VERITY GREENSLADE

JOSEPHINE GREY

FREYA SEYMOUR

I breathe out, eyes blinking in gratitude to see my name there and then I start to calculate. Verity I expected. Freya, though? I still can't make head or tail of it. Mrs Allen reads out the notice again during the service. She asks us all to stand up so she can read out our names. *Verity Greenslade* – polite clapping and a few whoops. *Josephine Grey* – the same and then *Freya Seymour* is called and I can feel the noise tingling through my legs. *They're cheering for the underdog,* I reassure myself.

'If you three could sit down now and please come and see me after chapel. Well done to you all again.'

I make my way, alone, to Mrs Allen's study. She is by herself in the yellow-painted room. There's a draught coming from somewhere, even though I've shut the door.

'Josephine.' She points to the chair opposite.

'Mrs Allen.' We sit in silence, both understanding the lack of need for small talk. I sit up straighter, clear my throat. After five minutes, three of which Mrs Allen spends flicking through a sheaf of papers, Verity rushes through the door.

'I'm so sorry,' she declares, grandly tapping her watch. 'Just had to quickly get my lacrosse stick ready for the match. Today it's us against St Cats. I'm Captain today because ...' Mrs Allen sighs which Verity mistakes for displeasure. 'Oh, I've left the lacrosse stick just outside don't worry ... it's clean...'

'That's quite alright, Verity. Just please sit down,' Mrs Allen throws me a look. A tiny lift of her eyebrows and I give a small smile, which Verity notices.

'Oh and Freya's just on her way,' she goes on, looking at me. Her mouth curls up in a smug little knot. 'She's just gone to the loo. Ha! Sorry, that's probably too much information.'

'Right. Thank you.'

My brain swells with the mention of Freya, until my thoughts are interrupted by her running through the door.

'Sorry, Mrs Allen,' she puffs, adjusting her tie. 'Late because, well...'

'Don't worry, Verity's filled us in beautifully. Sit down and we'll get on with things.'

Freya sits down; doesn't even acknowledge me. Just looks at Verity and squeezes her fists together in a show of excitement. Verity kicks her stubby little legs up and down in response. They are like two toddlers being offered a chocolate.

'Right, well as you know, the Anne Dunne Scholarship is up for grabs. The three of you have been put forward by the teachers' vote, and so I'd like you all to go for it, if you are interested?'

'Yes, yes,' we reply. Verity is now sitting on her hands. She then shifts her chair further away from me, towards Freya.

'We would be honoured,' I say, attempting to distract Mrs Allen from noticing.

'As you know, there are three other schools trying, each with three candidates having been put forward. I suspect, or hope rather, that it will go to one of you.'

'What do we have to do for preparation? I mean ... like, will we have extra lessons and stuff?' asks Verity.

'No, no nothing like that. The scholarship is all done on natural ability and general knowledge, so you can't really prepare too much, other than brushing up on your current affairs and getting a good night's sleep.' Verity is now picking a bit of fluff off Freya's jumper.

'You will be interviewed by Oxford's admissions department and that will take place over the course of two hours. You'll then be asked to write a short essay on a current news item, blind, by which I mean you won't know the topic or question beforehand. Obviously.'

Freya raises her hand. 'But what if it's about something totally random? I mean, something we've never heard of?'

'They're not out to get you. But we deliberately chose you three because you have a broad knowledge of things.'

But Freya doesn't. She is always complaining about it and how she wishes she knew more about international affairs. So why her? There's something so odd about her nomination. It worries me but, at the moment, I can't quite work it out.

'Right. So your interviews. I'll let you know when they come back to me with specific times but you'll be driving up to London with Mrs Kitts.' We all nod and Mrs Allen looks up at the large oak grandfather clock by the door. 'Right. Time for lessons. Please work hard. Don't disappoint me.'

Mrs Allen holds her arm towards the door and we all get up and walk towards it. Freya and Verity link arms and I wait for Verity to turn around and give me a 'look' but she doesn't even bother, too busy are they screaming and kicking their heels together.

The next few days I don't really speak to anyone. I'm busy sorting out Head Girl admin: who's going to be representing the school for the Big Debate, implementing a new Young Enterprise Scheme which will take the form of pupils swapping schools for a week, typing up notes for the next School Announcements, keeping staff informed of any relevant notices, drafting up pieces for *The Lens* and, all this time, a little metronomic tic occurs in my brain.

Freya and Verity, Freya and Verity.

Then I think of Verity's mouth puckering up with pleasure and I think of how Freya feels about this. Then a whole host of other thoughts enter my brain: *what if she tells Mrs Allen what happened that night? Will she speak to me again? How can she be friends with Verity Greenslade?* And then the upset disappears and is replaced by the most phenomenal rage. It tornadoes through me, whipping up my blood and organs until they feel as though they are shaking inside of me. I can't sleep with it and I can't eat with it and it's *still* distracting me from my work and that makes it even worse. Because then I won't get the scholarship and it will go to Verity and there really would be nothing more awful.

I queue by the phone that night, in the Upper Sixth corridor, to call home. I am desperate to make this call but there are three other girls before me. I tell them I have to go first because of an emergency. They all step back and one of the fifth-formers, who shouldn't be using the sixth-formers' phone anyway, gestures towards the handset. 'Go for it. All yours.'

'Thanks,' I say, frowning. They're all still standing there, though, and I tell them to wait outside in the corridor until I've finished.

'Sorry, sorry, of course.'

I've only got twenty units left on my phone card, so I don't have much time. The phone rings and rings but finally she answers. She falters a bit when I say, 'Ma,' as though I've called her by the wrong name.

She's very slow and, if I hadn't known better, I would have thought she was drunk. 'Yes,' she says, quietly. And then something that I can't hear. 'Ma, can you speak up?'

The line goes silent – I must have woken her up and she's fallen back to sleep. 'Ma, I would love to talk to you.' I sit there for five minutes, until the phone becomes slippery under my chin and starts beeping. Three units left. I sit, letting my ribcage expand and shrink. I shut my eyes against the flurry of girls that race past me on their way to supper. I try to let it all wash over me.

2014

It must be around five in the morning: the dawn light presses the day onwards. I'm lying on a bench in St James's Park. I've still got my phone and the small black envelope clutch bag that I took to the funeral. There's nothing in it except a fiver, some vanilla-flavoured ChapStick and a set of house keys. I like to travel light but today, the emptiness of my bag is unsettling. And then I remember I had my wallet. I do a quick check around me but it's gone. I lie still for a few minutes, heavy with dread at the unfolding day, until it crosses my mind that I can be seen by buses, people going to work. Imagine if someone I knew saw me sleeping on a park bench? I leap up, but then, stunned by my headache, I sit down and throw up in between my legs. Has it really come to this? *You buried your mother yesterday,* I tell myself.

I use the fiver to buy a McDonald's which I cram into my mouth, its salty deliciousness energising and heavenly. The last time I ate a McDonald's was probably eighteen years ago, with Freya. A night out where we had a competition to see who could eat the most chicken nuggets. Freya had won, pouching her cheeks with at least six in one go.

I swallow down the last of my breakfast muffin and remember that my Oyster card was in my wallet. With no battery on my phone, I have no way of calling anyone. I start walking and walking, with no destination in mind. My brain is not processing anything properly – thoughts clunk around in my head, and nothing seems very real – like I'm in some sort of parallel universe. It's only a hangover, I tell myself. By this time, everyone's walking to work, streams of people coming towards me. It's overwhelming and I have to get somewhere quiet. By now, I'm miles from home and the only person whose place I know I can go to lives a fair walk away. I end up doing it anyway, even though it makes me feel stupid. Going to someone who has been my main inconsistency. Right now, though, he feels like my only stability.

I find his street. He lives in a small, basement flat in a Victorian mansion house. What if his girlfriend, or whatever she is, is inside? Before I allow myself to think much further, I ring the doorbell. He appears pretty much straightaway, coffee in hand and then I remember he's always up by about four thirty every morning, scouring the day's news sites and pitching new article ideas.

'You're shaking,' are Toby's first words, pulling me inside. He doesn't question what I'm doing there, for which I'll be forever grateful. The flat is comforting. There's a huge world map in the hallway. It's curling at the edges and smells of old paper. I lean my face towards it and press my nose into the fading black lines. We go inside and he passes me a glass of water.

'Got anything else?' I ask.

'Like what?'

'I don't know. Just not water.'

'Just drink that then I'll see what I've got.'

I tuck my legs up on the sofa and he pulls a scratchy, red Afghan throw over me. An hour later and neither of us have said much.

'You're still shaking,' he says, looking at his watch. Then I lean over and retch into my hands. Nothing comes up but I retch again and again, folding myself up into the foetal position.

'Do you need help?' Toby is wedging a cushion behind my back.

'No. I'll be OK. I'm fine. I just had a bit too much to drink last night.' I can't remember much from after the funeral, only the guy from the pub whipping off his tie, lassoing me into his arms on the dance floor and then blank. It's a comforting blank. I feel safe knowing I won't get those memories back.

'No, I mean, professional help.' He reaches over to a small chest of drawers next to the sofa and pulls out a packet. He opens it, pops a pill out of a silver blister and hands it to me.

'Take this. Valium. You look wrecked.'

I glug it back with some water, retch again, and turn onto my back, realising that I don't know what happened last night and that I should probably get the morning after pill but at the moment, I'm too tired to care, or even to be disgusted with myself. Toby is taking off my shoes, which are inexplicably covered in mud and white lines, like dried seawater stains, and places them by the sofa. The pill finally takes effect and my head, arms and legs feel like they are melting into the cushions. Some reprieve.

'J, I think you need to see someone. I've never seen you like this. Look at you, you must weigh about seven stone.' He leans over and pinches the area above my hip bone. 'And your eyes. They look ... I mean, they look – you look sick.'

'Toby, I am sick. I've been on a massive night out, my mother's just died. You always used to accuse me of being cold and now I'm showing some sort of emotion, you tell me I need help.'

'It's not that. It's ...'

'It's what?'

'It's just, you seem so ...'

'Seem what, exactly?'

'I don't know. You've seemed disconnected for a while now. In Jordan ... At the Frontline when you did that weird thing in the audience. Now ... you seem ...'

'When you told me you had been shagging some other girl?'

'Well ... yes.' He has the decency to look ashamed.

'This is not about you.'

'I know. Sorry.'

'Have you got an iPhone charger I can borrow?' I hand him my mobile.

'Sure. I'll just get it. Stay there.'

By the time he comes back, I'm half-asleep. I hear the click of a plug socket, the kettle going and the jolted tap of a computer and Toby, whispering into his phone. I don't have the energy to hear what he's saying. That afternoon, when I wake up, Toby has gone. There's a cup of warm coffee on the table next to the sofa and a duvet has been heaped at my feet. I find a note on the floor, next to a pair of slippers that I use whenever I have stayed over.

Dr McKinnie, it says, alongside a nearly illegible telephone number. *GP but does some therapy-type stuff and deals with life problems and will give you prescriptions. Private practice but if you need help, I'll pay. I go and it helps. Call today. Back later. T.*

I feel strange holding on to this piece of information about Toby, like I'm inspecting his naked form whilst he sleeps. I've always wondered about therapy, what terrors someone would find if they looked inside my soul. Best left alone, except that now some sleeping pills or anti-anxiety medication wouldn't go amiss.

I crumple the note in my hand and stuff it in my pocket. Then I take it out again and get my phone from its charging point. Valium, I think. Valium, Xanax, whatever ... just something. I switch it on and there are three text messages from Father, asking if I'm alright. The idea of apologising for leaving him in the lurch makes my limbs ache, so I vow to ring him later. Before that, I punch in the number from Toby's note.

'Hello, Dr McKinnie's office?'

'Hi.' There's a long pause whilst I try to work out what I'm going to say.

'Hello?'

'Hi, yes sorry, I'd like to make an appointment. My friend, Toby, he recommended Dr McKinnie.'

'Lovely, and you are?'

'My name's Josephine. Josephine Grey.'

'Ah, Josephine, yes, of course. Sorry. Toby rang earlier. Said you'd ring. Of course. Come and see Dr McKinnie today if you'd like. We've had a cancellation actually.'

'Today?'

'Yes, today. There's a free appointment at six twenty. One of the last. We've just had a cancellation and, of course, because Toby's rung and all...'

It's three thirty now. 'OK. Thanks. I'll see you there. Whereabouts are you?'

'Sloane Street. Not far down from Harrods. Number 765.'

I hang up and think about sneaking around Toby's flat, looking for evidence of his girlfriend. The mother of his baby. In the end, worried by what I may find, I don't.

Instead, I lie on his sofa, the Afghan throw scratching my skin but I am too tired to throw it off. I keep thinking of Mother's coffin, and about her lying inside. Her toenails, of all wretched things. When I can bear it no longer, I get up and nearly kick myself when I remember I don't have any money. I could get Father to book a taxi on his account, but I still can't bear to ring him. I can send a text? But the guilt prompts me into total inaction – the guiltier I feel, the more paralysed I am to do anything about it. So I run upstairs and rifle through Toby's things to see if there's any change lying around. Toby's always been careless about his money and I leap on a twenty pound note that's lying on the side table by his bed. Reminding myself to tell him, I get dressed in yesterday's clothes, the dirt and stench a reminder of death and the funeral, and run out the door.

When I get to Sloane Street, my hangover has gone. It's been a killer but the shine on the doorknob of the doctor's surgery, the grand, carved wooden door slightly open and expectant, shames me into feeling nearly normal.

'Come in, you must be Josephine,' says the lady behind the desk. 'Are you covered with your insurance?'

'Insurance?' I remember from Toby's note that it's a private surgery. 'Oh, I ... No, I'll be paying ... can you invoice me?' I feel like a total fraud. Ridiculous. My pockets jangling with change from Toby's stolen twenty pounds.

'Of course.' She gives me two forms, and says she will let me know when Dr McKinnie is ready. I take a seat on one of the green leather chairs, breathing in the expensive smells of Jo Malone candles and wood polish. I lean my head back into the reassuring cushion and suddenly feel so weary I begin to nod off. The receptionist taps me on the shoulder.

'Excuse me, sorry to disturb you, but Dr McKinnie will see you now.'

'Oh, oh right.' Disorientated and heavy-limbed, I shuffle to where she is pointing. 'Thank you,' I say.

When I open the door, I'm really shocked to see a woman. Berating myself for the assumption, I sit down before introducing myself. I stand up again, reach over to shake her hand, which is heavy with semi-precious rings.

'Josephine, please, please sit.'

Dr McKinnie, or Diana McKinnie, as I can see on the headed cream paper on her desk, is beautiful. Perfectly plucked dark brows set off a face that is both angular but soft. Her hair as well is blow-dried in curls around her shoulders. There's a tiny beauty spot just above her lip and she's wearing a light-blue mohair jumper that I want to stroke. Her beauty feels like a betrayal. Has Toby sat here and pondered her? I become aware of the smell of my clothes, the itchiness of my unwashed scalp.

'Thank you, thank you.'

'Now, Toby rang and said you would come in. Would you like to explain a bit about what's going on?'

'Sure, I'm ... well, my mother just died.' I don't know what to say next, so I pick up a pencil from the desk. It's green and gold-embossed, and reminds me of Harrods. *Dr McKinnie, Sloane Street.*

'I'm so sorry to hear about that. When was this?'

'Last week. She was mentally unwell for as long as I have known her.' Dr McKinnie looks up from her paper. 'Paranoid schizophrenia,' I say, as matter-of-factly as possible.

'Right. And how did she die, may I ask?'

'Too many pills. Aspirated on her vomit, then contracted pneumonia.'

'Josephine, would you like the heating on? You're shivering.'

'No. I'm OK, thank you. I've actually just come to see if you would prescribe something for me. To help me sleep. I'm getting these flashback-type things ...' As soon as I've said it, I can see Dr McKinnie pick up pace with her writing. She thinks my grief has triggered hallucinations like Mother and I hastily backtrack. 'I mean, nothing bad, just repetitive, boring stuff.'

'Boring? Like what?'

'Nothing to do with my mother. Just to do with stuff from the past. Maybe in part triggered by her death.' I want her to think I've thought about it, that I'm on it, that I'm not so severely ill that I don't have control over my mental faculties.

'Would you like to tell me about them? See if I can help?'

'Oh, nothing too much. Just that ... I once nearly killed a girl. And I think it might be coming back to haunt me.'

There's a brief pause as she digests this, her pen stops moving. 'Right,' she says, kindly. 'Do you want to tell me any more?'

Shame punches my stomach.

'Well, it's not that I exactly nearly killed her. But she nearly died because of me. And she was my best friend.' I halt at this.

'Please carry on. I'm listening.' And because she doesn't look at me, I begin to do something utterly uncharacteristic of me: I talk.

I tell her an abridged version of the events with Freya – the drugs and ensuing fallout – and mention that she's been in contact, wanting to see me again and that I've said no.

'Why's that?'

'Just . . . Just. It's difficult.' Then I look around and see pictures on her desk and the wall. Kids, smiling husband, the whole perfect unit. I look back on my own life, the mistakes I made . . . the consequences. 'Anyway.' I stand up. 'Could I have a prescription, do you think? Oh and I need the . . . the morning after pill, so that as well. Please. I've actually got to get moving.'

'OK, I'll write you a note for the pill. And what else would you like?'

'Xanax. Anything.'

'To help you with anxiety?'

'Yes. Exactly.' I start picking up my bag and she motions for me to sit back down.

'Are you alright?'

'I'm fine. I'm fine.' I feel my cheeks flush and Dr McKinnie gets up and puts the fan on.

'Would you like to come back and see me next week?'

'Ah, no. No, thank you.'

'Well, I'll prescribe you a few pills for the short-term. Any more and you'll have to come back here.' She looks directly at me, eyes all wide with concern as though I'm about to take a massive overdose.

'I'm cautious. I mean, come on, I'm not going to ...' Then it strikes me that I've just told Dr McKinnie the cause of my mother's death. 'Fine,' I back down. I can easily cancel. 'I'll come next week then.'

I keep silent, don't want to disturb her from finishing that damn prescription, which I snatch from her and stuff in my bag.

'Wait ... Josephine?'

I stop. The intimacy of her calling me by my first name is nice, at first, followed by a flare of irritation at the presumptuousness. 'What?'

'Josephine, if it's OK, I'd like you to make the appointment now, with me.'

'OK.'

'So, it's Tuesday today. How about the same time next week? Is that convenient?'

'I'll probably be back in Jordan by then actually, so perhaps before then.'

She hands me a card. 'Ah. Jordan. I've got some cousins there. What is it that you do?'

'Archaeologist.' I don't want start any small talk, I just want to get out of here now.

'Great. Bet you get to see some amazing stuff. Anyway, Tuesday, a week today. Is that OK? Say, eleven o' clock?'

'Yes,' I lie.

I've got the prescription. I'll sleep well. Get the plane back to Jordan in a couple of days. Back to the dig. Will tell all my colleagues not to let on to a soul that I'm there. Won't see Freya. There's absolutely no excuse for me to be away, now Mother has been disintegrated into ash. Go back to normal.

I'll be damned if I have any reason to see Dr McKinnie ever again.

1996

It's been another two weeks since the scholarship announcement and I still haven't spoken to Freya. All the girls know something is deeply wrong. No one says anything but I detect it in the brittle energy, the falter before anyone talks to me, the slight incline of the head to see if anyone else is watching; judging them for interacting with me. Freya's got the edge in terms of popularity but as Head of School, the girls are still petrified of putting a foot wrong with me. There are some who try to talk me into telling them what's wrong. Gracie Lovell, sidling up to me after History, pretending to be concerned for my welfare. I catch her holding a finger up to her lips to Marge Bell before she turns to me with a shit-eating grin on her face. I don't say anything, just reply that I have to get going with my coursework. I see her shrugging to Marge, who nervously pulls her bottom lip to one side.

However, aside from the weird atmosphere, I'm coping well, I think. The busy routine of the day-to-day has settled the events of what happened with me and Freya and, on the surface, everything is calm. That is, until one night, I'm woken up to Eleanor from my dorm, holding her arms around my neck and then pushing my shoulders into the bed. 'Shhhh, shhh, you're OK,' she's saying.

I can't reply, her thumbs are digging down into my windpipe. 'You were shouting in your sleep and doing this weird jerky thing with your arms. You were saying all this stuff, about dancing? Freya? So weird. Something ... whatever it was, it woke me up. I was scared.'

'Shhhhh,' I say.

I try to grasp the edges of my nightmare but all I get are flashes of blood, sticky drips of it rolling down Mother's arm and the image shifts. The blackness around Freya's neck, which melts into slime and congeals into the blood from Mother's wrists. 'I'm alright. Must have been exam fear.' I try to laugh but the sides of my throat are stuck together.

'Do you want me to get Mrs Kitts?'

'No of course not. I'm fine. Thanks.' The shadows of passing cars turn sinister and I wonder if this is where it began with Mother. 'I'm fine. Absolutely fine.' I squeeze my arm, really, really hard and sink back into the warmth of the bed. It's only five minutes later, when Eleanor has heaped herself back into her duvet and my heart relaxes, that I realise I've wet myself. I wonder how I will get the sheets washed and back without any-one noticing and wait at least an hour, lying there until I am sure everyone is fast asleep before I act and, of course, there's no one to help.

Freya's always told me I have to be more open to other friendships. 'Not everyone's bad,' she used to laugh. 'It's not that,' I would say. 'I just don't want people asking about my family.' With no one else to really talk to, I try to see a flipside to the solitude – to use it as an opportunity to work. Firstly, *The Lens*: the initial proof needs to be in next week. I've called an editorial meeting in Mrs Allen's office. We run through the features, interviews and articles and I ask Dorian Marchmont, a Lower Sixth, to co-ordinate the first edits.

'Can those of you who've written opinion and features please leave me a headshot picture in my pigeonhole,' I say, looking around the room.

'I think that's pretty much it. I still haven't got any good stuff for the "Guess Who?" section, so please can you make sure you get something by Friday? That gives you two days. Come on, girls, I know you can do this. Gracie, you're always on the pulse – get me something by then?' She nods her head in a show of enthusiasm.

'Thank you everyone. End of meeting. See you all next week and don't forget head shots and "Guess Who?". If you don't have a photo then go and see Mrs Bloom, who'll do a quick snap for you and get it developed. See you next week then.'

Everyone leaves the room, except Sally Aylsford, who is waiting for me as I pick up my blue folder. *Please don't try and talk to me*, I think. Sally is in my year, in Larden House, and she's 'quite' everything. Quite funny, quite clever, quite sporty. But there's something I also find *quite* irritating about her. I haven't worked out what it is yet but I think it's to do with her jaw. Or lack of it and the way it makes her look timid. With her red eyes she reminds me of a myxomatosis rabbit.

'Hello, Sally.'

'Hi,' she says, pointing at a chair. 'Do you mind?'

'No, no go ahead.' *Christ,* I think.

'Mrs Allen won't let me try for Oxford.' I nod and thumb through the papers in the folder.

'She says she doesn't think I can do it.' I look up and lean my ear towards my shoulder. 'It's because I got that C in my History mock.'

'Oh.' *A C?* I want to say. I keep quiet.

'Yes. Quite. My dad has gone mad at me. Like, really, really mad. I thought he was going to hit me.'

'Oh.' I pull a grimace, which feels insincere even though I actually do feel sorry for her. I've heard horrible stories about her father. Families are always a hot topic at school – thank goodness no one knows about mine.

'Can you do anything? I've only got a few weeks until the application deadline. I've written the essay, though. So I can do it. I know you probably handed yours in ages ago, but there's time. I know there is.' She pulls at the sleeve of her navy blue school jumper.

'Do anything? Like what?'

'Well, like ask Mrs Allen if she'll change her mind?'

Of all the things I'm going to ask the headmistress, this is not one of them.

'I'll try,' I say.

'Really?'

'Really.' I get ready to leave the room.

'Because I can help you make *The Lens* the best one yet. I've got something that will make your "Guess Who?" section really quite explosive.' She stops me in my path and I can smell onions on her breath.

'Oh, thanks so much. I appreciate your help,' I reply.

'No. Really, I can.'

'I'm sure you all can. My father got me an interview with the PM. Of course it's going to be the best one yet, with or without your "Guess Who?" entry.' I frown.

'No. I don't think you quite understand,' she says. A hardening in her voice makes me stop.

'I've got something big.'

'Big?'

'Yes. Really, really big,' she says, folding her arms.

'Like what?'

'Like I told you. Something that will make the "Guess Who?" section the most talked about *Lens* piece the school has ever seen.'

'How?' I say flatly.

'I found out yesterday when I left the San. Remember I left English that day? Well I had a pretty high temperature.' I don't recall but I nod anyway.

'I found out then.'

'Found out what?'

'Do you promise this goes no further until we work out what to do?' she asks. I nod again.

'Swear? It's probably illegal, for one thing. I mean, if the papers found out, the whole school will be on the front pages. I mean, I couldn't believe it when I saw it.'

'Saw what? Spit it out.'

'Well, if you must know, it's about Freya.' A fountain of nausea rises up my stomach.

'Go on,' I say carefully. Sally leans forward and whispers in my ear, her hot breath warming up the hairs on my lobe.

'Freya? Sally, come on,' I laugh but doubt snakes through me. 'Freya? If anyone would know something as monumental as this about Freya, it's me. Don't you think? She's my best friend. If you think that's true and I don't know about it, you must be ...' Sally looks down, inhales. Reinvigorated, she steps closer.

'I know you two are best friends. I know how exclusive you are. How you tell each other everything. How your friendship is totally impenetrable. But I'm only telling you what I saw. And what I heard. It's true. Every word.' For a moment, I wonder if Sally's trying to come between us. Whether she has some weird motive or jealousy over Freya's and my friendship. Then I see her jaw frozen, her eyes unmoving from mine, and I can tell she's not lying to me. But I just can't accept it. Not the nature of what Sally's told me, even though if it's true, it would be the most explosive thing to ever have been contained in the walls of Greenwood Hall. It's the fact that Freya held this back from me. How long could she have kept this a secret? How long had she known? I could have reconciled myself to this if it was some-thing that had happened after our night out. But it wasn't. It was obviously happening all the time whilst Freya was calling me her best friend. My mind's going at high-speed, remembering things Freya said, did. Trying to connect them to what Sally's just told me and, although I can't seem to make sense of it, something resonates. A flash of something.

After all that's gone on in the past few weeks, it's this that makes me the most tired. I'm exhausted. I have nothing left. And then Sally interrupts the blanket of fatigue that hovers over me.

'I normally wouldn't have told you but I want something from you and, of course, I know she's been bad-mouthing you to everyone, so I thought you might be willing to help.'

'Bad-mouthing?'

'Yes. Bad-mouthing,' she repeats.

'Freya bad-mouthing is like everyone else's compliments,' I laugh.

'What? That you're like the devil incarnate? Without a soul?' Freya always says that kind of thing to me and I'm often inclined to agree, but then Sally takes a breath and what comes next is much worse. 'And that you are like your mother. Hateful, bitter, angry, cold. "Mentally damaged".'

I look at Sally and I know for sure she's not lying. About any of it. Freya, Freya – the only person who knows about Mother's illness, for her to say those things…

'How do you know this?' I laugh again but something is happening to my insides. They are collapsing.

'I was sitting next to her and Verity in chapel the other day. Verity was laughing when Freya was doing these weird impressions of your mother.' Sally uses her fingers to pull her eyes down and starts rocking back and forth. I am perfectly still but inside I am recoiling so tightly, it feels as if my insides are contracting into one large mass.

'Are you sure Freya was talking about my mother?' I whisper. I feel ice cold.

'Yeah. Definitely. She was laughing, saying sometimes you have that manic look in your eye as well.'

At last she registers the look on my face because she starts to look afraid.

'But I'm sure it's not true. About your mother, I mean,' she says hurriedly. 'I was quite shocked, you know.'

'I'm sure.'

'Verity was laughing, saying that she had always realised something was wrong with you.'

'Was she now?'

'But of course, Verity's an idiot. Doesn't know what she's talking about half the time. But she is your Deputy Head Girl, so I'm sure she's great.' Sally finally realises she's gone too far and is all tied up in knots, unsure of what she should be saying and who to trust.

'I need to think.' I sit down. We are both silent and I tear little rips into my blue folder.

'OK.' I stand up. My head hurts. The pain is spreading through my jaw and up my scalp and I remember Freya, pulling that clip through her hair and it all fits into place. What Sally's telling me. I'm beginning to see small hints, clues in Freya's past behaviour that mean I think Sally's got it right. And although I'm in shock, the seed of an idea forms in my mind. This idea, this cunning. I'm going to use Sally Aylsford's information as a little warning to my friend Freya. I will publish this prize-winning gossip in *The Lens*. It'll be anonymous. I won't name Freya. Won't tell everyone exactly what she's done. Hints, of course, yes. A little message from me to her. *Tell anyone what happened that night, Freya, and I will tell everyone what you've done.* Everything *that you've done.* After that, she won't dare, *dare* say a word. I will be safe. I will get into Oxford, things will go on as normal. The brilliance of it all feels like a smack in the face.

'Send me a letter,' I say. 'Put it all in a letter. Anonymous. And put it in my pigeonhole and I'll decide what to do.'

'And Mrs Allen and Oxford?'

I turn to her so fiercely, she leans back.

'Just do it.'

2014

I've told work I'll be back from my compassionate leave in a few days. I've told the crew of my plans, although there are a few more things I need to check up on: Mother's probate, her will and all her clothes and jewellery. Despite not having spoken to or seen him since I left the funeral, I call Father and ask him to help me clean out her room. Neither of us have stepped foot in there for, what, fifteen years? He doesn't mention my behaviour, just says he'll be along after work and so I head back home, where I'll make a start.

By the time he arrives, I've stuffed ten black sacks full of clothes – vintage gowns, fur coats and the newer stuff with designer tags still attached. The room is a tip. The dust is making my eyes water and I've got flakes of old paint on my clothes from where I've brushed up against the walls. I can smell gin on Father's breath.

'Can't do this sober,' he says.

'Didn't you think I might have to?'

'Sorry about that. You've got a stronger stomach than me.'

Father unearths three pairs of knickers that are inexplicably covered in talcum powder and two pairs of diamanté heels, one black and one grey, that have both been used as ashtrays.

'Good God, Josephine,' he says, sitting on the bed. 'Good God, what is this? Why couldn't we help her?'

'Well, you did your best. As much as you could with your job.'

He looks up and frowns. 'Do you mean … Do you think I wasn't there enough?'

'No. I think you … I think you did what you had to do. She had people looking after her.' I look over and he is using a black silk shirt to wipe his eyes.

I'm embarrassed for him and don't know where to look, so I get down on my hands and knees and crawl under the bed. The mattress sags in the middle and I'm forced to prop it up from underneath with a pile of books and magazines. There are photographs, diaries, three suitcases of God-knows-what and piles of pills, scraps of powdery paper, razor blades – some rusty, some still in their packets. I pull them out and ignore the noises Father is now making. The photographs are of the three of us. There's one where we are pulling faces; there's me on his shoulders; Mother looking like a fifties housewife, thin and perfect, making a cake and pulling a dainty pose for the camera; all of us on a boat in Battersea Park and, finally, one of me and Mother holding hands. There are later ones of her, puffy-faced and sleepy. I take one where she's holding my old one-eyed teddy bear in her arms and stuff it into my pocket.

'Why did no one clear this out before?' I ask.

Father doesn't respond, just takes the photo I've handed him of the three of us and presses it into his stomach.

Next suitcase. There's the clink of random medicines Mother used to stockpile, in case of full-blown war which, according to her, was always around the corner: little bottles of potions and lotions that would ensure our survival. There's a third, full of papers and letters and diaries.

'Look,' I say, flicking Father's elbow. He moves himself up off the bed and squats down beside me. I don't think I've seen her writing for more than ten years now, but I always remembered it as elegant, not spidery and illegible like this. There are pages and pages, none of it making any sense.

Father and I are both entranced. For four hours we flick through the documents, trying to find any clues, any insight into Mother's mind. Nothing. And then I find a piece of paper that is fresh. The blue ink is still bright and the date mark on the top is from last year. I cast my mind back and it's the same date as the last time I saw Mother before this visit. I was in London, giving a presentation on our excavation findings. She had been recently discharged from hospital, fit to go home after her meds had been readjusted for the fourth time that year. She had seemed less hollow, there was almost a shine of vibrancy about her. She wore a gold bracelet and, for once, her eyes had some depth to them. She had even asked about my dig, laughing when I told her about how I had nearly missed my plane. And then I had had a drink and a row with Father about something – and it's coming back to me now, the way she had looked at me. I had thought, at the time, that it was a look of love and protective-ness. Thinking about that look now, her eyes, dancing around in those fragile, yellowy sockets, it hits me that instead, she was very, very frightened.

I pull out the paper and read. I read and read again and again and I can't work out if I am reading the words correctly, so I pass it to Father, who looks at the writing that he recognises so well;

the curious way that the As change shape every time they are written, and a look of confusion crosses his green eyes and he looks at me, absolutely terrified, blinking like someone's about to poke a knife in his eyes. I don't look back at him. We read again. Both of us. We read the words, over and over, until they fumble in our brains, and Father reaches for a cigarette even though he's promised he will never smoke in the house, and in my head, I'm already going through the conversation I'll be having with Dr McKinnie tomorrow and I'm going to have to beg work to give me some more time off because at this rate, I won't be going back any time soon.

1996

So Sally Aylsford is in possession of Freya's secret. Who else has she told? I wonder. I'm guessing no one, if she wants my help with Oxford. Two days pass and I keep checking my pigeonhole for a letter from Sally for the 'Guess Who?' section. On Friday afternoon, just as I'm giving up hope, there are three anonymous letters, all of them written in block capitals. The first is about one of our girls who has apparently been kissing one of Eton's fellow drama students after weekly rehearsals. *Great. I know who that is,* I think.

There's a slip of paper that suggests that our Head of Art has been snogging the Head of Drama. Boring. Everyone knows that too. And lastly, there it is. The letter from Sally. It is entitled: *EXCLUSIVE: Freya's Dirty Little Secret* and signed off: *Best Wishes, Oxford Candidate.*

I scan through it and see details that I don't really want to know. The image of Freya sliding a tortoiseshell clip through her hair keeps jolting through my mind and I still can't work out why Freya wouldn't have told me. *Should I really be doing this?* But then I come to my senses. An ugly voice inside questions whether half the reason I want to make this public is bitterness that Freya kept this from me. But then I remember what's at stake. *Sorry, Freya, but you made me do this. It's for your own good. Yours and mine.*

There's only a week left until the first edition of *The Lens* will be mocked up. I shunt the plan to the back of my head, for fear that I'll change my mind. For now, I have to concentrate on the Anne Dunne Scholarship interview, which is in four days. This is what truly matters.

When the time comes, it's a freezing cold Tuesday. Freya, Verity and I get together after breakfast. We've been instructed by Mrs Kitts to meet her outside Main School so she can drive us all down to London, where we'll meet the interviewers.

'Hello,' I say as I walk up towards Mrs Kitts's dirt-streaked green Fiat Panda. Freya opens her mouth, just a margin, and I think she's going to say something, but she gets a warning look from Verity. I straighten out my Head Girl badge and pull down my jumper. None of us are wearing coats. Mrs Kitts rushes up ten minutes later.

'Quick, girls, sorry I'm late.' She wipes her nose and climbs into the car. Her heels get wedged in the door frame.

'Oh gosh. Ridiculous shoes,' she says.

'They're nice,' says Freya, quietly. She opens the door and folds herself into the front seat. Verity and I sit at the back, me pressed against the door, as far away from her as I can possibly get.

'So, girls, are you all prepped? Been reading the papers?'

'Yes,' Verity and I say at the same time. Freya keeps quiet.

'Are you all nervous?'

'No, no, it's fine. We're all just tired, I think, aren't we?' Verity leans forward and pats Freya on the shoulder. Mrs Kitts looks at Freya, eyebrows dipping.

'I haven't been sleeping great,' Freya replies, looking at me from the rear-view mirror. She looks awful. Her blonde hair has lost its glossy sheen and her face is pale. Even her freckles seem faded. She's lost weight and the red patch of skin on her neck has started to climb down her shoulders.

It's not just her face, though. It's a funny, empty look in her eyes. The usual green sparkle has been replaced by a dull flatness. Her mouth as well is set in a permanent crooked position, as though she's forcing a smile. *Maybe it is really getting to her after all,* I think and then dismiss the thought. Sally's 'Guess Who?' entry rolls through my mind and, looking at her, I can't ever imagine she would do something like that. I sit up straight and stare outside at the passing streaks of muted green and grey. I have no time to be vulnerable about her before the interview, especially given what I now know.

'You look tired too, Josephine,' Mrs Kitts says.

'I'm fine. All great, thanks.'

'Good. Well just remember, girls, this will all be over in about five hours. I've been instructed by Mrs Allen to take you all out for pizza afterwards, so you can relax.'

'Oh, I've got to get back Mrs Kitts,' I say. 'I've got some work to do, and *The Lens.*'

'Now, listen, Josephine. It's not often you have much fun. I insist. We'll make it quick and, anyway, we find out tomorrow morning who's won the scholarship so I want to treat you all before the announcement is made.'

'Tomorrow?' Verity sits up straight.

'Tomorrow. Of course. Don't forget it's automatic entry into Oxford so they'll need to let whoever wins know before the normal admissions process begins. There's probably loads of admin stuff that needs to be done too, for the next stage, so they've decided to tell everyone right away. So are you all set then? I think they're going to ask you all broadly the same thing, so you have equal footing. So don't worry if you don't know the answers now, you can't change anything. Alright?'

Mrs Kitts smiles first at Freya then glances backwards at us. Verity looks at me out the corner of her eye. No one speaks for the rest of the journey. London is coming into view, the grey buildings jostling for space. Verity's legs have been jiggling up and down for the best part of an hour, driving me mad. We draw up to a car park in Victoria, where it's started to drizzle.

'Right, girls, come on. Are you all ready? Just remember why you are all here. Because you are brilliant and you've been chosen as the best students that Greenwood has to offer. Now do your very best. I'm sure you all have your own reasons to want the scholarship, so keep those in mind. We are all rooting for you. Don't forget, we want someone from Greenwood to win!'

Mrs Kitts looks at all of us as she wraps up her little speech. She adjusts the belt on her pleated green skirt and gives me a small wink. Freya sees and slams the car door shut. Mrs Kitts draws her hand to her breastbone and jumps. I'm left to walk behind, whilst Verity slides over to Freya and the pair link arms. The London traffic slips by slowly, and it takes us a few round trips to find the entrance to the building. Freya points to a sign: 'Anne Dunne Interviews', with a makeshift arrow in highlighter pink. We walk towards it, greeted by a small lady, with orange hair and rose-frosted lipstick. 'This way. School?' she asks, wielding her clipboard.

'Greenwood Hall,' says Mrs Kitts, wiping her nose with a lace handkerchief. 'Cold, isn't it?' The lady doesn't respond, simply ticks off our school with a stab of her pen, and ushers us in. Mrs Kitts glances back at the lady and gives us a conspiratorial shrug. Verity guffaws. We're all directed to sit on grey plastic chairs and given water, pens and a small notepad. There are nine other girls waiting, none of whom I recognise. They all say hello when we walk in and then the room goes silent, apart from the occasional whisper of good luck. A big whiteboard lists our surnames names alphabetically, so Verity is first to go out of us Greenwood girls. She turns to Freya and gives an exaggerated thumbs-up, then looks at Mrs Kitts and holds crossed fingers in the air in mock salute. Mrs Kitts nods towards the door where the examiner is waiting. Verity skips off, clutching a plaid pencil case and a strange, greying, furry snake, which I can only assume is some type of mascot.

After about twenty minutes, she bounces back into the room and sits next to Freya, breathless and charged up. There's one other girl listed before me, so I've got another twenty minutes or so to get my brain focused. My thoughts won't crystallise into anything meaningful whilst Verity is nearby. I can almost smell her, she's so close. That smell that is at first sweet, blanching into a stale, almost moreish unpleasantness.

Verity casts her eyes around the room – looks towards Mrs Kitts and the other teachers, who are all now talking amongst themselves. She scribbles something on her notebook. Her gaze pulls Freya's eyeline down to the paper and I can't help but look as well. 'Israeli foreign policy', she is writing. Dangerous ground, I think. Verity is so desperate to shore herself up to Freya, she's willing to cheat. She sees me looking, makes a big show of covering the paper with her hands and writes something else. She and Freya both laugh like drains and my stomach turns. 'Shhhh,' says Mrs Kitts, holding her hand up in apology to the rest of the room. Israeli foreign policy? *I can do this*, I think. Each strand of policy assimilates and flashes up in my brain, along with dates and quotes. *Thank you, brain*, I think. *Verity you still haven't got the better of me yet.*

'Can I go to the bathroom, Mrs Kitts?' says Verity. She's balled up the paper and stuffed it under her jumper.

'Of course. It's through there, I think,' Mrs Kitts says. I wonder whether to say anything but then I remember the other plan, which is altogether more dangerous and explosive. If I told on this cheating, it would, after all, be Verity and Freya's word against mine. The girl who has gone before me comes out of the interview room after ten minutes, fiddling with her hair. As she shuts the door, she starts to cry. Her teacher rushes up to her and hands her a tissue. 'It's OK,' she's soothing. 'It'll be better than you think. These things always are.'

'Josephine Grey,' comes a voice from behind the door.

'Good luck,' whispers Mrs Kitts.

'Come in, come in,' says the male voice. I sit down without being asked. There's three interviewers, all men. The one opposite me starts. He keeps patting his stomach as though he's just eaten an enormous lunch.

'Right. Josephine Grey. We've heard great things about you. Head Girl at Greenwood Hall, I see? We've had a fantastic report about you from Mrs Allen.'

'Thank you,' I say. 'That's very kind.'

'So, are you ready to start?'

'I'm ready, yes.'

He pulls at his ear lobe and looks at the other men. 'Shall I go?' he says to no one in particular.

'Right,' he says, without waiting for a reply. 'So today, we're asking everyone about the same thing: we'd like you to talk a bit about your thoughts on the outbreak of mad cow disease and what should have been done to prevent it. If you were PM, what would you have done and what measures would you have taken to stop it?'

'About mad cow disease?'

'Yes, you must have seen it in the news?' *Verity, you bitch …* I think.

'Of course, yes. I have seen it in the news.' And heard Father talk about it non-stop.

'So what's your take on it all then?' I'm so wrong-footed by the misinformation from Verity that I begin to stutter.

'I … I, well, it's very interesting because…'

'Because?' The fattest of the three men crosses and uncrosses his legs.

'I mean…'

'Do you know anything about this? We can give you a helping hand?'

'Yes, yes of course. I mean, yes of course I know. Not that you need to give me a helping hand.'

'Great. So about the latest scandal specifically, if that helps.' It does and I'm back on track but I don't perform to my best. My answers are vague and I'm half shivering. Freya and Verity are there when I walk out. Freya's still laughing but there's a glint of guilt in her eye. Her meanness is the worst thing that's come out of all of this. Freya always used to pull me back if she thought I'd upset someone. 'How was it?' Verity asks, lightly.

'It was good. Thanks.' When everyone on the list has finished their interviews, Mrs Kitts comes and sits in an empty space next to Freya.

'How was it?'

'Fine. Good,' Freya replies.

'It was really good,' Verity says, giving me a sideways glance.

I can barely breathe. Shall I say something? Her word against mine. But then I realise they'll ask why I didn't say anything at the time, which makes me complicit. We spend the next couple of hours writing up essays on our blind news item and when the last of us finishes, Mrs Kitts comes and rubs each of us on the shoulder as she collects our papers.

'Phew. Finished. Well done, girls. Pizza?'

'Sure, Jenny,' Freya replies and then double blinks, 'Mrs Kitts, I mean.' Verity gives her a confused look but I am too sick with what just happened to take it all in.

We file to the car and go for food and sit, waiting for the hours to pass to find out who will be crowned with Anne Dunne's blessing. I look at Freya and see she's smuggled bits of pizza into the napkin beside her. She's always been sanguine about her eating, even after her mother died, but judging by the size of her at the moment, I'm pretty sure that pizza will go in the bin. She tries to put a small piece in her mouth, as Mrs Kitts talks to her but her hands are shaking and she keeps missing. She gives up and I see her throw it on the floor. Verity is inhaling great lumps of cheese, masticating from side to side.

I don't know why Freya set me up in the interview. Or went along with Verity. As an isolated incident, I could probably handle it. But coming off the back of mocking my mother in chapel, something has to be done. I think back to Sally, the way she told me about Freya pulling crazy faces. The image distorts to my mother, all blank-eyed and twitchy with drugs and the betrayal hits me twice as hard. I wonder what else she is capable of. Whether she'll tell someone just to spite me. And Verity, Verity hating me for being Head Girl, hating me for God knows what else. The way she's eating is making me feel utterly nauseated and by the time I've cut up my mouthful of food, by the time the tangy tomato sauce nips at the back of my tongue, I've already worked out *The Lens* headline that will bring Freya down, so no one would believe her if she said anything anyway. And now, after this, Verity is going down with her.

2014

'Why would a letter from your mother scare you so much?'

Dr McKinnie smells so clean and fresh it makes me think of apple orchards and meadows. It's almost hypnotic but I keep bringing myself to, with the image of Mother's snaky writing.

'Don't you get it? She's writing that I'm going to turn into her. I'm going to get ill. I'm like a ticking time bomb. Can't you see?'

'OK, Josephine. Listen, can you start again? Start from the beginning.'

I take out the note and start reading. Just one paragraph at first. I'm too ashamed to read the rest. Dr McKinnie doesn't know what to say.

I let her grapple for the right words. She goes and gets me a glass of water from a black ceramic jug on the white table next to the door. There's a purple orchid in a slim white vase. She sets the water next to me and sits back down, pulling her chair further towards me.

'This doesn't mean you are going to get ill.'

'I know. I know she can't categorically say for sure. But she can sense it. She was very intuitive, Mother, very lucid in her darkest moments. She knew, or felt things that no one else did. And anyway, even if I can't take this as gospel, it's like my soul has become the repository for her own fear, her own terrors. Her hallucinations. It's all me. I've caused her sickness.' I look down and read the note again.

Josephine, Josephine. I saw it that day you had the row with your father about some political thing or other. There was something there, in your eyes. Something that I saw in my own eyes before I got ill. I've seen it from when you were young. It's in you. The move of your hand. Your pale face, your soul. You are me. I am you. Don't you ever wonder why Father is always at work? Why he's too scared to look at you sometimes? Can't bear to be around you? And me? We have something in common there! It's because he knows what life has in store for you. It's not pleasant. It's not pretty. I know. But soon I won't. I'm going to save myself from any more. And one day, I promise you, you'll have to do the same. It's frightening, to have to live like this. But you will be OK.

'Really?' Dr McKinnie says. 'You believe someone can have that kind of power? To *make* someone become a paranoid schizophrenic? Can't you see? She wrote this when she was ill. She's bringing her fears alive on the page.'

'I know. But I *am* her fear. Her own daughter. I'm making her fearful.'

'No, Josephine. She loves you. Don't forget that. She might be incapable of expressing it but remember, where there's love, there's fear.'

I make a noise which sounds like a snort. Dr McKinnie hands me a tissue.

'And what about this girl, Freya?'

Why is she bringing her up now? Does she know her? Is she wheedling out information from me?

'That's OK. I'm hiding from her.'

'Hiding?'

'Yes. Hiding. I mean, I'm … she's everywhere.' I start to laugh because I can't really articulate myself properly and Dr McKinnie is making more notes and tap-tapping on this tiny little iPad she has.

'Josephine, do you think you might need a rest?' she says.

'A rest?' I'm laughing again and hiccuping.

'Yes. A rest. I think you've been through a lot. Your arms, you look as though you've been scratching them.' I look down and she's right. My arms are covered in red marks. I have no idea where they came from.

'Are you trying to section me? See? You do think I'm like my mother, don't you?' I swipe her iPad onto the floor. Dr McKinnie doesn't move. She reaches out and touches my arm in a strange act of compassion. I look down at the black screen on the floor and then back at Dr McKinnie's face. She's nodding at me, saying it's OK. I want to ask her if I really just did that but at this point, I'm too scared. 'No. Not at all,' she soothes. 'I just think you need a break.'

1996

I don't have much time to dwell on what happened at the scholarship interview. The next morning, I've got a half-hour phone interview with the Prime Minister for *The Lens*. Mrs Kitts has allowed me to use the private phone in her study. Thankfully, I don't see Freya to put me off my stride. Just thinking about her actions yesterday focuses my energy and the interview ends up going brilliantly. He says he remembers me well; he's chatty at first, asking about school and other things my father must have mentioned. Then we start discussing more serious issues and we rally back and forth for far longer than the allotted time frame. I end up with pages and pages of notes which I hug to my chest as he starts to wind up the interview. *The Lens* is going to be stellar this year. Unbeatable, I think.

'I so enjoyed our discussion,' he says as I start to say goodbye. 'Your father should be proud. Perhaps you could come and work for me one day.'

After he hangs up, I sit quietly for a moment, so happy that I am almost stunned. Working for the Prime Minister. Could anything be further away from turning into my mother, fretting anxiously, a paranoid wreck?

My joy is interrupted by one of the younger years waiting for me outside Mrs Kitts's study as I leave. She passes me a hand-written note.

Please be at my study straight after lunch, for the Anne Dunne Scholar announcement. Mrs Allen.

'Thank you for bringing this to me, Diana. You can go now.' I wave my hand at the timorous Upper Fourth girl and she runs off. After eating, I make my way, alone, to Mrs Allen's study. Freya and Verity don't look at me when they enter the room. Freya strides in, all airy and breezy, although I can see her lip twitching and Verity's squeezing a piece of Blu-tack in between her fingers. Mrs Allen isn't giving anything away; not that she ever does.

'Girls, thanks for coming. I won't make this too long,' Mrs Allen says. 'Firstly, we're all really proud of you for having been nominated. It was no easy feat.' I look at Freya, watching to see if she at least has the dignity to look ashamed. She's sitting on the edge of her seat with her hands all bunched up in her school skirt. *Think of who you've just interviewed,* I tell myself.

'Right. So I heard from the examiners that you were all particularly impressive. A couple of things that cropped up. Verity, they were very impressed with your knowledge of government policy. Freya, they loved your take on what you would do if you were PM. Highly original, said their notes.' Freya lets her hand drop from where she's been scratching her neck, and smiles. 'Really?'

'Yes, really. Don't look so surprised.'

'And Josephine, they said you managed to debate very well on new policies.'

'Thank you, Mrs Allen.'

'No, thank you. It must have been a tiring day and now I can put you all out of your misery.'

Mrs Allen takes off her glasses and raps her knuckles on the desk, in an obvious attempt to buy time. And from this tiny movement, I already know what she's about to say.

'Verity,' she says, but she is looking directly at me. 'You are the new Anne Dunne Scholar.'

'No way!' She high-fives Freya. The walls constrict, along with my heart and lungs and I want to run. To escape the vacuum of shame. I palm the heat in my cheeks, something that has only happened once before, last summer, when Freya's brother, Leon, saw me undressing in the Cornish pool house. 'Well done. Your application to Oxford will be withdrawn as you already have automatic entry with the Anne Dunne. You'll still have to get your A levels, though, so don't rest on your laurels. Well done again, all of you, for being put forward and best of luck with the rest of your applications.'

We all leave Mrs Allen's study and I offer my congratulations to Verity. She gives me a long stare. She tries not to smirk and Freya, Freya, who looks so thin, so blank, so wretched, finds it within herself to smirk at me too. Mrs Allen sends me a hand-written note two hours later, delivered by one of the first-formers, during a games lesson: *Come and see me for tea. Four o'clock, my study. Mrs Allen.*

It's five to four and I rush down, still wearing my lacrosse outfit: a short, pleated blue skirt and a white Aertex shirt. I don't even care that it's about minus two degrees outside.

'Mrs Allen,' I say, walking in before she's told me to come in.

'Josephine. Sit down, sit down.' Mrs Allen takes off her glasses and taps one of the arms on her desk.

'Don't let this affect your performance.'

'My ...?'

'Your performance. As Head Girl. As one of the best students Greenwood Hall has ever seen. If I'm honest, I'm not quite sure what happened. I was relying on you to win.'

I look down at my feet. 'So was I.'

'It's disappointing. But they were obviously looking for something specific. Eagerness, perhaps.'

'I don't know what happened,' I say, thinking, *I know* exactly *what happened.*

'Well, I'm not going to make a big announcement about it. I think everyone would have been expecting it to be you so we'll keep it relatively low key, shall we?'

'Mrs Allen, I ... I ...'

'Yes?'

'Nothing.' For a minute, just for one minute, I had thought about letting everything out; the horrors of that night, the argument with Freya, Verity. I know if one word slips out of my mouth now, I'm in danger of changing everything. Maybe Mrs Allen would help? Then I realise she is not built for that. Mrs Allen is about success. The righteous manner of the Greenwood Hall girl, the loyalty to the school and well ... achievement. If I change the nature of our relationship, I fear my own success will be over for good. I am her Head Girl. She expects nothing less from me than my utmost all. Dedication. Loyalty. Power. Results. With this in mind, I shut my mouth and look down.

'I'm going to be fine,' I say.

Mrs Allen takes off her glasses, puts them in her case; snaps it shut. 'That's what I thought. Now say no more. Just go back to work and forget this ever happened.'

I go to the phone box in Main School and call my father on reverse charge. The school is quiet, everyone's on tea break. For once, he comes straight to the phone.

'I thought you should know, before you hear from Rollo.' I swallow back the words, unable to continue.

'Josephine? I can't hear you very well. Speak up.' I clear my throat and tell him what happened with the scholarship, how I hadn't performed my best. How Mrs Allen had been shocked. 'She was really surprised,' I say, hoping this softens his disappointment.

'Well, I must say. I am quite surprised too. Did you work hard enough?' he asks.

'I did. Not sure what happened.' I haven't got long to talk. I can hear doors slam and the echo of voices. After-school clubs start soon and I need to get out of Main School before anyone sees how much I'm shaking. Father sounds alright. Not too upset but then he tells me to wait. 'Don't hang up yet,' he says. 'I'm seeing your mother tomorrow. Was hoping to give her some good news. Have you got anything else I can tell her?'

Freya, Verity, how dare you? How dare you be the reason I have to make this phone call? Showing me up in front of my father, Mrs Allen. Everyone else.

'Yes,' I reply. 'Yes. Tell her I'm working hard on the school newspaper. That it's going to be the highlight for the girls and the school.' I lean forward, ready to hang up. 'That should do the trick,' I say, before slowly placing the handset down.

The next day, I see Sally Aylsford walking down the corridor. She's linking arms with Minnie Adams. Sally is crying. God knows why. She looks up and sees me. I gesture for her to come with me.

'Hang on, Minnie. I'll meet you at choir practice, shall I?'

'Sure.' Minnie waves at me, with a big, inane grin on her face. I don't know how to react so give a small smile and turn back to Sally.

'Want to come to the Prefects' Room?' Sally looks thrilled and wipes away the last of her tears.

'Come on.' She holds her arm out to link it with mine but I ignore her.

'Hopefully it'll be quiet. There's no one around at the moment, everyone's in class or at games.' Sally peers around the white room and plonks herself down on a dark blue sofa which is laden with toast and biscuit crumbs.

'Wow. You're so lucky.' She points at a toaster and a cupboard full of tuck. I hand her a Mars bar, which she unwraps and stuffs into her mouth.

'Right. I'll make this quick. Bell's going to go in about ten minutes. Milk?'

'Loads.'

'Have you told anyone else about this?'

'No one. I swear. Pinky swear.' *Pinky swear?* For the love of God, I don't know how far I can take this conversation.

'Right. And everything you mentioned last week is true?' Sally nods her head up and down so hard I think her neck might break. 'Right. And so if this all goes ahead, you have my word I'll speak to Mrs Allen. In return, I want your word that I can do what I like with your "Guess Who?" entry.' There goes the neck again.

'This doesn't come from you, OK? Whatever happens, none of this leads back to either of us. What's going to happen, is that I'm going to be totally unaware of the whole piece. Someone will have tampered with the final proof edition. OK? I haven't worked out how yet. But I will, OK? I'll work that out. And your anonymous letter. You haven't saved it anywhere, have you?' Sally gives a small shake of her head.

'Sure?'

'Sure.'

'And where did you print it off?'

'At home.'

'So no one could have seen it at school?'

'Definitely not. I promise.'

'Fine. Good.'

'Anything else?'

'No, I'm just thinking.' I hold a finger up to my lips and Sally is now on the edge of her chair. I know she is about to ruin my train of thought so I turn my back to her.

'Josephi—'

'Shhhh. Give me one minute.' The bell rings so I motion for Sally to leave the room.

'Wait,' I say as she skips to the door. 'Remember. Nothing. Not one word. Just as I have the power to get Mrs Allen to let you apply, I have the power to stop her. One word is all it will take. Just remember, OK?'

Sally grins, gives me a thumbs-up and, with that, she's gone.

172

2014

In all my life, I've never been told I 'needed a break'. During my school days, I was always the person who could handle anything that was thrown at me. Until, of course, the events that happened with Freya. Even after that, though, I would bowl my way through the days using every second of every hour as an opportunity to do something useful.

So Dr McKinnie telling me I needed a 'break' at first made me feel gratitude towards her, followed by a storming defensiveness that makes me intent on proving that I don't need anything of the sort. I decide to hole up, do some research for our investors from my 'sickbed'.

Firstly, I stop off at the British Library and photocopy a whole load of articles. Stacks of them. I'm not really sure what information I'm harvesting but, when I leave, my rucksack is stuffed with paper. I catch a Tube and buy some archaeology books from Foyles on Charing Cross Road. I walk home, the weight of my purchases feels good, my emotional load balanced out by my physical stance.

Before I get to my desk I'm compelled to go to Mother's room. I dump all my stuff by the front door and shout for Father but no one is at home.

Her room is strangely warm, at odds to the rest of the house. I take off my jumper and collect the rest of her things, the stuff that Father and I didn't get round to sorting. I jam them in a pile in the corner, breaking bits of china from dusty bowls and mugs as I go. I throw half-torn up books onto the pile, along with all my mother's junk: her old make-up, shreds of old clothes, trinkets – rusting toy aeroplanes from flea markets, dog tags, dull brooches with the pins bent all out of shape. I run downstairs, bring up some bin liners and shove all the stuff in as fast as I can, cutting my hands as I go.

When I finish, there's blood seeping down my arm. I'm taken back to when it all happened, the morning after, when my head had started bleeding over breakfast. A little trickle worming its way down my arm. I remember not being able to work out what was ketchup and what was blood. Tasting it. Metallic, salty, sweet, all mixed into one. I start to heave.

The next thing I know, I'm overcome with a sense of foreboding, like I've been hooded, pre-execution style. It's so frightening, so overwhelming, that I go and search for my Xanax but can't find any. The Valium is useless, hasn't done a thing, even though the two I took earlier should have kicked in by now. I go and ring Dr McKinnie, on her private line, and request another prescription.

'Slow down, I can't make out what you are saying. I can't hear you,' she says. I say more stuff to her but she is still telling me I'm making no sense and that I must breathe, breathe, breathe. I can hear her sucking air into her lungs. 'Like that,' she's saying. I tell her, or at least I think I do, that I'm coming to see her, straightaway.

1996

The magazine flat plan is all done and *The Lens* is nearly ready to go to print. I've spent hours poring over text and photographs, perfecting the layout with the editorial team.

'No mistakes,' I tell them. I remind them that I've managed to interview the Prime Minister so we cannot afford to have anything go wrong. The *Prime Minister* for heaven's sake and I'm hoping it will make mainstream news. It's definitely the best edition yet and I'm ecstatic. After this, no one will remember Verity as the Anne Dunne Scholar. Freya's going to be silenced once and for all and I will go back to normal – I will be what people like Mrs Allen expect me to be. No more mistakes.

It's Monday lunchtime. The weekend had gone by in mad preparation, with me having to rewrite at least three pieces and gather up leftover profile pictures. I have to run through everything with Verity, since she's meant to be helping me edit. Not that she has done anything so far. She's shown little interest in any of the editorial, only telling me about her weekend at the lacrosse competition at St Margaret's.

'We won, with me shooting the winning goal,' she says at our final run-through. 'So, Margot comes in, knocking her lacrosse stick on some poor girl's legs and ...' I wonder why she is bothering to speak to me after everything that's happened. Has she forgotten? Or is she feeling guilty? Whatever, it's all a bit strange.

'Verity, would you like to read over this editorial? You can read all but the last pages, as you know. Tradition says that only Head Girl can look at those.' I'm referring to the 'Guess Who?' section, which still hasn't gone in.

'No. I'm sure you've got it all in hand,' she says. And then I think something is really strange. Normally, Verity would be looking over my shoulder, desperate for any chance to point out my mistakes. 'Do you really need that extra comma?' she would be saying. But then, I realise she couldn't care less about the magazine, or the 'Guess Who?' section. And then it hits me how this is going to work.

'Verity?' I say.

'I forgot to mention. I'm really rushed tomorrow. I know that you and I were both meant to be working on this thing together, weren't we?'

Verity pulls her neck muscles tight. 'Yes. I'm sorry ... I ... I've been a bit rubbish, haven't I? It's just not really my area of interest. Or expertise.'

'No worries at all, but obviously your name is going in the front as Deputy Editor. So if you could at least take the final proof tomorrow to the printer's, it would be amazing. I would appreciate it enormously.'

'Of course,' she gushes. 'Absolutely. Anything to make up for you having done all the hard graft. And thank you. For putting my name on the front. That's decent. Kind. When you know I haven't really been there. So yes, of course I'll take it to the printer's.'

'Do you want to go through the final proof now? Together, with me? So you can see what's gone in? Whether you want to change anything?' I know her answer though before she says it. It's why I've asked the question. Verity looks at her watch.

'Well, I'm so sorry but ...' And I know now that she will never, ever bother looking through the final proof before she hands it in tomorrow.

'Oh, that's absolutely no problem at all. As long as you just tell me it's signed off now...'

'OK. Sign off done.'

'Excellent,' I say. 'Excellent. And one more thing. You've got to promise me to show no one. Not Freya, not anyone. I'll meet you at ten to nine tomorrow by the school gates and give it to you. I'm going to send Sally Aylsford with you to make sure no peeking. OK?'

'Josephine ... I'm not going to look, I promise.'

'Swear?' I try to keep my voice light; I don't want her to become suspicious.

'I swear.' Can I trust her? Obviously not but at least Sally will be there to keep a check.

'OK, well I told Sally she could go anyway. She's been helping me out with some stuff and I said she would get a name check in the magazine if she did some odd jobs for me.'

'Right then. Am I free to go?' Verity asks, bored now.

'Sure.' Verity gets up to leave the room and, when she's nearly out the door, turns towards me.

'I think you've done a great job. I really do.' I can see she doesn't mean it, since she barely knows what has gone in but something doesn't sit right about her niceness. The effort she's making with me. The neck muscles sticking out further than usual as her grin begins to take on a maniacal look. I don't have time for it. I put away all the papers in my editorial file and, tucking them under my arm, I go for tea.

I see Sally Aylsford in the queue. She's looking sweaty. We walk into the dining room together, past Mrs McCready, who checks our names in at all meals.

'Sally. Come here.' She bounds over, wiping her face with her sleeve.

'Right. You're going with Verity tomorrow morning to the printer's. Ten to nine. Meet her at the school gates. I'll be there too. Make sure she's holding the proof copy all the way there. Do not let her give it to you for one second,' I say. 'Go on. Repeat what I've just told you.'

'I've got to meet Verity tomorrow at ten to nine. School gates. Do not let her give me the proof copy to hold, even for a moment.'

'Do not be late. Even if someone's having a heart attack, do *not* be late. OK? If you muck this up, I'm pulling your Oxford application. And no letting Verity look at the final draft. OK? I'm pretty sure she won't. She doesn't seem remotely interested. But if she tries, tell her you'll tell me ... Got it?'

'Pinky swear.' This time, I take the little finger she's offered and link it with mine.

'Pinky swear,' I sigh.

I've called a meeting after tea with Mrs Allen, in her study. She's wearing her home clothes, something I've never seen before.

Thick black corduroys, with a quilted coat. She's got a scarf wrapped around her neck that's a dark purple. It washes her out.

'You look ... different,' I say. 'Nice.'

'Thank you. Sit down. How are you? Coping alright? Application done, so we just have to wait and hear now.'

'Four or five weeks. Deadline closes quite soon.'

She nods. 'So, what did you want to talk to me about?'

Mrs Allen steeples her fingers and is expecting me to say something important. Instead, all I've got is Sally fucking Aylsford's plea case.

'Mrs Allen, I think you might have made a mistake with Sally Aylsford.'

'Mistake?'

'Yes. With her Oxford application. I think she could do it. She's been saying how hard she's going to work.'

'Is this really what you wanted to see me about?'

'Yes. But ... I just think she's got something else to her...'

'Like what?'

'Well, I'm not sure. There's a creativity there. A spark. Something. I think she just fell at that mock.'

'Fell? Dear, you can't just "fall" at Oxford University. It's not for people who "fall".'

She's called me 'dear'. Something I've only ever heard her use for the likes of Laila Hickman, who was always struggling to keep up with absolutely everything. I take a deep breath and play what I think will be my winning card.

'She's asked me to coach her for the application process and thereafter if she gets offered an interview. And I've agreed.'

'I see. Might I remind you about our reputation for getting girls into Oxbridge, though?' Of course – it's only ever about the school, how we appear. It's what I've always tried to explain to Freya but she never understood; no one ever expected anything of *her*.

'I know. I really think she can do it.' There's a silence of at least a minute. I'm trying not to hold my breath.

She stares at me, piercingly, and for a moment I think all is lost until, 'OK then. Well she's missed her Oxbridge UCAS application so if they'll accept a late one for whatever reason, you can go ahead and coach her. If you do a good job I'm sure she's got a fine chance. Are you sure you can do this? Have enough time I mean? Mrs Kitts said you've been a bit off pace recently. She's worried. Thinks you've got too much on your plate.'

'Too much? Not at all, Mrs Allen. I'm loving the challenge. I'm over the scholarship now. Look onwards and upwards,' I say, reciting one of Mrs Allen's favourite quotes. 'I'll have time, yes. I'll give her an hour twice a week. Just for History. It should be enough. In return she's going to do some admin, so actually it'll be helping me. I'll be going over my History notes whilst she takes some of the more menial work off me.'

'Fine. I trust your judgement on this one. Don't let me down.' She doesn't look up and I know it's my signal to leave. God, that was much easier than I thought it would be. She trusts me so implicitly, she trusts that I can actually get this girl an Oxford interview in a short space of time.

The next morning I wait by the school gates at ten to nine. Sure enough, there's Sally, who looks like she's been there for hours. Her hair is pulled back into a tight, serious ponytail and there's a sheen of sweat on the bridge of her nose. I tell her Mrs Allen's agreed to let her apply for Oxford and that if the university accept her late UCAS form, we'll start the coaching sessions soon, should she get an interview. 'They will accept a late form, they will. My father will make sure of it.' She lets out a small squeal, and then gives me a very small nudge in the ribs. Verity's running down the path, lacrosse stick in hand.

'Coming,' she shouts.

'Don't worry,' I shout back. 'Take your time.' I want to keep her onside, even though I can feel the blood trickling into my skin. Verity looks taken aback that I'm being so genial. She puffs up.

'Lovely, J. This is going to be a great edition,' she says, as though she edited the damn thing.

'Right. Sally,' I say, steadying my voice. 'I know you wanted to go too. Are you going to give the proof to Verity to hold?'

Verity frowns. 'She's not two! Nor am I!' She leans on her lacrosse stick for support. 'I'll take it anyway,' she says, taking the bait. I knew she could not resist being in charge.

'Sure. Anyway, Pete, the printer guy, is expecting you both. I rang and left a message with him last night.'

Verity skips off, holding the magazine, and it's only half an hour later and I'm waiting by the school gates for them to return when I see two figures in the distance, both dressed in school uniform. One is doing a stupid dance and the other is waving at me, giving me a huge thumbs-up.

I spend the day alone, thinking, wondering how everyone will react to what I've done. Will I be able to pin the blame on Verity? Of course. I have an alibi. Sally doesn't know what she's got herself into. My mind starts segueing into what could go wrong and so I mentally prepare myself by creating role plays in my head. That night, I have another nightmare again and wet the bed. When the others have gone to breakfast, I rush back up and hair-dry the mattress, methodically and without panic.

During supper the next day, I find myself in the queue next to Freya, who is already holding a tray full of beef stew, rice and three chocolate puddings. She makes a big show of holding the puddings, which, judging by the size of her, won't be eaten. I look up to the chalked blackboard and Freya's standing next to me, breath all jagged and hot.

By the time I've finished reading the lunch menu, Freya is wiping her nose.

'Josephine?' It is the first time she has called me by my full name in years. Her voice is so quiet I have to lean forward.

'What?'

'Can I talk to you? Tomorrow? It's important.' She's looking around at the other girls in the queue, worried one of us is going to make a scene. I feel a frisson of disgust. That's her recent modus operandi, not mine.

I raise my head, keeping silent. I can see Freya twitch. I think she's about to beg me so I hold out a little longer. I'm still thinking of the betrayal over Mother, the scholarship. All of a sudden, Freya looks totally lost and it's the best punishment I can think of for what she and Verity did to me. Then she makes a little movement, a small jolt where she nearly drops her tray and

I can see the impact it has on her. The fright. I relent slightly and open my mouth, as though mulling over her question. Her thick, dark eyelashes are fluttering away. I think I see tears forming and, despite all that's gone on, I am overwhelmed with wanting to reach out and hug her. To envelop her delicate frame and make things alright, like they used to be. To dissolve everything that happened. I'm also wondering what she wants; whether she wants the same thing. Freya can see I'm curious, strung up at that liminal point between yes and no and she seizes her chance.

'You have to,' she says. 'You have to hear me out. You have to hear what I need to say to you.' She's trying to keep the pleading out of her voice but, at the last word, she falls.

'OK,' I say, thinking of the old Freya, how she would have already been hugging me by now, telling me to hurry up, that we had things to do, laughter to make.

'Fine,' I reply. She exhales with relief.

'After tea? In the woods? Our usual?' she says. I'm desperate to make a snide comment about how nothing is 'ours' anymore, but I stay quiet.

'Fine. I'll be there.' She picks off a bit of chocolate sponge, puts it in her mouth and walks away. Freya is normally quite readable. At least to me. I know that the tiniest movement on the left-hand side of her top lip means she is nervous. I know that when she widens her eyes, she's excited, waiting for something to happen. I know that when she is happy and about to laugh, she pats her stomach. She is doing none of these things. And she's painfully thin, her little ankles rolling around in her blue school slip-ons.

There was no hatred there, just a resigned sadness, which makes me even more wary and then I think of Verity and all that weird nicey-nice behaviour and I think to myself then and there, as I'm asking for my prawn vol-au-vent, that something is desperately amiss.

2014

'Josephine?' Dr McKinnie says, standing aside to let me in. I walk through the big wooden doors and she looks at my mouth, my nose, my hands, curled up like a newborn's. 'Josephine, come and sit down.' She hands me a brown paper bag from behind the front desk.

I throw my hand at her, swiping away the bag and she forces me to sit down.

There's no one else around. After five or so minutes, my hands unclench and Dr McKinnie asks how long I've been feeling like this. 'I think, Josephine,' she says, rubbing my back, 'you need to seek some more help. Spend some time away. This Freya girl, your mother, it all seems too much. How about Cedars? I know you've probably heard about it because all the celebrities go there, but really, it's the best place for a holistic approach.'

'No, no, I'm not going anywhere.'

We sit in silence, Dr McKinnie rubbing my back and me wondering when she is going to let me go.

'OK then,' she says, 'what would you like to do?'

'I'm fine. Much better now,' I reply. 'Just came to see if you have any more medication you could please give me? Really, I'm fine,' I say.

'What are you scared of?'

'Nothing. Just ... please. Can I have some medication?'

'Come into my office. You'll need something for the immediate future. I'll write you a note. Come on, it's OK. Take my hand if you need to.'

I go with her, down the stairs and into her office.

'Please, sit there. Would you like some tea?' Dr McKinnie flicks a switch. I look over to the streamlined silver kettle that looks more like a miniature spaceship.

'Milk, two sugars, please.' I sit in silence as she makes it.

'Here we go,' she says, placing a black cup next to me. 'Drink that.'

'Do you have ...' I'm about to ask for some drugs then realise that I have to draw the line at quaffing pills back with my afternoon tea.

'Listen. Can I do anything else? Honestly, a break might do you good, force you to sleep – you can talk to people, rest, therapy? I can ring Dr Anthony now, if you like?'

'Sounds OK. But I need to get back to work soon. I'm on a dig and I can't just...'

'If you are in the midst of a breakdown, you can.'

'Breakdown? Are you sure? Isn't that a bit dramatic?' I can hear myself panting.

'I'm not sure but I believe you are caving in with stress, yes.'

'What do you mean by a breakdown though, are you sure it's nothing to do with ...?'

Dr McKinnie opens her mouth and throws her hands heavenwards. 'Oh, do I think you are having paranoid delusions, do you mean? Now I get it. Ah, your mother? This is what this is all about. No. I don't. You are OK.'

I start laughing, then realise I sound mad again and shut up. 'I'm fine then. I'll be fine. Just need a couple of nights' sleep, that's all. If you think I'm alright.'

The relief that my fear is out in the open, that Dr McKinnie thinks I'm OK, almost brings me to tears. But then she leans over her desk and puts her arm on mine.

'Josephine, I think you are OK in so far as I don't think you are having a paranoid schizophrenic episode. But I don't think you are alright. I think ... in fact, I'm sure, you need some more help, though. I need to ask, have you had any suicidal thoughts lately?'

I'm absolutely stunned by her question. 'I'm sorry.' She's looking at my open mouth. 'I really have to ask. To see how I can help.'

I'm moving my head but I can't tell whether it's going up and down or from side to side.

'And your arms, Josephine. I'm more than concerned about these.' She pulls my forearms to her and places them gently on the table. Under the soft lighting they look alright, but then she brings them up towards her face and I can see them too. Weird little criss-cross marks and smears of dry blood. I must look disbelieving because she looks at me and asks if I know how they got there. My head's still making odd movements, totally detached from my thoughts. Like my brain function has been severed from the rest of me.

'OK, Josephine, what I'm suggesting needn't frighten you. I think we need to find a solution apart from medication.

A longer-term solution to help you deal with these ...' I know she's about to say the word 'demons' and then I really start to panic, because my mother was so full of them. Real ones. Ones that I'm too petrified to even try to imagine.

She stops herself. 'These issues,' she finishes. 'Look at you. You can't breathe.' She hands me another paper bag and orders me to come back in two days. 'I'm putting an appointment in for you for nine thirty on Tuesday morning. I want you to go home, relax, call me if you need anything and think carefully about Cedars.' Her tone suggests I needn't do any thinking, that my stay there is as inevitable as if it were written in the stars. 'Here,' she says, realising I'm probably incapable of thinking about anything at the moment. 'Here's some more medication to keep you going. I've just given you enough to last until Tuesday. Try and sleep.'

When the Valium's kicked in and I'm in a taxi home, I think about Dr McKinnie and what she's told me. I think about going back to work in this state and how it's not an option. Even the thought of boarding a plane back to Amman; trudging up the metal steps onto the aircraft and climbing into the never-ending sky, leaves me winded. So when I get back home, I decide to luxuriate in a bath. It's something I never do – a waste of time. I run the hot tap, grab a book and a glass of red wine. I slop in some unused bubble bath from Father's bathroom – something that looks like it's from a five-star hotel. Then I pack on a sachet of cucumber face mask that I find in the back of my bathroom cabinet, curled and brown round the edges. It smarts my skin but feels good nevertheless.

I walk into my bedroom and light a cigarette, stark naked. I rearrange my pillows and duvet ready to welcome me out of the bath and go and get a piece of toast from the kitchen, smeared in butter and honey.

When I'm ready, I turn off the hot and dip my toe in. It's boiling, so I let out some water and put in a tiny stream of cold. I start to feel a little better. My thoughts are at least connecting. Whilst I'm waiting, I go into my bedroom and look at the latest news on the BBC website. As I'm reading a short piece about Michael Gove, my email pings. Since I've changed my contact details, not many people haven't written to me on this address – Freya that one time, Father, when he wants to send me reminders, and the occasional invite to something work-related. Before I can even see who it's from, I've opened it.

> *Josephine. I've made up my mind, I'm coming to see you immediately. I have a feeling you are still in London – Dad said he saw you at your mother's funeral, looking well. So I'm going to come and visit you here, or I'll find you when you are back in Jordan. I really, really need to speak to you. So please, no more excuses. Freya.*

I read it, close it, delete it. Then I climb into my bath, which is still hot. I dunk my head under the water, open-eyed, and globules of the cucumber mask release themselves from my skin, rising up and clouding the surface.

Soapy water slips down my gullet, expanding in my chest. I don't arise. I cough, bubbles of spit stinging the back of my throat. But even so I can't come up, I daren't; there's nowhere left to hide.

1996

Mrs Cape, who normally deals with the post room, sends me a note the next afternoon, to tell me that the printer's have rung. '*All in order,* The Lens *will be done early!*' it says.

I'm not as pleased as I should be – I'm due to meet Freya in five minutes and I'm still wondering what she wants. I keep thinking that she and Verity are going to pull another nasty trick on me, after what happened with the scholarship. I have drunk two coffees which have nearly sent me over the edge and, by the time it's quarter to four, I'm walking out of the dining hall, past the teachers and other girls. No one speaks or looks at me. I'm totally isolated but this is fine. Without Freya onside, I don't really care about anyone else.

The school grounds are still. There's a strange energy around. The woods are nearly dark. Branches scratch at my arms and knees and as the little clearing opens into view, I see bonfire remains still charred into the ground. There's a blanket under the big oak, a tradition from the older years. Freya sits beside it, legs under her chin. She's flicking the flint of her silver Zippo; it is the one I gave her for her sixteenth birthday. It's engraved: '*My friend Freya. With love on your sixteenth, J.*' She had taken to using another lighter more recently. A cheap purple one with a smiley face and '*Welcome to Cyprus*' on it.

'Josephine,' she calls.

'Yes.' *She's using my full name again.* I'm sweating and out of breath.

'Cigarette?' She pulls out her silver box.

'Fine.' I reach over and do a quick glance over my shoulder. 'Actually, no. Thanks. No. I won't. I'm surprised Verity isn't here?' I give a little laugh but Freya just turns and looks at me. Her eyes are doing this weird flicky thing, up down, to the side. She's hunched up, bony limbs folded all precariously, like a game of pick-up sticks.

A bright red woollen scarf is wound round her neck. I recognise it as the one she bought last year, when we went to Brighton for the day. Her hands are twisting around each other and she starts laughing and then sobbing and the sound intertwines, lengthens and turns into a wolfish howl. I don't know whether I'm expected to laugh or say something so I remain standing, muted. The noise stops and I can feel bits of soil trailing down my jumper and I look down and Freya is chucking little bits of earth and rock at me. I let her. And then the chunks of stone get bigger and one gets me near the eye, and I'm forced to hold a hand up. There's a high-pitched throb in my cheek. I can feel the pain all the way down to my toes.

'Freya, stop!'

She's too weak to get up, just curls herself back into a ball and makes another weird sound. 'I hate you,' she says. 'I really, really hate you.' She's now perched on her haunches, scraping holes into the ground with a large stick. She fills it with leaves, mud, twigs, whatever she can find. A small spider's web, just to the right of me, stretches and shrinks as a gust of wind hits my face.

'Aren't you going to say something? Why don't you say something? You freak!' She goes silent, stabbing the earth with her stick. And then, 'I guess I played my part too.' She gives a small, sad laugh which ends, if I'm not mistaken, with a hint of triumph.

'What do you mean?' I reply, crunching the toe of my navy school loafer down on a leaf.

'Just … never mind.'

I want to run away from all of this, but I wait, sensing she's going to say more.

'You just … you wouldn't help me out would you. Just as long as you didn't have your precious badge taken away. Your success. It's all about your success, isn't it? You didn't care about how I felt, did you? Because *you* don't feel anything do you?'

'Of course I…'

'Of course you didn't. You just wanted to make sure I didn't say anything to anyone. God forbid someone saw you as anything but perfect.'

It's getting colder and I want to go back inside.

'Listen, Freya, what do you want?'

'I wanted to see you. I wanted to try and sort this out. I can't carry it *here* anymore.' Freya brings her hand to her chest and then lets out a cry. A string of saliva attaches itself to her scarf. She wipes it away with the back of her hand. 'But now I've seen you, I've realised I can't forgive you for burying it all. For trying to shut me up like I was a nothing. I can barely look at you. You're weird. You're like a robot. You don't give a fuck, do you? I mean, it's weird. It's not normal. Why are you like this? Don't you have any feelings at all? Are you actually human? Say what you like about Verity, but at least she reacts to things in a normal way.'

She brings her hand up, pulling her elbow right back. She's holding a big rock this time. I sidestep and hold my hands up. The mention of Verity slices through me.

'Alright. Alright. OK stop. OK?' She places the rock by her foot, her hand still resting on it ready to launch at me again.

'I'm sorry.' I give her what I know she wants to hear. 'You know how I am, Freya. You know how different we are. It's not that I didn't, well, you know … I just, I was doing things the way I know how to do them. I was trying to deal with it for us both in a practical manner. Move on, so it wouldn't ruin us. Our lives. Our futures. Our careers. Both *you* and me, Freya. Not just me. It wasn't just about *my* success.'

Freya looks up. 'Is that true?' Her voice goes all small and shaky. 'Tell me it's true.'

'It's true. I promise it's true.'

'You didn't want to hurt me? You were looking out for me too?' she says. She's half standing up now, shivering and her fingers are all covered in filth.

'Yes.'

'Please tell me again you were. You are my best friend. You are the only one that gets me. You know me. You saw me – what happened to my family when my mother died. Everyone expects me to be this perfect thing, always perfectly turned out, looking good, smiling. You are the only one that knows me underneath.'

She's properly crying now. The tears are taking up her whole face and she's making weird, primal sounds.

'What about Verity?' I ask. I want to find out if she's told anyone what happened but keep silent, for fear of that rock.

'What about her? She saw we weren't talking after I came back from that weekend. Leapt on me, I guess. Probably to try and get back at you.'

'You really think?'

Freya nods. Innocent Freya, totally unaware of the malice in my voice.

'She's OK, Verity. She's been looking after me.'

'Oh?' I wait for her to tell me what Verity knows but she doesn't go on. She starts crying again and threading her fingers through her hair, pulling out long, blonde strands and letting them fly away with the wind.

'Stop,' I say. 'Don't do that.'

She turns back to me, smiling at the concern in my voice. 'Were you really just looking out for me?' she says.

'I guess.'

'What about that night? What can we do?' she says.

I crunch up a browning leaf on a nearby branch.

'I ... I don't know. Maybe we should just give up on Oxford altogether. Both of us. Come clean about the entire night? The whole lot?'

Freya doesn't look at me. Pulls her scarf down from her neck and thinks about what I've said. I hope my look of deference is enough, but not too much, that she doesn't see through my double bluff.

There's a sound of breaking twigs. I silently curse the noise for breaking Freya's train of thought. 'It's OK. Just a bird.' I point to a twitching robin red-breast. She looks up, renewed.

'No. No we can't. No, no, Josephine. Of course we can't. You were right. You were right all along about the drugs. All of that. We can't let it get out. You are right. It will destroy our future. Neither of us will get into Oxford. I would have to explain it all to my dad. He would be heartbroken. Really heartbroken.'

I let the thought silently proliferate, segueing on to her mother.

'And Mum too, of course. No, Josephine. You must never, ever let this out, OK?'

And then she stumbles towards me and she's taking my arms and draping them around her shoulders, like an extra scarf, and then she folds her own arms around my waist and squeezes. Squeezes for dear life.

As I soak up her warmth, I remember *The Lens*. And I realise I must leave, that minute, and get to the printer's and tell them to stop. Because at this point, I know she'll never tell anyone. But if the 'Guess Who?' section is published and she sees what I've done, my little warning, it'll all be over. It will have the opposite effect. She's too damaged, too unstable. It will shake her loose entirely and then she'll have nothing to lose. In revenge she'll probably tell everyone what happened. I've completely underestimated everything.

'Fine. Well let's forget all about it?' I say, trying to keep the panic from my voice.

'Is that it then? Are you going?' She lets go of me and drops her arms to her side.

'Yes. Well, it's not it. But I've got to go.'

She frowns and my heart breaks.

'But I promise you, we'll sort this out.' I'm edging away from her now. The smashing in my heart is making me veer off course. She drops back down onto the blanket and lies, face down, with her head on her forearm. Her blonde hair glistens in the weak sun.

'Bye, Freya. I'm sorry, I'm not leaving you. I'll come and see you later, OK?'

Her head moves up and down slightly and I shout that I love her and then I can't really hear anything else I'm saying because I'm running faster than I've ever run before, all the way to the printer's. I don't even bother signing out. No one's there when I arrive and I can't wait around any longer, because there's House Meeting. I scribble a note, asking for Pete to ring me, which takes a few goes as my fingers don't seem to be able to grip the pen. I slip it through the letterbox and, feeling sick and faint, I make my way back to school.

I take the first half of House Meeting because Mrs Kitts is nowhere to be seen. She flies in the room, apologising to us all. Her hair is crowned with an array of twigs and grass. She sees me pointing at her head, mouthing at her.

'Goodness. Sorry girls.' She's shaking her hair out onto the blue carpet.

'I totally didn't realise the time.' She lets out a bubbly giggle. After a few minutes, she takes control of herself and goes through the list of notices that I've already read out. Thankfully, it's just

the younger girls tonight, with the rest of the sixth-formers out
at revision.

'Right. Is that it?' She claps her hands and laughs.

'Yes I think so, Mrs Kitts. I'll take over from here.' I swipe at
the paper she is holding and motion for her to go to her study.
She skips her way over to her study door and waves everyone
goodbye. As soon as she's gone, the girls all slump back in their
seats and start talking about the next scheduled school dance
and the last *Friends* episode, and I realise that no one thinks anything is out of the ordinary. Thank goodness Mrs Kitts is out of
the way. I'll have to sneak out later and go back to the printer's,
and hope that she won't have clocked that I wasn't there for supper. I tell the younger girls that television time is over and they
are to all leave for study. I station myself on the sofa outside Mrs
Kitts's study and listen for any sound that means she's on her way
out. After an hour, I run to the sixth-form room, to find someone who'll sign me in and out for supper. There's no one in there
but, as I'm about to leave, Freya comes in and her eyes are black.
Freya hasn't been in to the sixth-form room since we got back
from exeat, so there's only one reason she's in here and that's to
find me. There's a green pallor to her cheeks and she's sweating.
She sits next to me and grabs the toast out of my hands. I can
smell booze and the remnants of marijuana smoke. I hand her
another slice and she tries to say thank you but can't.

'You OK?' I ask. She stares, searching.

'Freya. Are you OK?' And then she lets out a snort and I can
see she's trying not to be sick. It's too late and she hangs her head
over her knees and makes a tiny retching sound. 'Right. Come
here, with me.' I'm holding her with one hand, reaching for a tea

towel with the other, to wipe her down. 'Come on.' She doesn't resist, just flops right into the crook of my elbow. I drag her to the sixth-form bathroom, which is thankfully empty. I strip her, carefully unbuttoning her school shirt and unhooking her bra. I then pull down her skirt and tights; there's mud all over them, so I sling them in the bath too. 'Come on, get in ...' I have left her small white knickers on. They've got a tiny white bow on the front. 'Freya. Come on. Help me out here.' She's now struggling to even sit up and she throws up again into the water. I let the bath out and shower away the chunks of carrot and what looks like lumps of bread. I refill the bath and she's better now, sits up and looks at me.

'Josephine.'

'Yes? I'm here. Don't worry.' She catches me sliding up the sleeve of my school jumper, glancing down at my watch and, for some reason, this makes her cry.

'Please.'

'Please what?'

'Please don't leave me, Josephine.'

'Frey, I have to ... I have to go somewhere. I need to get something done. It's urgent. You have to sort yourself out.'

'Please. It's more important you look after me. I need you.' There's a loaded plea in her voice. It's now seven thirty and, without prior consent from a member of staff, I have to get down to the printer's and back by eight, otherwise it will be immediate suspension. And if that happens, I'll get demoted from Head Girl. 'Frey. I ... I just, seriously you need to trust me on this one.'

'I trusted you before. I trusted you. Look what has happened to me because of this. Look.' She rolls down her knickers and there's a zigzag of lines, so ornately etched into her skin that I think she's used a stencil. It's only when I look closer that I realise they are scars. Deep, shiny scars that are fresh. Bulging. I don't know where to look and I don't know if it's from that night or she's done this to herself but I start to feel sick as well.

'And anyway, there's something I need to tell you.'

'What?' I say, casually, although my ears sting with hot blood.

'I've told someone I shouldn't have. About us. That night. I had to.'

I stop what I am doing and stare right into her. 'You've told who?'

Freya shrugs but I catch her eyes slide to the door and I know instantly who it is.

'*Why?! Why did you tell anyone?*'

'Because I was so furious with you just now. So hurt we made it all up and you left me in the woods. Why did you do that? Why? I don't understand you. Just when I was beginning to think we could get through this together.'

I sit and squeeze my neck. How could I be so stupid as to think she was stable enough not to change her mind? That she wouldn't waver if I made one wrong move? I place my hands on my lap and breathe through the rioting thoughts. If this gets out, it'll spread quickly; I'll have no chance. No chance at anything. I cannot allow that to happen. 'Me too,' I reply. 'Me too.' I touch Freya's hand.

Freya leans over the plughole and is sick again. I rub her back and wash her face with a cloth that's drying on the radiator.

We sit there and it's nine o'clock before Freya can stand up again. I can hear the school bell going, and I can see the flash of torches – the sign that the caretakers are shutting all the gates up. It means it'll be too risky to leave the school premises. Even though I know most of the security team from our monthly safety meetings, there's no excuse I can give them that'll allow me to leave the premises without them alerting a teacher. I'm torn between relief at it being taken out of my hands and imagining Freya's reaction when she reads the magazine. It's made even worse by the fact we are here, together, holding hands whilst she's sick and she's trying to confide in me about that night. She talks and cries. I don't say much. The conversation comes out of nowhere and, at first, I'm not sure what she's talking about because as soon as she opens her mouth, she starts shivering. 'I don't know what happened, I just …' she says. I put some more hot water in the bath, squeeze her hand and tell her she has to be quiet or she's going to make herself sick again but she carries on talking, saying words that only seem to make sense to her. At this moment, when a level of trust has rebuilt, I want so much to ask her about what Sally told me. Whether it's true. I wonder if I should risk it, in the hope she'll have memory blank tomorrow but I can't. Most of all, though, I want to ask her why she felt the need to hide it all from me. The fact she's sitting here, naked and holding my hand, telling me her take on that night. And all the while she couldn't, wouldn't trust me with this other secret.

It's only two hours later when she feels strong enough to get out of the tub. I wipe her dry and wrap her in an old, green towel that's hanging on the back of the door.

'Come on.' I say, 'Let's go downstairs.' We walk down together and I tuck Freya into bed and fill her a glass of water. 'Here.

Drink this now and I'll refill it.' She looks at me as she drinks. I tell her to carry on. 'Finish. You'll feel better tomorrow.' I wait at the end of her bed until she falls asleep, checking that she is breathing. When she rolls over onto her side, I walk back to my dormitory and wonder what I'm going to do about *The Lens*. How I can stop this huge mistake.

2014

'I'd like to go to that place, The Cedars, please.'

Dr McKinnie doesn't say anything down the phone. I can hear her scribbling away; scratchy strokes against the paper. I wish she'd say something. I'm fidgeting, desperate to get off the phone and leave in case Freya turns up unannounced. After years of fear that Mother's madness might catch up with me, the fact that I'm willingly throwing myself into an institution to avoid Freya almost makes me smile.

'You would?' she says, finally.

'Yes, please. I ... I think it would be a good idea. Just for a few days. I told work I was ill. That I had the shingles so they won't ask questions.' There's a pause in the conversation. I can hear a small intake of breath down the phone and I consider a line of defence to the fact I've lied to my colleagues but Dr McKinnie starts speaking.

'Right. Well I'll arrange everything now, shall I? Do you want to come into my office first?'

'Yes, yes please. I'll be there in twenty minutes?' My luggage is already by the door. Amy has been helping me pack, asking me why I'm in such a hurry and why I can't fold my clothes properly. 'Let me do it,' she had said, throwing all my clothes on the bed and starting again.

'Twenty minutes? I didn't mean quite so soon. Are you OK? Is it that urgent?' Dr McKinnie's saying.

'Yes. Kind of.' I don't want to go into Freya's email and that I have to get out of the house straightaway, so I make a weird sob, like a little laugh.

'OK, come in now. I'll get things ready.'

Dr McKinnie hasn't asked how I'm going to pay and I don't want to think about how much it'll cost. Would probably be cheaper to book myself into a hotel but at least here I'll be protected. I've got some money, from my mother. A nasty little voice whispers in my mind: *how proud she'd be.*

I hand-write a note to Father – I don't want to go near my computer in case Freya emails again – and tell him a brief rundown of what's happening. '*Don't come and see me for a while,*' I say. '*Thanks. J.*'

When I've got everything packed and ready and called a cab, I say goodbye to Amy and tell her that I won't be contactable by email or phone. That I'm going 'somewhere with no signal'.

'I understand.' She winks as she misinterprets my reasons and hugs me. 'It's about time you did something like this,' she says.

The Cedars is a large, light building, set on the outskirts of London. It looks like a mini castle, complete with little turrets and stone doves chiselled on the roof. The front lawn is perfectly manicured, bordered with unduly bright flowers. There's a couple on the bench next to the main entrance. She's wearing a black and white miniskirt and her hair is dyed pillar-box red – the kind that was fashionable when I was at school, and, for a moment, I get the sense that I'm a teenager again. The sense that everything is a little too big for me.

The girl stares when I get out of the taxi. Gives me one of those timorous looks that I hate. 'New?' she says.

I nod and instruct the taxi driver to place my bags at the front door. I'm welcomed by Shona, who has a permanent grin on her face and a tone of voice like she's petting a dying animal. 'Please, let me show you to your room, dear. You'll be sleeping on your own,' she says.

'If you could also give me your phone and anything else? Any sharp objects. There's a love.' I'm tempted to leave there and then – it all seems a bit serious and I begin to panic that they might actually believe I am mad, and lock me up forever – but I can't face the alternative.

'Here.' I hand her my phone and she puts it in the front pocket of her uniform.

'Come on then, upstairs. Let me help you with your things.'

'No. I mean … no, thanks. I've got it.'

'If you're sure, love.' I nod and, together, we unpack, whilst Shona natters about the weather, her children, cleaning products. 'And I'll be taking you down to dinner now, love. Do you need anything else? Happy with your room?'

'Yes.' And I am – it's large enough to allow me to breathe but small enough that I don't feel overwhelmed. The dark brown furniture is ugly and cumbersome, the bedding a sickly avocado green with pink piping and the walls floral chintz, but, all in all, it feels like a generic hotel room, which I'm happy with.

Shona leaves the room and tells me to be downstairs in ten minutes for grace and supper. She leans forward to straighten out the bedspread and I can smell cigarette smoke and perfume.

'If you need anything else, just call me. You'll have time tomorrow to go through your therapy sessions and anything else. Oh, and Dr Anthony will be your consultant psychiatrist.'

'Psychiatrist? Oh ... I'm just in here for a ...'

'I know, everyone gets a bit fearful when they hear that, love, don't worry. It's perfectly normal. Sounds scarier than it is.'

'I'm not scared.'

Shona gives me a smile and shuts the door.

It's ten minutes before I can lift myself back off the bed. I hear echoes of laughter down the corridors, the coo of pigeons and the constant ring of the phone and beeping of the intercom. Again, I'm reminded of school but, this time, I'm not expected to behave in a particular way. I don't have to do anything except pretend to go along with all this therapy stuff. It's the most relaxed I've felt in years, hiding away in this weird place where everything runs to a strict timetable. I remind myself I'm still in charge though. I won't be surrendering myself any time soon.

The dining room is quiet, although the seats are full. No one looks up when I enter, even though the door makes a loud creak. I go and get a plate of food: chicken and gravy, with surprisingly crisp roast potatoes.

I take a chair next to a small lady with big, gold-rimmed spectacles. She doesn't look up, but I don't feel any hostility. We eat in silence and, when she leaves, she gives me a small, shy grin.

I'm one of the last to finish. I'm enjoying chewing my food, tasting the beefy gravy, the powdery insides of the potatoes. No hurry here. No need to hide. I get talking to a seventeen-year-old girl, whose bones jut out like knives. A nurse keeps waiting for her to finish her food and she's looking pained, so I tell her I don't like the gravy. She laughs and manages to swallow a crumb of chicken. I can tell she was once beautiful. Her hair, now straw-like, looked like it used to be thick and luscious, like Freya's, and then it hits me that I haven't thought about Mother, or Freya, since I've stepped foot in this place. Dr McKinnie has reassured me that I'm not going crazy and Freya will never, ever find me here. This makes me smile and the girl smiles back at me.

That night, I sleep right through the night, without fear of what lies in store for me in my dreams. I wake up, groggy and overcome with deep slumber, and, although the bell goes for seven, I shut my eyes and go back to sleep. A phone ring wakes me up and it's Shona, asking me where I am. 'Dr Anthony is waiting for you,' she's saying.

Dr Anthony's study is the kind I imagine you would see in a gentleman's dining club, all dark-red shiny leather and dimly lit reading lamps. He has an unusually low hairline, making him look like he's constantly frowning.

'Josephine,' he says, without looking up from the blue paper file on his desk. 'Josephine Grey.' I can't work out if he's smirking or not.

'Dr Anthony.' He spends the next few minutes flicking through some papers, humming and ahhing and taking sips of coffee from a china mug with an indeterminate blue logo on it.

'Dr McKinnie,' he says. 'Interesting.'

There's not one object here that's out of place. The books are all perfectly aligned, the certificates along his wall in straight rows. Even his pens are laid out in colour co-ordinated rows.

'Right. So Diana referred you. Thinks you might be on the verge of a breakdown?'

'I haven't heard that specifically from her,' I reply, nudging one of his pens across his desk. My stomach loops at the thought that all the staff here really do believe something is very wrong with me. He gives a tight grin, leans back in his chair. He realigns the pen and looks at me, daring me to do it again.

'OK. So let's start with the basics, how are you feeling now?' I'm suddenly too tired to play games. Paradoxically the long sleep has left me feeling mentally shattered.

'I'm OK, I'm OK. I slept last night for the first time in ages.'

'Really? Well we do try and make it so our patients are as comfortable as possible. So why do you think you are in here?'

'Well, for very unoriginal reasons. Mother just died, and you know ... I was probably burning myself out, working too hard, that sort of thing.'

'Right. And anything else?' Dr Anthony is still staring, expressionless, when suddenly I don't know what comes over me but I find myself saying –

'I'm hiding from someone.'

'Oh?'

'She's someone I had history with. Not that kind ... I mean ... something happened. Something happened one night and then, after that, more stuff happened. Bad stuff.'

'Can you tell me more about this, please? In your own time.'

Dr Anthony gives a small encouraging nod but I wish he hadn't because it makes me feel pressured to say something and, when it comes down to it, I find, as usual, I can't.

'It's alright,' he says. 'There's absolutely no hurry.' His eyes move towards the white clock above the door. 'We've got nearly forty-five minutes left.' It's another ten before I speak again. For the rest of the session, we don't discuss anything in too much detail. He asks me about other pivotal moments in my life: Mother being hospitalised, school, and I skate over his questions with brief, non-committal answers. He's writing fast and looking at me intently. It puts me off my stride. He calls the end of our session and says he's looking forward to seeing me again.

That night, I sleep well again, despite being able to hear the screams from the girl in the room next door. There's a patient day room which I visit for the first time the next day. It's got light-blue curtains and wooden chairs. Two beanbags lie, sunken and appealing, so I drag one to the window and take a book, and read before my next group therapy session.

I'm three chapters in when a girl walks in. I hardly hear her, but I can feel her presence. A weird prickle of energy, firing up my adrenaline. She's tall. Wearing brown loafers and light blue trousers, the exact same shade as the curtains. She's got long brown curly hair, a thin tracing of red veins line her cheeks. Something about her is familiar and I can't work out what. It's the way she holds her head, the cross of her two front teeth. The recognition is only a flash but it leaves me feeling off-kilter and I can no longer concentrate on my book. She hasn't seen me yet. Sits on a wooden chair and opens a book with a black and white swirling pattern on the cover. I don't know whether to move but

I keep looking up, trying to figure out where I've seen her before. I run through different scenarios and try to place her in them but none connect.

I get up and leave the room. Her image doesn't leave me all day. We have a group therapy breathing session and I keep thinking of her face, niggling away at me. That night, though, she's sitting near me at supper. I try to keep my head down so she doesn't clock me, just until I've worked out if I really do know her, but the hairs on the back of my neck stand alert and I know she's looking at me. Staring. When the meal is over, I rush and take my tray to be stacked and I hear someone walking behind me. I speed up and, as I do, I can hear footsteps, quickening in time with my own.

I get to my room, shut the door and slide down it, head in hands. I'm just imagining things, surely? She's probably just trying to be friendly and it's nothing sinister after all. Darkness sets in and, for the first time ever, I have to sleep with the light on.

The next day, I spend all my free time in my room, until a group therapy session is called. I don't want to go but Shona tells me I have to complete three stages before I can be discharged. When I arrive, there she is. I'm caught between running and sitting down calmly. By that point, everyone is waiting and Rosemary, the lady in charge, is pointing to the only empty stool and so I'm given no choice but to walk and sit, very still, with my hands on my knees. We go through a few exercises and we are all asked to speak a bit and I don't remember what I say because that girl, she's still staring at me, all the time, a half-smile caught on her lips as though she's about to say something to me.

She doesn't, and then Rosemary stands, pulls up her ill-fitting jeans and asks for a volunteer. No one responds and so she says, 'You, Josephine.' And when she says my name, the girl opens her mouth slightly, with a silent 'Ah' and nods her head.

'Right, here we are, Josephine, if you can show the rest of the group how to stand whilst we breathe, that would be great. Just like this.' She's pulling up my spine and straightening my neck but I'm curling myself back down because I can't breathe like she's asking me to.

'Josephine? Are you alright?'

'Absolutely,' I say.

'OK, well you look a bit faint, why don't you sit down?'

I go to my stool and the girl is now leaning forward, eyes open wide, hands mid-air.

'Josephine?' She's mouthing, 'Josephine!'

Shut up, just shut up, I will the loud monotone to stop. I'm focusing all my energy on keeping still. The second time she says my name, a flashback sparks through me. There's a residual terror connected to the visual image I have of this lady. The flashback lengthens and I can see who it is. It's her, I think. It's definitely her. Her face, once so clean and fresh, has now started to sag and crease but the defining quality of her is still there. That goading, smug look which jars me so much, I cannot move. She knows my past, is all I can think. She knows.

1996

When the morning gong goes I get dressed without showering. Mrs Kitts is waiting by the front door for us all to go to breakfast and I tell her I've got to go to the printer's.

'This early?' She looks up at the clock in the hall.

'Yes. The printer wanted me to have a run-through before they send back the copies.' She believes me and I make it there in less than ten minutes. I'm knocking again and this time Pete answers. He opens the door wearing a pair of dark blue overalls and heavy black boots.

'Josephine. I got your note. Tried to ring last night – a number for the main switchboard. About nine o' clock I believe it was. No answer,' says Pete. I smile and open my mouth, willing him to stop.

'I...'

'And then we rang again at about ten. No answer. Then the missus said I'd wake the whole school up if I tried any –'

'Pete. Stop. Have you printed?' I ask.

'Yes, miss. Of course we have. Delivery left. The van goes at six every morning. Thought you wanted early copies? Made an extra special effort to get them done quickly.'

Oh God. 'Thank you.' I rub my face. 'Where's the van now?'

'Hmmm. This time? Seven thirty. Should be nearby. You needing them urgently? I can ring and ask where they are? They've gone to do one delivery just before yours. Tesco. Leaflets. That'll be a quick drop, though.'

'And then?'

'And then your delivery, madam.' He's grinning at me, waiting for me to show my gratitude, which I can't quite bring myself to do.

'Right.'

'Great, young lady. I've billed the school and, in fact, Mrs Cape has already paid the outstanding. Very organised over there.'

'Great. I've just got something to change in the magazine,' I say. It's unlike me to be so uncontrolled but I'm hoping Pete will help me out.

'Change?'

'I know.' I force a laugh. 'Silly. I just printed something I shouldn't have done. I need to pull out each page.'

'Each one? There's a thousand copies, madam. Going straight to the school post room to be delivered to all the girls. Just as you requested, love.'

No one has any way of getting into the post room apart from Mrs Cape, whose study leads directly into it. Mrs Cape, who is only part-time, so she might not even be there. If she is, though, I'll have to tell her the truth. Tell her something needs to be taken out. It is my magazine, after all. I'm Editor.

'OK, Pete. I've got to go now.'

'Sure?'

'Sure. I'm just going to see if I can sort this out. Don't say anything, will you? My mistake. Need to sort this out myself.'

'Fine. I hope it's OK, madam. You have my word.' I wave goodbye to the receptionist who has just arrived. She's looking at me eagerly, hoping I've come to bring some excitement to her day.

'Just last minute things,' I say to her. She grins at me, holding crossed fingers in mid-air. I run back to school, to Mrs Cape. She's not there when I knock on her door. I wait for ten minutes and then run back to the school gates to see if the delivery van appears. It doesn't and, when I finally get back to Mrs Cape's study, she's sitting, sipping at a cup of tea from a school mug. '*Per Asperrimus ad Parnassum*', it says.

'Josephine,' she says. 'All excited? They've arrived!'

'They're here?'

'Yup! Arrived an hour ago. Said something about Tesco and how they were doing you a favour. You wanted them early? Delivery man said Pete would be chuffed. Something like that anyway.'

'Oh, wow. Thank you, Mrs Cape. Now I need to take them out, one by one. You're not going to believe this – it's totally mad. But the Prime Minister has told me I need to delete something in his interview. Told me we couldn't publish talk of his new manifesto. I promised I would take it out.'

'Prime Minister?'

'Yes. We got an exclusive with the PM. Didn't you know? This is why this is so important. Got to do what he says.'

'Oh. Oh dear.' Mrs Cape is clutching at a white hanky. 'Oh dear. My dear Josephine. That's terrible. What can we do?' She says. 'They've already been taken by the postman to all the houses. They'll all have their copies by now. It's past House Meeting time. I know how you all look forward to it for weeks on end. As do the staff. In fact, I've got my copy just here!' She waves her hand over to where she is sitting and indeed, just by her mug, is a copy of the magazine.

'I haven't started reading. Was waiting till I'd done Mrs Allen's post. Even saved myself a biscuit.' I walk over, pick up the magazine. It is beautiful. Thick, glossy paper with a picture of the PM on the front. The title font is in gold curlicue. '*The Lens*', it says. And underneath:

Exclusives!
Prime Minister talks to Josephine Grey
A look at the school 100 years ago
We talk to AKA Letz, the latest teen boy-band sensation
Guess who! We have the latest scandal from Greenwood Hall, right here!

I can't bring myself to open it. It sits, right there in my hands, for what seems like hours.

'Josephine?'

'Mrs Cape.'

'Shall I ring around the house mistresses? We can tell the girls to rip out each page from their own copy?'

'No. No, don't do that. Don't worry.' I manage to place one foot in front of the other and end up in the Mann Library. There's a little alcove with two green beanbags. I know everyone will still be getting dressed and making their way to breakfast, so

I'll get some quiet. I prop one of the beanbags up against the wall and sit down with the magazine. I don't open it. I just stare at all the books around me, dazed. An hour later, I haven't moved and it's still in my hand. I'm wondering what to do. I walk to breakfast. Gauge everyone's reaction.

The dining hall is silent when I enter. Not one person is talking. Every single head is buried in a copy of *The Lens* and I cannot cope. I leave. Go straight to chapel. I'm doing a reading today, in place of Mrs Allen, who has gone down to London for a headmistresses' conference. I sit at the front of the pulpit and force myself up straight. My badge is skewed so I unpin it, rubbing it clean. I put it back on and press it against my chest in an effort to stop the shrivelling near my breastbone. Freya will be coming to chapel in about ten minutes with all the other Prefects, ready to station themselves at the end of each aisle before the younger years file in. I will stand straight. Pretend nothing has happened. Pretend I don't know anything. That I am not to blame for any of this. Verity. It's all Verity. And I get ready to do this, when the Prefects arrive.

They are all silent. White. Margot Jones is nudging Alice Montgomery as they walk in and looking in my direction. They catch me watching and snap their heads back down. White. They are all white. Stand straight. I must stand straight. An invisible force seems to be pulling me towards the ground, tucking my legs underneath me like a broken string puppet. I manage to steady myself on the wooden bench in front of me. All I can hear is the whisper of Freya's name.

'Where is she?' Margot is asking.

'I don't know,' Kate Millington replies. Not one person can look at me. Margot has the magazine stuffed up her jumper. I can see the gold writing and the little logo – a magnifying glass – sticking out near her collar. The rest of the school come in, silently looking at me. Burning stares that crush my ribcage. Surely the entire school can't have guessed who it is that quickly, I think. I'd made it obvious, but not that obvious.

'Girls, do sit down.' My voice comes out louder than I expected.

'As you all know, Mrs Allen is away today, so I'm taking over chapel.' The girls sit. At this point, the Prefects are having to shush the younger years but, today, I can hear the echo of my voice from across the walls. I can hear Mrs Chambers's breathing. That loud, crackly, open-mouthed breath. I nod to Mr Cavendish to start the hymn and everyone breaks into 'All Things Bright and Beautiful'. I still cannot see Freya. And then I look to the back of the room and Verity is looking at me. Slowly moving her head up and down, as if to say: 'I knew it.' And then Scarlett Templeton's copy of the magazine slides to the floor right in front of me.

'All creatures great and small,' everyone sings. All I can see are the words: **'Freya's Dirty Little Secret'**. I have forgotten to edit out her name. I have forgotten. I had read over the piece so many times I had missed the most obvious thing about it.

'All things wise and wonderful...'

I had forgotten. I am Head Girl. *God, how could I make such a stupid mistake?!* No, stop it. Remember it is not my fault. Verity Greenslade – she took it to the printer's. Her name is on it too. *Oh*

God, Freya – I am so sorry. Freya, please, forgive me. I glance over, reading the upside down words.

> **'Freya's Dirty Little Secret'**
> *Female teacher and Upper-Sixth former's Naked Romps!*
> *It's not often you find yourself staring at a member of staff and a pupil getting hot and heavy in the san's isolation room. The Upper-Sixth former and the married lady teacher were locked in an embrace that can only be described as 'erotic'. The teacher apparently wanted to* **'See More'**, *but was told no. They were later overheard talking about their 'relationship'. It has been 'nearly eighteen months', according to the breathless pupil, who shall remain nameless.*
> *Who would have thunk it!*
> *Can you* **Guess Who?**

As I'm reading, I can see how brash the whole thing is. How utterly despicable. This thing with Freya and Mrs Kitts can't be that serious. Freya has never shown any inclination like that ... I was just so desperate to get back at her I would have believed anything. But then Sally was so convinced...

As one side of my brain is breaking down, the pragmatist with the voice of my father keeps telling me that it's a good move. It must have been Mrs Kitts who Freya told all about that night. It can't have been Verity, as she would have told everyone already. So if anything came out, no one would listen to them. This would mean I was in the clear. My future wouldn't be compromised. Oxford, my career. All intact. As the two sides battle each other, I can't stop the shaking in my legs. The realisation that, in spite of my excuses and my blaming Verity, I can never, ever look Freya in the eye again.

I carry on singing, loudly. 'All Things Bright and Beautiful.' No Freya. Not even in the back. Mrs Kitts is nowhere to be seen either. I look at Verity again and she is belting out the final verse of the hymn, looking up at the ceiling and smiling. I do the reading, which takes all of two minutes. We normally have reflection and prayer time but, today, I finish chapel early and tell everyone to have a good day. The girls leave, still silent. Still white. A few backwards glances from the Sixth-Formers.

Freya. What have I done?

And the pain is all over me. My hair, my bones. Inside. Everywhere. I can feel my skin cracking with it, but still I keep going.

'Right, girls, hurry up.' I clap my hands outside chapel and shoo a bunch of girls into the school. I walk, fast, to our English lesson. A week until my Oxford interview. A week. How can I get through the next second?

There is no one in the corridors, which is strange. Straight after chapel, everyone rushes to their lessons so loudly I can barely hear the school bell. The Science classroom door is ajar as I walk past and there's a crowd of Lower Fives, huddled and whispering around a copy of the magazine. Helen Graham is all puffed up in her white science apron, standing next to the Bunsen burners. 'A *female* teacher and Freya?' she's laughing and shouting, to no one in particular. 'What the hell? Can you believe it? This has to be the gossip of the century.' She catches my eye and shuts her mouth, shrinks back down. Whispers from the girls echo through my mind and it's hard to know whether the voices are real or not. Whether they are all talking about me or if my mother's illness is starting to take hold. I want to hold my hand over my ears and hide in a small corner where no one can reach me, but with all my effort I walk past and arrive at my English lesson. There are only two other girls in the room. Margot and Cressida.

'Morning,' I say. Neither of them reply. Just look straight down at their desks. Cressida is doodling and Margot is pretending to read. 'Morning,' I say, a little louder. Nothing. I sit down and take out my English file and my pencil case. Freya should be coming soon and I sit up, feeling a little sick and physically bracing myself for her reaction. *What will she do to me? What I fully deserve.* Mrs Bailey comes in – we all stand up.

'Sit down, girls,' she says, putting down her bags. 'Right. I understand a lot has gone on this morning. I know you'll all want to be discussing it. But please. You've got your interviews soon. Some of you as soon as next week. So we've got to concentrate. OK? Everyone here?' No one answers but we all make a big show of turning round and counting the people in the room.

'One, two, three … Ah, Freya. She's not here.' Mrs Bailey looks towards the door.

'She won't be coming. I'm sure,' says Margot. 'Let's just start the lesson.' At this point, I feel like running out the door. And then my whole body starts to feel totally weightless and I have the strangest impression that I'm completely drugged up – that familiar prickle in my scalp, my blood; that rush. That … that night. It's all coming back to me in a tsunami of panic and pain.

'Stop.' I realise I've spoken out loud and Mrs Bailey looks up from her desk.

'Sorry, Josephine? Are you alright? You're sweating. Shall I open the window?'

'Sure. That would be good. I'm fine. Thank you.'

'OK. If you're sure.'

'I'm sure.' The rest of the class goes by without incident and no one looks at me. I'm alright with that. I do not want to be looked at. We all leave when the bell goes and there's still this strange, disassociated feeling about the school. Post-apocalyptic. Like nothing really exists anymore and ... and ... as I walk down the corridor, I can see Mrs Allen outside on the school grass. She is not meant to be here. She is meant to be at the Headmistresses' Day today. What is she doing here? She is talking to a grey-haired lady, who I recognise as one of the governors. And then it hits me. This whole Freya business, her relationship with Mrs Kitts – she is probably going to be classed as a minor and, and ... it is only then that I'm embraced by the full horror of what I've done.

2014

Father, against my wishes, comes to visit me. He asks if we can sit somewhere light and have a coffee. It's a nice day so we walk outside to the garden.

'You seem on edge?' he says, as we find an empty bench.

'I'm fine.'

'Really? Well, if you were fine you wouldn't be in here in the first place. But you seem particularly on edge today. Why do you keep looking behind you, as though someone's going to attack you?'

'Do I?' I turn back to look at the hospital.

'Sorry,' he says. 'Sorry that you're in here. I should have talked to you more about your mother. I'm truly sorry.' He takes my hand and squeezes. My fingers all hot and rubbery between his.

'It's not just her,' I reply. 'It's everything.' I look out beyond the grounds of the centre. A child on a swing keeps coming into view. Up, down. Up, down.

'Heard from Freya?'

'Freya? Why would I have heard from her?' I sound defensive and Father looks worried.

'I don't know. No reason. Just wondering. After the funeral and everything. Rollo said she was trying to get in touch with you. I told him no, that you wanted to be alone. Just as you asked.'

'Great,' I say, light-heartedly, to stop any tension.

After that, we stick to talking about news, politics, what's going on in his job, and then he comes out with it.

'Josephine, I'm seeing someone.' He clears his throat and looks at me. I don't turn to look at him. My initial thought is that it's been a matter of weeks since Mother died. But the situation isn't as clear-cut as that. I should be supportive, as he is being to me now. 'Who?' I sound weary.

'Aren't you angry?'

'No.' I'm actually not. I'm surprised by my feelings about it all but then, I figure, I don't have the energy to be angry. I don't even have the energy to be upset about her death, really. I mean not consciously so. 'Who is she?'

'She's someone I work with.'

'Oh. Were you seeing her before Mother died?'

'Yes. Sort of. Your mother had been in and out of hospital so many times I just … we went for a few dinners. I needed someone.'

The admission of neediness makes me feel curiously better. That my mother's memory needn't be so frightening to me because I wasn't the only one who was fearful. Dr McKinnie's reassurance that I'm not going mad like her has also made me see things differently. I try to recall any times I had with Mother that were happy but I can't. Without warning I start to cry. Father sits next to me holding my hand.

As we're walking back, that girl appears again. Father walking tall, me totally emptied out.

She walks up to us and stops. What does she want? And, as she comes closer, I can smell her and, once again, the memory becomes sharper and more vivid and I'm almost bowled over by the force of it and I'm one hundred per cent certain it is who I think it is.

'Here, want me to take this to the bin?' she asks, holding out her hand for my father's cup.

'Sure,' he says, frowning. 'Thanks.'

The only way she knows he's finished his coffee is if she's been watching us. I don't want to cause a scene whilst Father is here, so I vow to find her when he's gone. He leaves half an hour later, patting me on the arm and handing me a rolled up copy of *The Economist* from his briefcase. 'Here,' he says. 'Keep this going.' He points to his temple.

'Bye. Thank you.' I practically push him out the door and, when he's gone, I run around the building, trying to find this girl.

She's nowhere to be seen until I go into the day room and she's there, lying on a beanbag with her legs up on a chair, head tilted back into the sun, her throat exposed and her teeth jutting out slightly and I'm brought back to the Greenwood Hall dining room, eighteen years ago, and I was right all along.

I sit down on one of the wooden chairs, waiting for her to look up from her book. When she does, she looks up at me, breaks out into an enormous grin and says, 'Josephine Grey. Well, well, well. I thought it was you. Then when Rosemary called your name in therapy, I thought hmmmm. Is it? Isn't it? And then I saw you with your father today and, well, obviously everyone knows who he is. You look totally different. Much thinner.' She sucks her cheeks in, hanging her arms, limp, by her side, in an impression of a skeleton, then she throws her head back and laughs and laughs and laughs.

1996

'Josephine. You have to tell me all you know. The Head Governor is outside, waiting to talk to you. You've got three minutes to tell me exactly what is going on.' Mrs Allen is staring at me. Her voice is calm but I can see her chest rising up and down.

'I don't know anything, Mrs Allen. I gave the proof copy to Verity, without the "Guess Who?" piece about Freya in it. And when the magazine was published, it was there.' My life is on the line here, I can feel it. But aside from a small tremor in my left hand, I remain composed: shocked but calm like a Head Girl should be.

Mrs Allen is scribbling down notes and I'm suddenly terrified Mrs Cape's going to tell her that I was trying to get one of the pages ripped out before distribution. I will have to find her after this, straightaway, and somehow get her to keep her mouth shut. And then I remember Pete and I realise I have to tell him too.

'Right. So you say you gave the proof to Verity Greenslade. What time was this?' says Mrs Allen.

'Hmmm, ten to nine?'

'Yesterday morning?'

'Yes.'

'And she took it to the printer's? Just her?'

'No. Sally Aylsford too. She had asked to be involved.'

'She asked to be involved?' Mrs Allen sits straighter. She is looking at my Head Girl badge.

'Yes.' I say, quickly. 'She just wanted something to say on her CV that would look good. I told her if she did a few things for me, a few odd jobs here and there, I would put her name on the magazine credits.'

'And did you? Put her name on the credits?'

'I did.'

'Right. So you can tell me honestly now that you had absolutely nothing, *nothing*, to do with this "outing" of Freya and this teacher? Because we need to know. We need to know who did it and so we can find out if this rumour is just a rumour, or whether it is true.' She looks at me. 'Because not only is Freya's welfare of paramount importance but we've got the school's reputation to consider. *The Good Schools Guide*. All of that.' Mrs Allen takes a huge breath. 'Freya is not saying a word. We can't get her to speak at all. And she hasn't told you anything at all? You being her best friend? You must know something?'

'Well, we haven't really spoken much lately.' I lean forward too. 'Busy. You know?'

Mrs Allen nods. 'I mean yes. Of course. You've had an awful lot on your plate, what with *The Lens* and everything. Universities. Mocks.' Then it hits me that if anyone finds out Freya and I have been fighting, I'll be incriminated.

'Yeah. We really haven't spoken that much at all because of all of that.' I'll have to think of a way around that too and my head is buzzing with all of it. *God, what a mess.*

Mrs Allen is now reaching across the table for my hand. I'm so surprised I let her take it.

'I think my daughter would have grown up to be like you,' she says. I know Mrs Allen had a daughter once. Died when she was eight. Hearing her say this makes me feel under pressure. Uncomfortable. I don't know how to act so I'll live up to her expectations. *All I've done has been to make you all proud of me.*

She must see the expression on my face because she says, 'Sorry. I didn't mean to frighten you. Just wanted to let you know that I'm keeping my eye out for you.'

'Thank you so much, Mrs Allen. I appreciate it, I really do. And I'll try and do my best to please you.'

'Right. Best call the governor now. Mrs Pownall. OK? She's going to investigate a bit further. Put some feelers out and find out what's been going on. If this is just silly gossip or we need to do something more serious about it. Which, obviously, I'd prefer not to do.'

'OK, Mrs Allen.'

Now I know Mrs Allen is rooting for me, I feel much more confident in telling Mrs Pownall what happened. *This can still be cleaned up, today's news tomorrow's chip paper and all that,* I tell myself, but it sounds hollow even to my ears.

'Mrs Pownall, please come in,' says Mrs Allen, waving her hand towards an empty chair. A tall lady with cropped, dyed blonde hair enters the room. She's wearing a very inappropriate skirt, tartan like she's imitating a young girl in uniform. She checks the chair twice before sitting, as though she's expecting to find it covered in dirt. She asks me over and over to tell her what happened.

'I told you, three times,' I say, looking at Mrs Allen then Mrs Pownall, who keeps scratching her head with horrible, long, spiky red nails. 'I gave the proof copy, without the "Guess Who?" section about Freya to Verity Greenslade and Sally Aylsford. They took it to the printer's together. That's all I know. I know nothing else.' Mrs Pownall is busy writing things down.

'So. Can I just clarify? You know nothing. I've spoken to a few of the other girls already. And they seem to think this ... *thing* between Freya and the teacher is probably true.'

'I have no idea what went on. As I told Mrs Allen, I've been really busy.'

'Right. And so, let me ask you this. Did anyone else have the proof copy before you gave it to Verity and –' she checks her notes '– Sally Aylsford?'

'Not as far as I'm aware.'

'Look, if this is some prank you need to tell us now. Then it'll all be over quickly. So let me ask you again – are you sure you didn't have anything to do with this?'

'I'm completely sure.'

Mrs Allen looks at her. She's starting to get cross.

'She's answered your question.'

'Right. Good! There's a lot more I need to do. To ask. This is just the beginning, so please be available for when I need to talk to you.'

'Yes,' I reply, thinking that if this is her line of questioning, I'm going to be just fine.

'Can you call in Verity next, please?'

I'm relieved. I've got time to find Sally and tell her not to say anything.

'Sure. I'll find her. She's just outside.' I leave the room and Verity is outside, sobbing; she doesn't look at me as I approach.

'I didn't do it, you know,' she says, still looking at her feet.

'Really? Well you had the proof last. Didn't you? Just remember what you did to me with the scholarship. People won't trust you if they know about that, will they?'

I'm risking a lot but Verity says nothing. Just wipes her nose with the back of her hand and I leave to find Sally and can't believe for the life of me that I'm lying to absolutely everyone. It's getting too big to control but I mustn't think of that or I'll panic completely. But then I realise first I should tackle the issue of Mrs Cape, so I make a quick detour. When I find her, she's reading *Woman's Weekly* under her desk and eating Garibaldi biscuits.

'Ah, Josephine,' she says.

'Mrs Cape. I've just had word from the Prime Minister,' I say breathlessly, not bothering with pleasantries. There isn't time. She sets down her biscuit, looks up at me.

'He's specified that you – he actually referred to you by name –'

Mrs Cape's eyes are jelly in their sockets.

'– that you must never, ever allow anyone to find out they were trying to cover up part of his interview. It might, you know, have an impact on future policies and the safety of the country. All that kind of thing. You know?' I sound ridiculous, talking about the safety of the country, whilst we are cocooned behind these four walls and I know I have to shut up right now before I lose total control, even though Mrs Cape looks petrified.

'Really?' she says. 'You mean, the PM, knows my name?'

'He does. He's asked me to make sure it's all kept quiet. It's really, really important no one finds out. Some of the interview wasn't meant to come out at all but it has now and the main press will use some of it. They'll be able to get their PR team to sort it out but it'll be much, much worse if anyone finds out they tried to pull it. Are you with me?' Mrs Cape nods. She's terrified. 'Of course. If it's for the safety of our country and all that ... Anything. You tell the PM I'll do anything.'

'Thank you so, so much,' I reply, almost wanting to laugh at her earnest expression and the fact she's fallen for this. 'And please. Again, Mrs Cape, I don't think anyone will ask but please don't tell anyone I've asked you to keep quiet on this. It'll be a disaster if you do. But I'll make sure he writes to you with a signed note, shall I? Make it out to you? Or is there anyone else?'

'Yes, ooh can you do that? Of course you can, thank you. And you have my word. I won't say anything to anyone.' I leave the room, ready to run to Pete and tell him the same thing. I turn to say goodbye once more and she's eating an entire Garibaldi biscuit, whole. I pray that she won't open her mouth and destroy this whole house of lies. I turn to go and find Sally. She's at the front of Main School, looking strangely calm.

'Sally,' I say, not bothering to wait for her to talk. 'They're talking to Verity now. Don't say a word. Just tell them what happened. You went with Verity to drop the proof off at the printer's. Don't give them any more information than they ask for. That's all they need to know. OK? And if you get stuck on anything just say you can't remember or something. Alright?'

She looks calm still. Happy, even. It's beginning to unnerve me and I wonder whether she's heard anything I've been saying.

'Sally?'

'Don't worry. I've got you,' she says. For good measure I remind her about Oxford.

'Listen, we've sent off your application, so if you get an interview, you'll hear pretty soon. So just be onside with me, OK? Let's do some coaching soon.'

'OK, Josephine. Thanks.'

'OK, good. You're being called in next to speak to Mrs Allen and Mrs Pownall – she's one of the governors. I'm going back up to the house. Can you come and find me afterwards and let me know what happened?' She nods and with a small smile walks off. When I get back, the house is very quiet, even though there are lots of people milling around. To avoid them I go to sit in the sixth-form study, as if I'm ready to do some revision and preparation for next week's interview, rather than desperately trying to get some peace so I can have a minute to just think. This will give me time I so need to try to foresee any hitches and, more importantly, work out how the hell I'm going to play them.

2014

Gracie Lovell gets up to hug me. I back away. Her leering face reminds me of the time at school when she tried to find out why Freya and I were arguing, all false sympathy and concern. And that girl she always used to hang about with, Marge someone-or-other.

'Sorry,' she says. 'Wasn't going to kill you or anything, was I?' She laughs. 'What are you doing in here?'

I sit on a wooden chair and, although she's a connection to Freya, it doesn't feel too alarming. She was never particularly good friends with either of us at school. She's changed a lot; I would never even have recognised her at first glance. Her eyes have become hooded, her chin sticking out, defiant against the weight of life. She's got a fine, straight nose, freckled and slightly snubbed, which I think I used to envy for its tomboyishness.

'Mother,' I say. 'She died and I, well, you know ...' I don't ask her what she's in for but she's keen to proffer me her life story.

'School. I think it actually ruined me,' she says, without giving any thought to what I've just said, or what will come out her mouth next. 'The success, the pressure. Everything. Didn't set us up very well, did it? I thought everything was so cut and dried and I would leave, become a lawyer or a doctor. And then I did leave, got married, husband cheated and I realised what I really wanted to do was set up an arts and crafts shop. Something like that. But by then it was too late and I had two kids to look after. School fees to pay. Cheating husband was made redundant. All that stuff. So I came in here. Work are paying,' she says defensively. I will her to breathe.

'Investment banking,' she says, as though I showed any interest. 'Do you see anyone?' she asks. She's wearing a white caftan top – the type we used to go crazy for at school – with penny-sized yellow stains on the sleeve and leather strings that she keeps winding around her finger.

'No not really.' I pick up her book to change the subject. 'Any good?'

'It's OK. Can't really concentrate on much in here. Always people coming in and out. Don't you find? Probably not. You always could concentrate anywhere, couldn't you? Anyway, so you don't see anyone, did you say?'

'No one from school. Anyway, no more about school. It's all in the past now.' I sound terser than I mean to.

'Is it? That's not what I heard,' she replies, looking pleased at having more information than me. I don't make any effort to ask her 'what she heard', although I'm dying to know.

'Freya?' she says, looking into my eyes for some sort of reaction. I get up to leave the room. 'She's been looking for you. Asking people things about you. Specific things. That's why I was so shocked to see you in here. Why I followed you with your father.' Gracie is now standing up too, crossing her arms over her concave stomach. 'Did she manage to get to you?'

'Get to me?'

'What's wrong? Why are you shaking?' Gracie asks. She's trying to sound concerned but she's almost laughing. 'What's the matter? All this school stuff getting to you as well?'

'Not at all. So long ago.' I attempt a laugh but it comes out as a hiccup and Gracie leans forward to pat me on the back. I smack her hand away.

'Josephine, are you alright? When you came in here I thought we could be friends, hang out. We never got to hang out much at school. I wanted to be friends with you and Freya but you always seemed so distant to the rest of us. How about it? We can get through our time here together?'

'Yes, of course,' I say, desperate to get her back on to my line of conversation. 'So, Freya, what about her?' I manage, somehow, to keep my voice from shaking.

'Ah, it's a long story, she's just been harassing all of us.' She's playing me and I wonder whether I should request a transfer of some sort. I can't be dealing with this.

'She was just asking this and that.' Gracie's fingering the smocking on her blouse.

'Ha, if I know Freya, I know exactly what she'll have been asking.' I say in a light-hearted way.

'Really?' Gracie replies. 'What's that?'

'Just this and that. As you said.'

Neither of us budge. Finally she relents.

'So, after all these years we can be friends? Come on, let's hang out. And then I'll tell you what's been going on. Everything.'

Gracie Lovell, after all these years, holds her arm out for me as if we were about to go for class and, for the first time in my life, I take it.

1996

I don't manage to find Pete before our next weekend exeat, so I spend two days at home jittery and unable to sleep. I'm safe in the knowledge that Mrs Allen is away, so won't be investigating. Mrs Pownall, however, who knows?

I sit in the British Library sipping at water, peeling oranges and thinking of Freya. I haven't heard anything from her since before *The Lens* was published. I had kept a close eye on my pigeonhole at school after the magazine was distributed, in case she had tried to contact me but every time I had checked, there was nothing. I remember vague plans of her family going to Rome for a treat; she had even mentioned asking Rollo if I could join them. I wonder what they'll be doing now. If Rollo was shocked at the news and if she managed to sweet-talk him into not being cross with her, her blonde head cocked to one side. My father is away, so at least I can avoid any questions from him and I feel a bit lighter by the time I arrive back at school. The first thing I do, even before unpacking, is track Pete down. He agrees to keep quiet. I tell him the same thing I told Mrs Cape before the break and he looks absolutely petrified. 'Well, Miss Grey. I would never let this fine country down,' he says.

'The school governors might be coming to question you about it, though. But that's about something else entirely. Just keep schtum.'

Pete takes a step back and clasps his hands together. 'Governors?'

'Yes.' He looks so scared I almost want to tell him the truth. Someone who knows nothing about me, my past, or the school. See what he would say and how he would react. But I can't, of course.

'Are you alright?' he asks. I smile brightly and tell him of course, that I'm great, I was just thinking about home. 'Ah yes, tricky,' he says. 'Not being with your parents and all.' He goes to his desk and opens an envelope, then pulls out a ten pound note. He presses it into my hand and tells me to buy something nice to cheer me up. When I see how genuine he is about giving it to me, I take it. When I get back to school, I put the ten pound note in a drawer and vow to pay him back one day.

But, as I turn the corner to make my way back to the main building, I see Mrs Kitts. She looks as though she's been waiting for hours. My first reaction is one of shock: I can't understand why she's still allowed on the school grounds. Freya is, after all, a minor. The school are obviously caught up in either trying to investigate before doing anything drastic, or they are trying to bury the whole ugly thing. Either way, Mrs Kitts looks around and, as though she senses nearby danger, quickly pushes me through the wooden door. It slams against my elbow.

'Josephine.' She stops herself from any more aggression. Smiles slowly and leans towards me, searching my eyes. 'Been working hard?' she says. I can smell the tang of alcohol and mints on her breath.

'Yes,' I reply. 'You obviously are too.' I want to add 'at seducing younger girls', but I manage to stop myself. I can tell she is desperate to ask me how much I know about her and Freya, but she can't risk a full-blown confession. Instead, she asks about my break. 'Speak to anyone when you were at home?' she says.

'Freya, do you mean?' I reply. Mrs Kitts doesn't say anything but she freezes for a second and I can see she's scared she's gone too far. 'Freya?' I say again.

'Freya? Oh you spoke to her?' Mrs Kitts feigns concern. 'How is she doing? Must have been terrible after that whole *Lens* episode. Poor thing. Nasty, vicious gossip.'

'Hmmm. Indeed. Surely I should be asking you the same question, Mrs Kitts. If you spoke to her?'

'No, no, I didn't.' As I'm looking at Mrs Kitts, the sharpness of her features and her dowdy clothes, I'm wondering what on earth Freya could have seen in her. She'd never, ever expressed any interest in girls before, was obsessed with that boy, Guy. Or maybe Freya and Mrs Kitts were in love and Freya never trusted me enough to say and I never saw the signs. Thinking about this is too painful – that our whole friendship was based only on what we had in common – our mothers, the fun times we had together, the boys we kissed – is too much to bear, so I am compelled to draw another conclusion about Freya. I wonder if Mrs Kitts has taken advantage of her after the death of her mother. If that's the case, then what I've done seems even worse. Exposed Freya for her vulnerability, shamed her for it, in front of hundreds of people.

Mrs Kitts sits down, wipes her black pleated skirt flat against her thighs. She looks up at me, pleading. 'How is she?'

'I don't know,' I reply. 'We haven't spoken. Why did you do it?' I decide to ask her straight. Gauge her reaction.

Mrs Kitts looks deflated. 'I couldn't not. You know her. You must know why. Who was it anyway? Who outed us?'

'I don't know. Whoever handed in the proof copy to the printer's.'

'Does anyone know it's me?' she asks, her voice hitching on the last note.

I shrug, keep my face a mask. 'Not sure.'

'Will you say anything?'

'No. I won't say anything. If you don't say anything either.' There's a pause. I can't stop myself from wanting to know if Freya's let anything on to Mrs Kitts. 'About things Freya might have told you?'

'About things she might have told me? Where do I start?' Mrs Kitts stands up, gains confidence that she's now got one over me, and starts counting on her hand. 'Drugs, cigarettes, alcohol.' She's mock singing. 'You've got it all haven't you? Head Girl, perfect life yet ... all this.' She's wiping dust off the shelves with her forefinger. 'And what if that came out?'

'It won't,' I reply. 'Because no one will believe you after this. Or care. You think people will take your word against mine now that you've been having it off with a pupil? Really?'

Mrs Kitts turns and drops her hand. I can't work out if she's looking vengeful, or remorseful but she's piercing me with her stare. I look right back at her.

'Bye then,' I say, in the same sing-song voice she's just been using. I walk to my books, take them off the shelf and leave the room.

The next week blurs by. The stale period just before the Christmas buzz. Two weeks before the holidays and the days are going painfully slowly. I try to avoid speaking to people on a day-to-day basis, and I haven't seen Freya at all since the magazine came out. I've been down to the san, to try to find her. To see if she'll talk, and to check that, at the very least, she's OK. To see if she'll tell me if it was Mrs Kitts who she told about that night, and if anyone else knows. I need to know to make sure I'm not on the back foot. To make sure I'm ready, with all the information at hand, to attack and discredit both Freya and Mrs Kitts, should anything come out. She's not there, though. She's not anywhere in the school at all. In her dorm, which I've been into a few times, her mattress lies bare and the only thing that's left of hers is a hair bobble on her bedside table, knotted with blonde strands. She must have temporarily moved house but I'm too proud to ask anyone where she is, so I spend my whole time eavesdropping around huddled girls, trying to pick up her whereabouts amidst the gossip. The rumours about who she was having the affair with are spiralling, becoming ever more ridiculous. There's a part of me that just wants to see her. To see how she reacts to me. Beneath all the plotting, the deception, the terror of being caught out, I desperately miss my friend.

Verity has been taking charge with a renewed vigour, trying to make a point to the staff and pupils that she's an upstanding member of the school, despite what's going on. She's there at chapel, standing at the front of the school, instructing the Prefects where to stand. She's there at games, wielding a lacrosse stick as though it's a sword; she's there at mealtimes, a whistle around her neck ready to blow at any pitch above regular-talking level. All this time she's grinning, teeth slightly sticking out. She's driving me mad. Mrs Pownall and some of the other governors come and go, questioning the girls about who has seen what. They then move on to the teachers. Everybody is questioned. Mrs Artington, Mrs Mayfield, Miss Berrymede, married teachers, single teachers, part-time teachers. No one gets off. There's still an atmosphere around the school. A strange negativity that's permeated the walls. Everyone walks round quietly hunched, whispering to each other. Mrs Allen asks to see me to go through school timetable.

'We've still got the governors asking questions,' she says, putting away the timetable that I've given her.

'And Freya's father has been on the phone. He is demanding answers. This has got to be kept in the school, do you understand that? If any of his competitors gets wind of this, it'll be all over the papers. And just ... Josephine, you know I've got to keep the reputation here.'

'I know,' I reply.

'And of course I'll have to work out what to do about you and Verity. No one knows exactly what has happened but you understand that the buck stops with you. And Verity.'

'I had nothing to do with anything,' I say.

'Well, I've called your father. He'll be here next week. We've got a meeting with him and Verity's parents. We've got to get to the bottom of this. Find out who published and who knew what about Freya and this ... *rumour*. I'm not suggesting you had anything to do with it but you understand, as Head Girl, you bear the responsibility. We've had a staff meeting and decided to wait until we hear if you've got an interview at Oxford or not. If you do and you get in and we decide to take punitive action, we'll have to deal with that then. The governors will all take a vote. But until that point we've got to give you all the best possible chance. Understood?'

'Yes. Yes, I've understood.'

'Good. You can go.'

'Wait,' I say. 'I mean, sorry, Mrs Allen. Freya? Do you know if she's ... is she coming back?'

'At the moment, Josephine, all I know is that Freya's father has been ringing me non-stop about his daughter being victimised. He's furious with the school for allowing it to happen and I'm having to calm him down as well as try and sort this whole mess out. I'm hoping she'll come back once interviews have finished and everything has calmed down a bit. Mr Seymour, I think, has agreed to that much and I think then we can try and get to the bottom of all of this with all four of you in the school.'

Mrs Allen's voice is all tight but, at the same time, it's comforting that she's confiding in me. It takes the edge off the fact she's said Rollo thinks Freya is being victimised. When I leave Mrs Allen's office I'm stopped by three teachers wanting to know answers to things I was meant to have organised weeks ago. It feels like a blessing, the fact I'm kept super busy with the run-up to Christmas. There's the carol service to arrange, charity functions and, all this time, I have to wait and hear if I've got a bloody interview or not, something that Verity doesn't have to worry about. The pressure has made me silent. Inconspicuous. After school hours, I've taken to wearing black. Black leggings, black T-shirt and black plimsolls. I feel anonymous. The badge is still there, though. Glowing and shining. Giving me hope. Power.

All this time I'd been gliding along the corridors terrified of seeing Freya, having to look her in the eye, but since Mrs Allen told me she's not coming back until after our Oxford interviews, I can stop thinking of her creeping up on me in the shadows. It feels like everyone's forgotten about the magazine, and I feel barely a day has passed when I find out from a weeping Sally that all three of us have got an interview at Oxford. Me, Sally and Freya. I wonder if Freya knows and, if not, who will be the one to tell her.

I don't have to wait long to find out. Sally tells me that, according to Verity, Freya's interview was listed for yesterday. Knowing I won't bump into her in Oxford gives me the resolve to stop thinking of her until the day is over. If I let too many thoughts of her into my head, about whether she could ever forgive me, I'll screw up my own interview tomorrow. At the same time, the idea of her return charges me up. Whilst she is not here I must take the opportunity to focus on succeeding, so once she's back I can face her knowing I've done my best, in the right frame of mind for any investigations that will take place. Pleased with my plan, I spend a fruitful afternoon in my room studying with the curtains shut, by torchlight, so no one can disturb me. Freya might well return to school whilst I'm at my interview and I want to stay hidden so I don't see her before I go, which might put me off my stride. The next morning I'm up early, ready to go. It's five thirty and I'm in the sixth-form study eating an apple and drinking black coffee. I go down to Main School, collect my books and check my pigeonhole. Nothing, although I don't really know what I was expecting.

By the time I arrive in Oxford, my body is bubbling with nerves but my mind is clear. It's something to do with the symmetry of the spires, the architecture, the light catching the golden stone. This city. This city that pulses through me. The place I've been working towards for so long. Over and above everything else in my life. I can't help but feel a part of it already. The students, milling around with books under their arms, biking to their next lectures, the little cafes full of people reading, talking, studying. I am made for this place. The energy of it all makes me feel high.

The interview is fine. Without Freya or Verity in my eyeline, I cope much better. Impressively, even. Something to do with being away from any reminders of school that sit heavy on my shoulders. The room smells of books and intellect and the chairs are upright and there's a thin, blue carpet which reminds me of Mrs Allen's study. The two interviewers are smiling when I leave, nodding between themselves. My Head Girl badge is on full display. They've asked me what being a Head Girl means to me. 'Leadership,' I tell them. Although I've never thought of the badge that way. 'Responsibility. A moral guide.' I remember the words Mrs Allen used when she first pinned the badge to my breast.

'It is a great honour to be a Head Girl in the top girls' boarding school in the country,' says one of the interviewers.

'It is,' I agree. 'Indeed. I hope it honours me with good courage for years to come.'

The hour-long session continues and, all the while, they are totally engaged with me. One of them frowns when I talk about a prominent historian's take on World War Two and says: 'I've never thought of that before. Impressive.' I leave the room and spend the rest of the day in a small cafe, steadying myself by reading books and papers and eating a slice of cinnamon cake. At five o' clock, I ring Father from a payphone. There's no answer and I leave a message, saying the interview has gone fine and then I meet up with Melody Swaffham, who had her interview straight after mine. We have supper and a glass of wine and get a taxi back to school. I'm still feeling high on the journey home and I'm ready to face Freya, who'll be back anytime now, and Melody and I don't stop talking, but when we pull up to the main gates, the darkness is interrupted by the headlights of four police cars, parked in the drive.

'What's happened?' Melody asks.

'I don't know. Nothing probably. Or they're probably still trying to work out what happened with Fr—' Her name gets stuck in my throat.

'Yes. Sure that's it,' she says. She's looking at me now, eyes wide and fearful. I don't want to leave the embryonic warmth of the taxi. It swings in to the school drive and we both catch a glimpse of an ambulance. It's careering up towards the boarding houses. It comes back down and swerves into the main driveway. Three men rush out, whilst Melody and I frost the car window with our breath. It's coming thick and fast and we have to keep wiping it clean with our sleeves.

'Josephine?' she says.

'Yes?'

'I'm scared.'

'Don't be so ridiculous.' I feel faint, my heart sticky in my chest.

'It's fine. It's just – it's just nothing I'm sure. Maybe a fire alarm?' I can hear windows sliding open. Girls are now hanging out of their dormitory windows, T-shirt nighties falling down their shoulders, hair wild, as the siren continues wailing.

'No. It's not. What's going on?' says Melody, again.

'Shhhh.' The paramedics throw their doors open and run into the school with a stretcher and first-aid paraphernalia. Someone has opened the door to them, we cannot see who.

'Shall we go out?' Melody asks.

'No. No, let's wait. We don't want to interrupt.'

In truth I am frozen. I cannot move. I am torn between getting the hell out of there and going to help but my limbs have solidified. I am still and everything around me hums. We are there for no less than five minutes and it seems like forever. We hold our breaths; there is no more frosting on the window. The door opens again and it is Mrs Allen, looking green. She is wearing a thick, plaid dressing gown, hair in rollers. It is an odd sight, the Headmistress in her night gear. I'd never imagined she needed to sleep. Mrs Kitts is behind her, I can see her gasping, hand up by her mouth. They are running and, behind them, flashes of green as the paramedics hold up the long stretcher. There is someone lying on it. Oxygen pumping into them. I can't see their face, or hair. The paramedics are leant right over her. There are shoes, though. Shoes, hanging off. They are grey shoes.

Grey suede trainers. New. I've never seen them before. It's a strange thing at a girls' school: everyone is recognisable by their shoes. The only sartorial identity amongst the navy uniforms. These ones though, I do not know.

The laces have been taken out and replaced with fluorescent string. The ankle is small, delicate. And Mrs Kitts is holding a note, waving it in the air and screaming. 'She's left a note. She's left a note!' She is hysterical, clawing at her top. She's also holding something else. What looks like a yellow rope, mixed with red. I can't work out what it is because Mrs Kitts is swinging it in the air like it's a shot put. As she comes nearer though, I can see the bit of paper she's holding. There are only three lines on it. And although it is not close enough for me to read, I have a distinctly uneasy feeling about who is beneath that oxygen mask.

2014

I have to play Gracie carefully. Last night, at supper, I had reminisced about school, trying to get information about Freya and what questions she had been asking. All Gracie had wanted to do, though, was talk about herself, compare our lives and be best friends.

Tonight, too, she's the same. We're at supper again and the atmosphere in the room is buoyant, as we've been told it is film night, with popcorn in the day room and that we get to vote on what we all want to watch.

'It's funny, isn't it? Where life has taken us. I mean ... who would have thought, you in here? I always thought how clever you were but deep down you and I were both struggling, weren't we?'

'Hmmm. I suppose,' I say, silently praying for her to shut up. 'So what other memories do you have from school?' I ask.

'I just remember working really. Working and working and trying to keep up. I never could quite keep up. I found it difficult. Not like you.'

'Yeah, me and Freya – everyone thought we had it easy,' I say, hoping it will help her open up.

'Really? Didn't you?' Gracie leans back from the wooden dining table, pushes her plate away and crosses her legs.

'Oh no. You know people expected a lot from us. We were so close and people wanted to know why we worked. As friends, I mean. We are ... were, rather, quite different.'

I look at Gracie, expecting her to say something but she doesn't. Then she starts crying. 'You were lucky to have each other, you know?'

I'm embarrassed that she's crying in front of everyone, so I quickly offer to go and get her some pudding.

'Yes, please,' she says. 'Sorry.'

'It's OK.'

When I return she shovels down great mouthfuls and glugs back a plastic tumbler of water.

'So how are you finding the doctors here?' She wipes her hand across her mouth.

'Fine,' I reply, not wanting to get into it. 'They're fine. Helping me with my mother.'

'Your mother. Oh yes ... wasn't she ill at school? I remember the teachers calling a meeting once, to tell all the girls we had to be careful not to mention her because you didn't want anyone to know, but that we had to look after you. What was wrong with her?'

'The teachers? Told everyone my mother was ill?' I'm shocked. I thought no one knew.

'Yeah. Everyone knew everyone else's business, didn't they? Whether you wanted it to be private or not.'

'She was fine.' I squeeze my fist, enraged. 'And yes, that was the way it went, wasn't it?'

'Are you OK? Did I say something wrong?' Gracie asks. Her voice has gone all flat and her eyes sunken and I realise that I'm making her paranoid. I need to make her feel as comfortable as possible if she's going to tell me about Freya.

'No, no, I'm sorry, Gracie. I didn't mean to snap. I was just thinking about something else entirely. What else then?'

'Nothing,' she says. 'I've got nothing. Really, I don't know why you are even talking to me. I'm just ... I'm useless, aren't I?'

I've lost her for tonight, so I get up and leave, saying I'm exhausted and I have to go bed.

'By the way,' I say, before I leave, 'you're probably not totally, a hundred per cent useless.'

When she smiles, I'm surprised to feel a quiet pleasure.

1996

Melody and I sit in the taxi for fifteen minutes. Neither of us talks. The driver is ashen. He keeps looking at us through the rear-view mirror.

'Alright to go now are we, girls?' he asks. Melody is clutching on to my coat, pressing in close. I'm still shivering.

'Want my scarf?' she asks.

'Thanks. I'm OK.'

'Here.' She takes off her blue school scarf anyway and winds it around my neck.

'Let's go up. I'll take you to your house.' Melody knows too. I saw her look at me when the stretcher went past. When we finally caught a glimpse of the slender outline of her body, the line of her chin beneath that mask. And then we saw her hair. It was all shorn and for the life of me I still can't work out why, and I feel like screaming.

'It's OK. She'll be OK,' she keeps whispering.

'Shall we go to the hospital?' I ask. I'm surprised I can't seem to make a decision.

'No. We won't be allowed. Let's go up to the house and find out what's going on there. OK?' Melody leads me through the grass and up the pathway. When we arrive at the house, all the lights are out. Mrs Sands, the matron, is sitting by the front door on a small plastic stool.

'Girls. You're OK. Thank God. I knew you were going to be late, Josephine, but Mrs Kitts has just rung. She's been ... she's been held up somewhere, so you'll have to lock up for her.'

'It's OK, Mrs Sands. We know. We've just been down at Main School,' Melody says.

'Well? What happened?' she asks. Her hands are ruffling her pleated skirt and the shushing sounds volcanic in my head.

'She's ... she looked dead,' I say in disbelief. 'Dead.'

I'm looking straight at Mrs Sands then I turn to Melody, who pulls her shoulders back.

'No,' says Melody. 'I'm sure she's going to be absolutely fine, Josephine. You don't know what happened. None of us do, so let's not be melodramatic.'

'Don't lie, Melody.' My voice sounds all strangled. 'She looked dead.' Melody looks down. Mrs Sands is crying. I'm now on the floor. Mrs Sands is stroking my hair and I'm pulling at my Head Girl badge. Tearing it out of my jumper.

Melody is holding my hair back and I'm retching into a little grey bin that holds three lacrosse sticks. My head is full of these weird little flashing lights: green, white. I can hear the music from that night and it's shooting down my spine in rhythmic beats. After five or so minutes, the phone rings. Mrs Sands picks it up and nods, making noises of acknowledgment to whatever is being said. Melody and I are looking at her. She holds up an arthritic finger. A shiny brown colour, like she's been oiling it with linseed.

'Right. I'll let her know.' She hangs up and looks at me. I'm now standing up. Regained my composure. I feel much better. Melody's right. I've overreacted.

'Josephine?' she says.

'Yes?'

'I'm sorry. You are to go and pack your things and take a small bag with you down to the san.'

'I'm fine, Mrs Sands. I just got a shock that's all. You know this isn't like me.'

'I do know, yes. And I'm glad you are OK but this isn't about that. I'm afraid Mrs Allen has requested that you are to go down and be in isolation. Not sure why but you're to meet her outside her office in ten minutes.'

'I'm to go down alone?'

'She's called Mrs Keats to come and walk you down. Left a message. Says if she doesn't turn up in five minutes, you're to walk down by yourself.'

I look at Melody. 'What about her?'

'This isn't about what you've just witnessed. I need you to go and get your things. Quick.'

I run upstairs. The younger girls in my dormitory are awake, wanting to know what's going on and I tell them Mother's ill. I can't think of anything else to say.

'Turn your lights out, quick. You know you're not meant to have them on after ten. If you get caught Mrs Kitts will make you get up early and collect the rubbish. She's on the rampage at the moment.' The lights go out and I'm relieved no one can see my face. *It's all over. I've been caught out.* When I come down, Mrs

Sands asks me why I've got so much stuff. Only two minutes must have passed and I have no idea what I've packed.

'Just … I don't know.'

'Right. Well, Mrs Keats isn't here yet, so if you could make your way down.'

'Of course.' *Get it together, Josephine. Deny, deny, deny.* 'Absolutely. Right, I'll see you tomorrow, Melody.' Mrs Sands opens the door, practically pushes me out into the pitch black. When I turn around to ask her if she's got a torch, the door has already closed. I can't lift up my feet too far, for fear of missing a step. Leaves slide under me and I think of me and Freya when we were young; ten or eleven or so; blindfolding ourselves in her back garden. She would demand I twirl myself around until I was nearly sick. We would play blind-man's chase for hours on end, until one time when I wrapped a black cloth round her head and span her, round and round.

'One, two, three, four, five, go, carry on twirling,' I had shouted. She did. Carried on for about twenty more seconds until I heard a thump and she lay giggling on the ground. 'Get up, more,' I said. She did as she was told.

'I'm going to be sick soon,' she laughed.

'OK. You can catch me now … try and catch me.' I had waited two or three seconds, then left the garden. I had gone up to the playroom, turned on her TV and forgotten all about her. Twenty minutes later her mother had come in and asked me where she was.

'Freya? Oh, she's in the loo,' I had said. When she left the room, I had run downstairs and found Freya sitting on the white love seat at the bottom of the garden. She had been crying; her dress was muddy and wet.

'Freya,' I had said. 'I only went upstairs for a bit.'

'Please can you take off my blindfold? I can't get it off.' I had knotted it four or five times so it had squeezed against her skull. It had left red marks either side of her eyes.

'You've got marks on your face,' I had said. She had looked at me.

'J, please don't do that again. You really scared me.'

'Come on. Let's go and get some lemonade,' I had replied. 'By the way, your mum asked where you were, I said you were in the loo. Is that alright?'

'Yes.' She had taken my hand and squeezed it.

I was now nearing the bottom of the hill and I realise I had never apologised to Freya for scaring her like that. If she pulls through, I will tell her I'm sorry. Sorry for leaving her alone like that. Her mother had come in, taken one look at Freya and her wet dress and told her to go and get washed. Freya had, of course, told her she was in the loo.

If she's alive, I will wash her now, I think. I will wash her if she needs me to wash her. I will wash her hair. I will wash her face. I will do anything. The recent events are looping in my mind and, no matter how much I try to distract myself, they won't stop. *Freya's Dirty Little Secret,* over and over, like a stuck showreel and the regret, the awfulness, is turning my heart into a cavernous black hole. I wonder if I will ever be able to forget this. The san is dark. No patients. Mrs Allen opens the door for me and points to a bed next to the window.

'There's a reading light there,' she says, pointing at a little table. I put my toothbrush and clothes in the bedside cabinet and sit down, waiting for her to say something. She doesn't. Just pats the end of the bed. Tells me to get some rest before tomorrow.

'What's going on tomorrow?' I ask, keeping my voice light.

'Just go to sleep,' she says.

2014

The next morning, I don't see Gracie. I'm wondering whether I should get Father to email Freya and tell her I've moved somewhere random, so she just leaves me alone for good. I banish the idea quickly. Too much. Too much to unravel. Too heavy. At lunchtime, Toby visits me in the day room. He's brought two bunches of flowers. One huge array of sunflowers and one small little bouquet that he's picked himself from the park.

'I brought them over here with no water. Look a bit dead,' he laughs and then looks nervous. 'You look really, really well. This place is doing you good.' He chubs my cheeks. 'You've even put on a bit of weight.'

'Thanks,' I say. It's true, I can feel my jeans getting tighter. I've even been eating a lot of cake at tea.

'It suits you, though. You look really well. Better than I've seen you look in ages.'

'I'm not wearing any make-up,' I laugh. 'I don't know how you can say that.'

'I've seen you without make-up plenty of times,' he says and we both go silent, thinking of the times he's seen me barefaced. Those times when we've spent days in bed, eating Arabic flatbread and drinking fresh coffee after fresh coffee and, and . . . I can't look at him anymore.

'How is your girlfriend?'

'She's fine. Morning sickness.'

'Right.'

And then it comes:

'She wants to get married.' Toby has sworn faithfully to me that he will never, ever get married. It is the one thing about him that I could be absolutely sure about.

'Really,' I say, calm in the knowledge that he's about to tell me how ridiculous it is.

'I've said yes, Josephine. I've said yes.'

It doesn't happen quickly but, when it does, my face folds in on itself without warning. That's the second time I've cried in this place in the past week. The second time I've cried in about twenty-five years.

'I'm sorry. I'm really sorry. I wish I didn't have to tell you here. Now. But there's an engagement notice coming out in *The Times* tomorrow. I didn't want you to have to see it without me telling you first.' I don't say anything for the next ten minutes. I just sit and cry.

'Congratulations,' I say, when I've finally stopped heaving.

'Thank you.'

'Thank *you* by the way.'

'For what?'

'For forcing me to see Dr McKinnie. Did you ever sleep with her by the way?' I feel carefree in asking him this, since he's put our relationship off the agenda.

'Dr McKinnie? No, are you joking, J? She's my *doctor*. Is that what you were thinking about all that time she was treating you?'

'Not all the time, no.' To his credit, Toby laughs.

'Toby, I need to ask you something.'

'Go on?'

'If someone was … someone from your past was trying to see you when you had told them no, what would you do?'

Toby stops and sits back down and takes my hand.

'What do you mean? Is this what's been troubling you all this time?' He looks all serious. 'What's going on, J? Do I need to get the police involved? Get someone to look after you? I know people, you know…'

'No, no.' The prospect of having told someone about Freya is so enormous, black spots appear in front of my eyes. 'One moment.' I sit and shut them, breathing, counting one to ten.

'I can't go into it too much. I just want someone to leave me alone. That's all. Dredging up too many memories…' As I'm saying this, my head starts swelling with noise. Trance music. For a moment I think someone's turned on the radio next door and then I realise it's in my head.

'OK, well, if you can't tell me what's going on, you can tell me why you are suddenly sweating so much. Here, let me wipe your forehead.' He trails the back of his hand underneath my fringe and shakes it out. 'You are absolutely soaking. What the fuck, J?'

'Nothing. Nothing. I wish I'd never said anything. I can't talk about it. Leave me alone. Just go.'

Toby stands up, points at the flowers. 'Want me to put them in water?'

'Just get out. Get the fuck out.'

Toby shuffles backwards and lifts his hands up. 'J ... I ... are you alright? I can help you, I told you. But you aren't making any sense. When you are ready, let me know. Alright? Just let me know. And I'll be there.'

I don't answer him. I'm too afraid to talk, the words are bulging in my throat, making me feel sick. *Fuck you, Freya, for making me feel like this.* I'm going to find out from Gracie, once and for all, what she wants and then I'm going to hatch a plan which means Freya Seymour will never, ever contact me again. Which means I can get on with my life in peace. Without the blackness of her memory, our memories together, rotting my core.

1996

I'm woken up by the drawing of the blinds.

'Wake up,' says Mrs Allen. It's six in the morning. Saturday. We're usually allowed a lie-in on the weekends until eight thirty. It feels strange, Mrs Allen seeing me in bed. Our relationship has never really evolved from past her study door and I feel uncomfortable, pulling up the duvet right over me, even though I'm fully clothed.

'Get dressed in five, I'll see you outside.' I get down off the bed. There's the big pile of clothes I picked up last night, and I go for a black gypsy skirt and smock top. Flat pumps to finish it off. The rest of the clothes, I fold back up and squeeze them into my book bag. It's been five minutes and I take out the clothes, repack them and put them in again to distract myself and stall for time. I can hear Mrs Allen pacing the corridor.

'Josephine?'

'I'm coming, Mrs Allen.' The school is freezing. The heating is normally on full blast but, when I touch the radiators, they sting with cold. We make our way to Mrs Allen's study and she offers me a seat before she sits down. The usual protocol of sitting after the teacher has gone out the window.

'Josephine. I can tell you want to know why you're here.'

'Freya,' I say.

'She's alive. Just. She's OK. We think she's going to be OK.' Mrs Allen looks down at her desk. Taps her hands on the wood. She brings out a note from her top drawer, unfolds it and passes it to me. I take it. Read it. It's the note that Mrs Kitts was holding when the ambulance took Freya away. I hand it back to Mrs Allen without saying a word.

'What do you have to say about this?' The words of the note are playing themselves over and over until they scramble before my eyes, and they make no sense at all.

Can't. Cope. Josephine. Blame. Kill. Josephine. Outed me. The Lens. My love. Kill. Myself.

I start to laugh. Mrs Allen looks at me.

'Well we're going to have to call Mrs Pownall in immediately. If not the police. But you know my thoughts on that. And your father. He'll have to come earlier than planned.'

'What about Verity?' I ask.

'What about her?'

'What about the part she played in all of this? I had no knowledge of the late addition to the "Guess Who?" section. None.'

'Well, that's good. But we need to get to the bottom of this. Need to find out what's going on. I don't want the press to get wind of this either. Do you understand? Otherwise we'll lose our standing.'

'I know. I know. I don't want that to happen any more than you do, Mrs Allen.'

She smiles. 'I know. Don't worry.'

'Am I being blamed for this?' I want to ask about Oxford and then suddenly I feel like I'm going to throw up. My best friend is nearly dead and it's because of me. I've nearly killed someone. This whole thing, this ugly, ugly thing has got so out of control that Freya's nearly lost her life.

'No. Not yet. We don't know what happened. It is a serious accusation to make from Freya's side. So we'll have to wait for her to get better...'

'She will?'

'I hope so. She's still unconscious but the doctors seem to think she's stabilised.'

Still unconscious? I thought she would be up and about by now. I'm nearly standing up, ready to flee the room.

'How?' I manage to ask.

'Pills. Pills and there are some rather deep cuts on her wrists. We think she might have had some sort of ... episode. She cut off all her hair, too.' I think of her long blonde ponytail and the shiny, pink scars on her pelvis.

'Who found her?' I ask.

I wish I had been there to find her. To look after her. To tell her it's OK. I want to take her in my arms and tell her that that night – it didn't need to destroy us both like this. That I am sorry for hurting her. I am sorry. But the guilt, this horrendous thing is too enormous. It's taken on a life of its own, formed into a mass of gruesomeness and, for that, I'm going to have to deal with the consequences. I fire through every way in which I can make this better. And the only solution in my mind is to carry on as normal. That way, Freya will recover, Verity will get the blame but she'll still probably get into Oxford and then Freya and I can be the successes we were always meant to be. She'll make her father – and her mother – proud. And I'll carve out my own career, my own life, away from the threat that I'm turning into Mother. As I've decided this, I look up at Mrs Allen.

'Who found her?' whispers Mrs Allen. 'That was Mrs Kitts …' she says, and her eyes light up. 'Mrs Kitts,' she repeats. She nods her head very slowly and opens her mouth.

'Mrs Kitts. Who would have thought … it's her, isn't it? It all makes sense now. Pushing me to put Freya forward for the Anne Dunne Scholarship. I had my reservations about that but she was adamant. Hounded me until I agreed. She found Freya after she … God. Mrs Kitts. All this time.' She's not asking me. And for a brief moment it all crystallises in my mind too and I accept it. That Freya had kept it all a secret from me. That of course it was true. That night, before the club, she was so adamant that she no longer fancied Guy. She was holding that secret then, I know it. That funny look in her eyes when I asked her if she was excited about seeing him and I wonder what else I didn't know about my friend Freya. What else she kept from me. 'Are you going to ask Verity what happened with *The Lens*?' I've got to appear as normal as I can, from now on. That means focusing on my work, focusing on getting into Oxford.

'Yes. At some point. We've got to wait for Freya to make a recovery, though.' Mrs Allen is now calling Mrs Pownall.

'Mrs Pownall, if you could come here, quickly, please. We've had further developments … No, absolutely nothing concrete so no need to call the police just yet … OK, many thanks. See you.' I open my mouth then shut it.

Curiously, I'm so certain that Freya will pull through that I don't give her a second thought. The idea that anything could happen to her is so … so … wrong that I simply will not accept it. Mrs Allen hangs up, still looking at the phone.

Father arrives that afternoon. He has driven himself, which is unheard of. His features look pinched, his shirt is crumpled.

'Josephine,' he says. 'Where's Freya?'

'She's in the hospital.'

'I've just spoken to Rollo. He's flown back from South Africa this morning. He's hightailing it to the hospital now. What happened?'

'She tried to kill herself.' Somehow, my voice comes out totally normal. 'What about Leon?' I ask, regretting how insensitive I sound. Father doesn't seem to care, or notice.

'Not sure. Last I heard he was staying with a friend. Good God. What are we going to do?' Father sits on the bench outside Mrs Allen's study and puts a red cashmere jumper next to him. I sit down and pick it up, putting it on my lap like it's a little baby. Underneath the sleeves, my fingers are pressed together so tightly I can feel the blood flooding to the tips.

'Why has Mrs Allen called me down here?'

'Because they think she tried to kill herself … because of me.' I watch Father's face as I say this. As I say the word 'kill', he goes red, then the blood seeps from his features. Saying the words out loud makes all this easier to deal with. They sound so absurd, coming out of my mouth that the whole thing turns into a farce in my head. But then, there's a strange, invisible force around my neck, as though I'm being garrotted and it takes me a moment to realise I haven't breathed for a long time and I start to choke.

'Are you OK?' he asks. 'Want some water?'

'No, thanks. Just swallowed the wrong way, that's all.'

'Why did she do it?' He's now taking off his watch and putting it back on again. 'Is she going to be OK?'

'I don't know. She's very ill.'

'What am I going to say to Rollo? His daughter tried to kill herself? My God. He's arriving soon. He said he didn't know any of the details. Just got a call from Mrs Allen telling him to come back straightaway. Suicide, Josephine. She's not yet eighteen? Josephine?'

'Yes.'

'Are you with me?'

'Yes.'

'Can you tell me what happened? Quickly. Before Mrs Allen gets here. She's gone to get Verity.'

'It seems Freya was having an affair with Mrs Kitts,' I say, hoping this will deflect from the suicide note.

'Mrs Kitts? Your housemistress?'

'Yes. But it hasn't come out for definite yet, so don't say a word.'

'And?' Bizarrely Father looks totally unperturbed by this piece of information.

'And then something was published in *The Lens*.' I look at Father to see if he has any recognition of my editorial triumph. Testing him.

'*The Lens*. What you wanted the PM for?'

'Yes. The PM.'

'Go on.'

'Well I sent the proof copy to the printer's and when it came back it seemed to have a piece about Freya. About her affair with Mrs Kitts.'

'Written by?'

'I have a few ideas. But it was there out of the blue. Ridiculous really. And then Freya tries to commit suicide. Left a note, blaming me. God knows why,' I say, quickly, in the hope this will somehow allow me to move on to his next question.

'Blaming *you*? What? This is all too absurd. I can't understand it. What's going on? You're her best friend.'

I don't know where to start with his line of questioning, so I keep quiet. I can hear the click of his watch strap over and over.

'Blaming you?' he says again, staring at me. I can't bear to look back at him.

'Yes. I have no idea why. I hadn't even seen her for ages. Perhaps she was a bit ... confused about what was going on? Not in the right frame of mind,' I say.

'Sounds like it. We'll find out anyway. Don't worry. In the meantime, who else knew about the affair?'

'Don't know.' I can't quite bring myself to admit to him that Freya hadn't told me about it, so I swiftly change subject. 'But I'm pretty convinced I know who's to blame for all of this.' I turn to look at him, gaining traction in my little speech.

'Who?'

'Verity.'

'Who's Verity?'

'My Deputy.'

'And why do you think it was her?'

Oxford. Oxford. It's got be Oxford. Perfect. I'm perfect and not like Mother.

'Because I gave her the proofs to take to the printer's and it didn't have the section about Freya in it. She's guilty. No one else could have got to it.'

'Right. OK. Well don't worry. We'll get this sorted. Sounds like it's got totally out of hand here.' I want to hug him for not questioning me further. For believing me.

'So yes, *The Lens* was good this year. The PM interview was great,' I say.

'Was it?'

'Yes.' He's distracted now, looking at his watch.

'What's the time?' I ask, although I'm not in the least bit interested.

'Twelve twenty. I've got a meeting at four.' With a sick feeling I realise Father doesn't believe, or disbelieve me. He's just in a hurry to get back to work.

'How's Ma?' I try.

'She's fine. Fine.'

'Right.'

'Is she at home at the moment?'

'Yes.' End of conversation. We sit for twenty minutes, me looking at the clock, Father tapping the chair. Finally Mrs Allen calls us in when Mrs Pownall arrives.

'Mrs Pownall.' She guides her hand towards Father. 'This is Mr Grey, Josephine's father, who has kindly agreed to come and speak to us.'

'Mr Grey,' says Mrs Pownall, as though she's at a cocktail party. She's wearing even more ridiculous clothes today – a frilled rah-rah dress that looks like something a cheerleader would wear, not a lady who's in her fifties. 'Thanks for joining us today. I know you are a busy man.'

'That's quite alright. No problem at all.' The edginess has all but disappeared. Father is now on form. The jacket comes off, but then he notices the crumples in his shirt and he puts it back on again. He sits up straight.

'Now, Mr Grey. I'm sure Josephine has filled you in but there seems to have been a bit of a commotion going on.'

'Yes. Josephine has indeed filled me in, haven't you, J?'

Mrs Allen makes a funny noise – a cross between a donkey's haw and a snort. She runs her fingers through her hair and looks at him.

'Right. Well we've got Mrs Pownall here waiting to ask a few questions. We would like to keep it in the school for the moment, just while we investigate. I'm sure you understand. Obviously there are these rather distasteful rumours, plus the awful events of last night. I understand you and Freya's father are very close.'

'That's right.'

'Great. Well he's currently on his way back from South Africa, so we'll expect to see him shortly. Last I heard he had just landed.' Mrs Allen gives Father a big smile. He smiles back and she puts a hand to her collarbone. 'Oh,' she tinkles.

'So, please do go ahead,' Father says. His eyes flicker down to his wrist. Mrs Pownall asks me why I think Freya would have written such a note. I tell her I do not know. That Freya seemed upset with the piece about her in *The Lens* and she probably named me because I was Editor and needed a scapegoat, or a deflection from what might get her into serious trouble.

'And I have no idea how that piece got in there,' I say.

'Right. Well then, do you have any ideas who might have done this? We need to get to the bottom of this soon. Was Freya the type who ... had ... how do I put this ... fixations?'

'No, no, she wasn't,' I say, surprised by my loyalty.

'And what about the note? Why would she do such a thing and blame you? Can you tell me what happened with your proof? You say you gave it to Verity Greenslade?'

'That's right. I went through the proof, which didn't have that piece about Freya in it, and then I gave it to Verity to deliver to the printer's.'

'Right. And Sally Aylsford can corroborate this?'

'Yes. She can.'

'And what was Sally doing there?'

'I promised her I would help her out. Give her a few things to do so she could get her name on the credits.'

'I see.' Mrs Pownall is chewing on a pen. Looking as though she's questioning me for murder. Which, in a sense, I suppose she is.

'She's fine, Sally. I don't think she even touched the copy when I left them both.'

'You think? How do you know this?'

'Because Verity took it from me and told me she gave it to the printer's.' I look at Mrs Pownall. Burn her with a stare and she stares back but then chickens out and looks down at her notes.

Father has started tapping his foot.

Mrs Allen notices and looks apologetic. 'Right. Mrs Pownall, shall we wind this up now?' She's looking at Father and taps her own watch, a conspiratorial rapport between two busy people.

Mrs Pownall is not quite finished. 'Jill, I've had a chat with the other governors, and we think it might be suitable if you called in a counsellor. In case any of the girls need to talk.'

Mrs Allen looks horrified but says yes anyway, that she will. 'Josephine and Mr Grey, you've been extremely helpful. Thank you ever so much for coming down, Mr Grey. I'll see you both out, shall I?' We all walk out the door and, as we leave, Rollo is stepping out of a big, shiny silver car. He's looking tanned and fat. His stride is abrupt but I can see his hands shaking as he grips on to his soft leather suitcase. He sees us. Sees Father shaking hands with Mrs Allen and stops where he is, crunching his toes into the gravel. Father strides up to him, arms open and, when he does, Rollo pulls his arm back, as though he's about to throw a punch in Father's face. We both step back and Rollo drops his arm. Tired. Bows his head and rubs his eyes. I don't speak. Wait for Father to open his mouth.

Rollo whispers to me, 'What have you done to my daughter?' he says.

Father holds up his palms. 'Leave Josephine out of this. She had nothing to do with it.'

'That's not what I heard. Mrs Kitts rang me just now. She told me about the note Freya left.' Rollo sniffs. More as an act of aggression, as though he is inhaling energy from the air, ready to throw another punch. 'Said you put something about Freya in the public domain?'

'It wasn't me,' I reply.

'Who was it then? How can Freya have got it wrong?'

'I don't know who it was. They're questioning Verity Greenslade.'

'Verity?'

'She's my Deputy.'

'Why would they be questioning her?'

'She was the last person to take the proof to the printer's.'

Rollo nods his head. 'Is there any reason why she would have wanted to do this to my daughter?'

'Me, I think. I think she was out to get me.' The lies are coming so easily I've begun to believe myself, that Verity is actually to blame. The deception feels frighteningly, deliriously exciting. *Catch me out if you can,* I think.

'She had a thing about me. Me and Freya. Wanted to be friends with Freya. Was out to get me.' Then I tell him about the Anne Dunne Scholarship – not all of it, but just enough to incriminate dear Verity – and his mouth opens and he stands up straight with renewed vigour and walks into the main school building.

'Rollo,' Father shouts after him.

'Yes?'

'She'll be OK.'

He says nothing, only nods. We watch as he walks into the school and Father looks at his watch one final time.

'Right. Great to see you. Don't let this Verity girl get the better of you.'

Is that all he has to say to me?

'I won't.'

'And when do you hear about Oxford?'

Oxford. Oxford.

'Interviews are still going on. After Christmas I think. I have no idea what's going on at the moment. I just hope Mrs Allen doesn't have to tell them what's going on.'

'That's not going to happen. I won't let it. You just make this go away. Do you understand? You make your own history. Alright? Don't be defeated.' Father places his hands on my shoulders and looks me in the eye.

'OK? Nothing will stop you.'

'Nothing,' I echo.

2014

I don't see Gracie for a few days. When I ask around, I'm told she's still here but that no one knows why she's keeping herself to herself. I spend this time writing letters, having therapy sessions and watching documentaries. In the silence of my surroundings, without the fear of Freya hunting me out, I start to think of Mother. The way in which I think she loved me, when she was able. I start to wish that I hadn't been so frightened of her. That her paranoid behaviour hadn't felt so threatening to me. That I had tried to understand it – her illness – a bit more. It was Father who once told me that, during her most paranoid times, she would often be lucid to the point of genius. I wished, more than anything, that I hadn't been kept away from her at those points.

Dr Anthony spends a lot of time talking about Mother with me, going through her symptoms, her feelings. It's helpful and her memory takes on a different light. He's a lot more receptive after speaking to me in depth. Today's session, he asks what I had wanted to tell him in our first meeting.

'Nothing,' I reply. The thought of Gracie being in here has made me unwilling to talk. He stares at me for a few seconds, unblinking but with a gentleness in his eyes. I feel my throat relax.

'It was just that someone is trying to find me. It's all tied up with the past and ... that's it, really. And actually, one of your patients knew the girl who has been trying to get in contact. Gracie Lovell. She's still here, right?'

Dr Anthony twirls his pen and places it at right angles to his notepad. Straightens it out and then adds another pen perpendicular to that.

'I can't talk about our other patients, sadly. But if anyone's making you feel uncomfortable, please do let me know. I can sort something out. Move either you or her to a different wing.'

'No, no, she's not at all. It's just weird, that's all. A constant physical reminder of the past.'

'And what happens when you see her?'

'Nothing. Nothing.' I don't want him to think she's having a detrimental effect on my mental state so I ask him when he thinks I'll be ready to go home.

'Do you feel any better?' he asks.

'I do, actually. It's nice being in here.' I look down at my clothes and realise I'm mixing up my wardrobe a bit. I'm wearing jeans and a T-shirt that I would normally wear with a skirt. Something must be happening to me. Then I ask him the question that has been haunting me since I arrived.

'Do you think I'm feeling better because I'm relieved Mother's died? If so, isn't that a bit strange?'

'No. I think you've lived under the fear of your mother's illness for so long that, in one sense, it's a relief she's gone because with her so is the threat. On the other hand, you'll find yourself grieving for the mother you never had. Grief is complex and the reactions we have are always different, which doesn't make them wrong or right – just right for us. Some people close down and others break down.'

'Hmmm. Which one am I?' I laugh and then I think of Freya and how she used to complain that I had no feelings. 'Like a machine'. That very second, I find myself totally desperate to find out what Freya wants from me, and before I can betray myself I tell Dr Anthony that I've got to go, that I've got a yoga session booked and that I'll see him soon.

'Fine,' he says. 'Just make sure you take it easy on yourself. And do those mental exercises I told you about. OK?'

'Yes. Of course. Thank you.'

I walk out into the corridor of the building and make my way to Gracie's room. It's locked and so are the doors of her next-door neighbours. I go round the garden but she's not there either. There's a teenage girl sitting there reading a book by the hedge, wearing hot pants and a lumberjack shirt tied up above her belly button.

She sees me looking at her stomach and pulls down the knot. 'Just relaxing,' she says.

'Don't worry. I couldn't care less if you were naked. Do you know where Gracie Lovell is? That girl I was talking to the other day at supper?'

'Oh yes, I know exactly the one you mean,' she replies. 'She was in my breathing class yesterday. She looked awful. All weird and haunted. Like, she had seen something that had frightened the life out of her.'

'Really? Like what?'

'She just had this strange look in her eyes. Like ... I don't know.'

'Do you know where she might be now?'

'No idea. Oh – wait, hang on, actually, there's those special therapy lessons going on – the ones where you learn those new techniques? I can't remember what they're called. But anyway, she's probably there. She's always in those classes. The list is up at the main entrance. You'll find the timetable there.'

'Thanks. Thanks a lot.'

'No worries.' She rolls over, pushes up her tartan top, right near her breasts even though it's freezing cold, and starts reading her book again.

The timetable is a large sheet of paper, full of illegible markings and highlighted sections. I look for today's session and find a class called 'Life, Body and Soul. Breathe yourself better.'

It's signposted as being in the Clareville Wing, so I make my way over through the main building. The corridors go from smelling of boys' locker rooms, to antiseptic and, when I finally reach the therapy rooms, the scented candles come as a welcome relief.

I can see Gracie through the door window and the girl was right. She looks dreadful. Everyone is standing up, all aligned and neat, and she's lying down. I can see her eyes shut but they are all red-rimmed. Her skin looks waxy, like she's dead and, for a minute, I can't see her breathing and I'm about to go in when I see her rolling onto her side and looking straight at me. She sees me, lifts her hand a couple of inches off the ground then shuts her eyes again.

I wait for the class to finish and she comes out, pushes past me with a white towel in her hands and runs off down to her room. I'm so perplexed by this, after how cosy she was with me the other day, that I don't think to chase after her.

'Are you alright?' says one of the patients.

'Yes, fine, I was just trying to speak to that girl there.' I point down the corridor but Gracie has gone.

'Ah, Gracie? She spent the entire class crying. Didn't do anything at all. Poor thing.'

'Oh.' I can't think of anything else to say, so I thank the girl and walk to Gracie's room before something else stops me.

I can hear a strange noise when I press my ear against the door and it's Gracie howling. I knock anyway and she opens up immediately, like she's expecting me.

'Come in.' She points to her bed, which has all the sheets rucked up at the bottom. There's orange make-up smeared over the sheets, which is really odd, given that she's been totally barefaced since I've seen her in here.

'Sorry it's a bit of a mess.' That's an understatement. There are empty water bottles filled with sweet wrappers all over the floor, ripped-out pages of magazines strewn all over the room and her clothes and shoes look like she's tipped them out and flung them all over the floor. There are even dead flowers stuffed in an open drawer.

'No worries.' I sit down on a red-leather-covered wooden chair and wait for her to do something. Instead, she just stands staring at me.

'My husband's left me,' she laughs. She's itching her nose in a manic fashion and then throws her head back and laughs even more in a freaky way. Then she starts crying and crying. I sit and look outside the window, until she's finished. There's not much to look at – a concrete wall and a long hosepipe taped up with plastic binding, presumably to stop people hanging themselves with it. The thought gives me a wry smile and then Gracie leaps at me. 'What are you laughing at? Me? Are you laughing at me? You always laughed at people, didn't you? You and Freya.'

'No, I'm really not laughing at you,' I say, still looking at the hosepipe. 'I was thinking of something else entirely.'

'Oh. I feel you were laughing at me.'

'I promise I wasn't.' Then Gracie lies on her bed and cries for what feels like an hour. When her sobs subside, I ask her if she's alright, whether she needs me to make her some tea, or bring her some water. She turns to face me, eyes all swollen.

'You're being kind,' she says, lifting her head up off the bed. 'Really kind to me. Thanks for sitting here with me.' Gracie seems genuinely shocked. It's nice to see her smiling a bit, so I move and sit next to her on the bed and tell her I'm sorry she's so upset. She cries some more.

'How come you are being so nice to me?' she laughs. 'You must have changed since school.' The slight hurts more than I would have expected it to.

'I guess school was … different,' I reply.

'It was, wasn't it?' Gracie finds the strength to sit up and I move her forward and place an extra pillow behind her. The intimacy of it is both strange and comforting to me.

'Gracie, I know you are feeling bad at the moment but I wondered if you could tell me what Freya wanted. When she was phoning everyone from school. Asking about me, I mean. I just, well … it's in my head at the moment and I thought you might be able to help me.'

Pleased to be asked, Gracie reaches out and pats my arm. She slumps back onto her pillow and starts to talk.

'She got in touch with everyone from our year. She's been ringing around for the past two months. So Sarah Maynard said. She's been really hunting you down. She's been harassing everyone about when they last saw you.'

'Everyone in our year? But that's over fifty people,' I say, shocked.

'Right. Well I don't know if it was *literally* everyone. But most. I was away at the time, with Felix's school. Volunteering at their summer camp.' Gracie starts crying again and then shakes her head muttering to herself to pull it together. 'So.' She takes a deep breath. 'On my last day at the school trip, Neil – that's my husband – actually, ex-husband, rang the landline at the cottage where we were all staying. Said there must have been an emergency of some sort because this Freya woman had rung so many times.'

Gracie stops there and reaches over to the bedside table and pulls out a tissue from a box.

'Do you want me to go on?' she asks.

'Yes. Please.'

'OK, so anyway, I think it's very peculiar but I can't do much about it because there's nigh on forty boys running around in this summer camp place and so I decide to wait till we're back home to ring her.'

'Go on, Gracie. You're being great. I appreciate it.'

'So then I get back and ring her and she is being really, really weird with me. I mean, I was never really very good friends with her but she says that she had to find you and that I was her last hope because she'd been through everyone else in the year whilst I had been away.'

The floor is spinning but I'm having to show Gracie I'm totally calm.

'OK, go on.'

Gracie gets up and picks out those flowers from her drawer. She sniffs one, tickling her nose with it.

'Well, so then the weirdest thing of all happened. And actually I had forgotten about this because of stuff with my husband and everything. But she said the strangest thing. She said that I had played my part in all of this. That I had been instrumental in nearly ... causing her to go six feet under. Because I'd given her the wrong stuff? Something that was too much for her? I couldn't really make sense of what she was trying to tell me ...'

As Gracie's saying this, I can tell she's remembering Freya, those sunken eyes after the suicide attempt, and there's a small gasp, a hint of a memory that I can tell has jolted her into the room. She looks at me, eyes huge, questioning, pleading.

'What you *gave* her?' I say. 'What did you give her?'

'Oh my God,' she says. 'Freya. She was getting at something in particular, wasn't she? About me being responsible for her nearly dying? I honestly had no idea what she was talking about on the phone. So I just sort of thought she was sounding a bit mad. That she wasn't making sense. I wasn't even friends with the girl, really. I always wanted to be, but really, I kept myself to myself, didn't I? I see what she meant now ... I see. I think she is blaming *me*? Blaming me for her suicide attempt?'

'How can she blame you for something she did, Gracie? Don't be ridiculous, you're just adding one plus one and getting four.'

'No, no, I remember now, Josephine. I remember all of it. I hadn't thought much of it but she's right, Josephine. She's right. What am I going to do? Does she know you're here?'

'No. No one does. I was worried you might tell her.'

'No, I haven't wanted to get back in contact. Especially not now. Josephine, am I really to blame?' Gracie wipes her nose on the edge of her top. Her fingernails are all grey.

'Well you haven't told me what you think you are to blame for, Gracie, I have no idea what you are talking about. Freya tried to kill herself at school; she blamed me for sending her over the edge. I've had to live with that for many years. I don't see what you've got to do with it.'

'Well, I'm not sure but I think she's talking about the pills. *I* gave her the pills. We had been in the san together for some reason I can't quite recall, so she knew I had them. She wanted loads, you see. Said she had period pains and could I give her all the painkillers I had. I had some left over from my appendicitis operation. I gave them all to her. They were super strong. Codeine. I didn't tell her the dosage or anything. I remember her hand, snatching the packet from me. And me being so pathetically grateful that I had been able to help her, I hadn't really given it a second thought. I remember her coming back afterwards with bandages around her wrist, so I didn't really think of the connection before. Thought she had …' Gracie makes a slicing motions towards her wrist. 'And now she's blaming me for giving her the wrong pills. I think she was telling me they nearly killed her? But if she meant to … I don't understand, if she wasn't attempting suicide, why would it …?' Gracie stops and looks at me. Her eyes have gone all fiery and she's trying to wipe her nose but her fingers are shaking. The impact of what we've just discovered seems to hit Gracie harder than me.

'Ah yes, she did both. Pills and cut her wrists,' I reply, thinking back to when I first saw Freya being wheeled out on that stretcher, fluorescent laces shining in the dark. And then I think of her afterwards, in the hospital, hair shorn and bloodied. Freya, I think. What did you do to yourself? I start to question everything in my mind and I look at Gracie and she's looking back at me, ready to speak but not wanting to break the silence. In the past ten minutes the memory of Freya is taking a more fluid shape and I can't pin down my thoughts enough to process this new information but a new idea forms in my mind. I open my mouth, stutter on my words and, when I finally manage to talk, I ask Gracie if she'll go and get me a drink of water.

1996

I say goodbye to Father and sit on the school bench just by the main gates. Mrs Allen has told me not to leave the school premises. Verity comes out two hours later. Rollo had left by then, in his big silver car, slowly leaving the gates as if he can't quite bring himself to go to the hospital. He had seen me waiting, sitting. Waved.

Verity doesn't wave when she sees me. Doesn't do anything other than walk right up to me and slap me across the face. I hold my head up high and stare at her, trying not to blink. Then she walks right off and doesn't turn back. I wonder if anyone's seen but not a soul is around. The sting burns my cheek. It feels good to have some physical pain. It's nothing compared to that night. Nothing. Maybe this is why Freya slices her skin the way she does. And then I feel anger. *How dare she?* I think. *I'm Head Girl - she is my Deputy.* I wonder if I should tell anyone then realise the moment is gone and I get up and go inside. I see Mrs Allen and she looks at my cheek.

'What happened?' she asks.

'Nothing. I just saw Verity,' I say, lightly.

She looks at my cheek again.

'Oh. I see. Well, we've had a long chat with her. She seems to think it's you. Trying to frame her, or something ridiculous like that. We're now losing sight of the real problem, which is Freya and the fact she might have been abused.'

I am horrified, the word feels like an electric shock. 'Abused?'

'By a teacher.' The word 'abuse' had never crossed my mind.

'Maybe they were in love?' I say. Mrs Allen scoffs.

'Mrs Kitts is being questioned now,' she says.

'And Freya?'

'She's pulling through. Seemed to rally round when she found out her dad was coming. She's been in and out of consciousness but she managed to sit up earlier, apparently.' Mrs Allen looks at me. Rubs the fleshy bit of her palm with her thumb.

'Josephine. You know I trust you. That's why I made you Head Girl. I trust your decisions. I trust your word.' I'm waiting for the guilt to kick in but it doesn't. All I can see is Verity's hand coming towards me.

'So I need you to tell me you are onside with this.'

'Of course, Mrs Allen. Of course. I just want Freya to get better, that's all,' I say. And I mean it. I feel bad that she's gone through all this. But now I know she's going to pull through, I've got to concentrate on the matter in hand.

And Oxford. And keeping my Head Girl badge. I've let the scholarship go, I cannot, will not, let anything else slip away.

'Right. Well we also need to find out what happened with *The Lens* sooner or later. Because of course whoever did this will be expelled.'

'Expelled?' It had never crossed my mind that the punishment would be that harsh.

'Of course. Expelled. And if that happens, we'll have to inform the appropriate universities, whether or not we've heard if you've got a place.'

'Of – of course, Mrs Allen.'

'Are you alright, Josephine? You look pale.'

'I'm absolutely fine.' I clench my stomach muscles. 'I'm just thinking about Freya, that's all.'

'Right. Well I'll let you know of any developments.' Mrs Allen reaches forward and squeezes my shoulder. I tense up and she moves her hand away.

'Don't worry, alright? I'll make sure Freya realises none of this is you.'

'Thank you,' I reply. 'Thank you very much.' I realise this is Mrs Allen's way of saying she believes me. Me and not Verity Greenslade. I'm still worried, though. Worried something will come out, somehow. In my head, I've covered all bases. Mrs Cape and Pete. Told everyone I had given the proof to Verity to hold from the moment she left the school up until it went to the printer's. The only fly in the ointment would be if Sally Aylsford said anything. The only way she might is if she doesn't get into Oxford. The realisation of this hits me harder than Verity's slap. She may feel duped. I have to make her think I've done everything to keep her onside. Immediately I go and find her and tell her that I'm going to give her coaching. That she is going to get into Oxford, her interview is going to be brilliant, and I'm going to help her. I will go over and over all her notes until she has everything drummed into her head. Her interview is in two days and we sit down for three hours, discussing possibilities of what might come up, and what they had asked me.

'You can't get nervous,' I say. 'Because that will make you fluff your lines.'

'I am nervous, though,' she says. 'I'm terrified.' She's pulling at her hair and putting the end of her ponytail in her mouth. 'I can't let my father down. And all this stuff with Freya. It's putting me off my stride.'

I ignore that last part. 'Right. So what are you really good at? What are you best at?'

'Lacrosse, I guess?' she says doubtfully. I will myself to be patient.

'No,' I say slowly, 'I mean as a person. In conversation. What are you good at?'

She looks down, sucks at her ponytail. 'Nothing.'

For God's sake. 'You are. Yes you are. You persuaded me to talk to Mrs Allen. You did a great job there. I wasn't willing at first but you managed to talk me round. That was really good. So persuasive.' She hangs her head. Scratches at her cheek.

'No, no don't look like that. It's a good thing,' I say. 'We've got to use this to your advantage. Use that in your interview. If they're trying to outsmart you, you can use those skills. Don't you get it?'

'Yes. Yes, I do.'

'Right. And don't suck your ponytail like that. Sit straight. Put your hands on your lap. Like this …' I place both hands flat on my thighs. She does the same. Already she looks better. 'Up. Sit further up. Straight. That's good. Now, when they ask you a question, look them directly in the eye. Answer. Don't think too much about their reaction. Just answer.'

She inhales. 'How do you know all this?'

'Watching people's reactions,' I reply. 'Now concentrate.' I ask her a series of questions. Difficult ones. The higher she sits, the better she answers. And she can see the nod of my head, the smile on my lips and she is bolstered. Sits up even higher, straightens her fingers out and she's beginning to really get it.

'What about the Cosmological Argument? What would an atheist have to say about that?' I ask. She looks flummoxed. Brings her hand up to her ponytail.

I scrape my chair forward and slap her hand down.

'Stop.'

'Sorry, sorry,' she mutters.

'Don't say sorry. Just do as I say. If you can't answer the question, think of a way round it. That's what you'll be good at. Just pretend you are in a social situation. OK? Pretend that you are with me, trying to get me to get you into Oxford. Don't think of yourself as Sally Aylsford trying to impress these people. Think of yourself as Sally Aylsford, Oxford candidate, with the cunning of a fox.' She laughs and so do I. It sounds odd, these bubbles of sound escaping from my mouth. Even Sally looks taken aback. I feel self-conscious and put the back of my hand up to my face. 'Now you're doing it,' she says. And we both laugh some more.

'Right. Let's go again. Ready?'

'Ready.' Hours later, when Sally's mouth is all sticky from talking and lack of water, we get up.

'I think you can do it,' I say.

'Really?'

'Yes. But only if you do as I say.'

'Thank you. Thank you. You are the only one to have told me that.' I want her to feel indebted to me, so she will never tell people the truth, but I also realise that I've had fun for the first time in ages and perhaps, just perhaps, I'm the one that should feel indebted.

2014

Gracie and I are still in her room half an hour later. My mind is curling around the fact that Freya never meant to kill herself. Beautiful, golden Freya, who was so desperate after what happened that she was driven to make it look as though she wanted to die and, unwittingly, she nearly did. I look at Gracie, who's rubbing my arm and telling me to stop shaking and that whatever I'm thinking, it's OK. She's feeding me sips of water from a white plastic cup and I'm grateful she's here to help me.

And then I think of Freya and that there was no one there to help her when she needed it most. No one. When she was shrinking into hell from the pain of what happened, I was the only person during that time who could really have done something and I wasn't there. Instead, I shut her down, over and over, so she could see no other way out. Freya, who would have given her right arm to make me happy. Who could hardly bear to even swat at a fly. To think that she was driven to this by ... me.

'Josephine? Do you want me to call someone?' I can hear the echo of Gracie's voice but I can't respond. Not just yet.

Freya still needs me. She needs to talk to me again and I'm doing the same thing, shutting her down again and even if ... even if she wants to hurt me, that's OK because I know if I don't, history will come smashing back at me. In trying so hard to cast away the shadows of Mother, I'm letting this whole scenario work its way into my life again, eighteen years later. When I think of this, Freya's beautiful smile fades from my mind and I'm left with the image of her snarling at me, red-eyed. Her shouting at me outside Mrs Kitts's study that time, telling me I was a bitch. Those red eyes, hunting me, willing me to come back at her so she could go on the attack.

I start thinking about Freya's suicide note that Mrs Allen handed me all those years ago.

The more I think about it, the more the words in that note weren't Freya. Just an approximation of her. They were never meant as a reality. A cry for help, yes. A cry for me to confess the events of that night in a public forum, just like I had done with *The Lens*. I claw back the memory of her writing on that crisp, white page. The smart writing paper she had used to leave her mark.

A confession: I'm sorry to do this but I can't cope anymore. I can't go on. Josephine Grey, you outed me and my love and this is what I have to do, to get away from it all … I'm going to kill myself. Sorry to everyone who I've hurt but I have to do this. Freya Seymour.

Dissecting her words now, I see that if Freya had truly intended on ending it all, she would never, ever have called Mrs Kitts 'her love'. At best, Mrs Kitts was a distraction for Freya. A distraction from her mother's death, a distraction from the fact she wasn't crazily academic in a school that prided itself on being so. A distraction from life. Mrs Kitts offered her the glamour of insight into adulthood. Except there must have clearly been something wrong with Mrs Kitts for her to have an affair with a student. I can see Freya now, toying with her, offering up her youthful flesh and the promise of exciting times when she left school. The reality was, Freya was set on going to Oxford, marrying a good-looking, high-achiever called Guy, and settling down into a boho-chic life of travelling and work. This note was not Freya intentionally wanting to die, to be disintegrated into the earth. No. It was a desperate, desperate clutch at survival.

A clarity seeps into me and I know that if I need to help Freya, and myself, I must resolve to see her. I know that if I don't she'll never let go, and that she's right not to. Because, otherwise, I won't be able to either.

1996

Sally Aylsford goes to her interview and I wave her off by the school gates.

As she gets onto the bus, I stretch my back up, making a pulling motion at the top of my head. 'Up,' I mouth.

She gives me a thumbs-up and, as I'm shouting good luck, I can see Mrs Kitts walking out the gates alongside Mrs Pownall and Mrs Allen. She's holding two suitcases and her husband is behind her. Her head is down and Mr Kitts is sliding his hands down his face. He is saying something, I can't quite hear but Mrs Kitts is shouting back: 'Nothing. Nothing.'

'A child,' he replies. 'Just a child.' And then I can see tears running down his face. Oh God, get it together, *please*.

Mrs Allen asks all the sixth-form Prefects for a meeting in the aftermath of Mrs Kitts's departure.

'Girls.' She's flicking through a copy of *The Lens*. Just watching her makes the sides of my throat come together.

'Girls, as you probably know by now, Mrs Kitts has left the school. She didn't admit much and Freya still hasn't said anything either other than what she wrote in her note, so we don't have anything to go on, but she's left voluntarily. Suffice to say she won't be coming back and I hope that'll be the end of it.

Now, it looks like Freya's definitely going to make a full recovery so, until she does, I suggest you girls go about your business. When she returns, we'll try and find out a bit more about what happened. If you decide there's any information you must impart, my door is always open.'

'Mrs Allen.' Verity's raising her hand high in the air, lifting herself off the seat as though she's begging to answer a question in class. 'Can we go and see her? Freya, I mean.'

'I'm not sure that's wise at the moment, Verity, given the circumstances. I'll tell her you were asking after her. See what she says.' It's at that point that I decide what to do next. I will go and see Freya myself. I need to see her face. To believe she is getting better and to see the life in her. Otherwise the last time I will have seen her, she would have been carried out on a stretcher, limp and, in my head, gone forever. The rest of the girls file out slowly. I stay behind. I can see Verity pause, desperate to know what I want, but I move over and wave her out, shutting the door behind her.

'Mrs Allen, do you mind if I go to the library now?'

'No, of course not.'

'Sorry – I mean the library in town.'

'Right. Fine. Just make sure you sign out and don't come back after … it's four o'clock now so just make sure you are back for supper.'

I make my way out of the school gates and up to the hospital. The receptionist tells me where to go and I ask if Freya's father is still there. 'You'll have to find out yourself,' she says, looking down at her magazine. 'Third floor. Ivy Ward, bed six.'

The lift stinks. A sweet smell of body odour and disinfectant. Most people hate hospitals. I love them. There's a certain type of security I get when I'm in one. Perhaps it's something to do with having seen my mother in so many. Knowing she's safer there than in her own home. There's the sterile smell, the swish of the mops, the human stench. Anonymity. That is, until I walk past the Ivy Ward. There is an old woman, in her own room, just before the nurses' station. She is caterwauling, with a piece of broccoli stuck to her chin and her legs are out of the sheets. Blotched red, blue, yellow. I can see her catheter filling up with yellow liquid.

There's no one at the nurses' station. I can see Freya's name in green marker pen, on a big whiteboard. *Freya Seymour. Ivy Ward, bed 6.*

I walk down a long corridor. It's quiet, apart from whispers, beeps of the machines and the rustle of newspapers and magazines. I see someone in bed six. Thankfully there's no one else there. This person has a shorn head. Where is she? Then, I remember Mrs Kitts waving that ponytail around. *Freya, what have you done?* Her hair? What happened to her hair? I step closer and can see little baubles of blood congealed into the scalp. There are marks, red lines, across her skull.

I sit down next to the bed. Her eyes are closed. The bed is narrow but somehow she looks lost within it. She looks quite peaceful. I've seen her asleep a million times and, for one moment, it's like we are hanging out together after a big night out. Freya would always nod off whilst we were talking, keen to stay awake so as not to offend me. I can see her eyeballs flickering ever so gently. I walk over. Sit down. Wait. A thin, loping nurse walks past and points to her watch.

'Visiting hours finish at eight, remember,' she says. And Freya turns her head, ever so slightly. There's a shift in her eye movement. I can see the shuddering stop. Peaceful now. *What were you dreaming about, Freya?* Was it a good dream? Or was it filled with horrors? The horrors of why you are here now, in this bed with your arm crooked against the wires and tape, your bloodied head. Your eyes that look like they did when we tried to do the 'smoky-eyed look' from *Just Seventeen*. It's perfect now. Did you really do this because of me? How could I have done this to you? I touch her hand. The skin is soft, like a kitten's nose.

Her eyes open, just a fraction, then shut. I find myself startled out of my reverie and I come to. What am I *doing* here? If Freya woke up and saw me, she'd probably have a screaming fit. Or call the police. I seem to have forgotten that I'm the reason she's in this place. I walk backwards out of the room, staring at her, willing for her to wake up and see me just for one second, so I can see her reaction. To see how much hate there is in her eyes. She doesn't. She stays peacefully asleep, so I run back to school, ready to behave as though everything is totally normal and that I haven't just come back from hell.

For supper, there's spaghetti Bolognese, chicken Maryland or baked potatoes with cheese and beans. I opt for the chicken. No one speaks to me as I make my way through the girls and then I see Sally. She's sitting with a load of girls from the year below and I go and join them. I remember I haven't yet found out about how her Oxford interview went. All the girls look up from their food, wondering why on earth I would be sitting with them – the younger years – and I offer nothing by way of explanation.

Sally looks at me a couple of times, frowning and leaning her neck forward, silently saying, *Are you OK?* I give her a brief nod. 'Fine,' I mouth, putting pieces of chicken into my mouth.

She looks worried. I try to reassure her. 'Sally, I bet you did brilliantly in your interview,' I say. 'Tell me all about it after supper?'

She gestures for us to go and I pick up my tray, leave with her. 'Is all OK?' She links arms with me.

'Fine. Fine. I just wanted to find out how things went.'

'Great. I think it went great. I don't know but I think they'll make me an offer. Unless I totally misread them.'

'I'm sure you didn't.'

'Really? Do you really think so?'

'I'm sure. Did you do everything I told you to do?'

'Yes. Everything. It helped so much. Josephine, thank you. I'm not getting my hopes up but thank you. For everything.'

'No problem.' Strangely, I want to confide in Sally. Want to tell her that I want this whole thing to be over. That I went to see Freya and that the whites of her eyes will haunt me forever. Instead, I ask her what questions she was asked in the interview.

'What about you?' she asks, when she's finished telling me. 'Do you think you've got a place guaranteed? I mean ... it's you, so of course you have but, I mean ... did you find the interview OK?'

'Yes,' I reply. 'Interview was fine. But, of course, I have to wait and see how this whole thing with Freya pans out.'

'Why?' she asks.

'Because if any of us are found guilty of *The Lens*, we get expelled. And that means we might get our offers rescinded from our universities. If we get an offer, of course.' I look at her and she doesn't react. Looks down slightly but other than that, nothing.

'Sally?' I say. I can't believe I'm actually in this position with Sally Aylsford of all people.

'Yes?' she replies.

'What do you think?' I ask.

'I think that we'll be alright. Just carry on. Just carry on as we are now and deny everything and we'll be alright.' She turns to me. Her cheeks have fired up. 'I can't let my father down. I just can't,' she says, mouth set.

She's with me. She feels the same way so now I can't go back. I can't ruin Sally's life too.

2014

The doctors and nurses are worried about me. They say I'm not eating enough again. In truth, I'm totally preoccupied with the idea of seeing Freya. I'm starting to feel weightless with the idea of it. But at the same time, I don't want to leave the comfort of this place; the thought of not being told what to do and how to fill my days fills me with dread. I've grown used to not having to think about where to go, what to do next. No pressure to perform and no responsibility. But I'm going to have to leave here at some point and all I can think about is what Gracie and I discovered together and the thought that Freya is never going to give up tracking me down. I decide to get someone else's take on the whole thing.

'You seem ... lighter,' Dr Anthony says at our next session, as he hands me some water.

'I'm just trying to work a few things out. I'm ... this girl ... the one from my past. She's called Freya. I'm wondering whether to see her. Things have changed. The idea of her in my head has changed and I'm just trying to work out how to best deal with it.'

'Would you like to tell me a bit more about her? What happened with her?' Academically, I want someone to talk through it with, the events that followed that night – *The Lens*, the attempted suicide. Emotionally, though, I'm not sure I am capable.

'What's stopping you?' Dr Anthony leans forward and taps the desk with his right hand, a movement that makes him seem impatient, even though I know he just wants me to talk.

'It's just quite a lot to go into. That's all. I can't even be sure I've got all the details right. Remember everything correctly. It was so long ago.' I give a nervous little laugh.

'That's alright. Why don't you start with how you met this girl? What you remember about her. Those first impressions. Then we can go on from there. Stop any time you feel uncomfortable.'

I talk about the Freya I used to know. Before all the horrid stuff. The innocence of her, even when bad things happened. Those eyes, alight with hope and joy. And the confidence, even when her mother was dying with all the surrounding ugliness, that of course everything would be alright. Her body was like a gilded cage that no amount of hurt could penetrate. The buttery tone of her skin. The straightness of her nose. The rich curve of her lips that always hovered on a smile. My friend Freya.

'You look sad,' Dr Anthony says. 'You look as though you want to tell me more.'

I don't really, but Dr Anthony's voice is hypnotic. And I feel so, so tired. Too tired to resist.

'Well, she was just Freya. Everyone at school wanted to be her. She would come in wearing a new pair of shoes and, the next half-term, everyone would come back wearing the same ones. I made her wear a pair of her mother's old platforms once, just as a joke and, of course, they came in fashion the month after. She was just one of those types. And she just got people. But then she changed. Something in her changed.'

'Why did she change, do you think?'

'I don't know.' I dare Dr Anthony to accuse me of lying. To tell me I do know.

'Can you think of any occasion that led her to change? Or was it that your relationship became different?'

'Both. Probably. Just that … we, we drifted apart and then there was this whole thing where I published something I shouldn't have done in the school newspaper and…'

Dr Anthony is drawing lines on a notepad. Long, strokes of black pen. 'And?'

'And then she attempted suicide and all this time I never realised but I think, perhaps, that she didn't mean to do it. I thought she just got lucky. That she got saved in time but…'

'Oh?' Dr Anthony's now making sharp little lines on the page. I can't even begin to explain about Gracie and how we found this all out, so I let it lie.

'I think … Well, I think that …' I stop for a moment. Dr Anthony tells me to take my time. 'I think she might have felt betrayed by some of the things I did. Felt that her suicide attempt might have been the only way she could get through to me. Didn't mean it to go so far but wanted my … or someone's attention. It's just so…'

Dr Anthony nods and stares at me with an expression I can't work out. Concern? Trying to make sense of the things I've told him?

I sit and wait for Dr Anthony to speak but he doesn't say a thing. Just scratches a point on the page and hovers his pen over the desk.

And, out of nowhere, it happens. A flash. It happens so quickly I can't grasp it back. A flash of that night. It's the first memory recall I've had of that time, beyond blurs of lights and sound and drips of red and the roar of the dance floor. Freya is standing over me, smiling, as I take a drink she's bought for me. Her hips are swaying in time to the music, in that slow, sexy way of hers, as though she knows absolutely everybody is looking at her. I remember being in awe of her then and, still, now.

I remember feeling short next to her, as though she was the tallest goddess in the world and then thinking it was probably the half a pill I had taken kicking in. But no, she really was like that. Like she was the tallest girl in the world. Then the memory fades and it's replaced by a blackness that seeps through me. 'Here.' Dr Anthony passes me a tissue. I wave his hand away until I realise I'm crying. Again? What the hell is wrong with me?'

'Don't worry. Just carry on talking.'

'I've got nothing else to say.' I'm distracted, obsessed with getting back to real life. To get this meeting sorted quickly, face things head-on and pray Freya isn't trying to destroy me, so I can rid myself of this noose around my neck.

'Josephine? How about telling me more about your mother then?'

'Oh, my mother? Well, I didn't see her much. I didn't want ... or rather, don't want, to become ill like her, put it that way.'

'And have you ever thought you were?'

I think back to all those times at school, where I was paranoid, convinced my mind was turning, convinced other students were out to get me and then realising it was just my mind playing tricks but how would I know? How would I know if I was ill or just...

'I have. Yes. All throughout my school years. I would have this image of my mother, screaming that the devil was in her. And when I was at school, I was always frightened that I would end up doing that unaware in class. I lived that fear, breathed it. It became alive in everything I touched and did.'

'That must have been very exhausting for you,' Dr Anthony says. 'And yet you still managed to excel?'

'I did. Although I was always fearful, in a strange way the school routine away from home gave me stability. But I guess I burned out. Then all this stuff with Freya happened. And that was it really.'

I can't go on any longer. My voice has gone. It's like all the speech has been sucked back inside me. All the ugliness. I've got too much to think about and, even though the lights are dim, they feel way too bright. I shake my head and Dr Anthony beckons for me to go. He looks up at the clock and says, 'Only five minutes left anyway. Well done. You did well today.'

I didn't do well, but I shut the door and, as I'm leaving, I hear Dr Anthony shouting after me. 'You'll have to think about what changed. What changed your relationship with Freya, I mean. For next week? OK?'

'OK,' I whisper. I walk away, as fast as I can. I'm going to do one better than that.

1996

We've all been sent back home – Verity, Sally and I.

Mrs Allen called us all in and told us that the school governors thought it best that we stay away until Freya is out of the hospital and all this has blown over.

'It's not a suspension, as such,' she had said, looking at each of us. 'Think of it as an enforced break until … well, until things calm down.' She runs through the practicalities – how we will sit our mocks, who we may contact if we have academic queries. 'And you can always get someone to collect anything you need.'

Sally and I had looked at each other. 'Get someone?' And then it hits me that we aren't even allowed on the school grounds.

Home was both the best and worst place I could be. Amy is away until just after Christmas and without her the house is a heap of mess. None of Father's shirts have been washed so I collect them and take them to the dry cleaner's. There are half-drunk tumblers of whisky everywhere, which I collect and take to the kitchen. Nothing's been washed up for long enough that the steak rind on one plate has shrivelled yellow.

But with no one around, I'm not reminded of Freya and, for some reason, with nothing or no one to live up to at school, the terror of Mother subsides. Instead, I can focus on working. But when night-time falls and the wind starts raging, I start to feel alone. Father often doesn't get back until after midnight and I spend my time anticipating the click in the lock, the soft humming and the clattering of his keys on the mantelpiece.

There's a constant noise in my head, but the sharp flashbacks of that night and the constant sense of threat and paranoia over this whole Freya business subside now I'm away from school. There's still moments when I'm jolted into panic – triggered by things that I can't often connect and, sometimes, I'm woken from a deep sleep either by Freya's contorted face lunging at me, or from a time in the club just before everything goes black.

It's only after three days that I realise I haven't left my bedroom. I've been down to the kitchen once or twice to bring up some supplies – a few apples and some leftover curry that Father's brought home from the night before, but aside from that, I feel embraced by the four walls that separate me from the rest of the house. It's the day before Christmas that Father shouts from outside my door. 'J, your mother's back tomorrow.' Just like that. I can't remember the last time we've been home together.

When she arrives, I can hear her downstairs. There's what I think is the thump of her suitcase then Father saying in a loud, falsely cheerful voice that 'Josephine's upstairs and I know she'd love to see you.'

I don't hear anything in response. Just some shuffling and then the crash of china and Father saying, 'Please, please don't worry it's only a vase.' It takes me nearly two hours to go to her. When I go down, she's curled up on the sofa. She looks well. She's filled out a bit, enough that there's a line of flesh under her chin that was never there before. Her cheeks have become softer and fuller and she's wearing big, red apples of blusher. Her hair's brushed over one shoulder and she's wearing a coral-pink T-shirt with a large beaded necklace that looks like it's been made in an arts and crafts class and she's holding a magazine. When she sees me, she leans over to put it back on the table. It's the *Radio Times* and she's folded over different pages.

'Darling.' She opens her arms, barely wide enough for a three-year-old to squeeze into, but I lean down into her anyway. Father comes back with a tray of tea, the first time I've seen him make any in years. 'Your mother was saying how excited she was to see you.' He looks at Mother, who has put her feet up on the sofa. She's wearing a large pair of trainers that make her look like a teenager. 'Please,' he says, pushing them off. 'Not on the furniture.'

'Shall I turn on the television?' Mother asks.

'Sure,' says Father, handing her the remote control. 'Not sure how it works but do go ahead.' Mother spends the next hour flicking through channels until she settles on a programme that makes her gasp. 'I love this one,' she says. By the time the credits roll, she's asleep. When Christmas comes around, we open our presents on the sofa. Our family have never been very good at getting gifts but, this time, Father excels himself, buying me a set of first edition history books that I love. Mother gives me a little address book. When I open it, I find random scribbles inside.

Mother has a few moments when the torpor clears but generally we sit in silence and, although I try to be awake, I can feel my energy sapping and anxiety kicking in about the quality of work that I'm doing now that Mother's here.

I haven't been able to sit and study properly for days now and I'm beginning to feel resentful. I'm unable to conjure up any desire to read or make notes and even Father's telling me that I have to get to work. I make half-hearted attempts at highlighting pages in my textbooks but it's nothing compared to the usual flash cards, mind maps, books of notes and quotes that are usually filed in crisp new folders, ready for the term ahead. I don't even seem to have the energy to wonder when I'm going to get back to normal.

It's not long after Christmas when Father tells me I won't get into Oxford if I carry on staring into space. I'm sitting a few feet away from Mother, watching the same daytime programme that's been on loop for days. 'Josephine, what's wrong with you?' My father pulls me out of the room and points back inside towards the sofa. 'You are turning into her. She's ill, Josephine. You aren't. Get back to work. Get to Oxford. Get your life back on track. You need to do the best you can so you don't ... so you have as many opportunities as you can.'

I look through the doorway to the sofa where Mother's lying and I am overcome with a fear so great that I'm catapulted into doing something drastic. Something unlike me. Something to take me out of myself before I have to face all this crap back at school and before we find out our fate. I go back inside, tell Mother that it's been lovely having her around and then I go upstairs and sit with the house telephone on my lap, ready to make the phone call.

2014

I don't last long enough to make Dr Anthony's next session. The decision to see Freya is like a magnetic pull that almost throws me out the front door. I leave the clinic two days later, after I've had enough yoga and breathing lessons to feel I might combust. Gracie's nowhere to be found, but I leave her a note.

> *I hope you make things up with your husband. You were very kind to tell me the things you did about Freya. I'm going to find her myself. If she contacts you again, please don't tell her we met. I want to try and start afresh with her. Make yourself a good life.*

When I discharge myself from the clinic, I tell them I'll come in as an outpatient for a few sessions a month, even though I'm sure I'll be back in Jordan before then. The thought of seeing Freya fills me with strength now, instead of the terror that came with the idea of us meeting and the outside world stops feeling so frightening. I even notice the grey, naked trees, clawing at the sky, and the lake next to the hospital that manages to look beautiful, despite the sludge. I still wonder about how Freya managed to get my email address after I had changed it but instead of being fearful, I resolve to ask her myself.

When I get home, Father is back. He's sitting on the sofa, watching television. The same sofa where Mother used to sit all those years ago. The room he refused to go into unless she was at home. He wouldn't even go in there when he wanted to watch a film; instead he had bought a small television that he put at the end of his bed.

'What are you doing?' I ask.

'J, you're home?' He beckons me to the sofa. 'I didn't know you were coming back. It's good to see you. How are you feeling?'

The television is coated in dust and I go and get a hanky and give it a wipe. 'You're watching telly?'

'I know. I just felt like, well, relaxing. Want to join?'

I hover in the doorway, not knowing where I would sit, so I tell him no, that I'm going upstairs.

'Wait,' he says, patting the sofa again. I move towards him, perching myself on a small stool next to the coffee table. 'How come you are back so soon? I thought you might have stayed a bit longer? What did they say? The doctors, I mean.'

'Well, it's a long story. But everything's fine. Good, even.' Father's looking at me, unsure, so I tell him, in brief, about my breakthrough with Dr Anthony and about decisions I've made. I don't go into detail but the idea that I'll be rid of Freya hunting me down makes me chattier and more open with Father than I can ever remember. In turn, he is smiling at me and leaning forward, totally engaged with what I'm saying. I stop, half embarrassed when I realise how much I've divulged but he doesn't seem to care. Just tells me that if I feel unsteady again, I'm to come to him and he'll do what he can.

'I'm going to go and sort my stuff out and rest,' I say, walking to the door.

We both give a shy, half-wave. When I look back, he's still smiling, lifting his feet onto the plump, cream cushions.

I walk slowly up the stairs back to my room and open my computer. There's nothing there. No emails from a single person. It makes me feel sad, which takes me by surprise. Then I start crying for real, thinking about Mother and the lack of friends she had.

I start typing quickly, before I change my mind:

Freya, I don't know how you got this email address but since you have, here goes: I've been thinking about seeing you. About what it might be like. I know a lot has happened since we last saw each other and I've managed to shed some light on a few things. Let's meet. I'm in London at the moment and due to get back to Jordan soon; in the next couple of days or so, so let me know where and when. Best, Josephine.'

I manage to press send before I chicken out.

A whole day goes by and I'm still waiting for her to reply. I keep opening my computer, checking my phone. Nothing. All this time she's been waiting to see me and now she hasn't even responded. What is she waiting for? What more does she want from me? In an effort to distract myself, I spend the time reading, walking aimlessly around the house and emailing work to find out what's been going on. '*I'll be back in three days,*' I tell Jeremy decisively. If Freya hasn't got back to me by then, she'll have missed her chance.

'*Brilliant. We've all missed you,*' he replies.

I stay awake all night, reading the same page of a book, over and over. I haven't had so little concentration for years. I'm furious for ceding control, for allowing Freya to make me feel like this again, especially when I had felt so much better in the past few days.

At four in the morning, I go downstairs. It's totally dark in the kitchen bar the winking blue lights of the Wi-Fi. I can't even find it in myself to switch the side lamps on, so I find my way around the counter towards the kettle, using my hands. I make some coffee, which seems like a stupid thing to do, but then I'm too wired to sleep and I don't feel physically awake enough to do anything useful. I'm wearing one of Mother's old silk dressing gowns that's a bit moth-eaten and smells of make-up, but I'm pleased I can wear it now without freaking out. I wonder how old the gown is, whether Mother wore it before she got ill, and then I remember that it was my fault, my birth that triggered the worst of her schizophrenia. Would the same happen to me if I were to have children? Then I remember a conversation Freya and I had, one night in the woods at school.

'I want four kids,' she had said, pressing her hand against her stomach. 'Two girls and two boys.' She said it in the bold, confident manner that only a teen could have. She had looked so luminous in the dark, her hand circling her belly.

'What about you?'

'I'm not sure I would be a very good mother, you know,' I replied.

'Balls,' Freya had snorted. 'You are the best friend anyone could ever have. In the entire world. That means you'll be an incredible mother.'

At six in the morning, I get her reply. I've been watching a history documentary on my computer and an email from her pings right up on my screen. For five minutes, I can't read it then I calm myself using the breathing techniques Dr Anthony taught me.

Josephine, thanks so much for getting back to me. I've been wondering if you would change your mind I'm pleased you did. There's so much I need to talk to you about. Let's go for a walk and then, depending on how things go, lunch?

Depending on how things go? I think. What the hell is she thinking will happen? My gut begins to swoop.

Let's meet Tuesday morning, Hyde Park at twelve? I work not far from there and I'll take a long lunch. See you at the Kensington Gardens exit – the one where we used to meet up on our school holidays. Freya.

I stay in bed until 1 p.m. the next day. Then I go and get my hair cut. I've spent the past sixteen years trimming my own hair with a pair of nail scissors so I'm shocked when I'm charged fifty-five pounds for the pleasure. This time only a month ago, I would have found the whole experience intrusive, ugly – all the reasons I stopped going to the hairdresser in the first place. Now, though, I let the young man with the tight black jeans and crazy black hair go to work. He massages my head, shampoos my hair and then cuts, holding up my brown locks before decisively snipping off huge hunks which land all over my hands. I keep sneezing and he's laughing, asking me when I last came to the hairdresser. When I tell him, he puts down his scissors and goes and gets me a glass of champagne. 'Here. You need this.' I drink it and laugh with him about how my hairstyle is actually in style now. 'You're so out of fashion, you've come full circle,' he laughs.

When I get up, my whole head feels light. I can feel a breeze on my ears and my fringe has been swept to the side so I can see my forehead properly for the first time in years.

'Stop looking at yourself,' the hairdresser says. It's true, I can't stop staring. My whole face looks totally different and my hair doesn't hang like stringy rope either side of my face. I don't stop there. I go and buy some new make-up from Boots. I don't want Freya to think I've been revelling in my own misery all this time. I spend an hour at the Chanel counter, spending the last of my pay cheque from before I left Jordan. Having bought only two or three items of make-up in the past few years, it feels justified. The saleswoman behind the counter offers to do my eyes and I let her. 'The green in them. Wow,' she says. 'This colour looks fantastic on you. Brings them out. Hasn't any one ever told you that before?'

'Not for a long time,' I reply, smiling.

I'm tempted to meet up with Toby, to see his reaction and then, as I sit down for another coffee, I realise how bloody stupid I've been. Behaving as though this is a first date? God knows what Freya has in store for me, and I don't know why I'm acting as though I'm a love-struck teen. The full force of what is about to happen hits me and then I get an odd feeling that something bad is afoot. I try to shake it, blame it on too much coffee, but it's there, and my make-up feels really garish and my haircut ridiculous. Freya's email plays through my mind: '*and then, depending on how things go, lunch?*' Rationally, I know that, of course, Freya is hedging her bets that we might not want to spend much time together. But what if ... what if she has something else up her sleeve?

Freya, I wish I could still read you, I think.

1996

I ring Freya's house. I'm not quite sure why I'm doing it. Just to hear her voice? I'm not even sure she's home. I recall Mrs Allen saying she was to spend time in psychiatric care, so I'm probably not going to have much luck. I tap the numbers quickly; my fingers work without having to think too much – I know Freya's number as well as, if not better, than my own. It's Leon who answers, and I nearly hang up.

'Hi,' I say.

'Hi,' he replies.

'It's Josephine.'

'I know.'

'How is she?'

'She's alright. She's doing alright.'

'Listen ... I ...'

'Josephine, I think it's best we don't really talk. Don't you?'

'Leon ... I ...'

'Bye, Josephine.' The phone buzzes in my ear. I think about ringing him back. Shall I? And then the phone goes and I know it's him.

'Hello?' I say, coolly.

'It's me.'

'Oh,' I say. 'Hi.'

'Listen. Sorry about that. Things are just … things are mad here.'

'It's OK. I just wanted to tell you something. I needed to speak to you.' Although I rang to speak to Freya, I start to realise how much I need Leon.

'I can't. You nearly killed my sister.'

We go silent and I feel his words like knife slashes.

'I … Leon … I – I need to explain.' I'm desperate for his reassurance. For him to put his arms around me and tell me it's OK. That everything will go back to normal.

'What do you need to explain? My sister nearly topped herself. Blamed you for it. How can I possibly see you? Josephine, you were family. You belonged to our family, do you know that? How could you do what you did?'

'Please, *please*, if you just let me explain?' My voice is cracking. I don't want to have to beg Leon but I need his strength. I need to feel his calmness. 'Please. Give me five minutes. I won't tell anyone we've met. You need to do this. For Freya. Let me just speak to you.' I hate begging but I can't fuck things up with Leon.

Half an hour later, we meet at the bench in Hyde Park where Leon taught me and Freya how to smoke. He's sitting there already by the time I arrive, his bike flat on the grass beside him. He's wearing soft, scuffed leather biker boots and his hair's grown. It's freezing but his leather jacket is slung over his lap. His arms, those arms.

'You've got three minutes,' he says. 'Then I'm going. I'm doing this for my sister. To see if you can help. If you can't, I'm never seeing you again, do you understand?' A burning sensation shoots from my heart to my throat, up the back of my nose and I begin to cry.

'Leon, I ...' I'm overcome with a desperate need to kiss him and I don't know whether this is because I need some sort of physical affirmation that everything is OK but he's looking at me with such a burning hatred that I have to take two steps back.

'I'm sorry,' I say. 'I'm really sorry. But you don't know the full story. I can't tell you what it is. But just so you know. It wasn't just me.'

I start crying and open my arms to him. 'Please. Please help me,' Leon looks around him and takes a step forward.

'It's OK,' he's saying. 'It's OK. I know you're hurting.' He relents, just like Freya would, then his face goes all pinched.

'But you have to remember, my loyalties ...' he says. For the first time ever, I have more than a superficial surge of jealousy towards Freya.

'Don't you have any loyalties to me?' I reply. He puts his hands in his back pocket and looks at me, unsure of what to say. 'Is she OK?' I ask.

'She's having some pretty hard-core treatment at the moment. She's not great. She'll be fine, though. Dad and I want her to go back to school. To get some sort of normality back, so we'll see what happens.' I wonder if she's told her doctor everything.

'How is your dad?'

'He's OK. He's fine. Doesn't really know how to handle this. It's not his fault. But I've been looking after her quite a lot.'

There's the jealousy again and I'm worried about saying something spiteful. To stop myself, I look over at a passing dog, chasing a bright yellow ball.

After a while, he says he has to go. That he can't be seen with me. That if he were, his family would never speak to him again. 'OK,' I tell him. 'OK.'

Then he turns away, wheeling his bike off into the distance, and I am left to wonder if I'll ever see him again.

My offer letter comes in the next day. Father comes to my room just after lunch, where I've been at my desk working since six in the morning.

'What are you doing at home?' I ask.

'I thought you'd be asleep. Glad to see you're working. Anyway – I wanted to see you, of course. And I've got this.' I sit up, take the envelope with the Oxford University emblem stamped on the front. There is a sheath of papers inside. I already know what this means. I take it from him, weaving it through my fingers.

'Hurry up,' he says.

'What are you really doing at home?' I ask.

'Had to change my suit. Spilt my lunch.' I look down at his white shirt and it's spattered with what looks like steak gravy and red wine. 'Come on then. Shall I?'

'Yes.' I hand him the letter and he opens it. Reads it. Looks worried. Puts his hand to his mouth in a bid to show me he's sorry and my heart blips. Then he leans forward, gives me a hug and says, 'Only joking. You didn't really believe me, did you?' Deep down, I didn't but I've never seen my father play the fool like this. So swept away am I by this that I forget to look at the letter.

'Here. Read.'

Dear Miss Grey,

Further to your interview with us, I am pleased, on behalf of Somerville College to offer you a place for admission in October 1997, to read History, a three-year course. This offer is conditional upon your obtaining the following grades in your forthcoming examinations:

I don't read any further. I have to keep looking at Father's face, at the gleam in his eyes, because when I don't, and I remember everything I've done and how bad the situation is, I get this horrid, flat disappointment seeping through me, like someone's punctured all the life from me, and Freya's face keeps appearing. Us, laughing at something that no one else would understand and my feelings are made worse because I can't share this moment with her. And I wonder if my father's pride, me trying to get away from the fear of my mother and the joy I should be feeling at my dreams coming true, is enough to make the pain go away.

The next morning, Mrs Allen rings to congratulate me on my offer.

'Josephine, I've had word from the Dean that your History essay was the best they received in years. Well done. Truly.'

But this feels hollow in light of the suspension. 'Any news on when I can come back?' I ask. I sound agitated.

'Josephine, let's just concentrate on your news for the moment, shall we? I'm sure you and your father … and your mother, must be extremely happy, Josephine?'

'I'm here. What about Oxford. Did Sally get an offer? And what about Freya?'

'Josephine I'm not at liberty to say. I'm sorry. If you want to know you'll have to ask the girls.' I hang up the phone and ring Sally. She picks up after half a ring.

'Hello, Aylsford residence,' she sings.

'Sally,'

'Jo! I got in! Three A offer of course but I did it! I've been trying to ring. Got the letter yesterday. Did you? Get the letter, I mean?'

'I did, yes.' She doesn't ask any more, safe in the assumption that I got in.

'Have you heard about anyone else?' I ask.

'No, no, I haven't. Haven't spoken to anyone. My dad and I were celebrating all day yesterday. He took me for pizza and the cinema. First time we've spent any time together in ages.'

'Good for you,' I say, and mean it.

'What?' she says. 'I can't hear you, you've gone all muffled.'

'Oh sorry. Anyway, I had better go. Let me know if you hear about the others. Oxford, I mean.'

'Will do. Loads of love, Jo, and thanks. I keep telling Father, you are the reason I got in. You don't think they'll stop us, do you? Stop us from going if this all gets out?'

'I hope not,' I say.

'OK. Call me if you hear anything then. Don't forget.'

'I won't.'

'Lots of love then,' she says.

Sally rings me back later that night.

'Freya got in.'

'Oh, great,' I say. 'How did you find out?'

'I heard from Marge. I have no idea how she knew.'

'Ah thanks a lot for telling me.'

'No probs. And I think we're allowed back to school tomorrow.'

'How do you know?'

'My dad. Lawyers.'

'And Freya? Did Marge tell you anything else?'

'Marge didn't know any more but my father spoke to Mrs Allen. Apparently she's doing absolutely fine. Walking around and stuff. She's got to do some more psychiatric tests but they're going to question her about everything tomorrow, before we get back. I don't know if that was the whole story but I don't think she was allowed to tell him much more.'

'Right.' I want to ask Sally if she thinks it'll be OK but she gets there first.

'She won't say anything, will she? I mean this is more about her and Mrs Kitts, right?'

'I think so. Listen, Sally. Just remember, Oxford. If you are tempted to say anything at all, like I told you before: Oxford. I'm going to coach you with our mocks and I'll do A levels too. OK? I got you the interview, so you have to trust me on this.'

I can almost hear Sally nodding down the phone. 'Yup. I will. Don't worry. I've got this far. I'm not going to let it go now.' I believe her and hang up, relieved.

I think of Freya having psychiatric tests. Whether she'll be in a fit state to be questioned and I wonder if she's thought of me at all. The next day, Father gets me a taxi back to school and waves me goodbye before he sets off for an afternoon meeting. He strides off, looking at the sky, waiting for it to rain.

There is no rain, though, for days. Only sun, bright blue skies and grass blades bending back and forth. All the girls are smiling. Picnics outside. Lacrosse games, swimming championships. It's all wonderful. No one mentions *The Lens*. The buzz of gossip over Mrs Kitts and Freya seems to have died down. Soon this will all be over, Freya's getting better and I'm pretty sure I'm going to Oxford.

2014

I'm twenty minutes early for my meeting with Freya, so I walk around the park. It's drizzling and I haven't an umbrella, so I stay under the canopies of trees, away from the cyclists and runners. By the time midday comes, I work my way back to the Kensington Gardens Gate.

There she is, I can see her, leaning on the railings.

She looks perfect. Absolutely perfect. She's got her back to me but I know it's her. All that time searching the crowd for her face when if she was truly among them, I wouldn't have needed to, she would have stood out immediately. She's wearing tight-fitting jeans, crocodile-skin loafers, a pink cashmere jumper that hangs just underneath a loose-fitting blazer. That beautiful hair as well. It's tied up in a chignon, in a tortoiseshell clip, the luscious thickness making her look even taller.

She's got sunglasses on her head, which, despite the rain, she manages to pull off. She's holding a see-through umbrella and a black leather bag with a gold buckle and, when I turn to look at her, I can see everyone else is also staring. She's oblivious though. Even when one man whistles and gives her an up and down, she just smiles back and I can see her mouthing 'hello' to him, like he's offered to carry her bags.

As if she senses me staring she turns around. Scans the park. But somehow she doesn't see me. I am slightly hidden from view, deliberately so I can watch her unchecked. She smiles at a passer-by. Her teeth glow. Her whole being glows. She is luminescent in the grey drizzle. I stop and drink her in for a few minutes. I feel dowdy in my black boots and my black jeans. I'm wearing a thick, woollen jumper that looks like I made an effort but not so much that it's obvious. I ended up wearing minimal make-up. Just a slick of mascara, blusher and a tiny dab of nude lipstick that I find in my bathroom that's probably over ten years old. It's the same colour I used to wear when we were at school. I feel more confident in it. That Freya will be able to recognise me. The old me.

I see her looking at her watch. She pulls up the sleeve of her jumper and I wonder if the scars on her arm are still visible. She looks around for me and I can't quite bring myself to go over yet. After a few minutes more, I finally move. I bump into two people, who both stop and swear at me. 'Sorry,' I mutter. 'Sorry.'

As I pull away and apologise to the second person, she sees me. She sees me, dammit, walking into someone. I'm sweating and I try to look as though they've been the ones to bump into me. I hold my hands up in mock reassurance. 'Don't worry,' I say to them, smiling.

I look over and wave. She waves back. Smiling. She's smiling so widely I can see her back teeth. White and perfect.

The sun comes out and the noise of the rain stops. I can hear the beep of a lorry reversing, the screams of some kids playing football and then, my name.

'Josephine,' she's shouting. 'Josephine!'

I walk over and she starts to pull me into a hug but sees me step back a touch. She drops her arms and, as she does so, I change my mind, walking into her embrace. We end up clashing. Freya makes a little sound, like a bird. We both pull away.

'Freya,' I whisper.

'Josephine,' she says. 'I can't believe it's you, after all this time.' There's something false in the way she's talking. The smile is too forced, the twitchy hand that keeps pushing back the two locks of hair that have come loose from her chignon.

'Me too. Me too.'

We both stare at each other until someone pushes me aside.

'Move out the way, will you?' he shouts, scowling. Then he notices Freya and attempts to pull back his words. 'Oh, sorry, sorry ... Just ...'

She shoots him a look and he slides his eyes up and down her before walking off. 'Dick,' she says. We both laugh.

Then her face becomes serious. 'I'm sorry about your mother, by the way.'

'Thanks.'

'Bench?' she says. 'Here. I bought you a coffee. I remember you used to drink yours black. I hope you still do.' She turns around and picks up a cardboard tray with two cups from the base of the park railings. 'Here.' She hands me one.

'Thank you,' I say, taking it. The paper burns my fingers, so I let it rest between the flesh of my palms.

We walk in silence. I'm standing a few feet away from her. She keeps moving towards me but I'm finding her presence all too overwhelming.

'It's been so long, hasn't it,' she says. A skater speeds in between us, causing Freya to jump.

We reach our old bench. Leon used to sit in the middle and pass a lit cigarette to us both. 'Suck it down like this,' he'd say, gasping air into his lungs.

'Look,' Freya calls. 'It's still here, look!'

I look over and Freya's holding out a beautifully manicured nail on the slats. 'I can't believe it's still here,' she's saying. 'That time you, me and Leon etched that funny symbol into the wood. Here, just on the edge of the bench arm.'

I look and there it is. A small round circle with two squiggly lines through it. We had vowed, on that day, that that would be a binding symbol, our calling card. That if any one of us needed help throughout our lives, we would use the symbol and the others would come to the rescue.

'Wow. I had forgotten about that,' I say, smoothing my fingers over it. Leon had carved it into the wood, with a Swiss Army knife. I think about his long, brown fingers, working into the wood. Leon.

'I've always avoided this part of the park,' she says. 'Ever since ... well, ever since we last saw each other.'

We sit. Freya takes out her hair clip and puts it in her bag. She looks like she's going to give me something but decides against it.

'I don't know where to start,' she says, looking at my face.

'Me too. I don't know why you wanted to meet me so much,' I reply. The sun's out now, making me squint. Freya hands me her sunglasses.

'No. I'm OK thanks.'

'Don't want to show any weakness?' she laughs. I only realise what she's said a few seconds later, when she looks like she's about to start crying.

'What do you want from me?' I ask.

'It's ... it's a long story. I wanted to talk to you about things. I wanted to tell you things. And ask you about that night.'

'Why? Why now? What good can this possibly do?'

She doesn't say anything, just stares down at her feet. After all the hounding and emails I am finally here and she can't answer the first question I've asked.

'Why?' I ask again. I'm practically shouting and Freya looks up at me, frowning.

'It's still in my head, I just needed to ... I've got a kid...'

Freya has a child? 'So?'

'And I just needed to lay my ghosts to rest.' She winds her hair around her fingers and lets it drop on her shoulder.

'What do you mean?'

And then Freya starts crying. Just a small trickle at first, and then the tears splash out, landing on her cup.

'I just keep thinking about us. We weren't even eighteen,' she says in a small voice. 'We were young. And then I think of my child. And how alone I felt and what I would do if ... Like I said, it's just in my head at the moment. That's the main reason I was so desperate to work this out. So I could move on. Look after my child without *it* being here.' Freya points to her chest and then her head. 'Haven't you ever felt like that? Aren't you tired of carrying it too?'

And just like that, all my suspicions of Freya, my fears of her seeking revenge evaporate. Her emails, which all seemed so sinister at the time, now looking back in a different frame of mind, take on another hue: not onerous, but desperate – pleading.

'We were, weren't we?' I say. 'Young, I mean. I felt so old at the time, like I'd lived ten lifetimes. Now it just seems so ridiculous. We were babies.'

'Yes, yes that's exactly it.' The agreement brings back some of our old comradeship and Freya seizes upon it. 'Did you ever feel bad? About what you did to me, I mean? With Mrs Kitts and everything? Did you ever regret it? Any of it from that morning the next day to … to the very end? I never understood any of it. I thought we knew each other so well.'

I can't look at her as she is saying this. There's so much bubbling under the surface and I know if I don't keep my cool, or if I give her a loaded answer, the whole meeting will end horribly. So I try to speak truthfully but sparingly.

'Yes I do. If I could go back, I would undo a lot of things,' I say carefully. 'I don't look back on any of that with any sense of pleasure. To be honest I can't bear to look back on it at all.'

'Really?' She seems surprised, hopeful even. 'What would you do differently?' I'm wrong-footed by this and I'm about to flare up, but I realise she's not being accusatory.

'I would have … I think I would have told someone. I think you were right. But at the time … Now though I think maybe it would have worked out in the end. I was just so focused on …' Freya's frowning, nodding. I start to whisper the last, 'Focused on not being my mother.'

'What was that?' Freya's saying. She's cupping her ear but I can't go any louder.

'My mother.' I was all set on reciting a whole load of things to Freya. I'd been practising them in my head all week. In fact, since she got in touch. But none of it comes out.

Then I think about how we once were. Me and Freya. And I'm looking at her face and she's barely aged at all, really. Her skin is still totally smooth, the light in her eyes is still there and that same smile on her face too, even when her mouth is set. I think of the old days and I'm overcome with a sense of nostalgia and I want to make it right. To grab back those heady, hilarious times of friendship and laughter which I've never since been able to share with anyone else. And Mother. I'd never even intended to mention Mother to Freya. As it is, I'm already starting to feel this is the best thing I could do to let go of the fear of her. Releasing the sadness surrounding my mother's life that had turned malignant inside me, so long ago.

'It hurt, you know,' I continue, unable to stop. 'I was even jealous of you that your mum had died, when I was stuck with my own mother being so ill. I'm sorry to admit that. I was devastated, of course, for you and your family, but her death gave you a freedom that I could never have. Well, until now.' Freya looks horrified, then her eyebrows relax and her mouth turns upwards.

'That's some admission there,' she says breathlessly. And then she cries again.

I want to reach out and comfort her but I daren't. 'I know. I wasn't expecting to be so honest with you. I guess there's no point in all the deception anymore.'

'Yours, you mean? With *The Lens* and everything?' Freya is asking without nuance.

'I'm sorry. I'm sorry about *The Lens*,' I reply. I'm crying now and seeing her here, in front of me, I realise how much I have missed her, how much in trying not to think about her for eighteen years I have done nothing but. 'I didn't mean for it to get so out of hand. I mean, firstly, there was that night. Then, part of it was because I was so cross about you and Verity. Jealous. And then I'd become so obsessed, so focused on being this success, being different to my mother, that I became totally blinded by it. I didn't think there was any other way. When, of course, there was. We were a team, Freya, and then all this stuff happened and suddenly you were my enemy and I guess I was even more of a prisoner to the way I felt. I made so many mistakes, and the stupidest thing was that I really did think, or at least convinced myself, that it was all for the right reasons, but it wasn't. I am so sorry.'

Even though the tears won't stop coming, my entire body and mind unclench for the first time in years.

We are both silent. It's strange to be talking so openly with Freya, after everything. After not having seen the girl for eighteen years, after hiding from my own truth for ... well, my whole life, really.

'You've no idea how long I've waited to hear you say that.' Freya takes my hand and I hold my breath. 'I'm sorry too. I'm sorry that I pushed you so hard. I should have tackled it differently. I was being selfish. Thinking only of how I was reacting. I know ... knew how you were, I should have thought you would be dealing with it in a different way to me and I should have managed that properly, but I was just reeling from what happened.' She stops talking. Her features bunch together and she blows out a stream of breath. 'And I'm sorry,' she says. 'About using Verity against you. She meant nothing to me. Did you know that? I felt such a bitch after school. She's been in touch quite a lot and I only talk to her now really out of guilt. I used her to make you feel bad. Saying those words out loud makes me seem like such a nasty, nasty person. I should be apologising to her too.'

'Don't worry,' I reply. 'You were hurting. That's why.'

'Do you think? Do you think that's both why we did the things we did? Because of that, not because we were ... you know ...'

'Maybe,' I say. 'I think when you're nearly eighteen it's a pretty good reason, don't you?'

'I do. I really do.'

'Freya?' I ask, leaning back on the wooden bench. She turns and offers me a piece of chewing gum. I'm reminded of when we both used to come back from smoking cigarettes in the woods.

'Yes?' she says, crumpling the foil wrapper into her hand.

'When you ...' But I can't quite bring myself to say the words, though I know I must if this conversation is to ever take hold. She's looking at me, worried.

'When you tried to ... you know ... kill yourself ...?'

I let the words hang between us. Freya smooths her hand across the bench and picks up a little ladybird. She blows it off her finger and I think she's about to ignore me but then she starts to speak.

'That. That was so stupid,' she says eventually. 'I mean, I can never begin to explain that or rationalise it.' She looks at me, takes my hand. 'I'm sorry. I'm really, really sorry. That got out of control too. Needed some sort of ... I don't really know what. Acknowledgment? Stupid.' She gives a sad little laugh, pulls up her sleeves and holds them up for me to see. The scars are still there, faded and white.

'You didn't deserve that, and you know what? I was the one that probably hurt the most from it. Seeing what it did to my father. To Leon. I've never got over that. We did such terrible things to each other.'

'And all in the name of survival,' I finish. Freya looks at me with a little smile then drops her head. I reach over and squeeze her hand. She looks wary at my physical affection and then laughs. 'God, things really have changed, haven't they?'

'I guess so. They had to, though. Didn't they?'

'Thank you. Thank you, Josephine, for coming here and being so open. And kind.'

'That's not something I'm very good at,' I reply.

'It is, J. It is. You have no idea how kind you are underneath. You just have a funny way of showing it sometimes. Or did, at least.' We both laugh. And suddenly, like a rusty squeeze box, the creaky dynamics of our former friendship begin to fall into place again. It's an amazing feeling. Something close to euphoric. And then we both go quiet. A good, peaceful quiet. The tension rises out of my body. I'm nearly floating and I find I want to hug her. She's looking at me too and she looks so happy, like the old Freya, but then she rubs her arms as though she's chilled to the bone and a weird expression crosses her face. It's one I've seen only once or twice before. I think it's something close to shame and then she slides herself away from me so she can turn and face me properly.

'Josephine,' she says. 'There are things I need to tell you about that night. Things I never told you. Things I couldn't tell you.'

I look down and walk my fingers through a pool of coffee on the lid.

'Like what?'

'Well ... I need to ask you, do you remember any of it?'

'I think ... I ...' How can I explain? It used to dance at the fringe of my thoughts but then I just pushed it away, kept pushing, kept burying. I didn't want to see what was there; I didn't want to believe.

'All this time I thought you were pretending, compartmentalising. But you can't really, can you? Or have you just blocked it out?'

She's looking at me in a strange way and suddenly I am reminded of that moment back at school in the spare classroom just after chapel, and that expression on her face that I couldn't decipher.

'I need you to listen to me, Josephine. I need you to just shut your eyes and try to remember with me,' she says.

'Look, I can't remember.' I am panicking now, my voice rising. 'And quite frankly I don't want to. What good does it do?'

She shakes her head. 'No. No, I remember everything, you see. Absolutely everything. And I had taken a lot more than you. I know you remember, and it's time you stopped pushing it away. I need you to try. Just shut your eyes. For me. Please. Shut them for one second.'

I feel too vulnerable with my eyes closed in the middle of the day, so I sit, eyes wide open into the sun and, all of a sudden, Freya's holding my hand again.

'Go on, shut them. I'm here, with you.'

For a moment, I'm tempted to pull away but the squeeze of her fingers feels nice. I shut my eyes.

And with the warmth of her hands, after all this time, I finally allow myself to be taken back to where it all began. All those years ago. Freya and me.

1996: THAT NIGHT

'I love you.' Freya clutches my hand.

'That's nice,' I reply.

'Come on, just say it back. Go on. I dare you.'

'No, don't be annoying.'

'Want some?' Freya pats her bra and mouths something to me.

'What?' I cup my ear.

'AMAZING,' she's saying, rubbing her hands down her chest. 'They're amazing.'

'No. I'm only drinking tonight. You know that.'

The club is filling up and we're both smoking on a beanbag upstairs from the main dance floor.

'Come on, don't be so boring,' she says, pointing at the large black speakers. 'Come on. The music ... it's amazing. You'll feel amazing. These pills ... they're ...' She rests her head back on the wall and rubs her temples.

'No.'

'You are so lame,' she laughs. 'I'm not on your wavelength tonight so you'll just have to get drunk. Wow, this music.' Freya's tapping her foot and looking blissed out and I start to feel left out of her elation.

'Oh for fuck's sake,' I say. 'I'm Head Girl, though.'

'Oh don't get all uppity,' she laughs, pulls herself up and crouches over, fiddling around in the dark. She takes my right hand, puts crumbled bits of pill into it. 'Here. Here's half. Barely counts. No one will know and you can still be Head Girl.'

OK. Half. That's basically nothing so I can still wake up tomorrow and pretend I've been totally sober all night, can't I?

My throat closes around the bitter taste and I swig back some water. More water. I fall back into the floor and shut my eyes. An hour later and Freya's taken another half and, by that time, my thoughts have finally faded from my consciousness. They are separate from me now and, as soon as I try to clutch on to that very notion, it drops into a dark abyss. I try to catch it back but it's gone. I start to laugh.

'What?' says Freya. She looks like a cow chewing on grass. Mouth side to side, forwards, backwards.

'Nothing. Can't talk. I love you, Frey.' *I do love her*, I think to myself.

'Love you too.'

'Shall we go and dance?' My foot is tapping against the sticky floor.

'Are you feeling any effect?' Freya asks. I'm no longer really aware of the time but it can't be more than half an hour since I took it.

'Yeah ... it's nice. Not too much. I still feel quite normal. Just a tiny bit.'

Freya gets up and tells me to wait.

'I'm going to get you another drink then,' she says, pulling out a note from her sock. 'Wait there. To be a bit more on my level.' She leans her head back again and pushes back her hair from the sides of her forehead. 'Phew,' she says flicking her hips from side to side in time to the music. I can't help but think how effortless and beautiful she is. 'Wow. Wait there, for one sec, OK?'

'Yeah, OK then.' I wait for what seems like twenty minutes and then Freya's back holding two drinks.

'Here. Sorry about that,' Freya says. We stand by the beanbags, half dancing and finishing our drinks.

'What is this by the way? It's pretty rank.' I hold out my empty glass.

'Oh some weird cocktail mix thingy ... I can't remember what I asked for. It's rum, vodka ... can't remember what else.' Freya says she needs to chill out for a bit and so it's an hour later before we walk downstairs. I feel like I'm walking on a huge, bouncy castle. Green laser lights and flashing strobes startle my eyes and I start convulsing to the rhythm. This is weird, I think. 'What the fuck was in that pill?' I shout. 'I only took half ... you must be feeling absolutely wasted.'

'Ha,' she says. 'Told you they were amazing.' She holds her hands up to her mouth in a girlish giggle and, when she pulls them away, I can't tell where her face ends or begins. If I laugh, the image won't be frightening, so I giggle and that makes me feel like I'm pissing myself. I quickly wipe my hand down there and feel nothing.

'Freya, can we go for a breather in a minute, please?' I'm shouting but she can't hear me because the music has just gone up a notch. The vibration from the speakers is riding up into my pelvic area.

Boom. Doof. Boom. Doof. Boom. The crowd roars and whistles.

'Freya?' I look around for her and she's four rows in front of me, dancing and laughing with some dreadlocked guy. She's whispering in his ear. Everyone's faces suddenly start melting into the floor. I shake my head to purge the image and gulp back some water.

Boom. Doof. Boom. Doof. Hold it together, I think, as my heart punches my breastbone. And then I can feel someone's hands up my top. Freya, I think, but I turn around and she's not there. I have no idea how long has passed from when we hit the dance floor.

'Freya,' I mouth and then I catch a glimpse of her and she's standing in front of the guy with dreads now, weaving her hands through her hair and twisting it in her fingers. She's reacting to his gaze, eyes half shut, sliding her hand down her stomach.

'It's me. I'm here.' I hear a deep voice and I can feel a pair of hands snaking down my skirt. I cannot talk.

'Freya,' I say, again.

I look down and don't see anyone. There's a curtain of laser beams blocking my vision. And then I see. A flash of a large, shaven-headed guy with a lip ring and an enormous dragon tattoo emblazoned on his chest. With the lights in my eyeline, he's spectral. He's there and then he's not. There and not. I feel his hands again. I try to push them away but it feels sort of nice. Relax into it, I think.

'Freya,' I say. Now his hands are actually in my stomach, scooping out chunks of flesh, intestine and food. He makes a throwing motion and my innards splatter against the crowd of people. I look up and see the man and he's grinning at me although there's no intestine, no food, no chunks of flesh. Just people dancing, grinning, waving their hands in the air and having a good time.

'Freya,' I say. I feel something hard, like a stone, pressing into my back. I try to walk away and then the stone is inside me, isn't it? And now I do see Freya, two people away from me. She's being kissed by the sweaty, dreadlocked man with yellow face paint on his cheeks and he's giving a thumbs-up to the guy with the dragon on his chest. I can't see his other hand but I think it's down somewhere near Freya's skirt. As the music gets louder and peaks I start to cry. I haven't cried for about ten years but when I wipe my face, my hands are dry.

We stand there, me and dragon man, swaying. To any onlooker, we must look like lovers. He's whispering to me but I can't understand what he's saying. My heart is going nuts and I'm too frightened to move. And what I think is about two hours later, Freya tugs at my hand.

'Come on, let's go,' she says. 'I'm beginning to freak out. Let's just go for a cigarette somewhere quiet. The music. It's too much. Those guys. He's nice but starting to freak me out. Think I'm just a bit ...' She pretends to slit her throat with her hand. I see blood gushing from her neck. I blink and it's gone and her neck is flesh-coloured again.

'Me too,' I'm trying to say but I can't respond. So I nod and follow her. We end up leaving the dance floor via one of the green emergency exit arrows. It glitters.

'Here. Come on. We can get upstairs this way I remember. It's where we used to smoke joints on that landing.' I walk behind her, body swooping up and down into the floor, the ceiling. Lurching forward. I think I'm going to be sick, so I pull Freya into a cubbyhole, off one of the emergency stair landings. It's covered with a thick, red velvet curtain which stinks of mould.

I swallow hard and try to breathe. Freya gestures for me to inhale deeply, which I do and I am nearly sick again. We sit down, me behind the curtain. She rubs my back. The curtains are ripped apart. Two men. Both topless. One with the tattoo, staring eyes, lip ring and torn black combats. The other with the dreadlocks. Handsome. Ripped bodies. Freya is the only body they can see. They shut the curtain and one of them places his foot on the hem. I try to get up, because I know something's wrong, but if I move, my head, my heart, my lungs, my guts will explode, so I stay where I am. And then I can't hold it back any longer.

Freya gets up to help. The movement alerts dreadlocked guy to me. I feel a steel boot in my groin. I don't see what happens next, but Freya falls.

Then Freya's skirt goes. Denim. Glint of the skulls and cross-bones. Sparkles. Beautiful. Shimmering. My skirt goes too. Torn down my leg. Pain. Then my cheek is being rhythmically squashed into the wall. Back and forth. All I can think about is that my neck feels like it's going to be cricked. I feel my head smash further and further into the wall and then I see Freya standing behind dragon guy, leg in the air, and she's kicking him. I can hear music. Roar of the crowd. Whistles. Voices at the top of the stairs, funnelled by distance.

'You dirty little bitch,' someone says. I can feel something thwack my skull. Blood. The dripping sensation makes the drugs kick in again and I begin to rush.

I turn my head and I can see Freya, she's also now on all fours. Man behind her. One hand wrapped tightly around her mouth, the other squeezing her neck. I can see her neck, bulging out of those hands. Her eyes, shivering inside the sockets. She is moving, back and forth back and forth. There is blood pouring from her nose. Blood red, like my Head Girl badge, I think. Pain. Pleasure. Pain.

Freya is now cheek on floor, arms forward like a cat stretching. Her eyes are no longer moving but the pupils are black. Endless. Zipping sound. Another zipping sound. Then a clapping above our heads. *Boom. Doof. Boom. Doof.* Thick curtain is pulled back and we are left alone. I wipe my mouth.

'Shall we go?' Freya whispers. She is crying, haloed in an eerie green glow. I can see the tears in the dark. I reach out and touch them and my fingers come away wet and then I realise it's mixed with blood and I wipe my hands on the wall. We hug and she leads me out of the club. The cool air blasts on our faces and we remember we've left our coats in the cloakroom.

'I can't.' She shakes her head.

'Let's go then.' We leave. Nose still bleeding, Freya runs into McDonald's and picks up some napkins. She cleans us up and we get a taxi home. The next morning, Freya is curled up at the end of my bed. Father is still away and Amy hasn't come back. Freya is holding my foot and there's half a cigarette stubbed out in an ashtray by her head. I lean over and stroke her hair.

She looks up at me and gives a half-smile and then frowns.

'What happened?' she asks.

'We're OK,' I reply, sliding off the bed and patting my stomach. 'Shall I cook bacon and eggs?'

'No thanks. Jo, I need to speak to you about ...' And then Freya's crying so much she can't get any words out.

'Come on. I'm going down. I'll meet you in the kitchen.' The eggs and bacon are cooking and Freya comes down and goes to the CD player. She puts on Nirvana, *Nevermind*, and the bass line echoes around the kitchen and she's crying. And she looks so pretty, despite the smudged make-up, the smears of dirt, the black round her neck and the grazes. So pretty, still.

2014

Freya's pushing my head down between my knees. 'Sit down like that,' she's saying. 'You look like you're going to pass out.'

I sit like that for at least ten minutes, neither of us speaking and then I throw up, all over the ground. I'm shaking, my legs are jerking, just like Freya's did that night, and I seem to have lost total control of my body.

'What's happening?' I ask Freya. She rubs my back and pushes my head back down. We sit like that for about half an hour. I'm shaking and sweating and very breathless.

'I think I need to go to a doctor,' I say.

'No, no. You're fine. It's just a physical reaction. It's what I had. The day after. Do you remember?'

I do, but I'm too ashamed of myself to admit it. Ashamed that I didn't help her. Ashamed that those marks around her neck were bruises and all that time I had convinced myself it was dirt. Those hands around Freya's neck. Squeezing. Flesh bulging. And I'm sick again. Freya hands me a hanky. It's embroidered with her new initials. I take it, wipe my mouth and I want, more than anything, to lie down.

'Josephine? Are you feeling better now?'

'I'm fine,' I say.

'I thought you'd say that.'

Freya pulls something out of her bag. I lift my head and have to drop it again. 'Are you alright?' she asks again.

'I'm fine. Just give me a moment. Thanks.'

I can hear Freya humming very softly. It's that hum she does when she's getting trying to fill a silence. I know the exact notes she's going to sing and it's reassuring to hear that even that hasn't changed.

'You're doing that hum, you always used to do,' I say, when I've caught my breath.

'Hum?'

What was meant to be a fond reminiscence sounds like a recrimination. There's silence again, and it grows. It's been eighteen years and, on the surface, nothing's changed: the intonations and the flickers of her features. The way her hands rest lightly on her thighs. She probably thinks the same of me, the tight way in which I hold my arms to my sides, my straight back and the impenetrable force around me that Freya used to laugh at, preventing people from standing too close. I make a concerted effort to sit in a more relaxed way but it feels so odd and Freya gives me a funny look. I can tell she knows what I'm doing.

Neither of us talks for about five minutes. We watch the people walking past us. A fat woman struggling to pull a large suitcase behind her. A small child throwing his toy teddy on the grass. A group of young men who wolf-whistle at Freya, aimlessly high-fiving each other. My legs have stopped shaking and my stomach has settled but, if I stand up now, I'm pretty sure I'd fall. We wait another twenty minutes or so and then Freya motions to another bench, away from my vomit. I manage to stand up and stagger across to it. When I feel like I can talk, I can't think of anything to say. The boys have caught sight of Freya again, walking. Another wolf whistle sounds.

'Men never did notice me when you were around,' I laugh.

'You think they didn't. But they did. Anyway, the teachers never noticed me when you were around,' she says with a small smile.

The old joke between us brews and turns slightly hostile, despite the earlier forgiveness. It's all still so precarious.

'Here,' she says, pulling something out her handbag. 'It's my daughter.' She holds out the peace offering and I smile and take it.

There's a little creature who looks exactly like Freya did when she was young, except she's absolutely covered in freckles. The sunlight bathes her mini arms and blonde hair and she looks like one of those kids in those aspirational clothes adverts. The ones in striped dungarees that you think couldn't get more perfect.

'Evie,' she says.

'She's lovely.'

'Kids?' Freya asks me, as she strokes the photo before returning it to her bag.

'No.'

'She's just like me,' Freya says.

'Really?' I don't know what else to say.

'Yes. She's going to be like me as a teenager. Which is why … Which is why I needed to see you and to sort this thing out. And why I need to clear everything up. Everything from that night. I need some sort of closure. Don't you?'

'I guess so.' I laugh inwardly. If only she knew where I'd been for the past week.

'We've done well, so far, haven't we?' she asks. I nod my head, wondering what she means by 'so far' then I remember she said she had something to tell me.

'There's just a bit more, though. Some stuff I need to talk to you about. Stuff I need to tell you.'

In truth, I'm worried about how I'm going to react to whatever it is she's going to say. I wasn't expecting to feel so physically bad when thoughts of that night came back to me. I wasn't expecting an iron weight across my chest that made me think I was going to die.

'Go on then. What?' My voice comes out all constricted.

She looks down and then up at the sky. Her lip is moving to the side and I know she's dreading telling me whatever it is.

'I'm so sorry,' she says, closing her eyes.

'So am I. About the whole thing.' The words surprise me and she takes my hand again.

'It was something that just happened, wasn't it? I mean neither of us could do anything about it. Isn't that right? Even though we were both high?'

I nod my head.

'Look, J, you know how much you meant to me.' Even after all these years, the past tense of her words hurt me. 'I wanted so much for you to be happy. To have a good time. To enjoy yourself, even with all the pressure you put yourself under.'

I don't know what she's getting at, but I sit and listen.

'You know, with Head Girl, your mother. Everything like that. I just wanted to you to loosen up sometimes, you know?'

I don't know but I turn and look at her and she's gone a weird colour. A chartreuse tinge is spreading across her face.

'That night. That night…'

'Go on.'

She opens her mouth to talk and the words freeze somewhere between her throat and the air.

Her eyes, they are all shaky and they've gone a weird black colour. What, just what on earth could be that bad that her eyes have turned black?

1996

Verity, Sally and I are all in Mrs Allen's study. There's a lacrosse game going on just outside the big window against our biggest rival, St Margaret's.

'It's good to have you all back here. To maintain some sense of normality,' says Mrs Allen. 'I wanted to have a meeting with you to discuss Freya.'

'I spoke to her,' Verity says, looking around the room, all pleased with herself. 'Yesterday. She's doing much better. Said she was with her father and brother. And of course, as I'm sure you all know, her father is due to go away again so she's thinking about coming back to school ... I think she's got to have some ... treatment or something at some point, but hopefully she'll be able to see us all before that.'

'Verity, thank you for that info,' says Mrs Allen. 'As Verity has filled us all in I won't bother to repeat it but we'll have to see what happens.' A distant cheer comes from the lacrosse field. Mrs Allen turns her head and looks through the glass, to see who has scored.

'Iris Delamere,' she whispers, turning back to us, rubbing her eyes beneath her glasses. 'Right, as I was saying. Freya. She's much better. Now, I've spoken with the school governors, who have come to a decision. If this gets out, it'll be a disaster. As you all know there's *The Times Good Schools Guide* coming out soon so we need to be top of our game. Keep our number one spot … So, I'm really sorry to say, and this has been a very, very hard decision to make, given that it might affect the league tables. And our reputation. But we realised we would do even more damage if this got out and we'd done nothing. So, again, I'm sorry to say but it's been decided that if none of you comes forward, you'll all be expelled and your universities informed. They can make the decision as to whether you'll still be welcome.'

Verity jumps up. 'That's not fair, though, Mrs Allen. I wasn't involved. It could have been absolutely anyone.'

'Verity, sit down. That may be the case but as you three are the only people who could have possibly been involved, we have to take due action, unless something drastic happens and someone else turns up with some evidence.' My skin feels as though it's burning up. She's bluffing, I think. I'm sure she's bluffing, in the hope that one of us will come forward and save the day.

'Girls?' Mrs Allen is looking at Sally, then me.

'And what about Freya and Mrs Kitts?' I say. It's the first time Mrs Kitts's name has been spoken in a while.

'We're conducting a final investigation and, whilst it continues, Freya will be allowed back at school, if she's up to it of course, and until then, everything carries on as normal. When the governors file their reports, we'll work out what comes next.' Another cheer. Iris again. I can see her from a distance, lacrosse stick bobbing up and down.

'All four of you. I can't believe it,' says Mrs Allen. 'Four of Greenwood's star pupils and this is what happens.'

'Nothing's going to happen, Mrs Allen. We're all going to be fine,' says Sally, looking flushed.

'Is that so?'

'Yes. I'm going to Oxford whatever happens. My father will be sure of it.'

'Let's hope that's the case,' Mrs Allen replies. We all wait for the game to finish. Greenwood Hall win, by the sound of things, and Verity stands up and does a falsetto cheer. I feel like kicking her. It dawns on me, as the sun retreats into cloud, that if Freya comes back none of us will know how to behave. Will she talk to me? Will she even look at me? Mrs Allen wraps up the meeting and asks me to stay behind in her study.

'Josephine, I need to speak to you alone please. Head Girl matters. Girls, thank you for meeting me. Now get back to work, you've got lots of revision.'

She waits until they have both left. 'I've spoken to Freya's father. He rang last night. Late. She's made a good recovery but, of course, she'll be feeling ... out of sorts for a while. Mrs Kitts. All that business. Will have scarred her.' Where is she going with this?

'And so Mr Seymour thinks it's best if you two don't talk whilst the investigation is going ahead. In fact, he's requested that if she does decide to come back, Freya moves boarding house. So she'll be down in the main school, near the san.'

'So you don't want me to communicate with her if I see her? Is that right?'

Mrs Allen wipes her nose with a lace hanky. 'That's right. I'm sorry, Josephine. I know that must be a bit of a blow.' It's not. It's a relief. The possibility of awkwardness has been taken from me.

'That's OK. I'll stay away from her. What about classes? Oxbridge lessons?'

'We've sorted this all out. Don't worry. Freya will have separate classes. There was talk of her going to a different school if she's up to studying at all, but her father thought it would be even more disruptive for her to be away from her friends at this time.' I wonder what it would have been like if it had been the other way round, given that my only real friend was Freya.

'Right.'

'Josephine, is there anything else you'd like to tell me? Anything at all?' Mrs Allen starts so stand, as though she's expecting me to say nothing at all.

'No. Ask Verity the same question,' I reply. My head fills with thoughts, all jostling for attention, and my scalp starts prickling.

'Josephine?'

'I'm here. Sorry. Right. I'd best get going, Mrs Allen.' My voice is crisp.

'Right you are. Please do come to me if you need anything.' The study is hot, sunlight streaming through the windows. I'm dripping cold sweat.

The next day Freya's back. I don't see her but I can tell by the high-pitched chatter around the school. Girls nudge each other when I walk past and bury their heads down, as though I won't notice. I walk past them, back straight, books under my arm. Sally catches up with me on the way to History.

'Have you heard?' she asks.

'No,' I reply, looking out the window, pretending not to care.

'About Freya?'

'No,' I sigh, as though her silly gossip means nothing but I'm covered in goosebumps.

'She's leaving. Was here for three seconds apparently. She's packing.'

'Where's she going?' I'm still looking outside the window.

'Don't know. Home again, I suppose. To that psych place she was meant to go to? Don't know. But do you think that means all this will blow over?'

'I hope so,' I reply. 'Oxford.' Sally links my arm.

'Hope so too. Want to come and stay next weekend?'

'OK.'

'OK?' she replies, extracting her arm from mine in disbelief.

'I said OK, OK?'

'Are you serious?'

'I'm serious.'

'That's ... that's amazing. Cool!' She turns, giving me a huge grin.

For a moment, I feel I'm being disloyal to Freya. It's replaced by a cool relief that I won't need to be on the constant lookout for her presence sliding around the school corridors. The whispers of girls. I'm so happy she's alive that all the guilt, resentment and hurt over recent events floods back.

'So, I'll organise something fun, yes?' Sally says.

'Sorry?' I reply. 'Oh ... yes. Sorry, that'll be great. Just something low-key. Cinema or something would be great.' I smile. I need to keep Sally onside, but more than that, I've grown rather fond of her. She's not a replacement for Freya, but her presence is comforting. Labrador-esque. I think of Freya and what she would say if I told her that.

2014

'You remember you hadn't wanted to take anything that night? I mean, you said no to any drugs?' Freya says. She's squeezing my hand. 'I think you wanted to keep on the straight and narrow as Head Girl and you were frightened by your mother. I had pretended not to understand why you were freaking out at the time. Always felt bad about that. I knew perfectly well you were scared that it would trigger something that meant you would get ill like your mum. I saw the report too, the one you mentioned. That drugs cause mental health problems. Anyway...'

I wonder how many other times Freya played dumb with me.

'I felt things were going to change when you were made Head Girl. Like you wouldn't be able to mess around with me. I was scared. I was scared we would drift apart.'

Freya's pulling out the picture of her daughter again. She's looks at it and then quickly shoves it back into her bag.

'So that night, when you said you wouldn't take anything. Or just half a pill ... I went to get you a drink.'

I know what's coming next but I have to hear Freya tell me herself.

'I ...' She breathes, a controlled, steady breath which judders into a cry. 'I put some stuff in it,' she says.

354

'What stuff?' I already know what she's talking about, but I'm biding time to process the blaze ripping through me.

'That night. I took loads of pills. But as I said, I was pissed off you wouldn't go all out with me. So I crushed some pills up and put them in your drink.'

'How many?'

'Two. Maybe three?'

I remember the drink now – the sweet fizz of the Coca-Cola, followed by a bitter, stringent taste blossoming around the back of my throat. Trying to cough away the taste and then, soon after, the prickling of my scalp, the blood warming up my veins.

'So that's why I was too … to do anything?' She turns and nods. The light bounces off her hair. Silence. A bird trills and the sun gleams.

I want to ask why she's waited to tell me all this until now. Why she didn't tell me before we talked about everything. But the crushing sensation across my chest has returned and I can't talk. It's even more painful, given the conversation we've just had, the level of closure we reached. I hunch over myself, squeezing away the pain. It goes soon after. I'm thinking back to that night and, when I do, I can't say I'm that surprised about what Freya's just told me. I think, deep down, I had always known she had done something like that. There was something not quite right about how paralytic I had been. I wonder how things would have turned out if I had been sober. I think back to how I hadn't been able to control myself. How I had not even been able to stand up to stop those…

She's looking at me, eyes pleading and she's reaching again for the photo of her daughter.

'Don't,' I say. 'Don't use your daughter here.'

Freya bites her lip and puts the photograph back. Looks at me again.

'I don't know what to say, Josephine. It's something I haven't been able to forgive myself for. All this time later, it plagues me, every single day. I've felt trapped with it ever since because it's always with me. With every movement I make. That guilt. The happiness of Evie, I keep thinking I don't deserve it. Don't deserve her, for being such a bad person for what I did.'

Freya's ripping up bits of tissue, rolling them up and putting them on the bench beside us.

'I did actually try and tell you. You know that? I tried to tell you the next morning. You wouldn't listen though. I wanted to get us the morning after pill, but you wouldn't even let me look it up. I thought that was so risky, by the way. So stupid. I'm not trying to avert any blame. Or excuse what I did. Not at all. What I did was a horrendous, awful thing to do that I'll live with to the day I die. But if you'd talked to me that day after, instead of shutting me up … instead of closing down, we might have reached some sort of closure earlier on. Do you see? I felt so, so alone. I couldn't talk to you, let alone anyone else, and you just didn't seem to care.' Freya's really sobbing now. Her eyes are shining, tears catching the sunlight. 'Do you know what I thought?' she says. I shake my head. I don't know anything anymore.

'I thought you were so lucky. I thought you were the luckiest person in the world. To be able to act as though nothing had happened. To seem unaffected by what happened to us. I used to think nothing could hurt you at all.'

I don't say anything. I want to say to her if she hadn't been so stupid, I could have prevented all of this happening, I would have been sober, we would have been fine. But I can't, because how can I tally up that one act against all the others I committed myself? We are in a web, she and I, so interlaced with recriminations you can no longer tell where it first began to be spun.

'Could it?'

'Yes. Yes it could.' The pain gives way to a throbbing tiredness.

She breathes out heavily. 'Why, how could you have not talked about it then? I needed you so badly. I know it's your way of dealing with things but wasn't I important enough to you that you felt you could help me? Help yourself too? We could have gotten through it together.'

'I told you,' I say. 'I told you just now. It was all to do with my mother. All that stuff.'

She leans back, contrite. 'I know. It's really helped, seeing you, having you explain that to me. I've got to spend time recalibrating my whole idea about that time. Think of your viewpoint. Think of how much stuff you were going through too. And how differently we felt about that night. I can see it now.'

'I don't think we did, underneath,' I reply. 'Underneath it all, Freya, underneath the things we did afterwards. I don't think we felt differently at all.' I look at her and, as I'm saying those words and making that admission, she's reacting to me as the old Freya would. She's looking affectionate and her nose is all red and there's a kernel of the old friendship there.

'It's good to hear you say that.' Freya wipes her nose. 'Really good. I feel like I've got some semblance of you back. All those good memories of us growing up together, like sisters, they were obliterated by how we both behaved straight after what happened. But knowing you felt it all too, that makes it so, so much better. That I wasn't mad, that I wasn't completely alone.' And there's something about the way she says that, about being alone when I have been so alone for nearly two decades, that I feel my body buckle and my arms are around her and I let her put her arms right back around me and she tells me it's OK and that it's over.

We sit like that for a few minutes. Then she gasps and looks at her watch and says that it's already two o' clock and we've talked right through lunch.

'I thought we'd only be here for a bit,' she says. 'I couldn't imagine us going through all of this.'

'Me too.' She's resting her head on my shoulder.

'Did you ever want to see anyone again? From school, I mean?' she asks, lifting her head up and smiling. The old Freya.

'No. I won't be going to any reunions soon that's for sure. But I'm less fearful about the old memories being dredged up now we've seen each other. What about you?'

'Nah. Not particularly. I never really spoke to anyone again after everything,' she says. 'Apart from Verity. Mrs Kitts wrote to me at home a few times, to say sorry. If that had been now, she would have been hung, drawn and quartered, wouldn't she? I guess they had nothing to go on.'

'Was that serious then? You and Mrs Kitts? I can't believe you kept that from me all that time.' I try and fail not to sound bitter, all these years later.

'Well, no. For me it was just comfort. And she seemed so ... together. Like you but not quite so unyielding.' She gives a rueful smile. 'Looking for the right things in all the wrong places. The last time she wrote to me years ago, it was four pages long. Memories. Her and me. She was more damaged than I was.' Freya's biting her lip again. 'I didn't tell you on purpose, by the way. The whole Prefect, Head Girl thing was beginning to happen. I didn't want you party to anything that serious. Smoking and stuff … fine … but that … you could have been in real trouble if they'd known you were aware of what was going on. If it came out and they questioned you.'

'Really? That's the entire reason you didn't tell me? To protect me?' I think of all the hurt her not telling me had caused me, when all this time…

'Really,' she says. 'I thought about telling you for ages. Thought I had given you some hints but I guess it was too random for you to just guess.'

And this makes me feel worse for not protecting Freya when she needed it most. I let her kindness settle over me.

'It was Sally who told me, by the way. About you and Mrs K.'

'Sally? Oh … that makes sense, now. You and her. *The Lens.*' We are chatting like we're in her bedroom once again, lying on her duvet and gossiping as if we are talking about other people, which in a way, I suppose we are.

'How's Leon by the way?' I try keeping my voice casual.

'He's well. In America as I said. Music A and R. He discovered loads of people. That big boy band that sang that song, you know the one that came out over Christmas. *Bang bang di bang.*' I raise my eyebrows and laugh. Freya laughs too.

'He's separated. Married that girl Rosie, do you remember her? And she couldn't have kids.' My heart nearly dies at what could have been.

'I can put you two back in touch if you want?' she says. 'He would love to hear from you. He always had a soft spot for you.' I don't know whether she's joking or not.

'Ha,' I say. 'Maybe.'

'What about you?' she asks.

'What about me?'

'What happened after you left school? I always used to try and find you on Facebook and then Verity told me she had read about your dig.'

'How did you find me by the way?' I ask. 'It scared me so much. I got rid of our … my old email address. The one we set up together.'

'Oh, when I got a response from your old email saying it was no longer in use, I rang your house and spoke to Amy. I got hold of your father a couple of times and hung up. Eventually Amy replied. I knew she was still with you. Or that someone would have been. She cried when I told her who it was. Said she had missed me so much and that I had been like a daughter to her and a sister to you. I made her promise she wouldn't tell you that I had been in touch. Don't get angry with her, J.'

'I'm not. I'm relieved it wasn't more sinister, frankly. I spent all that time looking over my shoulder, thinking you were some-how watching me.' We both laugh again.

'So go on,' she says, 'tell me. Tell me what you've been up to in those years we didn't see each other. Did you go to Oxford in the end? What happened?'

I sit and tell her everything, not knowing if we'll ever fully rekindle what we once had. I don't mind, though. We did good things today. We recaptured the good memories, came to terms with the bad. And there's a part of me that still loves her. Always will. The beauty of her.

1996

The minute we are allowed back to school I decide to blitz my work. For the past two days, I've been revising all day and all night. The school takes on a studious air before our mocks, quiet and self-important. There's total silence round the corridors. All I can hear are the rustle of books and nibs, pawing at blank pages. Everyone makes their own timetable and daylight holds no sway. Heads down, no eating. Everyone's nervy.

'Work hard, do all you can,' says Mrs Allen in chapel that morning. 'This school prides itself on academic achievement and so I expect all of you to fulfil your ambitions both here and afterwards. Make us proud. Make yourselves proud.' Limbs twitch, eager to get back to books.

My first History exam is later that day and I've memorised the entire curriculum textbook, and read a whole load else too, which I hope will stand me in good stead. The exam goes well. Hints of panic drip into my brain but I steel myself against them. Panic can wait, I tell myself. My body is totally fired up, but to the onlooker I am calm. I can't stop thinking about Freya and the fact she should be here.

It's another two days until we are all gathered again: me, Verity, Sally, alongside our parents. A meeting has been called to determine our fate.

I'm early and wait outside Mrs Allen's study for ten minutes. I inhale, stand up tall and unpin my Head Girl badge from my jumper. The gold edge has kept its shine and the pin is still sharp. It's left two holes in the wool.

Head Girl.

I breathe on the badge, misting it up and rubbing it until there's no fingerprints, no smudging to be seen. I repin it to my jumper, threading the badge through the same two little holes.

Whilst I'm waiting, Caroline Dawes, a freckly, energetic fifth-former, comes to pin up a note on the door of Mrs Allen's study.

'Your meeting,' she says to me. 'Mrs Allen's asked me to pin this up on her door. It's been moved to the Mann Library. It's still starting now ...' She looks at her watch. 'Well, in a few minutes at least. Mrs Allen's study's being repainted and everyone's in lessons at the moment,' she explains, looking at my face.

'Thanks,' I say and make my way to the library.

Soon after, Verity arrives along with her parents and then Sally. My father is last, looking unshaven and red-eyed. I feel bad that he's had to come all the way here when he's probably had to cancel a load of meetings just as General Election fever is about to start. He presses his keys down onto the nearest wooden table. He smiles at me then Mrs Allen and I can see his chest rise. He slides his hand down his stomach, straightens his tie and sits down.

'All, thank you for making the effort to attend today's meeting,' says Mrs Allen looking around the room. We're seated on wooden chairs, apart from Mrs Allen, who is on a big green velveteen armchair.

'We've got three governors with us today.' I've barely noticed the other people – all women – in the room. There's Mrs Pownall;

a round, short-haired lady with huge, red glasses who keeps picking fluff off her black and white dress; and a small, blonde woman, probably in her early forties, who looks like she can barely contain her glee at being important enough to attend.

'Now tea? Coffee?'

Everyone nods.

'Mr Grey?'

'Tea. Please.'

'Mrs Balfour, please could you ask everyone what they want to drink and do the honours?' The blonde governor looks crestfallen at being asked to serve.

'Right,' Mrs Allen says. 'As you all know, this meeting has been called as a last-chance saloon. Mr Seymour has instructed us to have it; he believes that one of you girls is responsible for what happened in *The Lens* and thus what drove Freya to her suicide attempt. So, one last chance for your daughters –' Mrs Allen taps out a rhythm on the desk '– to tell us all what they know. Anything. And if none of you confess to anything, we're going to probably have to take punitive action against all three of you. Depending on what's said at this meeting, of course.' She looks up, daring anyone in the room to challenge her. 'We are, of course, in a difficult position where none of these girls can be proven guilty. They all had a hand in *The Lens* prior to publication but, apart from that, we have no proof. Only their word. But at the moment, there was no one else involved in the whole thing, so it's likely they'll have to take a collective hit.'

None of the parents say, or do, anything, apart from my father, who is standing up, very slowly.

'Mrs Allen, excuse me for interrupting, but I will not have my daughter used as a scapegoat so this whole affair is kept quiet and buried. Mr Seymour will not use our children in return for his child's salvation, or whatever he's looking for. Do you understand?'

'Mr Grey, please...'

'No pleases. Our daughters' whole careers are at stake here. Their futures, Mrs Allen. Isn't that what you pride yourself on as a school? Setting your girls up for their futures? If that's the case, you'd better take it upon yourself to do just that, before I call in my lawyers. Do I make myself clear?' My father doesn't look around the room for approval, for reassurance. Doesn't need it. I catch Verity's mother bobbing her head up and down and Sally's father shifting in his seat as though he wants to say something too, annoyed that my father got there first.

'I am extremely proud of my daughter.' Father is getting louder. 'Head Girl, an offer from Oxford, she's had a stellar education here at your school and I will not let some silly little girl's affair with a woman twice her age affect it.' Mrs Allen, I can tell, agrees with him.

'Mr Grey. Thank you for that. If you could sit down please,' Mrs Allen barks. 'If we could get back to the matter in hand. We need to hear one last time from the girls if they have anything they want to say, before we ... that is, me and the governors, decide what to do. I would like each of you to take some time, think about what it is you want to tell us, if anything. Let's take a few moments, shall we? Let's reconvene here in five minutes.' Sally's parents both leave the room. Verity has started to cry. Her mother leans over her talking in a babyish voice, telling her she's the best girl in the world and that noth-ing will change that. I'm trying to work out in my head what to say but I keep wondering if something will incriminate me. Keep it simple, I tell myself. Just as we are all settling back down for the meeting Mrs Cape enters the library, holding a huge batch of post.

'Mrs Cape, sorry, we're having a meeting here,' says Mrs Allen.

'Oh terribly sorry, Mrs Allen. It's your office and all. Your study, I mean. I don't have anywhere else to sort this lot. Might you let me sit in the staffroom?'

'Of course, that's fine. You know the code? Ah actually, Mrs Cape. I have a request. As I said, we're just having a meeting. A confidential one. I've just remembered I said I would make it all official and present it to the rest of the governors in our next meeting. Could you make yourself useful and type it up? And can I trust you that none of this goes any further?'

'Absolutely, Mrs Allen. I'll write shorthand notes and type it up afterwards. Secretarial college – that went to waste!' Mrs Cape grimaces. I'm starting to feel uneasy.

'Great. Apologies for this, everyone. Shouldn't take long,' says Mrs Allen, waiting for Mrs Cape to collect some paper and a pen.

'It won't. I'm good. Just watch.' Mrs Cape wiggles her fingers around the room, smiling at everyone until her gaze stops at my father. She recognises him, it's obvious. Recognises him from the news. Her eyes light up in that way when people see him in the street and want to stop him but are too embarrassed. She looks down and blushes.

'Right,' says Mrs Allen. 'Let's get a move on. Josephine, do you want to do the honours?'

I start talking. My heart is clacking around because I know something here is not right. I carry on, looking only at Sally, who provides me with some sort of comfort. I tell the room how I had nothing to do with the 'Guess Who?' entry and that I'd already been through the whole ins and outs of my where-abouts, about what I did after the proof went to the printer's and that if anyone had any questions, they were welcome to ask. I look up and Mrs Cape is staring at me, giving me a reassuring nod and then she goes and gives me a bloody thumbs-up sign.

'Is everything alright, Mrs Cape?' Mrs Allen says.

'Yes, yes it's great. I'm getting everything down, don't you worry. I'm just wondering about Josephine here and the PM. I hope you didn't end up getting in trouble with him!' Mrs Cape is looking thrilled to have been privy to this information and is beaming at my father.

My mind is speeding. I'm trying to think of ways to stop the meeting – faint, maybe? Ridiculous, I think. Tell them I know more about Freya and Mrs Kitts?

No. No more. I'm tired. My mind is going too fast for me to think straight anyway. My field of vision is skewed with fluores-cent green lights and I can hear my breathing getting faster and faster.

'Josephine? Josephine?' My father is shouting.

'I'm fine. I'm fine,' I manage. Breathe. And somewhere, in the distance, I can hear Mrs Allen going over the same old story that we've heard a million times but, of course, this is all new to Mrs Cape. I've given the proofs to Sally and Verity, Sally doesn't touch them but they go down to the printer's together and blah blah blah. *Blah, fucking, blah.* And that's where it happens.

'Just imagine the Prime Minister himself!' Mrs Cape's voice has gone all jaunty. 'Josephine, your dad's here now so it's OK for us to talk about it, isn't it?' Mrs Cape winks at me and nudges her elbow in my direction. The pinprick of vision I have left is directed at Father, who is frowning and looking at Mrs Cape. She is grinning away, panting like a dog. 'Your daughter here rather heroically tried to save the nation!' she chortles.

'My daughter? I'm a bit lost, sorry Mrs ... Cape.'

'The manifesto that the PM was desperate to take out. Could have ruined the country your daughter said, when the first copies arrived from the printer's. Ruined the whole place! Dust to dust, I thought to myself.'

Mrs Allen is standing up, creasing down her pleated skirt. It's pink. Flesh-coloured. Most unlike her. She's normally a dark-green, grey or black type of person

'Mrs Cape, please. We've got a lot to get through and, if you don't mind me saying, it's not really your place to comment at this meeting.' If I'm not mistaken, Mrs Allen knows. She's sounding panicked. 'Please could you be quiet and concentrate on finishing the notes.' There's a cough lodged in my throat and I can't release it. If I do, I'll look like I'm trying to cause a distraction. I hold on to it, bulging in my windpipe.

'No, I'd like to hear what this lady has to say,' my father interrupts, thinking he's doing me a massive favour. The room falls silent but I can practically hear the blood whooshing through my veins. I take a quick look round the room and every single person is frowning.

'Well, when the copies of The Lens first arrived at the school all ready to be distributed to the girls and all –' Mrs Cape has her hand on her chest and she's all breathless with excitement '– Miss Josephine comes running up saying there's been a huge mistake in the magazine and could we stop giving them out to all the houses and that. She'd been speaking to the Prime Minister himself that very morning! Said he'd stepped over the mark because she was a personal friend … a personal friend! Imagine that! And of course could she please keep all the copics of the magazine and rip out the bits that weren't meant to be seen. Then she told me to be quiet about it but I guess with your father here, now, it's OK … That's why you're all here, isn't it?'

Everyone is now standing up. Staring at me. Mrs Cape, oblivious, carries on.

'Anyway, I said, "No, Miss Grey. I'm terribly sorry, they've all gone out already." White as a sheet you were!' She looks at me. Then she looks at everyone else and realises something's wrong. I lift my head up high and look Mrs Allen straight in the eye. She doesn't say anything at all. Doesn't look cross. Or upset, or disappointed. Just walks over to me, slowly. Looks me in the eye and holds out her hand.

I raise my hand and unpin the badge from my school jumper. I give it to Mrs Allen and she takes it. Holds it in her palm, squeezes it. Father is walking towards me, arms open but I don't have the courage to look at him.

'It's OK,' he is saying. 'It's OK.'

'I know,' I say. 'I know.' And I feel it is OK because now the truth is out. Verity is staring at me, and Sally is holding her head in her hands. She lifts her neck up at me and I can see the pleading in her eyes. I give her a small reassuring nod and she falls back into her chair, thankful. Nothing matters.

Father is standing opposite me now, hand outstretched. I take it. His fingers and palms feel swollen and hot. He pulls me up and we walk out of the room. My footsteps are slow, like I'm walking through treacle. I can hear Mrs Allen asking the other parents to make their way out of the room. By that time, I'm already closing the door behind me and walking out of Main School, into the fresh, blue air. I take a deep breath.

'Please can we go home?' I say to him.

'Yes. Your mother isn't here at the moment so we've got the place to ourselves.'

I breathe in the coldness, sucking it down into my lungs. I'm ready, I think. I hope.

I have no time to pack; Mrs Allen says she'll get all my clothes sent home. No one says goodbye. Mrs Allen follows me and Father outside and holds open her palm.

'This,' she says. Red and gold sparkle in her hand. 'This was your curse. Maybe it's my fault. Maybe I expected too much.' I open my mouth and then shut it. I want to say I'm sorry but I can't. Her face scrunches up. Like she needs the loo, or something. Her glasses have steamed up but she doesn't clean them.

'Thank you,' I say. For what, I'm not quite sure.

'Come on, Josephine.' Father pushes me into the car. The journey back is silent. There's a Radio Four programme on, about university, and I can feel the air expanding with thoughts of my education. Eventually, Father switches it off. We edge into London. The street lamps are on and there's a mist descending over the city.

'Why?' Father says, looking straight ahead.

'Why *what*?' I snap. But he doesn't say anything, just rubs his right temple. We never speak of the incident again, other than when Mrs Allen rings up to tell me that I've been formally expelled and that she's had to inform Oxford.

'They'll tell us in due course,' she says, 'whether your offer will be rescinded or not. You'll still take your A levels, though, when the time comes. We've arranged for you to be invigilated somewhere in London. Just you. I'll let you know details in due course.'

'Right. Thank you. What do you think? Do you think they will? Rescind, I mean.'

'I don't know. I really … I just don't know. I really don't. I can't even think about any of this.' I hang up and Father appears from nowhere.

'What did she say?' he asks.

'I've got to wait to find out what's happening with Oxford. She didn't say. Can't you speak to someone?'

'Speak to someone?' I know he's considered it. 'After this whole sorry mess? I don't think so, Josephine. It's just too wrong. I think it would be too wrong. And what if it got out? My job would be on the line.'

The next week is spent in the Kensington library. I walk past Freya's house a couple of times but there are no lights on and the blinds are down. I think I see Leon at the end of the road but it's not him, just someone else with dark hair. It's good to be away from the school grounds though. It allows me to focus. Being on my own feels nourishing in a way that I could never get at Greenwood. My father and I don't see much of each other – he spends all his time out and that's also fine with me: whenever he's in the house, he keeps looking at me and then the phone.

I don't hear from Mrs Allen for a few days. I receive a bumper package from her on Tuesday, with carefully photocopied notes and test papers. She's filed everything and I know she's done it herself because she's made little markings where she thinks something is important. There's no compliments slip or anything, but at the end of one of the notes she's underlined a quote, double lines, in red. 'Success is not final, failure is not fatal, it is the courage to continue that counts.' It has no relevance to the text and I read it again and again, waiting for it to buoy me up. It doesn't.

It is not until the end of the week that Mrs Allen calls again. Father picks up and asks how she is and, without waiting for her response, hands me the phone. He accidentally hits my chin with the receiver.

'Mrs Allen.'

'Josephine. I hope you are well?'

Father is pretending not to listen. Goes over to the drinks cabinet and pours himself a large whisky.

'I'm well, I'm good, thanks. Working hard.'

'Good. Now, I've sent you some more stuff in the post. It should help with your History exam.'

'Thanks so much.' I wonder if there's a reason she's ringing.

'Now, about Oxford.' Father has sat down and is flicking through the *Radio Times*. Front page, through to back page. And again.

'We've had a long discussion with them. Me and the governors …' Hurry up, I think, before Father rips that fucking magazine apart.

'And we've come to a conclusion together. Now it's a strange one …' Of course it's strange, I think. Father gets up and hands me his whisky glass. I wave him away.

'They've left it in my hands.'

'Your hands?'

'Yes. My hands. They've left it up to me and the school to make a decision. About you. About your future.' Neither of us speaks.

'What's she saying?' Father is mouthing. I hold a finger to my lips.

'So, what have you decided?' I laugh a brittle, hopeful laugh.

'We haven't yet. I – I have to think of what is best. Greenwood Hall must come first. But you know I have … well, I'll have to let you know tomorrow.' She hesitates and then, 'Goodbye, Josephine.'

I hang up and sit down next to Father. He sets his whisky back on the table and for the first time I can remember puts his arm around me and holds me tight.

Montreal, Canada
22 December, 2014

Dear Mrs Cape

Please find enclosed a signed and framed message from the Prime Minister. I'm writing to apologise for the terrible way I behaved at Greenwood Hall all those years ago. I sincerely hope you can forgive me.

Best wishes,
Josephine Grey

Montreal, Canada
28 January, 2015

Dear Verity

I hope you are well. Freya and I finally managed to meet after all this time – she told me you two are still in touch. I'm writing to say that I'm deeply, deeply sorry for the way I behaved at school. For trying to frame you for something I did. You have to believe me when I say I look back on that time with great shame. I can't blame it fully on things that happened in my life but some events made me go down paths I might not normally have taken.

I hope, truly, that you have not carried this in your heart for all this time, as I have in mine.

I wish you great happiness.

All my best,
Josephine Grey

Montreal, Canada
28 January, 2015

Dear Pete

You may not remember me. I probably saw you about nineteen or so years ago. I was Head Girl at Greenwood

Hall. I know this may come late but I'm writing to everyone I think deserves an apology from me. Everyone I hurt in some way, or misled, and one of those people, which I'm so ashamed about, is you.

You helped me print the copy of *The Lens*, our school magazine. I was hugely indebted to you. I asked you not to tell anyone I'd come asking if I could change the magazine's print run. I told you this was because the Prime Minister would get involved, and I'm writing to tell you that I lied to you. This wasn't true. I did something very bad to hurt someone I once loved very much. I suspect you may have always guessed I hadn't been entirely truthful but perhaps didn't want to believe it of me. I'm sorry.

I can only imagine what you must think of me. For all these years, I have felt so awful, and guilty, about what I did to you. I have learnt from all of this though – and I hope you'll believe me when I say it – that, truly, I'm not a bad person. And I'm trying, whole-heartedly, not to let the guilt consume me and take me down even uglier paths.

I really wanted to write to you because you were so kind to me that day and you tried so hard to help me out. I wanted not only to say I'm sorry, but that I got my come-uppance, which I thoroughly deserved. I ended up getting expelled by Mrs Allen, the school's headmistress. I was unable to go to Oxford University – something I'd worked towards all my life.

I now live in Canada, doing academic research, and lecturing at a good university. I don't know why I'm telling you all this but I'm really trying to be good. To be kind, like you.

You also gave me ten pounds. Here is the same ten pound note you gave me, all those years ago. The exact same one. I never could bring myself to spend it.

Yours sincerely, with gratitude and apologies,
Josephine Grey

Montreal, Canada
28 January, 2015

Dear Freya

I don't know where to start with this letter. I'd been wanting to write to you for all these years. To tell you things
I knew you'd laugh at, to share my thoughts with you but,
all this time, I haven't been able to. I know how much we
both fought through to get to this point in our lives and I just
wanted to say that I'm so, so glad we shared what we did
when we met in Hyde Park last year.

It made me feel so nostalgic for our old days, before all
the bad stuff happened. Didn't you feel it too? I also felt that
we came to an understanding about what happened that
night. And about everything that followed. I hope with every
shred of my being that we don't allow it to ruin us again and
again, like it has done for all these years. We must not let
this be bigger than us. I know I've failed at things in my past
but I am sure, both of us, will be able to succeed at this. By
seeing each other we have already, in part, won.

I know that we won't be able to recapture what we once
had. Those glorious, carefree days. But I really, really would
love to be a part of your life somehow. To meet little Evie one
day, who looks so like you. So beautiful and radiating such
goodness. Maybe it's too late, but maybe not. I spent so
long not saying the things I should have to you, I don't want
to continue that any more.

Freya, you will always be a part of who I am and I will
always hold you with such fondness in my heart.

Thank you, for being able to see me as I truly am, even
when I wished it otherwise.

With fond love,
Josephine

Acknowledgements

With thanks to:

My agent Nelle Andrew, whose incredible wisdom, editorial insight and kindness helped bring this book to life. Also to the fabulous Foreign Rights team at PFD: Rachel Mills, Rebecca Wearmouth, Marilia Savvides and Alexandra Cliff.

Joel Richardson, Mark Smith, Robert Woolliams and Claire Creek at Bonnier and Twenty7. Thank you for taking the book on and Joel, for your hawk-eye editorial skills and for all your support. Becky Short and Fliss Denham at Midas and Annabel Wright at whitefox.

Kerry Hudson, who set up the WoMentoring Scheme. I'm very grateful to have been taken on by Alison Hennessey, whose time and efforts were invaluable.

To my Faber Academy tutors, Esther Freud and Tim Lott, who kick-started this book. My fellow writing buddies, Neil, Richard, Bernadette, Jo, Jude, Mike, Jill, Kate and Jackie. And also to Ian Ellard.

Adrian Thornton, Jamie Evans, Hetty Cavanagh, Matthew Heath and Annabel Mullin for your introductions, inspiration, knowledge and help. Any mistakes are my own. Emily Heath and Cyrus for the amazing reflexology sessions.

Jo Bloom for answering all my writing-related questions and for the encouragement.

My family. Special thanks to my parents, as always, for your unending love.

My in-laws, Karen and Ellis, and to Zoe, Nick, Jamie and Carly Spero.

My godmother, Anne Kriken Mann, for the support, generosity and wonderful suppers.

Isabel Benson, Elizabeth Day, Jasper Thornton, Elizabeth Thornton, Asia Trotter and Charlotte Wilkins. I cannot thank you enough for your friendship, endless writing advice and editorial suggestions along the way. I love you and couldn't have written this book without your input and support.

And also to: Emilie Bennetts, Daniel Cavanagh, Gemma Deighton, Maria Guven, Caroline Jones, Philip Taylor and Isobel Wield.

Finally, Olly, Walter and Dominic, for everything.